MURDER UNDER MOONLIGHT

IRIS LOWE MYSTERIES BOOK 2

DELPHINE WOODS

PEPPER POT PUBLISHING

Copyright © 2021 by Delphine Woods

All rights reserved.

No part of this book may be reproduced in any form or by any electronic or mechanical means, including information storage and retrieval systems, without written permission from the author, except for the use of brief quotations in a book review.

Created with Vellum

For Madam Pigott, and all those who have suffered alike.

PROLOGUE
1900

They were watching him. He couldn't back out now. He hesitated only a second as his small ice shoes cramped his aching toes and a crow was buffeted out of the bare branches above his head. Inching forward, the surface squeaked, like hazel trees in a gale. Sniggering came from behind him and heated his blood. He pushed one boot forward, then the other, his stomach muscles tensing as his balance wavered.

The edge of the lake was a notorious mire of reeds and sucking mud. While most of it was blanketed in white ice, this section was blacker. Trees twisted out of it, their trunks curling around each other like the limbs of the damned he had once seen in a drawing in a book.

He must just touch the bark and he would be accepted, but everyone knew it was not really that simple. Two years ago, a boy a few years younger than himself had fallen through the ice. The reverend had found the body after the snowdrops had shrivelled and the daffodils had bloomed.

'Hurry up!'

Vibrations skittered across the lake towards him, and he glanced over his shoulder to find the mean little congregation stamping on the ice. All but one. His only true friend stood biting his strawberry-red fingertips at the edge of the group, eyes wide, shaking his head. But it was all right for his friend because he had already proven himself, two weeks ago when the ice was at its thickest and safest. Now, though the wind remained bone-chilling, spring was beginning to waft through the air. The thaw was approaching. He must act now or he would have to wait until next winter, and he did not want to face another lonely summer.

He pushed on. Best to do it quick, get in and get out. So he dug in his heels and propelled himself towards the blackness, arm outstretched, breath held, body tensed.

The end of his third finger grazed wood. He had done it.

A cheer rippled through the boys behind. A wave of euphoria crested over him, and laughter burst out of his lips. Gripping his knees, he took a moment to catch his breath. In and out, in and out, staring at his broken leather skating boots and the silver-black ice beneath him. Hairline cracks were beginning to form, but the elation from his victory blocked worry from entering his mind. For now, he was victorious. He was one of them.

'Come back,' his friend called, and the sound echoed off the twisted trees. 'Come back!'

He rolled himself up, wiping the sweat off his forehead with the back of his sleeve, turned, and glided towards his peers. All of them were smiling. All except one.

The sight of his friend's scrunched face distracted him.

His skating blade caught on a frozen reed protruding from the surface. His knee cracked against the ice before he knew he had fallen, and in less than a second he was screaming as his legs speared into the water. Clawing on to the ice by his fingernails, he managed to keep his torso clear of the lake, but underneath, his legs kicked uselessly, his blades slicing through water like butter.

The other boys reeled back. They glanced between themselves as he yelled for help. All of them dashed away, back to the safety of grass, not bothering to change out of their skating shoes as they jumped over the wall and into the street. All except one. His true friend remained, seemingly paralysed.

His legs were slowing down; his shoulders were screaming. He would not be able to hold himself up for much longer.

'Help me,' he said again, but this time he could only whisper it. Fear and cold had already robbed half of his life; the water would take the rest.

Something clattered towards him. He lifted his chin off the ice to find his friend running at him, brow wrinkled and breath smoking the air. His friend gripped his arms and pulled. There was a moment of nothing, when Mother Nature and his friend battled and held their ground. Then he was moving forward.

He pushed with all his might as his friend's fingernails bored into his forearm. The pinch of pain roused him, and he worked harder. Eventually, the chilled air bit his wet backside, then his thighs, then his calves as he slid out of the water and onto the ice, panting and juddering like a newborn lamb.

He and his friend lay on their backs, their glazed gaze

on the iron sky above, and silently thanked the Lord for their salvation.

He dragged himself upright and stared at his prone legs. Pinpricks were starting to tickle his soaked skin; in a moment, his thighs would be ablaze. He readied himself for the pain.

'What's that?' his friend said, pointing at the jagged hole in the ice, breath misting the air.

'I think… a bottle?' He did not want to go an inch closer to that hole, but curiosity stung him. He clutched his friend's hand to anchor himself to safety, then leaned towards the water.

It was just out of reach. He stretched and stretched until his joints throbbed, until the ice moaned, and with one last grunt, his thumb and forefinger closed over the cork. He plucked the bottle free, and they scuttled to the grass before they dared examine its contents.

'Green's for poison,' his friend said as they twirled the bottle before them. It was empty but for a sliver of black liquid in the bottom.

Without thinking, he popped off the cork.

'What did you do that for?' his friend sniped.

'There's nothing in it.' He tipped the bottle upside down, and the black liquid trickled out, staining the frosted grass beside him.

What were they doing wasting time looking at empty glass bottles? His arse was freezing, literally; when he stumbled to his feet, his trousers cracked after stiffening with ice. He chucked the bottle into the undergrowth by the stone wall as the church bells chimed three o'clock. Grasping his friend's arm for support, he staggered over the wall and off Buckley property. He was too preoccupied with the thrashing he would receive from his father to give the bottle another thought.

1
1956

'Iris? Iris!'

She peeled her head off the pillow. In her sleep, she had buried down under the eiderdown, and she tugged it off her face to find the day had faded to night. The closed curtains rattled with a cold, autumn breeze.

The door creaked open, cutting Iris's eyes with a shaft of yellow from an electric bulb. She flinched and brought up the eiderdown once again.

'Are you asleep?' Her mother waited in the crack of light.

'No,' she moaned, without the strength to point out the obvious, that there was no chance anyone could sleep when Pearl Lowe shouted.

'How are you feeling?'

Like a thousand needles were bearing into the soft, grey bubble of her brain. Like cats' claws were scraping down her throat. Like lava was roiling in her stomach, not knowing which way to erupt.

'Bad.'

'Still? Should I call the doctor now? It's been five days.'

Her mother was not going to get the hint and leave. Iris eased herself up the bed. Squinting, she made out her mum's silhouette and the tray in her hands.

'It's just the flu. You shouldn't be in here.'

'I brought you some stew to get your strength up.'

She could smell it wafting towards her. She pinched her lips and swallowed the nausea. 'Thanks.'

Her mum set the tray on the floor, lingered, and sighed.

'I'm better than yesterday.'

'That's good, then.'

It was good, because despite being semi-unconscious for the last five days, she had still been disturbed by her mother downstairs: vacuuming, going at the mangle as if it were a masked intruder, dicing meat and vegetables on the chopping board, slamming plates and throwing cutlery into their drawers, banging the door shut each time she went out for the groceries, guffawing with the rag-and-bone man on the front step directly below Iris's window. So much for rest. Iris would have got more rest if she had set herself up next to one of the women on her ward and been treated as a member of the chronically insane.

'I'll be back at work by Saturday,' she promised both her mum and herself.

Saturday – another two days to endure. Maybe she should force that stew down to try to speed along her recovery.

'Don't you rush into it.'

'They need me.'

'It was that attitude that knocked you down in the first

place. You're only one woman, love; you can't do it all. They've been running you ragged these last few months.'

Would her mother have put her bout of flu down to overwork if she had been a factory girl or a typist? She didn't think so. Not only was Smedley an undesirable mental hospital; according to her mother, it was also physically dangerous.

'Can you shut the door, please?'

'Yes, yes, all right. Night then, love. If you need me, just shout.'

She dragged her lips into a smile, then scooted back down to her pillow. She'd eat the stew later, once it had cooled, for she couldn't face its beefy steam drifting up into her face just yet. And then she'd give herself a wash, try to freshen up a bit, try to stop her limbs from shaking involuntarily. Because she could not stand more than two days cooped up in this house with only her thoughts and her mother for company. They were already driving her to distraction.

Strapped up in her biggest coat, with her mum's knitted scarf and hat thrust on her head, Iris bustled out of the back door. The air hit her like a train – a wall of ice after being under blankets and an eiderdown for a week. She almost longed for those first sick days of soaring temperatures to warm her up now, to battle the chattering of her teeth and the goose pimpling of her flesh. For a moment, she nearly lost her nerve and crawled back to her bedroom, but when she glanced at the doorway, her mum was there frowning. Iris turned away and, with all the strength she could muster, marched through their backyard and out into the alleyway.

It took her twice the time it usually did to reach Smedley, having to stop every five minutes to catch her breath, but when she saw its golden stonework looming above her, she smiled. She had missed it, which was odd – she doubted anyone ever said they missed such an establishment. Usually, everyone was trying to run away from its echoing Victorian corridors, both the patients and the staff.

Not Iris.

The weight of her sickness lifted as she passed between the avenue of lime trees, whose leaves looked as if they'd been caught in a fire and were carpeting the ground in red and amber.

Her colleagues were already rousing the women when she arrived on Ward 13. Scooting past them, she found the charge nurse, Miss Carmichael, behind the desk as she slipped off her outdoor clothing and fixed on her cap.

'You're late.'

'Sorry, ma'am. It took longer than expected. It won't happen again.'

Carmichael raised a brow at the damp sweat on Iris's forehead. 'Are you well enough to return? Influenza could kill most of them off in here.'

'I'm feeling much better, but if you think—'

'You're here now. Might as well stay.'

In the ward, she helped a fellow nurse with the patients. They worked in almost silence. She found that most of her peers fell quiet around her now, although they chatted easily enough between themselves. It was just Iris, then, who no one really took to.

It was probably her own fault. During training, she and Shirley had met and become unbreakable. No one else had been able to get close to either of them. The others had formed their own groups, gone to forbidden parties without inviting Iris and Shirley, whispered gossip over Shirley and Iris's heads. Back then, it hadn't mattered; she'd had Shirley. But now that she was gone, the chasm between Iris and the others yawned wide open.

In the last three months, she had often heard heels on the floorboards and a titter of laughter in the distance and looked up expecting to see blonde curls and twinkling eyes, but the sight had disappointed her. Shirley had seemingly vanished, and with her last words ringing in Iris's ears – *I never want to see you again* – Iris hadn't yet built up the courage to track down her whereabouts.

Iris and Nurse Bennet approached the next bed. Louisa Edwards stared at them, hooking her sheets up to her chin as if petrified. Iris smiled as warmly as possible as she neared the woman, and slowly the terror dissipated. Perhaps there was even a hint of recognition.

Iris helped Louisa on the commode. 'How have you been, Louisa?'

The woman nodded, but before she could speak, Bennet startled her by whisking the commode away as soon as her bottom had inched off it. Iris wrung out a wash cloth.

'Let's freshen you up, shall we?'

She sat Louisa on the bed and gently wiped her arms, neck, and chest. Finally, after some coaxing, she cleaned between her legs.

'That's better.' She stood, and for a moment the room

spun. Taking a deep breath, she smiled down at Louisa and saw her frowning up.

'Matilda? What are you doing here?'

'I'm not Matilda. I'm Iris. Remember?'

Louisa blinked.

'Who's Matilda?' Iris asked.

'It's not him. I'm sorry.' Louisa's eyes became hazy. 'I was wrong.'

'Eh' – Iris stroked her arm – 'it's all right.'

Louisa's stare broke off. She took in her surroundings. 'Where am I?'

'Smedley Hospital.'

'Where's Abigail?'

Louisa was always asking after her daughter, even though she had turned up almost every afternoon for years. 'She'll be here soon.'

'Then I can go home?'

Iris smiled tightly but kept quiet. No patient usually left the ward unless it was feet first.

* * *

Iris was waning by the afternoon. A whole morning of lifting and cleaning and marching about had left her with trembling limbs. It had been an effort just to butter the bread for the lunchtime sandwiches, and she had nearly dropped the teapot too many times. She leaned against the wall, pressing her clammy forehead to its cold plaster.

'Go and sit down, Miss Lowe, otherwise you'll drop.' Nurse Carmichael placed her hand on Iris's shoulder for a brief moment, a hint of compassion in her eyes.

Iris didn't need to be told twice. Staggering, she made

Louisa sipped her tea. 'Have you put sugar in this?'

'Yes, Mum. Always.' Abigail laughed and dabbed the wetness from her eyes.

Louisa looked at her daughter. Her gnarled hand cupped her chin and her thumb brushed away a tear. 'There's no use crying, darling. Tears don't get you anywhere.' She dropped her hand, smiled briefly, and turned back to her tea. 'That's what I used to say to my daughter when she was little. She's called Abigail. I named her after my grandmother. She's a teacher, bright as a button. She's getting married soon.'

Abigail feigned interest, as if it was completely normal for her mother to have forgotten who she was. Iris noted the absence of a ring on Abigail's fourth finger, something she hadn't paid any attention to before.

'The longer I'm away, the more she forgets,' Abigail said when her mother's interest had dissolved. 'I try to come most days, but sometimes it's just too difficult.'

'Do you live far?'

'Close to Ludlow, so it can take a while to get here. It's getting harder to leave Dad now too. He's sharp as a pin, up here' – she tapped her head – 'but he can't get around by himself anymore.'

'I've never seen him.'

'He won't come. Him and Mum had… a trying marriage. He prefers to stay at home.' Abigail's voice cracked and trailed off. 'Anyway, he's probably right. It's never pleasant having them in the same room together.'

'Are you taking me home today?' Louisa asked.

Abigail patted her mother's hand, smiled, and sipped her drink. Louisa's attention drifted away once more.

'You'd think she'd have stopped asking by now. You

her way to the chair by the window, the chair which only months ago used to be one special patient's favourite spot in all of Ward 13. Beyond the glass, the oak tree's leaves were rusting and peppering the grass. A shimmer of fluff ruffled the branches, and a grey squirrel darted head first down the trunk and ferreted at the base. Not too far away, a blackbird stood proudly on a raised root and opened its yellow beak to sing.

'Are you all right?'

Iris wiped the tear off her cheek. Beside her, a woman not much older than her mother gazed down. She wore a plain wool skirt and a blouse, which had most likely once been a curtain. She had a round, softly wrinkled face and rich brown eyes, and her thin lips bit each other as she waited for a response.

'Yes, fine. Thank you, Miss Edwards. Just… a memory, that's all.'

Miss Edwards nodded, relieved, and sat in the chair next to Iris. 'It's Nurse Lowe, isn't it?'

'Iris, please.'

'Then you must call me Abigail. Miss Edwards was what the children used to call me.'

Abigail's mother, Louisa, fiddled with the handle of a teacup on the nearby table. 'Have you put sugar in it?'

'Yes, Mum,' Abigail said. 'How's she been? My father's been poorly, so I haven't come in the last few days.'

Iris sat up in her chair – slouching was unprofessional – and cleared her throat. 'Actually, I've been off ill this last week too, so I can't say I've seen much of her. But she was asking after you.'

Abigail plucked at the bobbles on her skirt, sniffed, and blinked. She fished a handkerchief out of her handbag.

know, it was ten years in August – her anniversary here, I mean.'

Iris nodded. She had known, but she had paid it no heed. She had been too busy mourning the death of her favourite patient, Katherine Owen. Just the thought of Kath was enough to make her eyes sting even now, and so to distract herself, she asked Abigail who Matilda was.

The woman cocked a brow. 'Matilda? I don't know. Should I?'

'Your mum mentioned her. I thought she might be a relation, but I've never seen her here.'

Abigail took a moment to think. 'No. The name isn't familiar. We're a small family.'

'Patients who are... like your mother tend to remember the past better than the present. Perhaps Matilda was someone she used to know?'

Abigail swallowed. 'Perhaps.'

'Look, maybe she's just getting confused. This disease only worsens. Have you got anything at home she could remember you all by? It might help if she had it with her here, to bridge the gap between your visits, so to speak.'

'I'll bring some things in tomorrow. Sorry, I've completely forgotten – what's your name?'

'Iris.'

'Iris, yes, of course.' She laughed. 'Like mother, like daughter.'

2
1956

Rain fizzed against the windows and shrouded the afternoon. The lights were turned on by half past three, smearing the day room in flickering yellow, making the old women's complexions even sallower. Those whose minds still functioned hugged their shawls tighter and glared at the weather, while the others stared unseeing at the empty tables before them. The visiting pianist tried brightening the atmosphere but, after a few upbeat tunes, gave up and settled on something more melancholy. The notes played out against the sounds of nurses' heels on damp floorboards and the unrelenting moans of the patients.

Louisa's inanimate face melted into a smile as she saw her daughter heading her way.

'How are you today, Mum?'

'Are you taking me home?'

Abigail set her handbag by her mum's feet. 'You're resting.'

Louisa soured. 'I'm fine. How many times do I have to tell you?'

Abigail glanced guiltily at Iris before taking the seat next to her mother. She forced her voice to be light. 'I've brought you some things, Mum.' She opened her bag and brought out a knitted blanket. Louisa took it and gently rubbed it against her cheek.

'My baby's favourite.'

Before getting upset, Abigail took out two framed photographs. Both held old pictures, one from the twenties judging by the fashions and the young faces staring out.

'My brother Samuel's wedding in twenty-nine,' Abigail explained. 'It's the only one to have all of us in.'

Five people stood stiffly before rolling countryside. The bride and groom were in the centre. Abigail was between her brother and mother, and a man, who Iris assumed must have been Louisa's husband, stood next to the bride. Only the two young women smiled.

The other photo showed a couple with a baby. The man could have been mistaken for the groom in the other photo, but no, Samuel was the baby here, so Abigail explained. The man was her father, a dashing fellow with thick black hair and a moustache. Iris recognised a young Louisa sitting beside him and holding the baby. The face shape was the same, the eyes just as unapproachable. Youth had made her interesting, somewhat arresting, but not exactly pretty. Unfortunately for Abigail, she had inherited more of her mother's qualities than her father's.

Louisa held out her hand for the photographs. She peered at the wedding picture and smiled, then showed Iris.

'My daughter. She's a teacher. Bright as a button. She's getting married soon.'

'How lovely,' Iris said, because Abigail had turned away with a sigh.

Louisa's attention fell on the baby picture. Her smile withered. A frown etched her forehead. 'But it was on the wall.'

'That's right. I brought it from home.'

Louisa shook her head. She blinked, studied it more closely. Confusion creased her features as she faced Iris. 'The picture on the wall.' Something was on the other side of those wide, mud-coloured eyes. A memory sifting through the silt of a demented mind and rising to the top.

'On what wall? Where?'

'Bodnem.'

'Mum and Dad used to live there,' Abigail said. 'I've never been. I wasn't born there, but she talks of it sometimes.'

'Did you like Bodnem, Louisa?'

'Horrid. All those girls…'

Iris looked at Abigail, who could only reply with a shrug.

'Will you put the photographs by her bed?'

'Of course.'

But for now, Louisa was too engrossed with the baby picture. Iris would take them later, once Abigail had gone and it was time for tea.

'I hope you don't mind my asking, and please feel free to say no.' Abigail snapped her bag shut. 'Normally I pay a lady from the village to help, but it's so last minute.'

Iris raised her brows. Abigail cleared her throat, as if embarrassed.

'My brother and his wife are visiting this weekend. Only told me today.' She rolled her eyes skyward. 'Mum likes to see him and I try to take her home for the day, but I can't do it on my own. She's too much work now. I wondered if you would mind coming along. If you're not working, that is. Or,' she added as an afterthought, 'have other plans. I wouldn't want to get in the way of anything.'

Iris smiled. 'I have nothing going on that you could possibly get in the way of.'

Iris wore her most formal outfit of black skirt and blouse, with her coat brushed and batted of day-to-day grime and her hair slicked back beneath her hat. Why she felt so nervous, she didn't know, but it was the first time such a request had been made.

Rain smoked the air. Instead of mid-morning, it felt like dusk. The street lamps remained on, glimmering dimly through the fog and casting sickly, syrupy light on nearby objects. Already, her feet were cold in her finest pair of black shoes, and raindrops condensed on the patent leather like boils on flesh.

Finally, headlights glowed between the lime trees. Iris rubbed her hands together, igniting warmth and confidence, as Abigail parked her bottle-green Morris Minor in front of the hospital. She, too, had dressed for the occasion. Gone were the old, tattered skirt and lace-up shoes. She wore a teal coat, buttoned tight at the waist and trimmed at the collar and cuffs with mink fur. Dainty, low-heeled court shoes elongated her legs and slimmed her ankles. Her hair had been in rollers and was set to within an inch of its life.

Iris breathed a sigh of relief; she had not overdressed. Obviously, Samuel warranted far greater effort than a woman in a mental hospital.

Abigail rushed to where Iris stood under the hood of the hospital entrance. She shook her head. 'Sorry I'm late. It's just been one thing after another.'

Iris had already got Louisa ready. On the ward, the woman sat by the window in the best skirt and jumper Iris could find, even though they didn't belong to her. The shoes definitely weren't hers. They swallowed her feet whole, and despite how tight Iris had tied the laces, they still shuffled around loosely.

'Sorry, these were the best I could do.'

Abigail frowned at the sight of her mother. 'We'll change her when we get home.'

Twenty minutes later, Louisa was staggering out of the doors clinging to her daughter, while Iris dawdled behind carrying the bags.

It was an uneasy journey cramped in the back of Abigail's car, knees buckled up to her chest so her legs didn't batter into the back of the passenger seat. Abigail took the bends on the country lanes too fast for Iris's liking. Thrown from left to right, Iris did not manage to make idle conversation to fill the silence. Not that the erratic driving seemed to bother Louisa. The old woman sat contentedly next to her daughter as if she were used to it, gazing out at the passing fields, never flinching when a wheel dipped into a pothole or the exhaust spluttered phlegmatically with each shift of gear.

'I love driving,' Abigail shouted over the din of the

engine, flashing Iris a crazed smile in the rear-view mirror. 'Cars are my guilty pleasure.'

Iris nodded, holding her tongue in case more than just words came out of her mouth.

An hour later, they finally slowed to a more acceptable speed as they approached a little village. Dipping into a shallow valley, Abigail pulled onto a gravelled drive and parked in front of a large, detached house next to a black Rover P4. Raindrops blanketed the front garden's grass, and the clipped evergreen shrubs drooped and dripped from the downpour.

For a moment, none of them moved. After the whirring of the engine, silence descended, allowing everyone to take a breath. Abigail and her mother stared at the blank, leaded windows of the house as if unsure whether to enter.

'Home,' Louisa whispered, and stirred the atmosphere.

Abigail jumped out of the car as if propelling herself forward in an effort to get the day over and done with as quickly as possible. Louisa shrugged off her daughter's aid and strode to the front door, marching inside without hesitation.

Pea-green wallpaper lined a dark hallway, where glass figurines sat atop the shelves and a grandfather clock crouched next to the stairs. The smell of roasting meat warmed the air as Iris brushed her shoes on the mat and waited for Abigail to lead the way.

Louisa marched straight for the kitchen and filled the kettle. A bowl of uncooked, peeled carrots and potatoes sat in cold water in saucepans on the centre table next to a glass bowl filled with trifle, the whisked cream frothing all the way to the rim.

Abigail peeled her mother's coat off her shoulders, shrugged out of her own, and held out her hand for Iris's coat too. She set all three of them on the stand back in the hallway, then wiped her palms on her salmon-coloured skirt as she bumbled around in the kitchen, taking out cups from the cupboard and preparing the teapot.

Iris wrung her hands, not knowing what else to do. Louisa lumped herself on the kitchen chair and picked a carrot baton from the pan. Male voices drifted from another room, growing louder and forcing Abigail to acknowledge them.

'They're in the parlour. We'd best introduce you. Mum, come and say hello to Samuel. He's up especially to see you.'

Louisa nibbled the carrot but got to her feet all the same. Abigail led the way, and Iris trailed behind them both.

The parlour was large, dominated by a Victorian fireplace and a painting of a moonlit lake which hung above it. A glistening cherry-wood table held three glasses of sherry which belonged to the two men and one woman who sat about the room. All of them fell quiet as Abigail guided her mother inside. The only sound was Louisa crunching the crudité between her teeth.

'Mummy,' Samuel said after a long pause, rising to his feet and kissing Louisa's cheek, 'you're looking well.'

The other woman, who Iris assumed to be his wife, copied his actions with a mew of agreement, before ogling Iris who remained in the doorway.

'Who's this?' The old man in the corner of the room peered at Iris over his spectacles.

'The nurse I was telling you about. Iris, this is my father, Tim Edwards.'

Iris stepped forward, plastering a smile on her face as she approached him. He was not what she had been expecting. He was smaller and decidedly frail. Flesh draped from his cheekbones, causing stubble to cluster in the deep wrinkles around his jowls. Only one thing was as she had expected – the eyes. Shrewd and sharp, as they were in the picture.

He took her offered hand limply. 'Are you taking care of my wife?'

'Better care than you ever did,' Louisa said, her first words snipping like scissors.

Tim let go of Iris. She hurried back to her place beside the door.

'Now, Mum, let's not start. We're here for a nice lunch and to see Samuel. But first we need to get you into something more… fitting.' Abigail ushered Louisa back out to the hallway, rolling her eyes so only Iris could see. 'Will you help me?'

Gladly, Iris left the grim company and headed upstairs.

* * *

A small double bed took up most of the room, squashed in amongst fitted wardrobes and a vanity table. A thin window looked down on the back garden and fields beyond. Louisa went to it, gazing out at the rain which dented the pond and waterlogged lawn.

'Always losing her things in that place,' Abigail muttered as she threw open the wardrobe doors. 'And I stitch her name into them all.'

Iris flushed, feeling as if she were being told off by her teacher.

'Oh, I don't blame you. It's been the same for years. The clothes I don't mind so much, but the shoes.'

A smattering of skirts and blouses swayed on the rail as Abigail forced her way to the stack of shoeboxes at the bottom. She began taking each one out at a time.

'Mum adored shoes. Her only vanity. Every Christmas I'd buy her a new pair. Good job, I suppose, although we're getting through them now.' She lifted the lid off the first box and revealed a pair of cream-and-brandy-coloured Oxfords. Judging by the pungent smell of leather and their quality, they had hardly ever been worn. 'Too nice.' Abigail replaced the lid and moved on to the next. 'There are cardigans in that drawer.'

Iris found a wine-coloured cashmere cardigan. 'Is this your father's room too?' she asked, hoping she didn't come across as too nosey.

'No.' Abigail sighed over a pair of navy brogues. 'He's across the landing. Mum and he… liked their own space.' She moved on to the next box.

Iris plucked a cream blouse off its hanger and coaxed Louisa out of her jumper. She fastened the blouse on quickly, for Louisa's skin had pimpled against the cold, then tugged on the cashmere. When she turned, Abigail was no longer holding up shoes for inspection. Rather, a thin piece of paper trembled between her fingertips. On the bed, a notebook sat on top of a pair of burgundy peep toe heels.

Abigail's eyes scanned left to right as she read the words on the page. As she did so, colour drained from her cheeks. She looked up at Iris, dazed.

'What is it?'

Abigail picked up the notebook and leafed through. All of the pages were filled with scrawling handwriting. She dropped onto the bed and showed her mother the paper.

'You wrote this?'

Louisa stared at it vacantly.

'You wrote this for me?'

Louisa's crooked fingers reached for the notebook. Without understanding, she flicked through the first few pages until something dawned in her eyes. 'Read it.' She pushed it at Abigail.

Mother and daughter regarded each other warily. Iris, although intrigued, backed towards the door. 'I can go if you'd like?'

'No. Stay.' Abigail pushed a shoebox aside so Iris, too, could sit down. The piece of paper lay between all three of them, waiting.

'What does it say?'

3

1946

27th August 1946

Smedley Mental Hospital

My dearest Abigail,

This is not a letter like the others. You must show no one. Not your father, nor your brother. What I write here is for your eyes only, for I know they are the kindest eyes in all the world.

My darling, I fear I am losing my mind. Your father tells me I am, but I stopped paying attention to him a long time ago. Grief is what they say is responsible. This lapse in judgment, the low emotions interspersed with maniacal outbursts. They are not maniacal, and I am not grieving. I had no love for that woman. I am sorry for you to hear it, but you will have known that already.

It is not grief which plagues me. It is guilt. So much guilt. I fear it has gnawed at my brain and pocked it with holes.

I know what is coming: a slow decline, the way my own grandmother went. My father sent her to Winson Green Asylum when she could no longer recognise him, and we never saw her again. Promise me you will not abandon me so when I have gone the same way.

Now I must write, while those vague shadows circle only the edges of my mind. I must tell you, for there is no one else to tell. I hope, in the telling of it, in the explanation of what happened and what I did, you will understand us better – your father and me. At the heart of it all, I hope you will forgive me for what I did to you and Samuel.

My sweet boy, Samuel. I weep now and blot the ink. To think of how I have treated him. My love for him calcified because I made it so, because I thought that was the only way of putting things right.

How I was wrong.

How I wish to hold him as a babe once more and kiss him. How I wish to delight in his first words, first walk, all the firsts, instead of view them with fear and trepidation.

It was never the case with you, Abigail. You, out of it all, were my salvation. A light in the darkness. And yet you only deepened the ridges between us all.

None of it is your fault. It is all mine and your father's. So many lies have entwined between us and bound us tight, unable to live with each other and unable to live without.

And so I write to you.

I do not know when I will get out of here. If I ever will. I could not speak this story; I would not be able. The words would stick in my throat, come out all wrong, and surely you would run from me for good. Better to have it on paper. Then it is only mere words. Then it is a tale from a novel, easier to ingest, to break apart, to understand.

I was wrong.

I believed a lie, and it has carved the heart out of me.

But now I know. Now I, too, understand, although that does not diminish the hurt. The waste of it all.

I will tell you everything. Every detail I can recall. It is the only thing I think about as I stare at these walls.

Sometimes, I wonder whether this life is a dream. Am I still living in Bodnem? Am I sleeping upstairs in the cottage, with Tim and Samuel either side of me? Do I only need to open my eyes to step back into that time?

Who truly knows what is nightmare and what is waking life?

Read, my darling. From the start. Only if you see it all will you be able to understand, and perhaps – I hope – sympathise.

Your ever-loving mother,

Louisa

4
1900

Bodnem was the type of place which looked inviting until you were stuck there.

The houses were black-and-white wattle and daub, with thatched roofs and crooked door frames. They spilled out around a crossroads where once, so Mr Edwards told me over my very first dinner in the village, they used to bury suicides. An old coaching inn nestled in one quadrant, and in another and beyond a low stone wall, a lake, which I was told was beautiful in summer and a death trap for skaters in winter. The lake belonged to the squire called Buckley, who lived at the end of Church Street in a great manor house. My new home was at the start of this lane and in the third quadrant, facing the crossroads. Behind it loomed St Luke's Church, whose sandstone bricks looked decidedly dull on a drizzly March day, with headstones at odd slanting angles. Everything was untidy in Bodnem.

Everything, except my new mother-in-law.

Mildred Edwards was a short, stout woman who never

smiled. She reminded me of the ponies I once saw on a day trip to the Long Mynd with my charges. Small, stocky, stubborn, and unapproachable. I did not get too close for fear she would bite. She kept her house spotless and did not employ a maid or a cook, which I found bizarre and discomforting; would Tim expect the same from me? It seemed as much. But then, I had not married him for money.

'Mother asks if you will peel the potatoes,' Tim said as he crept into the parlour. He made for the fire, holding his hands towards the flames, and stared down at his son.

Samuel slept in his cot before the fire guard, his cheeks rosy, his breathing deep and contented. He was one month old, and try as I might, it was impossible to imagine how he had ever fought his way out of my own body. The horrific ordeal seemed like a lifetime ago, and yet when I let my mind wander towards it, I could feel the ripping of my flesh all over again.

In the kitchen, Mildred started banging pots and pans.

'Is there no one in the village who can help her?' I whispered.

Tim did not answer. He was wearying of my criticisms and how I had pestered him for our own house. He had dashed my hopes and told me he had no intention of living elsewhere; the whole point of coming back was to take over the role of village doctor from his ailing father.

I rose with a sigh and slipped into the kitchen. Mildred was mincing the leftovers from a joint of mutton and nodded towards a bowl of sprouting potatoes. I took up the knife.

We worked in silence. After the mutton, she chopped

an onion, then set it over the range to fry. Beyond the kitchen window, the sky grew dark.

'I could always take notes for Tim,' I said. She slid the minced mutton off the board and into the pan, her back to me. 'I should be happy for the work.'

She sniggered.

I stabbed a potato and sliced it through the middle.

Really, I had never been so bored in all my life. The only books in the cottage were medical, nothing to serve as a distraction from the endless hours. And I would not entertain the notion of housework; if I started, Tim would believe I'd do it forever.

A bang came from above. From the cracks in the ceiling, dust trickled down and landed on the potatoes.

'Louisa!' my father-in-law shouted too loudly; one would have thought he would have known there was no need to shout in such a tiny house. 'Louisa, can you help me?'

Smirking, I stood from my half-peeled vegetables.

'Stay where you are.' Mildred jabbed the wooden spoon in my face.

'But he called for me.'

Mildred plodded upstairs. Their voices were murmurs, but I knew they were close to arguing. The baby must have been able to sense it too and began to cry. I left the table and found Tim prodding Samuel uselessly. I scooped Samuel up and smelt him.

At least cleaning him got me out of the kitchen. One small victory.

* * *

'What did you say your father did, dear?' My father-in-law bent over his mutton pie, his fork hovering halfway to his mouth and dripping mashed potato onto the plate. He had asked me that question the very first night, and again the second. He must have forgotten in the intervening three days.

I wished his memory were better, for then there would have been no need to mention my family ever again. As it was, I could not help the blood rising to my face as I recalled my father's disgust and my mother's dismay the last time I had set eyes on them. But he didn't need to know that. I would make sure he never knew that.

'He's a senior clerk for a toy company, Mr Edwards.'

'Ah, yes.' He nodded. 'In Birmingham. I remember now.' He shovelled food between his thick, pale lips. Potato frosted the ends of his greying whiskers, and I had to look away.

Judging by the photograph in the hallway, my father-in-law had once been rather dashing. He'd had wavy black hair, black brows, a sculpted face; his son had inherited all those things. But Mr Edwards was larger than Tim, broad and heavy whereas Tim was wiry. Even as he hobbled around on his cane, he was a few inches taller than my husband, and when he entered a room he seemed to fill it completely.

At least he had welcomed me. On arriving, he had embraced his son as I had never seen a man do before. He then turned to me, and I was consumed by his tobacco-cloyed wool jacket.

His wife had not even said good day. Her dull, pinched eyes scanned me from top to toe as Tim introduced me, rather sheepishly, as the new Mrs Edwards. She grunted, then turned on her heel to lead Tim inside.

Whenever the subject of my parents came up, I felt those horrid, mean eyes upon me again, scrutinising me, wondering why I blushed and squirmed. She did not trust me.

'How are you feeling now, Mr Edwards?'

'Please' – he touched my hand – 'call me Howard. I am better, thank you, my dear. Although my damned eyes never improve. My breathing is easier; the milder weather and my medicine is helping. As are you. Isn't it wonderful to have young blood in the house again, Mildred?'

Mildred did not meet her husband's gaze.

'You have caused quite a stir in the village.'

'Father,' Tim warned.

Suddenly, I was alert. 'Why? What are people saying?'

'People say all sorts of things when they don't know the truth.' Howard's eyes sparkled mischievously. 'They are just jealous. We don't often have new women in the area.'

I swallowed as I imagined the rumours that might have been spreading. I had done nothing to allay such gossip; I had hardly stepped out of the front door. Most of the time I was exhausted from Samuel. He didn't sleep well through the night.

'Perhaps you should talk to them, get to know them,' Tim said. 'Why don't you do the shopping some time instead of Mother? Once they realise you are… one of us, they will take more kindly to you.'

Already, I resented them.

* * *

I took Samuel with me to the shops, thinking he might be some kind of protection. No mother could be termed uncaring when she had her son in a fine pram and wrapped in the softest muslin.

The wind bit my cheeks. It was odd stepping outside, as if I had forgotten what the world was truly like; I had been observing it through a windowpane for too long. The smell of cows wafted from the nearby fields, and coal smoke ribboned out from all of the chimneys. My shoes echoed as I stepped into the crossroads, the place eerily quiet but for the odd door shutting now and again and the clanging of a hammer in the distance. I glanced over my shoulder and found Tim watching me from our bedroom window. He smiled when our eyes met, then ducked out of sight.

Mr Powell's grocery store was in the middle of a cluster of shops on what was a bad excuse for a high street. Tins and jars lined the wood-panelled walls: tea from China, coffee from the Americas, Lyle's golden syrup, Huntley and Palmers' biscuits. It was an assault on the senses. I had never had to do the shopping before – there were always maids for that sort of thing. My mind turned blank. What did Mildred say she wanted? I perused the shelves and picked up a bag of powdered sugar.

The woman behind the counter and the two in front of it fell silent. I fixed my gaze on the garishly coloured products, hoping the women would resume their conversation, but it was useless. Gritting my teeth, I turned to face them and found only one smiling. She was the youngest, not even twenty judging by the roundness of her cheeks. There was a simpleton glimmer in her eyes which gave me little hope.

'Good morning,' I said, and I had to clear my throat before I spoke again. 'Mrs Timothy Edwards, from the doctor's cottage.' My introduction was pointless; of course they knew who I was.

The young woman lunged towards the pram, her grin spreading to show all of her crooked teeth. 'I'm Jenny. Pleased to meet you. Oh!' She leered over Samuel, and as he wriggled, her grubby finger darted to his neck and tickled him. 'Isn't he a bonny lad?'

I manoeuvred the pram away from her and set the sugar upon the counter. 'Two ounces of coffee. Do you have any almonds?'

The woman, short and rotund and whom I assumed to be Mrs Powell, trudged to the jar of coffee and then to the scales. She nodded in the direction of the almonds.

'And a lemon?'

She ducked under the counter and produced one brown-speckled specimen. Jenny slid towards the pram again and made faces at Samuel, who stared up at her, frowning.

'How are you finding Bodnem?' the other woman in the room said as she leaned against the counter and clutched a paper bag in her bony, gloved hands. She looked at me with too-big eyes in a mousy face. I assumed it was from her that the faint scent of carbolic soap emanated, and from Tim's descriptions of the villagers, I surmised she was Mrs Dunn, the pharmacist's wife.

'In truth, I have not had the chance to explore it yet. Samuel has been a little sickly.'

'He looks fat enough for such an early baby,' Mrs Dunn said, flicking her gaze at Mrs Powell. She spoke with a smirk in her voice. 'What have you been feeding him to make him grow so quickly?'

My cheeks flushed.

Mrs Powell scrunched up my paper bag of ground coffee beans. 'Your mother-in-law says you were a governess in the city. The work not suit you?' Her gaze sharpened on Samuel. I snatched the coffee bag and lemon from her and placed them by his feet. 'When was it you married Master Edwards?'

'He is *Doctor* Edwards,' I muttered, heat rising all the way from my boots. 'And he will be settling your account at the end of the week.'

I made for the door and emerged into the street like a drowning woman. I could not face the butcher's or the baker's. Let their imaginations run wild for another day; for now, I needed to be on my own.

I marched towards home but stopped at the crossroads. I did not want to go inside. I had been cooped up in there for far too long already, and now that I knew my mother-in-law had done nothing to quell the vicious gossip about me, I could not bear to face her. Perhaps she had been the one spreading it. Perhaps she thought if she made the whole village resent me, I would magically go back to where I came from. Unfortunately for both of us, I feared that was impossible.

Looking left down the south road, I saw a group of boys playing with sticks in the street. To my right, a man readied a pony and trap. I did not want to pass either, and so I headed straight on, along Church Street.

'You don't sound like you're from Birmingham.' The close proximity of the voice startled me. I jumped backward and whirled around to see Jenny not a foot away from me.

'Beg your pardon?'

'Your accent. It's posh.'

I took a deep breath and collected myself. 'Do you want something, Jenny?'

Her attention fell on the churchyard to our right. 'My sister's just over there. Mary. Do you have any sisters?'

I didn't know whether to apologise for her loss or not. She did not seem particularly bothered by it herself. I decided to keep the conversation short. 'Four.'

'I bet that's nice. I would have liked a little sister so I could brush her hair and dress her up and all that sort of stuff. I've only got boys now.'

Again, I did not know if I should console her. She was grinning, though, so I decided to move on. Just as I was about to wish her good day, she fell into step beside me.

'Where you going?'

'For a walk.' Alone, I wished to add.

Her arm shot before my face, almost swiping my nose in the process. 'That's Buckley Lake. We could go skating next winter. Do you have any skates?'

'No.'

'I'll ask Ma if she'll lend you hers. She doesn't like skating on there, not since Madam Buckley got put in the water.'

I stopped, confused and horrified. 'What on earth do you mean?'

'Madam Buckley's evil spirit,' she explained to me, as if I were the idiot. 'Long time ago now.'

'Evil spirit?' I laughed when I said it. Bodnem truly was the armpit of the world.

'That's what got Mary. That's why Ma doesn't like skating on there. But it's all right because the spirit's in a bottle and can't get out.'

I stared at her. Did she honestly believe what she was saying? I pitied the girl. There was no place in society for someone like her. Fear stirred inside me. What if Samuel turned out like her, as God's way of punishing me?

'Jenny, are you not needed at home?'

She shrugged.

'I'm going to continue on my walk now.' I inched onwards, sighing with relief when she remained where she was.

'You watch out up there, Mrs Edwards. Don't let old Buckley catch you on his land.'

The road narrowed and the hedges grew dense after I left her. Soon, I could not see the church beyond the shrubbery and trees. Old leaves scattered the road, soggy from the endless drizzle, but it was blissfully quiet, with nothing but birdsong. To my left and on the other side of the stone wall, the marshy lake area vanished and instead green fields rose up, strewn with sheep. The scent of cows and coal disappeared too, and the air was like a glass of cold water on a summer's day.

The church bells told me it was ten o'clock. I had been out of the house for a whole hour. How long did this road continue? My boots were making my heels sore, for I had not walked so far in over three months. And yet, there was enjoyment in that simple, lonesome activity.

Always, I had enjoyed my own company. At my childhood home, I would hide in Father's study at the back of the house, curled up in the window seat overlooking our neat patch of garden while I read a book. I would be in there for hours, even when I could hear my mother and sisters searching for me, as I imagined my husband might have started to do now. I could not bring myself to care; it had been his idea to get me out of the house, after all.

I crested the hill. Below, the road spilled open, the hedges falling away to grass. I quickened my pace until I emerged into a grand garden. Trees stretched into the sky. The grass was long and shaggy. Dishevelled bushes slumped after a long winter. Branches had snapped off the trees and lay where they had fallen, like broken bones.

I ventured further along the road until it veered right and I came across a hand-painted sign: *Buckley Manor. Keep Out.*

I paid it no heed, and before long the house rose up over my head. Below it, there was a brick wall, with steps on the sides which led to the manor. The house itself was one long, jagged oblong of red brick, with whole walls devoted to windows, although the curtains inside were drawn. A few chimneys squatted on its roof, but none emitted smoke.

It seemed incongruous with Bodnem. The house was too large and angular – too even. The modernity of the red bricks seemed to mock Bodnem's wattle-and-daub cottages. Indeed, the manor appeared somehow cruel.

Samuel squirmed. He clenched his fists and opened his mouth, about to cry. I turned around quickly, not wanting his noise to alert whoever might be inside. I ran back along the road, lifting my heels to be as quiet as possible. Glancing back, I was sure there was a pale face in the upper-floor window which I had not seen before.

5
1900

Howard was improving by the day. No longer did he hack up half of his lungs or stagger on unsteady limbs. He wandered about quietly and serenely, and smoked his own special mixture for his asthma, dousing the cottage in that peculiar sweet smell of dried herbs and tobacco he stuffed into his pipe. He let Tim take care of the bulk of the work and enjoyed leisure time with his first and only grandson, upon whom he doted.

As it was, Tim spent most of his days out in the pony cart making calls. He left early after a quick breakfast and often did not return until dusk was approaching. And so, after just two weeks, my routine was horrifyingly dull; I did whatever Mildred asked me to, unless I could get away with it.

I found the best way to dodge her was to run the errands.

The first time I met Mrs Powell's daughter, Daisy, was after Mildred had challenged me with scrubbing the copper pans. With my fingers stinging from the vinegar and my nails blackened with old grease, I had eagerly dashed out of the house when my mother-in-law had moaned about her lack of onions to fry for that night's dinner.

'A pound of butter, please,' I said breathlessly, as Daisy squinted at me as if I were something the cat had dragged in. 'And two onions.'

She was as plain as a loaf of bread and just as podgy. A sore had cracked the corner of her lips, and white face powder had crusted over it. I shuddered, imagining those flecks speckling the butter.

'That all?' She did not meet my gaze but stared out of the window in boredom. Slight bruises shaded the skin under her eyes as if she had not enjoyed a restful night. She did not say another word as I made my way outside.

'Want to see what I found?' Jenny emerged out of nowhere, giving me a fright. She grinned devilishly as I composed myself, then fished something out of a stained cotton bag and held it before my face. I batted her hand away.

'Isn't it pretty?'

'It's a bottle.' The kind I had seen many times before. The kind that lined every pharmacist's walls on every high street. 'What are you doing with it?'

She returned it to her bag, shrugged. 'Pretty.'

We walked back towards the cottage. At last, the weather had brightened. Overhead, a thin layer of white cloud could not disguise the blue beyond, nor the watery sun hanging low in the sky. The puddles in the road rippled blue and glossy, and in the patches of woodland that lined Bodnem's roads, splashes of yellow daffodils bent in the breeze.

'Fancy going for a walk?' Jenny said, looking hopeful.

I didn't fancy it, but then I fancied being under Mildred's watchful eye even less.

We stopped in the middle of the crossroads. 'Which way?'

Jenny headed north. I followed, and we did not speak as we passed the short row of houses and Mr Griffith's smithy at the edge of the village. Smoke chugged out of the flue, but inside all was silent.

'You seen him?' Jenny asked, as woodland built to our left and a field spread out to our right – the communal field for the villagers' horses. Mr Griffith earned a few extra pennies by taking care of them. Sometimes, so I was told, Squire Buckley let his own fleet of equines graze in it too.

'Who?'

'Old Buckley. Is he back yet?'

'How should I know?' I kept my gaze on Samuel, although I felt Jenny watching me.

Of course, Jenny watched everything. She must have known how I had wandered too many times up Church Street, inexplicably drawn to that manor and whoever might have been inside it.

'Anyway, back from where?'

'The big smoke. He's down there all the time, almost. Can't stand Bodnem.'

That made two of us, I thought. But then another thought occurred to me – if he had been in London, who had I seen at the window?

Jenny shushed me before I could voice my concern. She stopped, forcing me to do the same, and pointed to the stables.

My cheeks burned as the muffled noises became clear. A man and a woman, breathing heavily, groaning, shuffling.

Jenny crept closer to the sound, trying to see who was making it, but I grabbed her arm and yanked her back.

'Come away now.' My ferocity startled her; suddenly, she was little Catherine, her cherub cheek blazed red with my handprint, her eyes wide and wet with shock.

I shook the image from my mind until I saw Jenny once more. I let go of her, turned on my heel, and marched all the way home.

By Thursday, I could not stand another minute in the cottage. Things were worsening between Mildred and me. A tension pulled between the two of us, so tight I was afraid it would break if we only looked too long at each other.

Once out of the front door, I set Samuel in his pram. Mildred took out her anger on the rugs in the backyard. Each slap reverberated off the houses and seemed to smack me in the face. I stomped towards the high street. The sign of the Black Heart Inn swung and creaked in the gaining breeze.

Public houses were odd places in the daytime. Empty vessels, haunted structures with windowpanes as black and dull as dead fish eyes. Only in the evenings did they come alive, shining with candlelight, laughing with men's voices and a girl's lusty song.

Betty Crook's voice snaked into the street each night, acting as a lullaby for the women left at home. From my bedroom, I could only decipher the tune, which was best; the words were not something I wished to hear. Indeed, Betty was an audacious girl, but then, having been raised in such an establishment, what else could one expect?

I was surprised to find her that morning in her backyard – typically, she was a creature of the night. I saw only a slither of her skirt at first, for she was hidden behind a half-open gate, but then she stepped back, bent from the waist, and vomited. She eased upright, wiped her mouth on her wrist, and, with that odd sixth sense we all possess at some time or other, felt herself being watched and turned to look straight at me. Her pale face rippled into a scowl.

'What?'

'Ginger tea helps, so I hear.'

She sniffed and swayed, but swallowed down whatever had been threatening to come up. 'Don't know what you mean.'

She looked dreadful, not at all like the fresh and vigorous young woman who paraded around after dark. The effect of drink was heinous, and decidedly worse on women.

'Do you think' – she stopped me as I began to walk away – 'Master Edwards might see me?'

'My husband is out. I don't know when he will return. Dr Edwards Snr should be able to fit you in.' Although I doubted she had the money to be seen by either of them. And what she was hoping they would do for drunkenness was anybody's guess.

'I'll wait.' She disappeared inside the inn without another word. I let the insult pass; one should not feel insulted by a barmaid.

A shadow slipped up the side alley of Powell's grocery. I approached, slowing a little, a sense of danger creeping over me, but it was only Jenny pressing herself against the wall.

'I can see you.' My voice echoed.

We had not spoken since Monday after the incident by the stables, although I had seen her flit past the house and gaze through the windows. Guilt had plagued me, scratching at the back of my mind when I least expected it.

'Look, I am sorry for grabbing you like I did,' I said quickly. 'I didn't mean to frighten you. I just can't stand it when people sneak around spying. Do you understand?'

She muttered something but remained where she was.

'Why don't we go for a walk together?' I began, trying to tempt her. Why I should have felt the need to lure her into conversation was somewhat of a mystery. I should have been glad of her avoidance, and yet I had the urge to speak to someone. Anyone. Tim never listened to anything I uttered, and I couldn't bring myself to say more than a few words to Mildred. Howard was welcoming enough, but there was something in me which desired female companionship, a silly need for gossip, if you like. 'You can tell me all about Squire Buckley.'

Still she did not move.

'Jenny, come out now. This is ridiculous.'

Reluctantly, she shuffled towards me, head down, and came into the sunshine. Raising her shoulders so that half of her face was concealed, she twisted in such a way that I was forced to address her ear.

'Well? What interesting titbits do you have for me?'

She shrugged. I sighed with frustration and moved on

to peruse the grocery store's window display. Seeing her reflection in the glass, I finally realised why Jenny had been hiding herself.

I dived in front of her and, although she tried, she was too slow to shield herself. The left half of her face was swollen and bruised; her eye peered through two giant mounds of reddened flesh.

'What on earth has happened?' I held her by the shoulders as she tried to squirm out of my grip. 'Jenny, who hurt you like this?'

'It was for her own good.' Mrs Powell's nasal voice startled me. I whipped around and found her standing in her doorway, arms folded across her chest.

'She is little more than a child.'

Mrs Powell laughed. Jenny tugged out of my grasp, pushed her hands before her face, and wept.

'Who did this to her?'

'Her father, so you can unscrew that face of yours. He's every right.'

'What were his reasons?'

Daisy crept up behind her mother and stared at Jenny, scratching incessantly at her palm as she did so. The three of us waited for Jenny to explain.

'The bottle,' she wailed, spittle hanging from her open mouth.

'I don't understand. She was beaten for collecting a bottle?'

'Not any old bottle,' Daisy Powell said, stepping out of her mother's shadow. The sore at the corner of her mouth appeared to have cracked, and her skin there was raw. 'Madam Buckley's spirit bottle. And she opened it.'

I stood, dumbfounded for a moment, then laughed.

'Shame on you,' Mrs Powell spat. 'Laughing at the devil's work.'

'Oh, for goodness' sake, there are no evil spirits. And they cannot be trapped in glass bottles.'

Our argument had caused a stir. In the surrounding shop windows, gaunt faces watched our altercation. Mrs Dunn scurried out of the pharmacy next door and, to my surprise, stepped in before Mrs Powell could launch her attack. 'Mrs Edwards doesn't know what we know.'

Mrs Powell snarled at me one last time. 'You wait and see, Governess. Your little friend there has let the devil loose on our streets again.'

Tim and Howard had gone to the Black Heart Inn. I'd asked Tim to stay, for it felt as if we never had a spare minute to ourselves anymore, but no matter what I said, he was powerless to refuse his father.

I was beginning to worry I had married a weak man.

Neither did I think his profession suited him. At dinner that evening, I had raised the subject of Madam Buckley's evil spirit. Tim had turned quite white when I mentioned how the bottle had been found and opened. Surely a man of science could not believe in such superstitious nonsense?

His father sided with me and shook his head as I told him of Mrs Powell's idiotic ramblings about devils loose in the streets. Mildred said nothing. She laid her knife and fork on her plate and pinched her lips shut.

'So, what happened to Madam Buckley?' I said when Howard had finished ridiculing his patients.

'Died in childbirth.' He patted his lips with his napkin and clasped his hands over his stomach as Mildred cleared away the plates. 'Terrible end for the poor girl. The baby, it... well, it wouldn't come out naturally. Wasn't facing the right way. She lost too much blood.'

I shivered, thinking of my own ordeal and remembering the forceps. Tim rose and excused himself. I heard him leave through the back door, making for the privy.

'Were you there?'

Howard nodded. 'And Tim. We tried everything we could.'

The room felt very brittle. Howard stared intently at the empty table before him, and as the silence dragged, I gently squeezed his arm. He looked up at me, surprised by my tenderness, but in the next instant, Mildred returned and I retracted my grip.

Tim returned and asked his father for some help in the medical office. After they had left, Mildred and I passed a couple of uneasy hours alone before the fire. She sewed while I read. Samuel slept in his cot, which was why, in our chamber just before the chiming of midnight, he was still wide awake.

In the bed beside me, he kicked his legs in the air and held on to his feet, cooing and gurgling to himself. Both of us watched the moonlight stream in through the open curtains and listened to Betty's voice leaking in through the windows as she sang in the Black Heart.

Despite her cheery tune, I could not stop thinking of that bottle, and of Mrs Powell's last words to me.

Your little friend there has let the devil loose on our streets again.

Again. What did she mean by again?

I recalled Jenny mentioning her sister being taken by Madam Buckley's spirit. I wished I had probed Jenny further, or paid more attention to the newspapers in previous years. Perhaps her sister had merely died of the influenza, or pneumonia, or some other common ailment, and everyone had blamed an evil spirit. People found it easier to believe in God and heaven if devils walked the earth.

Downstairs, the clock struck midnight. It was only because of the dark loneliness that my imagination was running so wild. In the morning, I would laugh at my fevered thoughts.

Samuel stirred, his forehead wrinkling. Betty's singing had ceased, and now only men's voices tumbled into the night air. I scooped Samuel into my arms and paced the room, rocking him gently.

Looking out of the window, I saw that Bodnem's black-and-white houses had taken on skeletal shapes under the moonlight. The road glistened, reflecting gold specks of candlelight from the inn's windows. In the Black Heart, ruddy-faced men were finding their coats before stumbling into the icy air.

Another man emerged, alone. I recognised him as Daniel Griffith, heading towards his cottage beside the smithy, glancing back at the pub too many times and hesitating. In the end, he marched to his front door and kicked the wall before crashing inside.

Foolish man. He would not thank his beer-induced rage in the morning when his toes were bruised.

My gaze returned to the public house and settled on two unidentifiable figures moving in the shadows outside. I squinted, but the moonlight did not reach them.

Really, I should have returned to bed, but something made me remain. A moment later, one of them sauntered into the light. Betty. I knew her at once by her black mop of loose curls and the way she strutted. The other figure waited beside the curtain of ivy. Two drunk men fell out of the pub and leaned on each other as they staggered along the south road and then, finally, the person in the shadows emerged.

My husband.

* * *

Dawn was breaking as Samuel woke for his feed. I had come downstairs just after one o'clock in the morning. It was easier to deal with him in the parlour, without Tim groaning at me to be quiet. Although why I should have cared, I didn't know; he had not tried to be quiet when returning to the cottage in his cups.

Yesterday morning, he had apologised for the state of himself, believing my coldness was due to his drinking. It did not stop him returning to the inn for a second time last night.

Now, the fire I had stoked was once again dulling to orange embers. I threw on a few pieces of coal and blew on the golden glow until a flame took, then slumped in my chair and tried to resume sleep.

Through the leaded window, the Black Heart was dark and lifeless once again, but the images from two nights ago came to me. I had not decided what to do about it. Perhaps there was an innocent explanation for Tim and Betty's covert midnight meeting. I hadn't seen them doing anything physical together. And Betty had said she wanted to talk to him.

I resolved to have it out with him at some point soon; I had been putting it off long enough. In all honesty, it was not infidelity which bothered me so much as his secrecy about it and, indeed, whom he had chosen as his mistress. I dreaded to think what other men Betty had entertained, or what diseases she harboured.

The clock chimed six. My eyelids lowered, until a scream shook the house.

I could not move as the sound echoed in my mind; I did not know whether it belonged to my dreams or reality.

It came again, a heart-twisting screech.

Fear gripped me. I held Samuel tight and ran to the front door.

Miss Sutton, the schoolmistress, stood at the crossroads in her black skirt and jacket, her hair neatly styled under a black hat. Her grey eyes bulged as she stared at the ground, and the collar of her blouse shook; she trembled all over.

An instinct within me told me not to look. There was something familiar, something right at the back of my mind, which told me that nothing would ever be the same again if I did.

I forced my gaze to the middle of the crossroads. Betty lay on the ground with her arms splayed out, her hair a tangle of black curls. The skin of her face was pure white, her lips pale and blue, her eyelids blushed mauve.

I waited, believing she would wake and cackle and boast about what an actress she was.

She did not.

Howard and Tim approached the body. Tim stopped several feet away, but Howard checked for a pulse.

As he did so, other villagers tiptoed out of their homes. Pounding came from my left, and I turned to find Daniel Griffith running our way. He glared at the scene.

Howard rose, shaking his head.

Soon, the Powells emerged. Next, Mr and Mrs Dunn, although their son, Pat, held back. The reverend hobbled from the vicarage, his clothes in disarray, his white hair dishevelled, and gasped at the sight.

'She's back,' Mrs Powell whispered. 'What did I tell you?' I sensed the question was directed at me. 'It's starting all over again.'

6
1956

'Abigail? Should I put the potatoes on now?' Samuel's wife opened the bedroom door.

Abigail slammed the notebook shut, causing a cloud of dust to fog the air. Three sets of eyes turned on the woman lingering in the doorway, who frowned with suspicion.

'Everything all right? You've been up here a while.'

'Yes. Sorry, Henrietta. We've been searching for a pair of shoes.' Discreetly, Abigail hid the notebook under a box. 'Would you mind?'

'What?'

'The potatoes.'

'Oh. Yes, of course.' Still eyeing them, Henrietta slipped out of the room. Both Abigail and Iris waited to hear her footsteps on the stairs before letting out their breath.

'What on earth was that all about?' Iris nodded at the notebook.

Abigail skimmed through its pages. 'It's full.'

'A girl was murdered?'

Abigail glanced at her mum. 'Why didn't you tell me this before?'

'Read it,' Louisa said, turning her gaze to the wall.

Abigail pulled it into her hands and ran her thumb over its cover.

'Are you sure you want to do this?' Iris asked.

'Abigail?' Henrietta shouted from the kitchen. 'What about the carrots?'

'Coming.' Abigail snapped the lid over the burgundy peep toes and thrust the notebook into Iris's reluctant hands. 'Will you take it for now? I don't want any of them downstairs seeing.'

Abigail ushered her mother out onto the landing. Iris trudged behind, dashed to the coat stand, and slipped the letter and notebook into her handbag.

* * *

The plate was meagre compared to her mother's generous portions, but it was for the best. The beef was too hard, overcooked, and full of gristle. In the present company, she could hardly spit it out, and by the time she was halfway through, her jaw ached from the effort. The others must have felt the same, although no one said anything. Louisa gave up on the meat, opting instead for the vegetables; her teeth were no longer used to such battles after a decade in Smedley where the food was unidentifiable mush.

Iris sipped from a glass of water. She had refused a pre-dinner sherry, and then a glass of cold red wine. She was here as a professional more than anything else. Smedley's reputation should not be further smeared by one of its staff getting tipsy in a patient's home.

Conversation had been limited, almost as hard as the beef. Discussed topics had consisted of the safest bet of all, the weather, and a few odd remarks about what was going on at the Suez Canal. Not that Iris had much to say on that. She kept her head out of the newspapers and away from the wireless as much as she could. It was taxing enough dealing with a ward full of chronic patients without having to face the world's crises as well.

'How is the surgery?' Abigail asked her brother as she sawed into her dinner. She had been on edge ever since reading the start of Louisa's story.

'Good,' Samuel muttered, his jaw otherwise occupied.

'You're a doctor on Harley Street, Mr Edwards?'

Samuel flashed Iris a smile for the first time. 'That's right. It runs in the blood. Got to keep the Edwards's reputation intact.'

Louisa snorted and set down her cutlery with half of the food uneaten.

Brittleness descended over the table. Tim dropped his napkin on his plate and turned to look out of the window. Tired, bored, angered: it was impossible to tell.

Abigail pushed out her chair and stacked the plates, snatching Henrietta's dinner away as she raised the last forkful to her lips.

'Let me come home, Tim,' Louisa whispered.

Tim continued to gaze outside.

'Please.'

The final plate cracked on top of the others. Abigail lifted a trembling hand to her forehead and pushed back a curl. A pained smile distorted her face as she picked up the stack of crockery and headed out of the dining room. 'I hope you like trifle, Iris.'

The faces turned to her, seeking a distraction. She nodded eagerly, too eagerly.

Abigail returned with the pudding and scooped it into bowls as she redirected the conversation. 'I was showing Iris the photograph from your wedding, Samuel. It was such a lovely day.'

Henrietta smiled in agreement, flicking her eyes nervously between her husband and Iris, as if searching for approval.

'You looked beautiful,' Iris added, and Henrietta's worry vanished. Judging by her clothes and jewellery, she was a woman who cared about beautiful things above all else. 'And you looked so like your father,' Iris said to Samuel, who took his bowl of pudding from his sister's hands. He raised a brow.

'I showed her the other photograph too. Of you as a baby.'

'The picture on the wall,' Louisa mumbled, frowning at the place mat. She drew confused eyes up towards her husband. 'It was on the wall, Tim.'

Tim's bulbous knuckles crunched into the table as he forced himself up. Standing, he seemed to shake, and Iris didn't know if that were due to his weak muscles or something else. 'I told you not to take it,' he spat at Abigail. He turned, trying to walk away, but his legs were no use. He couldn't lift his feet off the carpet. 'Help me!'

Abigail jumped at her father's command, supporting him under both arms and walking him out through the kitchen. Everyone at the table listened to shuffling shoes, the parlour door opening, the gentle sigh of a cushion giving under a light weight.

'I hope you're happy now, Mummy. You've done a fine job of upsetting him.'

Louisa stared at her son, tears brewing. 'Where am I?'

'At home. And you say you're not mad.' He shovelled his last mouthful between his lips.

'Where is my daughter? Abi? Abi!'

'I'm here, Mum.' Abigail rushed into the dining room and hugged her mother.

Louisa burrowed into her daughter's side and whispered, 'Who is that man?'

'Jesus Christ.' Samuel tore the napkin off his lap and threw it on the table. Without another word, he stormed out to the parlour and muttered his complaints to his father. It wasn't long before Henrietta departed too.

'I'm so sorry,' Abigail breathed to Iris, stroking her mother's hair off her face.

Iris cleared away the plates and ran a bowl full of soapy water. There was nothing else she could do to help, and it saved her from trying to pass the time with Samuel and Tim.

'I'll do that later; you're a guest.' Abigail helped her mother into the kitchen chair and picked up a tea towel.

'It's the least I can do.' She eyed the mountains of crockery, glasses, cups, roasting dishes, and saucepans piled up on the kitchen counters. A pang of pity stewed inside her. All that effort, and for what? An argument. Half the food untouched, none of it appreciated. The people whom Abigail had gone to so much effort for were rooted in their seats with no intention of helping clear away the mess.

Iris set a pan on the drying rack with a bit too much force.

'I shouldn't have mentioned the photograph.' Abigail wiped the potato masher resignedly.

'Why didn't he want you to take it?'

She shrugged.

After washing up, Iris helped Louisa to the bathroom, telling Abigail to go and sit down. Louisa did her business quietly, but when Iris helped her up, she pulled her close.

'He knows I know,' she whispered.

Iris flushed the toilet and washed their hands. 'Know what?'

Louisa bit her lip and said no more.

Inside the parlour, talk ceased as Iris led Louisa to her seat. She sensed she had walked in on a private conversation, but private from whom she couldn't tell: herself or Louisa.

'When do you head home?' Iris asked when the silence stretched for too long.

'We'll go after supper.' Samuel would not meet her gaze. He was on his third glass of sherry now, by Iris's reckoning.

'When will you come back?' Abigail said.

'Christmas, I suppose. If I'm not needed down there.'

Even Iris inferred the reluctance in his words and the disappointment in his sister at being left alone to cope with their parents for so many weeks.

The clock on the mantelpiece chimed two.

'They hanged him,' Louisa said to no one and everyone.

'What are you going on about now, Mummy?'

Louisa's gaze rammed into her husband's. They glared at each other across the room.

Tim took a deep breath. 'Abigail, your mother is worn out.'

'All those girls.'

'Take her back now, Abigail. She needs to rest.'

'Yes, Dad.' She lifted up her mother.

'What is going on?'

'I'm going to take you to Smedley now, Mum. Say goodbye to Samuel and Henrietta.'

'I want to stay. I'm home.'

Tears filmed Abigail's eyes. 'You're going there for a rest, remember, Mum? Just for a rest, not forever.' The breaking of her voice undermined her promise.

'No!' Louisa tore out of Abigail's grip. 'I won't go, Tim. You can't make me!'

It took all of Abigail and Samuel's strength to grapple their mother to the front door. It was a harrowing thing to witness: two children bundling their screaming mother into the back of a car.

'I'll tell them, Tim. If you make me go, I'll tell them everything!'

Abigail shut the door and leaned against it as Louisa plucked at the handle. Tears poured from her eyes, staining her blouse, and she took a moment to try to compose herself.

Samuel placed his hand on her shoulder. 'It's for the best, eh, Abs?'

Very slowly, she nodded. He brushed a tear off her chin, then waved at his mother who had slumped in her seat, defeated. 'See you at Christmas, Mummy.'

She didn't wave back.

Iris didn't have the nerve to return to the parlour and wish Tim goodbye. She could hardly say it had been a pleasure meeting him, after all. Instead, she grabbed their coats and bags, smiled at Samuel, and scurried for the car. Abigail had started the engine and turned the heating up as high as it would go, and as Iris slid into the passenger seat, she rammed the gearstick into reverse.

'Read it,' Louisa whimpered from behind them.

Abigail glanced at Iris.

It was a long drive back to Smedley.

7
1900

The coroner requested Tim do the post-mortem. A constable cleared the road, shooing off gawping children who battled against him for one last look at the dead girl, before Tim, Howard, and Mr Dunn and his son carried Betty into the cottage.

Mildred and I watched from the kitchen door as they shuffled over the floorboards, Betty's hardened body unyielding. Her hip banged against the door frame as they tried to twist her around the corner. Her black curls brushed the floor, and it was as if death had scuttled its fingertips across us all.

'He needs boiling water, towels, bowls, jars.' Mildred was talking to me, although I couldn't take my eyes off Betty.

'What will he do to her?'

'Go and put a pan of water on to boil now.' With a shove, she sent me into the kitchen. I did as I was told.

Taking the towels into the medical room, I had to squeeze between the men. They had dragged in the kitchen table and had laid Betty's body on top of it, and what with that and so many people, there was hardly an inch of space in which to breathe. As I set the towels on the desk, my arm knocked against Betty's shoe, and I jumped with fright. The men regarded me, as if they had only just noticed my presence. Mr Dunn's son stared as if I were the Reaper hovering beside Betty's body come to steal her soul away.

'Bowls, Louisa.'

I nodded, glad of Tim's instruction. When I left, I heard their low mumblings, my husband thanking the Dunns for their help, their feet shuffling out the same way they had come in.

I gathered all the bowls we had into my arms, thinking of the few times I had mixed pastry or beaten eggs in them. What would Tim put in them now? How would I ever mix pastry or beat eggs in them again?

Tim, Howard, and Mildred stood around the body, unspeaking. I placed the bowls in a pile on the desk beside the towels, then lingered.

The bare skin of Betty's hand lay against our table. The same table on which I had chopped carrots, gutted fish, and scooped marrow out of cows' bones. Would Betty end up just as hollowed out? Her innards set in glass jars which had once held blackcurrant jam?

'You should go,' Tim whispered to me. His palm flitted over my shoulder without landing. 'Feed the child.'

'In this house of butchery?'

'What would you have me do? Cut her open in the street?'

I shrank away from his annoyance. She was pale, yes, and still, but could she not have been alive? Could she not have just been sleeping deeply, like something out of a fairy tale?

'Should you wait? What if she isn't dead?'

Tim retrieved his metal instruments from the glass cabinet, then threw open the windows and doors, searching for as much light as possible.

'Rigor has already set in, my dear.' Howard lifted up Betty's rigid arm to prove his point.

'But you should wait. A day. Surely?'

Scalpels and knives glittered with the sunlight which slanted into the room. Tim removed his jacket, his waistcoat, his collar, and cuffs. Mildred found an apron from one of the cabinets, clean but stained with residue from years before.

'What if she wakes up?'

Mildred settled herself in the chair behind the desk, testing a pen in the ink well, opening her notebook. Tim tied the apron tight, rolled up his sleeves, and came to Betty's side.

'We'll start with the exterior examination.'

'Tim, you should wait.'

'Do not tell me what to do!' He glared at me over Betty's bodice, his voice ringing out in the silence, then pushed his fists into the table. 'I am a doctor, Louisa. I know when someone is dead. Betty is dead.'

Once again, my gaze drifted to her face. So white, so calm, so sleepy. Would her eyelids pop open when she felt the blade pierce her chest?

'My dear.' Howard wrapped his arm around me, his heat and strength somehow comforting, like an anchor of life in that room of death. 'We should come away now.'

'You aren't staying?'

'My eyes are no longer good enough for such a thing. Tim knows what he is doing. He trained in such things in Edinburgh.'

Tim took a breath. 'I will be gentle with her. I promise you, Louisa, I will not hurt her. No one can hurt her anymore.'

Howard guided me to the hallway, then to the parlour where Samuel lay in his cot. Looking down on him, I noticed the soft glow of his cheeks, the faint threads of blue veins across his skull, the throbbing of his creamy skin under his jaw: the signs of life which had been absent in Betty.

'I'll make us some tea,' Howard whispered.

I lifted Samuel into my arms and snuggled him close, trying not to imagine the knives slicing through Betty's flesh in the next room.

* * *

I watched the crowd growing from the parlour window. All the village had turned out, so it seemed. Every woman garbed in black, even those who had barely spoken a word to Betty. Even I had donned my only black gown, the one reserved for this kind of time.

A line of twelve men lingered beside the ivy of the Black Heart Inn, waiting to go inside. Almost half of them were from the village. The other men looked about themselves uneasily, plucking at their lapels as the weekend's rain dripped from the leaves and spotted their bowlers.

In the hallway, Tim prowled. His heels tapped incessantly, faster than the ticking of the clock. The sounds were out of balance, chaotic, and made me feel dizzy. I clutched the windowsill as the room began to swirl and finally, with a sigh of relief, saw the carriage carrying the coroner arrive.

'He's here,' I called, but Tim was already out of the door. He marched over the crossroads as if a body had not been discovered there only days ago. His foot landed right where Betty's heart would have lain.

There was a commotion, a swarming of skirts and hats and canes as the crowd swallowed the stranger, and then the jurymen and witnesses followed him inside, my husband at the head of them.

Dashing into the hallway, I peeled on my gloves and fixed my hat.

'No place for a woman,' Mildred muttered from her seat in the dining room. In the cot beside her, Samuel slept.

'Are you sure you want to go?' Howard met me in the doorway. 'These things can be upsetting.'

'I shall be fine. I should be there for Tim.' And then, just to placate him, I touched his hand and added, 'If anything upsets me I shall leave at once.'

I did not wait for him to try to dissuade me. Striding for the public house, I slipped on to the end of the congregation filing inside and secured a position squashed between the door frame and a female farm labourer, with the brass bell clanging against my hat in such a way that I had to tilt my head at a right angle for the proceedings.

Betty's corpse rested in the centre of the room. I had not seen it since it had first lain on our kitchen table, fresh and intact. Her mother must have washed the body and dressed it in her Sunday best. Her hair was spritzed with oil so that it shone as it rippled over the woodwork.

Her mouth had been threaded shut, and she looked as peaceful as she always had. As if she were, once again, sleeping. But I had heard the knives sawing the bones of her. I had heard the sloshing of her insides into bowls. I had smelt the contents of her stomach and bowels as it had drifted through the open doors.

Was she hollow inside? What had Tim done with her lungs and heart and stomach and brain? Was she nothing more than a shell of skin and fractured bone as she lay in front of us all? If one of the children were to jump on her, would the air seep from between Mildred's stitches until she was flat?

Swallowing, I forced my eyes away from Betty and to the jury. Beside them, a few strangers prepared their notepads and glanced around the room with eager eyes, jotting down the scene. Reporters. One of them, to my amazement, was a young woman.

A makeshift witness stand was positioned beside a window. The coroner organised himself next to the taps. And then it began.

Miss Sutton walked serenely to the stand, dressed as she had been the morning of the discovery. No longer did she tremble, despite the eyes upon her. Perhaps it was all her years as the schoolmistress which granted her such poise in front of the congregation – many would have sat before her ten, twenty, thirty years ago to receive their lessons.

'I found the deceased just after six o'clock in the morning of Friday the twenty-third of March as I was making my way from my home to the school hall on the north road.'

'What did you do when you found her?' The coroner

spoke with a yawn in his voice and earned himself a stern look in response.

'It was a shock. I believe I screamed.'

'You didn't touch the deceased?'

'No.'

'How did you know she was dead?'

'Well…' Miss Sutton gestured at the body on the table. 'It seemed obvious. And at that time in the morning.'

'Had you ever seen the deceased at that time in the morning before when you had gone to the schoolhouse?'

'Never. She kept late hours, what with working here in the evenings.'

'What happened when you screamed?'

She paused, took a breath. 'Mrs Edwards, the young doctor's wife, was the first to arrive, followed directly by her husband and his family. Dr Howard Edwards checked for a pulse, so I recall, and made out she was dead.'

Briefly, faces angled my way. I ignored them, and shortly Miss Sutton was dismissed. Mrs Crook made her way, staggering and sniffing, to the stand where she was sworn in.

'The deceased is my daughter, Betty.' Her voice broke on the last word. She pressed a black handkerchief to her swollen eyes.

'Can you tell us what happened on the evening preceding your daughter's death, Mrs Crook?'

'She was working. It was just a normal night.' Mrs Crook struggled to swallow. Her throat waved and her jaw clenched.

'What time did the deceased go to bed?'

'Perhaps just after one o'clock.'

'Did you see her go to bed?'

Mrs Crook shoved the handkerchief into the corners of her eyes. 'I had gone to bed already.'

The coroner paused, considered, and repeated, 'So, did you see her go to bed that night?'

Mrs Crook shook her head. 'But I heard the floorboards. They creak on the landing at the top of the stairs outside my door.'

'You had closed by the time you heard those floorboards?'

She nodded.

'Did you hear anything else after that?'

'I… I think… maybe voices.'

The coroner sat up straighter, his drooping eyelids suddenly lifting. 'Whose voices?'

'Betty's and… someone else's. I can't be sure who.'

'What time was this?'

'Shortly after two. I'd heard the bells, then some voices.'

'Where were the voices coming from?'

Mrs Crook sighed. 'I can't be sure.'

'How long have you lived here, Mrs Crook?'

The question confused her and dried her eyes for a moment. 'Almost thirty years.'

'And yet you cannot locate the voices you heard?'

For the first time since Friday, Mrs Crook's cheeks found some blood. 'I was tired. I thought nothing of it.'

'But your daughter was talking to a stranger at two o'clock in the morning.'

Another flurry of whispers flamed through the crowd.

'It was the spirit,' Mrs Crook cried, and silenced everyone. 'Madam Buckley's spirit. My Betty was frightened to death.'

The coroner did not have the manners to hide his laughter. His ridicule made his audience hostile; once again, Mrs Crook was favoured by her neighbours.

'Why should you think such a thing?'

'The bottle was opened. And now the spirit is out and hunting for girls again.'

Pens scratched at paper. The reporters filled their pages quickly.

'Besides this evil spirit, is there anyone else who you think could have harmed your daughter?'

Mrs Crook sniffed, her composure crumbling as she gazed down at Betty. She shook her head and, in the next instant, dashed through into the back room, sobbing.

The coroner checked his watch, then called Tim to the stand.

My husband had less resolve than the schoolmistress. Like Mrs Crook, he was pale, shaking a little, unable to meet anyone's eye. His shoulders curled inwards as he took the oath, and his fingertips tickled the chair backs as he waited to be addressed.

'You conducted the post-mortem on Miss Crook, Dr Edwards?'

'That is correct.'

'You were also one of the first people on the scene. What were your initial impressions?'

Tim cleared his throat, then cleared it again. 'The deceased lay in the middle of the road. There was no disturbance to the clothes. She had no possessions on her, but I do not think it was a robbery as her purse was found in her room by her mother. There was no blood at the scene. It is clear why the idea of the deceased having been scared to death would seem plausible, if the neck was not visible.'

'How long had she been there?'

'Rigor mortis had set in by the time she was moved to my office. When she was first discovered it was only just starting, which suggests she died within one to four hours before six o'clock in the morning.'

'Do you believe she had died where she was found?'

'The shoes were clean and unscratched. The clothes, as I said before, were not dishevelled or torn.'

'There was vomit found in the public house's backyard. Was there any sign of illness within the deceased? Had you known of any sickness before death?'

I peered more closely at my husband over the farm worker's shoulder. The daylight struck whitely off the sheen on his forehead.

'There was a small quantity of alcohol in the stomach contents of the deceased. There was no food. I would suggest the vomit was caused by nothing more than that.'

His fingertips had whitened on the chair back. Had anyone else noticed it? The female reporter scribbled something down, and, as if feeling himself under scrutiny, Tim pushed his hands into his pockets.

'And the results of the post-mortem?'

'The eyes were bloodshot. That is a general sign of strangulation or suffocation. There being a thin, red line around the neck showed likely strangulation. On internal examination, the blackening of the heart and other organs confirmed my suspicion of asphyxia.'

Suddenly, I was keenly aware of my own breath moving in and out of my lungs and the restriction to my chest from my corset. I wriggled uneasily as the woman before me decided it was too much to bear. With a grunt of horror, she pushed past me and out of the door, allowing me to step out from the under the bell and straighten my spine.

'To clarify, Dr Edwards, what do you believe caused the death of the deceased?'

'I believe, judging from my medical examination, that Miss Crook was strangled with a thin cord or rope of some kind. She was killed between midnight and dawn and left in plain sight. She died in the same way as Miss Witcombe, Miss Carr, and Mrs Smith were killed several years before.'

Gasps rippled through the crowd. Tim rolled his shoulders back, buoyed up now, but by what, I did not know. Perhaps the fact that his interrogation was coming to a close. The coroner called order in the room.

'Why should that be relevant, Dr Edwards?'

'Because I believe,' Tim continued, his voice stronger now than it had ever been, 'that Miss Crook was murdered by a copycat killer.'

8
1956

Both of them fell quiet. In the chair, Louisa's head drooped from one side to the other as she muttered about paintings on walls and dead girls.

'A copycat killer?' Abigail mused. 'How have Mum and Dad never mentioned this to me before?'

Iris squirmed in her seat. 'Look, I'm not sure I should be listening to all this.' She pulled her collar closer. She had become chilled sitting in the day room, hearing about women-murderers as dusk settled outside. A shiver juddered down her spine. 'It's your family's business, not mine.'

Abigail glanced away and fiddled with the edges of the paper.

Iris excused herself and made for the toilets. Water rushed over her palms like a thousand ice picks. She flicked her wrists, spraying the green tiles and the square patch of mirror on the wall.

She should not get involved with Louisa's tale. She should not embroil herself in more dramas that had nothing to do with her. It would only cause more grief, as had happened with Kath.

The months following Kath's death had been hard. With the loss of Shirley's friendship and Simon keeping his distance, Iris had carried the burden alone. She still visited Albert sometimes and would sit in his front room and share a pot of tea, but neither of them talked about the past.

She had worked herself raw at Smedley, taking on all the extra shifts, staying later and arriving earlier, anything to keep herself busy. She kept her mind focused on soiled sheets and sedatives so it didn't wander back to the blister of rage which sat at the top of her spine. The rage which made her scrunch her sheets at night and bury her scream in a pillow. The rage which came from knowing about Kath's injustice and not being able to do a thing about it. Her body had been wound as tight as a banjo string, and it had snapped as soon as the first frost brought with it a bout of flu.

Now that she was recovering she didn't want to fire up that rage all over again. She didn't want to delve into a past that didn't belong to her, searching for secrets that had been happily buried.

She wanted a quiet Christmas. After such a year, she wanted the last remaining weeks of 1956 to be beautifully dull. In truth, she wanted to rewind the clocks to the time before: before she had known of Kath's tragedy, before Shirley had met John and lost herself, before Simon had stumbled into Iris's life and plagued her thoughts at the most inappropriate of times.

Before was simple.

But before was irretrievable.

The reflection in the mirror stared back with hard, dark eyes. Sickness and fatigue had mottled her skin. Cold air had chapped her lips. It would take all the contents of Shirley's makeup bag to make this stranger pretty.

She smiled as she thought of the last time Shirley had tried to perform such a miracle; it made those hard eyes soften.

Wiping her hands on a towel, she chastised herself for the melancholic thoughts. Did she really want to turn back time? Did she really wish she had never met Kath or Albert or Simon? Of course not.

She was being too hard on herself. Fighting through the pain, she remembered Kath's smile when she had kissed the photograph, the peace it had brought her. Not justice as Iris would have liked, but a certain kind of happiness. Wasn't happiness something of dreams, when it came to the end of life?

Kath had transformed from a shell of a person to a woman who loved again. After all she had been through, she had been capable of that.

Yet, with Louisa it was different. No amount of truth could cure her disease. Perhaps, in some odd way, it was best her illness was allowing her to forget the past. A dead girl, a suspicious husband, a whole book filled with secrets. Perhaps it should have stayed in the shoebox after all.

She straightened the towel on its rail. There was no use hiding away in toilet cubicles. With a deep breath, she returned to the ward, hoping that Abigail might have left for the day, but she still sat next to her mother.

'I'm going to have to get back to work.'

'I don't want to read it without you.'

Iris took one last look at the notebook. 'Then don't read it.'

'You must want to know who was responsible.'

'Not really.' Even as she said it, she knew it was a lie. She was too curious by nature to not be interested.

'Iris, a girl died.'

'Well.' Iris plucked strands of hair off the back of the chair. 'We can't do anything about it. It was almost sixty years ago.'

After all, people were always dying. On battlefields, in concentration camps, locked up in places like this. Why did one girl matter?

'It wasn't him,' Louisa murmured.

Abigail ignored her mother. 'Fine. I'll leave it. Pretend I never saw it.' Lips pursed, she got to her feet and shrugged on her coat. 'As you say, what does one dead girl matter?'

'Abigail, please. I didn't mean it like that. I just don't want anyone else to get hurt.'

'No, you're right. It isn't your family; it isn't your problem.' She headed for the door and Iris hurried to catch up.

'Wait. I just…'

Abigail paused.

'I've got involved in things before and they didn't turn out great. I don't think I can put myself through it again.'

Abigail sighed. The anger drained out of her. 'I can't expect you to either. I'm sorry. You're just a nurse. I shouldn't have asked for more.' Although it hadn't been intentional, Abigail's remark hurt. 'I'll do it on my own. Thank you for all your help.'

It was a dismissal. Exhaustedly, Abigail turned for the

corridor. Her heels dragged over the tiles, and her shoulders tilted to one side as her handbag weighed her down.

'Hold on.' Iris ran to her. She couldn't bear to see her leave like that, as if Iris had cast her off without a thought. As if Iris was just like all the other nurses on Ward 13. 'What are you doing tonight?'

'What I always do. Going home and making Dad his dinner.'

'My brother's having a bonfire party.'

'You don't sound pleased.'

Iris tested a smile; Abigail returned the gesture. 'If I know my brother, it will be raucous.'

'Raucous?' Abigail laughed. 'I haven't been to anything raucous for decades.'

'Then why don't you come with me?'

Abigail shook her head. 'You don't want me at a family get-together.'

'I do.'

'Surely you can find someone better than an old woman?'

Iris pushed Simon's face out of her mind. She was desperate to make up for the rift she had caused with Abigail. The bonfire might go some way towards an apology. 'There is no one better.'

9
1956

Abigail's car was the only one on Iris's brother's estate. She parked at the entrance because of the bonfires in the road and looked as unsure as Iris felt about leaving it so far away; fireworks were likely to do as much damage as thieves tonight. With tight smiles, they walked away from the car, glancing back every so often to see its green paint winking in the light from the flames.

A gang of children ran around in shorts and skirts, as if it were summer, carting a straw man between them. 'Penny for the guy,' they shouted. The littlest ones begged at their neighbours' doors with pleading eyes, rattling their tins.

The heat from the fires was a welcome relief after days of lashing rain and biting wind. She and Abigail held out their hands to the orange crackles, nodding to and wishing strangers a happy November the fifth as they wound through the warren of streets and finally came to Alan's house.

Of course, his had to be the biggest fire. He stood before it, hands on hips, admiring his creation. His son, Adam, zoomed around the spluttering logs, hissing at the flames, picking sparklers out of a bucket, and lighting them one after another.

'Aunty Iris!' Adam yelled, and charged at her. She dodged out of the way of the sparkler just in time and picked it out of his fingers as he hugged her legs.

'Who are you?' he said to Abigail.

Iris blushed at his rudeness. Her brother should have taught him better manners than to talk to a lady like that, but then Alan had been the same. His lips tended to work quicker than his brain.

Abigail crouched down and introduced herself with a smile. 'I'm Miss Abigail Edwards. And you are?' She held out her hand.

Delighted to be treated like a grown-up, Adam shook her hand. 'I'm Adam Lowe. I'm five years and four months old, and I'm going to be a bus driver like Granddad.'

'Well then, it is a pleasure to meet you.' Abigail eased herself up as Adam ran off to alert his dad about Iris's new friend. 'Your nephew is a credit, Iris.'

Abigail's face had warmed, brought to life as much by the heat as by the child. Iris glanced at her nephew and felt an odd jolt of pride. She'd never experienced it before. She'd never thought Adam had much to do with her – she was, at best, an aloof aunty. Her place was on the side lines, there to observe but never interfere. To be credited with some of his charms was both undeserved and surprisingly pleasant.

'Penny for the guy, misses?' Behind them, the gang of children from earlier had caught them up. The straw man lying crookedly in the wheelbarrow had lost half of its body now, and spiky guts trailed in the road. Nevertheless, she rummaged in her purse and found a coin. Abigail studied the quality of her pennies, plucked out the shiniest specimen, and dropped it in the waiting tin. Sensing they'd got a soft one, the children lingered, gazing up at Abigail hopefully.

'Get on with you!' The children scurried away with shrieks of laughter as Alan ran at them, brandishing a sparkler as he did so. He shook his head and smiled at their cheek, then tugged Iris into an embrace.

'How are you, sister mine? Glad to see you're still kicking.' He tweaked her arm and held her fast as Iris struggled to break free. He spoke over her head to Abigail. 'Never comes to see her big brother. Anyone would think I've got something catching.' He released his sister and scooped Abigail into a hug, much to Iris's horror.

Abigail tittered an awkward hello, pushing her hat straight as soon as Alan let her go.

'Thought you'd be bringing that Simon. I wanted to get a look at him, see if he's up to scratch for my little sister.' He winked at Abigail.

Iris pushed past him, beckoning Abigail to follow as she headed for the kitchen to get a drink.

The place was crowded. It wasn't just the family here, as Alan had promised. A small get-together had morphed into a swell of all of Alan and Janet's friends and neighbours. She didn't recognise anyone until she heard the shrill cry of her mother cracking over the conversations. Standing on tiptoes, she saw her parents stuffed up in the corner of the living room as Mum rocked her new-born granddaughter.

Battering her way through into the kitchen, where her shoes stuck to the cheap vinyl flooring and young mothers stifled the air with cigarette smoke, Iris found the drinks' station. She poured them both a cup of cider, guessing that Abigail's more sophisticated palate would appreciate that rather than a flat pint of lager. Wine and sherry were not on offer.

'I'm sorry it's so busy,' Iris shouted over the screams of too many excited children and their gossiping mums.

'It's nice.' Abigail sipped her drink and winced. 'Who is Simon?'

'Oh.' Iris hoped the blood wasn't rising to her cheeks. 'Just a friend. We haven't seen each other for ages.'

Abigail's eyes glinted as she gulped more cider. In a moment, her cup was empty, and she asked for a top-up.

Pushing her way through the open-plan living space, Iris led Abigail to her mum and dad, introducing her as the lady who had invited her round for Sunday lunch.

'At the posh house?' Mum looked Abigail up and down and pecked her cheek. Her nose was glowing – the sign she'd had too much to drink. 'Nice to meet you.' Astonishingly, she sounded genuine. 'I'm sorry to hear about your mum, but Iris takes good care of them in there.'

'Your daughter has been a real help.'

Both of them smiled at her. Squirming under their praise, Iris feigned interest in the latest addition to the Lowe family. Jane the baby had a scalp coated in ginger tufts and a face much prettier than her brother's had been at that age. Adam had been a spindly thing, all long legs and arms and gaping fish eyes. Jane was plump and soft, with rosebud lips and a button nose. And all of a sudden, she was being lumped into Iris's arms.

She tried to protest, but her mum was having none of it. Before she could stop it, Jane's toasty, swaddled body was pressed against her chest. The baby gazed up at her in surprise as Iris stared down in horror.

It was the first time she'd held her niece. She'd seen Janet a week after the birth, along with her mother who had galloped all the way. Thankfully, back then her mum had been too besotted to let Iris even get a whiff of the baby. Since then, Iris had either been too busy or too ill to visit.

'Eh! Looks good on you, Iris.' Alan prodded her shoulder as he sauntered towards the kitchen, sniggering as Iris sent him daggers.

'Give her a little rock,' Mum urged, shaking her head. 'Babies don't like being still.'

Iris did as she was told, stiffly bobbing the child up and down. Jane began to mewl and struggle, and just as Iris started to panic, Abigail cut in. 'May I?'

Iris quickly handed the baby over. Abigail took her easily and gurgled nonsense, swaying from side to side as Jane's frown smoothed away.

Mum caught Iris's attention and nodded at Abigail's left hand. She mouthed so that no one could hear, 'No ring.'

Iris needed another drink.

By the time she'd returned, Jane was snuggling into Mum's embrace again and everyone was making their way out to the street. Iris slipped beside Abigail and, once in the shockingly cold evening air, handed her a hot potato from the fire's ashes, cut open, buttered, and salted.

'Everyone ready?' Alan shouted. The crowd roared back their excitement.

A short way down the street, a few rockets were propped up in empty milk bottles. After a few quick drags on his cigarette, Alan used the glowing stub to light the fireworks before scarpering away. With a shattering of glass, the rockets took off. To everyone's relief, they went skyward. Ear-splitting bangs caused dogs to bark throughout the estate and babies to wail. Mum hurried inside with Jane.

It was over in seconds, the blooms of golden light in the sky quickly fading to black. Alan lit the Catherine wheel he'd hammered into the nearest tree, and Adam scared his friends with a jumping jack.

'Fantastic. Brava!' Abigail called to Iris's brother and scooped potato into her mouth with a teaspoon. She'd lost the gauntness from before. Fire smuts smeared her cheeks and the drizzle had flattened her hair, but she seemed far happier and more relaxed than she had done for the past few weeks at Smedley.

'I've had a wonderful time. Thank you, Iris.' When nothing but the charred skin of the potato remained, she continued, 'I was thinking I would like to pay Bodnem a visit.'

Iris's smile petered out.

'I know what you said earlier about getting hurt, but I want to see what it's like now. See if any of the people Mum mentions still live there.' She put the potato skin in the bin that overflowed with beer bottles.

'I don't know if that's a good idea.'

'What harm can it do?'

'There might be nothing there.'

'Exactly, so what's the problem?'

Iris took a breath and checked her watch. 'Your dad might be wondering where you are.'

Reluctantly, Abigail nodded. She waved goodbye to Alan and Janet. 'Will you walk me to the car?'

Iris wished they hadn't parked so far away; it gave Abigail longer to dig at her.

'Aren't you just a little bit intrigued?'

'Not particularly.'

'Don't you like secrets?'

Iris hastened her steps. 'Look, if you want to go to Bodnem, I can't stop you. But I don't want to get involved.'

They passed another bonfire in the street, and as Iris's attention drifted to the flames, she tripped on a kerbstone. Abigail caught her by the elbow, and a group of people cheered and laughed. They continued at a more sedate pace.

'Dad always said we should never encourage these… stories of hers. Perhaps he was right.'

Iris stifled her sigh. She knew what Abigail was doing – dangling bait right in front of her.

Do not get involved.

'You know, Mum has always been spiteful to Dad. She's been cold to Samuel most of his life, although the notebook suggests she wasn't always like that. You see, Iris, ours is not a family like yours. We can't all be blessed with love. But I have often wondered why.'

Abigail rummaged in her handbag and retrieved her car keys.

'I know she's stubborn. She's always wanted things her way. It was she who pushed me into teaching. Not that I minded, but I would have liked to have had an opinion on my own life. And when I was due to be…' She shook her head. 'She's selfish. Always has been. I know that. But she's proud too. She's never said sorry easily. So that letter, the way she apologised, the way she urged me to read it… I think I have a duty to do as she asked.'

They were coming to the end of the estate and approaching the – thankfully intact – car. Abigail grabbed Iris's hand and pulled her back. 'Whatever happened at Bodnem has haunted my mother nearly all her life, clearly all of my life. I could try to put it right.' A flame of hope twinkled in Abigail's unsteady gaze. 'It could help her. She might get better with Dad. She might be able to… come home.'

'She won't.' Iris shot the hope out of Abigail's mind. 'This is a disease that cannot be cured.'

Abigail blinked, shocked by Iris's honesty. She retracted her grip. 'It might help, in some small way. She wanted to make amends. She wanted to tell me something, something she has never told anyone else. She wanted – needed – me to understand.'

She took a quivering breath. 'Look, it's just a book. It's just a visit here and there, some questions. I know it's a lot to ask, but I would really like you there with me. I don't have anyone else.'

'I'm just a nurse.'

Abigail shook her head. 'You've been a friend to me. I haven't had one of those in a while.'

Iris pinched her lips, uncertain.

'Please.'

'All right, fine. I'll come with you if that's really what you want.'

Abigail smiled, and the tension oozed out of her shoulders. 'Thank you.'

'As long as you're prepared.'

'For what?'

Iris sighed. 'There's usually a reason people bury secrets. You might discover something you wish you hadn't.'

10
1900

An inspector arrived on Tuesday. Quinton was his name, and I didn't like him.

He started his rounds in the village and came to our house just before three o'clock. Mildred only let him into the dining room, not wanting one of his sort in the parlour. We each took our seats, and the inspector perched on the spare stool. Mildred poured his tea into the plain china cup.

'How long have you known Miss Crook?' His voice was thick with a Birmingham accent, and for a moment I felt as if I were back in Edgbaston, listening to maids whispering on the stairs.

'Years. Nice girl.' Howard sipped his tea. The cup was ludicrously small in his large hands.

'Do you know of anyone who might have wished her harm?'

Howard frowned at the air before him and shook his head. Quinton turned to my husband, and Tim copied his father.

'Can you give me a sense of her character?'

'She was a nice girl,' Howard said. 'Although, we didn't know her well. We saw her at the Black Heart. But then…'

Quinton leaned forward. 'What?'

'I don't wish to speak ill of the girl. She was always friendly. Sometimes too friendly, if you understand?'

How Mildred blushed! Even I felt myself burning. Tim's chin dipped, and he stared at the floor. Did Howard know of his son's indiscretions?

'Too friendly with whom?' Quinton asked, his eyes lighting.

'She never seemed particular.'

Mildred slammed her cup into her saucer and excused herself.

'Did you see anything that night? Your windows overlook the murder scene.'

Again, my father-in-law shook his head. 'My chamber is at the rear of the house.' He turned to Tim.

Tim shook his head, but the movement was barely perceptible.

'Did the child wake you, Louisa? Might you have seen something when you dealt with him?' Howard asked, and Quinton's gaze slipped past Tim and landed on me.

'I fed him just after midnight. You had both just returned from the inn, and Samuel was restless after being woken.' I glared at Tim, but he didn't notice. 'He wouldn't go back to sleep, so at about one o'clock I came downstairs and changed him. Then I fed him again and that settled him. I made myself a cup of cocoa, and then I must have slept for a few hours. I fed him again at half past four, and then again just before… the scream.'

'Did you notice anything when you came down? Anybody lingering outside?'

'No.'

'What about at half past four?'

'I didn't look. I was half-asleep.'

'And you didn't hear anything until the scream? No noise at all? Nothing else woke you, even for a moment?'

'Inspector, I have a new baby. Sleep is a luxury, and I take it whenever I can. If he does not wake, then neither do I.'

Quinton nodded, stood, and shook hands with Tim and Howard. He was shorter than both of them, reaching only to their shoulders, and his hands were thin with arthritic knuckles. Working hands. He made his way to the front door, walking with a rolling gait, his legs bowed. I imagined it had taken him years to claw his way up to his current position.

He thanked us all and headed off into the village. Tim and Howard turned back inside, but I had seen the shadow in the bush by the stone wall. I told them I would join them soon.

'He won't find no one.' Jenny slunk up to me as she sunk her teeth into a sugared bun. We watched Quinton hobble into the Black Heart, which was now draped in crepe the same colour as its namesake. 'It's Madam Buckley.'

'Oh please, Jenny. There is no such thing as an evil spirit.'

'Then why did the same thing happen five years ago? We had her for two years back then. No one walked the streets after dark, not if they could help it. And if they couldn't help it, they wound up dead in the morning.'

A chill rippled down my spine. 'Your sister was a victim?'

She nodded. 'Ma told her not to go out, but she was like you and didn't believe in such tripe. We found her on the wall by Buckley Lake.' Jenny's eyes filled. She blinked the water back, sniffed, and continued to eat her bun.

'Where had she gone?'

Jenny jerked her head in the direction of Church Street. 'The manor house. She was in love with him. Said she was going to marry him. Her and Ma had a big row. Mary stormed out of the house, and that was the last time we ever saw her alive.'

I glanced over my shoulder, saw the Buckley wall, and imagined the mirror image of Jenny lying prone on top of it.

'It's girls what Madam Buckley takes. Happy girls. She steals their happiness because hers was stolen.'

'Tragedies happen in childbirth. It was an accident.'

Jenny shook her head. 'Buckley said to save the child. He didn't care a jot about his wife. She heard him telling Dr Edwards. That was the last thing she heard, and that's why she haunts us all. It's what happens when people die in anger.'

* * *

At seven o'clock, Tim returned home from his calls, damp from the rain. He snatched the collar off his shirt as he climbed the stairs, and while Mildred finished dinner, I dashed up to meet him. He had dropped his jacket and waistcoat on the floor and was leaning over Samuel's cot.

'Why did you lie to Inspector Quinton?'

Tim jumped at the sound of my voice and spun around to face me. 'What?'

He crept to our bed and unfastened his shoes.

'You agreed you didn't know Betty well, but I saw you talking to her outside the Black Heart the night before she died.'

His shoe toppled to the floor, waking Samuel, but the child only mewed before sleep took him once more.

'What were you talking about?'

Tim covered his face; his stubble rasped against his palms. He shook his head.

'She told me she wanted to speak with you, but you said she hadn't been ill at the inquest. Was that a lie too?'

He remained silent.

'Or was there something else going on between the two of you? Was she your…?' I could not say the word aloud. It made my skin shiver, not with jealousy but with shame, shame that I had become what I had pitied and despised in other women. A suspicious wife.

'Was she my mistress? Is that what you're asking?'

'What should I think?'

'I cannot tell you anything. I have a duty to my patient.'

'So she *was* ill?'

'That is not your concern.'

'What was wrong with her?'

'I cannot—'

'She's dead, Tim. Does it really matter now?'

He wavered. 'Will you leave me be if I tell you?'

I nodded.

'And you must not repeat this to anyone. I mean it,

Louisa. If people think they cannot trust me, there will be no future for us here.'

I nodded again, eager to prise the information from his lips.

'She thought she was with child.'

He let the information sink into my mind. How had I not guessed? The early morning sickness. The need for a doctor.

'She wanted me to get rid of it for her.'

My breath faltered. I imagined a knife, long and thin, sticky with blood. 'Did you?'

'Of course I didn't. And I said there was no way I ever would. She was not pleased with me.'

I remembered Betty strutting out of the shadows. I had thought she had been strutting, but perhaps she had been storming away, angry.

Someone else had been angry that night. My gasp of breath made Tim squint at me over his shoulder.

'I know who killed her.'

'What?'

'Daniel Griffith. She was pregnant with Daniel's child. It was Betty and Daniel who I heard at the stables—'

'She was not pregnant with anyone's child. She was not pregnant at all.'

I stalled, shocked.

'Do you not think I would have mentioned a child at the inquest had I found something? Her womb was empty.'

'But why would she be so certain otherwise?'

He shrugged. 'Sometimes these… thoughts occur. If a woman is particularly fearful of such a thing, or even so desiring of it. Clearly, Betty was the former. The mind plays tricks on us, Louisa, tricks that are very hard to identify and understand.'

'Her lack of a child means nothing, though. You only found out she was barren when you cut her open. It could still be a motive for Daniel Griffith to murder her.'

Tim raised his brow. 'He wouldn't have it in him.'

'He was angry with Betty the night before her death.'

'There is a difference between anger and having the rage to kill someone.'

'What if, after you told her no, he made sure he would never be burdened with a child?'

Tim stared into my eyes. The vanishing light had made his pupils black. 'You are talking nonsense.'

'I should tell Quinton.'

Tim sprung at me. His hands fastened around my upper arms, pinching the soft flesh there. 'You will leave this be, Louisa.'

'But—'

He shook me so violently that my chin smacked into my chest. The room darkened.

'Leave it, Louisa. Do you understand?'

I could not speak. When he dropped me, I reeled back to find solidity and comfort in the wall.

He pushed on his slippers and checked himself in the mirror. 'Come. Mother will have dinner waiting for us.'

11
1900

Sunshine painted the town in a pale-yellow glow. I closed my eyes briefly as I raised my face to the rays, soaking in the warmth. When I opened them again, Samuel smiled at me encouragingly from his pram.

I knew I shouldn't. Tim had told me to leave it, but with the breeze pushing at my back, urging me on, I remembered my promise: I would not become my mother. I would not pander to my husband's every whim, nor flinch whenever he raised his voice. I would not bow and obey. A new century was upon us. A new era for women. If Tim thought he had married someone with no mind and no will of her own, he was wrong.

Bodnem was quiet. In the scattering of houses along the north road, there were no sounds of life beyond the cottage doors. The smithy was closed, and no smoke plumed from the flue. Only my footsteps and the steady squeak of the pram's wheels filled the air.

As I approached the stables in the field, all was quiet. To the side of the hut, the horses and ponies gathered around a small pile of hay and stooped to eat. They raised their heads when they noticed me, and their glassy brown eyes passed over me vacantly before they returned to their feed.

I fixed the pram by the fence, then let myself in through the gate. The ground was muddy, and I raised my skirts to tiptoe through the sludge and into the stables.

Inside was dark but for one shaft of sunlight falling through the open door. Particles of dust and hay lingered in the air and tickled the back of my throat. The sweaty, warm scent of horses brought flashes of life as governess at the Pendleton's manor back to me. I saw two hands, both chubby, one slightly larger than the other, holding out an apple core and a wedge of carrot. Two sets of white velvet lips brushed against those open palms, and children's laughter echoed in my mind.

'Can I help you?'

I had to squint to make out the shape of Daniel Griffith in the corner, dwarfed by stacks of hay. He slapped his hands against his thighs and edged closer but did not enter the beam of light. I rolled my shoulders back, breathed deeply, and faced him, trying to shake off the memories that had made me tremble.

'What do you want?'

I did not know how to begin. If my theory held any truth, I should not have been alone with him. But I was, and I was not going to walk away.

'The inspector's left,' I said. 'No evidence to go on, so he says. He's sure someone will remember something and come forward soon.'

'And you're telling me this because…?'

'Because I know you were angry with Betty the night before she died.'

Silence dragged for minutes. I clasped my hands together to stop them plucking at my skirt. When he did not speak, I continued, 'I saw you walking away from the Black Heart Inn. You kicked your door and cursed.'

He inched closer, and I stepped back.

'What are you getting at, Mrs Edwards?'

I swallowed. 'Did you kill Betty?'

Daniel laughed. He marched towards the hay bales and tore them down. They plunged to the floor, smacking into the earth and making more particles scatter through the air.

'Did you know she was pregnant?'

He stopped. Through the flecks of hay which swirled in the sunbeam, he was even harder to see. 'No.'

'I think you did. You didn't want to be burdened with all that trouble.'

Daniel stormed towards me and into the light. 'It could have been anyone's bastard.'

'But what if it was yours?'

'Should we be calling you detective now, Mrs Edwards?' He emphasised my real title, hissing it into my face.

'Was it the baby that made you angry?'

'It wasn't mine,' he growled. 'You think I went near her without a sheath? She was riddled.'

'You seem to be implying that Betty was—'

'A whore.'

He smirked at my shock.

'That's absolutely what she was.'

I had considered Betty might have been loose, but to have taken payment for it made me nauseous.

'So you were angry because she was on the game and you weren't the only one. You were jealous.'

He turned from me to lean against the timber walls and laughed. 'I don't get jealous over whores. I was the only one she didn't get coin from. I don't need to pay for that sort of thing, Mrs Edwards, if you understand?'

I ignored his slippery tone. 'Then why were you angry with her?'

'It wasn't anything to do with Betty. I'd lost a bet at the inn, that's all – you can check with Mr Dean if you like. I wasn't in the best of moods. And since I'd told Betty it was over between us, she'd turned nasty. The night you spied on me, she'd called me a scrub and a lobcock as I left. Women get like that when you tell them to piss off.'

'I did not spy.'

He snorted. I raised my chin.

'Where were you the night she died?'

'At home with my father. I didn't go to the inn. We played whist. I needed to get back the money I'd lost the night before.'

'And did you?'

He nodded.

'So, your father is your alibi?'

'It was good enough for the inspector.' He pushed himself away from the wall and bled into the shadows. 'Now, if you'll let this scrub get back to work.' Picking up a fork, he dragged its metal tongues over the stones and into a horse block.

I turned for the door, patting spikes of hay off my skirt as I went.

'I should say a punter who got his wagtail in the family way would've had more to be angry about than I did.'

'Which punter?'

He peeked out from behind the wooden board. 'Patrick Dunn.'

'The pharmacist's boy?'

'The very one.'

'Paying Betty for…? Surely, he wouldn't. He wouldn't have it in him.'

Daniel grinned. 'Then he's fooled you too.'

* * *

'Is something the matter, Mrs Edwards?'

I halted in the middle of the road; I'd been caught. In front of me, Mrs Powell peeked between the shelves in her window display. She caught my eye in such a hostile way that I was almost relieved to face Master Pat Dunn.

I hadn't paid him much attention when he'd helped carry Betty's body into the cottage. Now, I wished I had taken more notice of his actions around the corpse.

He was a fleshy boy, only a few years younger than me but the chubbiness of his face made it seem more, and his eyes appeared squashed by his cheeks. Whiskers the colour of mud sprouted from his upper lip and chin, and his pallor was decidedly ashen.

'You've been walking up and down here for the last half hour.' His voice was soft and weak.

'Could we talk about Betty?'

He stiffened. 'Pa will be back soon.'

'It'll only take a minute.'

Wavering, he scanned the street. 'Can we go to the yard? Everybody has two sets of eyes in this village.'

I followed him down the alleyway that cut between his family's shop and Powell's grocery store. We stopped at the far end of it, in the darkness.

'What were you to Betty Crook?'

He swallowed. 'Sorry?'

'Did you see her after the Black Heart closed? Did she meet you somewhere?'

'Are you implying that Betty had a habit of meeting men at night?' Was that a hint of sarcasm in his voice? In the shadows of the alley, it was hard to read his expression.

'Did you pay Betty for…'

'What?'

I ground my teeth together and folded my arms. 'Sexual relations.'

'How do you know?'

'Doesn't matter. But is it true?'

He slumped against the bricks. 'Yes. To my shame.' He wiped his forehead with his sleeve. The scent of carbolic wafted from his clothes.

'Did she tell you something you didn't want to hear?'

'Like what?'

I paused. I had made a promise to Tim not to repeat his words – a promise which I had already partly broken by speaking to Daniel.

'A baby, you mean?' Pat said, shocking me into silence.

He had known about the child.

'It was yours?'

'I hoped so.' His face was white where it was not hollowed out by shadows.

'You wanted her to keep it?'

He nodded. 'I said we could have the banns read and be wed in a month, and we could say the child came early. So what if people talked? We'd be together by then.'

'She refused you?'

He took a shuddering breath. His shoulders sagged and he turned from me, weeping. From his jacket pocket, he brought out a flask and sipped. He offered me some, but the smell of bitter gin made me gag. I forced myself not to think of the last time I had drunk too much of it.

'She said she didn't love me.'

'What if it wasn't yours?'

His wet eyes flashed at me. 'But it could have been. That was enough.' He fixed the top on his flask and returned it to his pocket. 'I could never hurt her, Mrs Edwards. Even if she didn't love me, I loved her. And I loved the baby inside her.' Sniffing, he wiped his tears off his cheeks. 'I best get back, before Pa catches me here.'

He ushered me back up the alleyway. I kept a couple of paces in front, the hairs on my back lifting as he closed the space between us until I emerged into the sunshine.

'Good morning, Mrs Edwards,' someone sang, and I glanced to my right to find Jenny skipping towards me. She froze when she saw Pat and didn't come any closer.

'Have a good day, Mrs Edwards. Jenny.' Pat nodded at the girl, then ducked into the shop.

'What were you doing speaking to him?' she whispered.

I checked over my shoulder in case anyone should be nearby, but only Mrs Powell simmered up to her window to watch us once more. Jenny looped her arm through mine as we strolled towards the doctor's cottage.

'I asked him about Betty.'

'Why?'

'To see if he had something to do with her death.'

'Pat Dunn is as mean as a goat and he's a bully, but he wouldn't murder anyone.'

'A bully?'

She blushed.

'He just cried in front of me. I can't imagine him bullying anyone.'

Jenny's lips twisted. We stopped outside the gate of the cottage, and she found interest in the moss on the wall.

'Does he bully you?'

'He says I look like a donkey.' She scratched the lichen. Green dirt stuck beneath her nails. 'He says I'm as stupid as one too. They all do. All the boys.'

I wondered at how cruel children could be. How cruel Pat Dunn could be, according to Jenny. How deceptive he could be, according to Daniel Griffith. And yet, to me, he had wept and pleaded his devotion to a common whore.

Which of them was lying?

I took her hand so she would stop ruining her fingers. 'Come inside for a cup of cocoa. My mother-in-law might leave me in peace if she sees I have company. You know, Tim won't tell me anything about the other victims. Perhaps you could shed some light for me? We have biscuits.'

* * *

'Georgina Witcombe was the first.' Jenny picked a biscuit off the plate that Mildred had begrudgingly allowed me to take in. My mother-in-law was working in the kitchen, banging around, making her displeasure known, but at least she didn't interrupt us. 'Georgina died in the autumn of ninety-five. The reverend found her next to Madam Buckley's grave on a Sunday morning.'

'What was she like?'

'Never saw her much. Kept herself to herself, not like Madam Buckley when she was alive – she was always in the village. Don't think Georgina liked Bodnem. She was from Bath. Preferred the city, so Mary told me.'

'Then why was she here?'

'Madam Buckley was her cousin. She came as her companion when Madam Buckley got married.'

'Did she have any enemies?'

Jenny shrugged.

'The man who hanged for the last three murders, his name was Reg Smith. He was the husband of the third victim, Connie Smith.'

Jenny nodded. 'He only hanged for her death, not the other two, but people here thought he'd killed Georgina and Mary as well. If they didn't believe in the ghost, that is.'

'Did he ever have anything to do with Georgina?'

Jenny snorted. 'Not likely. She was a lady. Although she was a bit...' Jenny tapped her temple and pulled a face. 'I'd see her at church after Madam Buckley died. She was there in the dark, chattering away all nonsense. She never slept. Old Buckley had to fill her with chloral just so she'd rest, so Mary told me.'

She reached for another biscuit.

'And your sister?'

She never faltered as she took a bite. 'Died in ninety-six, in the May. Ma wept for months. But then…'

'What?'

Jenny sighed, and crumbs sprayed from her mouth. 'I know I'd rather have gone quick like that than linger.'

I frowned, but Jenny did not enlighten me until I asked her to explain.

'Consumption. Your fellow found it in the post-mortem. Ma said we should have known – always coughing, she was, no matter the chlorodyne she took for it. Horrible way to end, as if you're drowning. I wouldn't have wished that for her. Better to go quick. A short fright on a summer's night doesn't seem so bad.'

I wondered if she'd said such a thing to her mother and what kind of beating she'd received if she had.

'And your sister, did she know Reg Smith?'

'She'd look after his little 'uns sometimes before she went to the manor. Just to help Mrs Smith out. He was no use at all.'

'Did your sister ever say what Reg was like?'

Jenny forced her mouthful down. 'She didn't like him, but she never told me why. She just said he felt… wrong.' She brushed the crumbs off her skirt, then took up her cup of cocoa.

'What can you remember of Connie Smith?'

Jenny licked the chocolate moustache off her lip. 'Nice woman. She always looked worn out. Ma said that was because she was poorer than us. The last time I saw her, we'd all gone out blackcurrant picking. I remember because she told me how to make a pie out of them, and it was lovely. I wanted to thank her, but I never got the chance.'

'What was their marriage like? Was Reg ever violent towards her?'

She slouched back in her chair, her toes scuffing the floorboards. 'Men are allowed to beat their wives, but I don't know why he did it to her. Mrs Smith never put a foot wrong.' Jenny finished her drink, all the while watching the breeze tinkle the foliage through the window. 'Ma said he was cruel. He liked to hurt people.'

Shivers whispered over my neck. I thought of Tim's fingers squeezing my flesh, of the faint bruises he had left me with. Was that how it started? A heavy touch at first, then a fist, then a hand around the throat?

'Still' – Jenny sniffed – 'doesn't mean he killed her.'

'There had been no other deaths after they hanged Mr Smith until Betty. Now, my husband and the inspector are saying it's a copycat. Can't you see that if it hadn't been Mr Smith – if it had been the ghost as you say – then the killings would have continued?'

Jenny shook her head. 'The reverend exorcised the ghost not long after Mrs Smith died. He put Madam Buckley in that bottle. That was why no one else was killed.'

I pinched my lips. Nothing I could say was going to change her mind.

She gazed out of the window again. 'And now Betty's dead because I let the spirit out. Who knows when she'll stop this time?'

12
1900

'Fire! Fire!'

My eyelids peeled open. For a moment, my surroundings confused me. The ceiling seemed too close, as if it were falling in on me. I squinted at the beams, trying to understand what they were in the dim dawn light. Cold air sliced into my right arm, and I turned my head on the pillow to find Tim jumping out of bed.

'Fire!' the voice shouted again.

Samuel screamed, and suddenly I was awake.

I ran to him and scooped him out of his cot. There was no time for slippers or dressing gowns. Tim yanked my arm and dragged me, stumbling, out of the bedroom as Samuel writhed in my arms.

The landing was almost pitch; no candles lit the way. Tim helped me towards the stairs just as his mother emerged from her bedroom. The three of us met, panicked and panting.

'Give him here.' Mildred snatched Samuel out of my

grasp and, before I could argue, Tim pulled me down the stairs.

My feet were numb as they slapped on the floorboards. Tim flung open the front door, but his father cried again from deeper inside the house.

'Fire!'

We ran to the parlour, and I braced myself to confront great swathes of smoke choking the ceiling, but there was nothing. The scene was as normal as ever. There was nothing but ash in the fire grate. A book lay half-open, face down on the table beside two small glasses flecked with port. A blanket lay untidily over the back of a chair.

'Howard?' Mildred called. She clutched Samuel, crushing his face against her chest. She edged towards the door to the kitchen and pushed it open with one finger, as if she couldn't bear to see what might be inside.

Howard stood in a silk dressing gown and slippers, his cap slanted to one side, his smile reaching from ear to ear. He laughed when he saw us. He laughed so hard and for so long that he had to use the tip of his cap to wipe the tears from his eyes.

Mildred crumpled into the nearest chair. In her plain cotton gown, the skin on her bare forearms was slack, wrinkled, almost translucent. Without her high, tight collar, her neck reminded me of one belonging to a turkey, and her flesh there wobbled as she composed herself. I felt something akin to pity for her.

'Here.' I placed my palm on her bony shoulder as Samuel struggled to break free of her fierce embrace. 'Let me take him.'

'April fools!' Howard cried, but his voice was cut off by

a coughing fit. None of us helped him. 'What's wrong with you all? It's only a bit of fun.'

I should have smiled; after all, Howard was usually my only ally in the house, but I was too tired and cold to move. And in my stomach, a ball of rage burned.

I hated this day. I had hated it my whole life. Always, I had been the victim of my sisters' games: honey drizzled into my hair as I slept; the toes of all my stockings cut out; the last pages of my book slashed; arsenic in my bowl of porridge which made me rush for the pot, until they told me it was sugar and to stop being such a spoilsport.

It was a day of madness. Indeed, cackling in his nightclothes, Howard could have passed for a lunatic.

Tim set his hand on the small of my back and whispered into my ear, 'Go back to bed.'

The clock read just after six in the morning – not enough time to return to sleep before the tasks of the day began.

'I'll try to settle Samuel, then I'll dress.'

In the parlour, Howard sat and caught his breath. He dragged the blanket over his knees. 'Best start up the fire, Mildred. It's cold this morning.'

None of us had recovered properly by the time we filed into St Luke's. I did my best to keep my mouth closed whenever a yawn moaned from behind my lips, and each time the reverend led us in prayer, my eyelids fell gratefully.

In the front pew sat a figure I did not recognise. His shoulders were broad, his frock coat the deepest shade of black, his upturned collar piercingly white and stiff. His brown hair was fuzzy around the back of his head but thinner on top. Everyone watched him.

Everyone, apart from those who glared at me. Across the aisle, Mrs Powell scowled. Behind her, Mrs Crook's red, hostile eyes flickered in my direction.

Resolving to look only at the ground, I focused on the criss-cross of the wooden floorboards until we had sung the last hymn and risen from the pews. Briefly, I noticed a flash of black as the stranger marched down the aisle. Everyone dropped into curtseys or bowed their heads as he went. Tim's gaze followed him and stayed just a second too long on the empty doorway.

I wanted nothing more than to go home and settle my weary bones before the fire. I did not want to talk to anyone, but to my dismay, as we spilled out of the church, Howard sauntered off to speak with Mr Dunn and called Tim over.

Mildred and I lingered near a leaning gravestone as villagers sidled past us, and as the seconds stretched, I feigned interest in Samuel so I did not have to think of something to talk about. Mrs Crook prowled our way.

'I'll thank you not to spread vile gossip about my daughter.' Hatred laced her voice, and her black crepe dress trembled as she glowered at me.

'Mrs Crook,' I began, trying to keep calm, 'I fail to understand your meaning.'

'My meaning?' she erupted, and heads whipped in our direction. 'You've been going round telling everyone my Betty was a—' She pressed her hand against her mouth, unable to say the word.

'I have done no such thing, Mrs Crook, I can assure you.'

'Liar,' Mrs Powell spat, crawling to Mrs Crook's side and wrapping an arm around her. 'I heard you myself, asking Master Dunn all kinds of things, making out she was that kind of girl.'

'I did not,' I lied.

Behind them, Pat crept by. He could not have missed the altercation, but he kept his eyes to the ground as he shuffled for the lichgate. He was not going to come to my aid.

'Who are you, to come here and call our Betty such names? You didn't know her. You don't know any of us.'

Soon, all the women who had gathered to observe the spectacle viewed me through suspicious eyes. The ground wobbled beneath my feet.

Jenny fought her way through the crowd. 'That's not what happened,' she cried, but her mother pulled her away by the collar before she said any more.

'Yes, I admit I was talking to Master Dunn about Miss Crook, but it was only because I wanted to ask him if he had seen her the night of her death.'

A gasp of indignation swept through the women.

'I did not mean anything by it.' I searched for saliva, but my mouth was dry. 'I am only trying to uncover the truth, Mrs Crook. Surely you want justice for your daughter? Surely you want to know what really happened to her?'

I had silenced the crowd. Mrs Crook finally began to quieten and raked her sopping handkerchief across her eyes one last time. I dared to breathe again, but when Mrs Crook met my gaze, I recoiled.

'The only whore around here is you. Keep your nose out of my business.'

Mrs Powell smirked as she took Mrs Crook's arm. They slithered away, leaving a semicircle of village women ogling me and trailing off in groups of two and three, gossiping. For a moment, I did not know if my legs would hold me up.

Tim barged into me, knocking me off balance. He grasped my arm as I stumbled, squeezing too hard, and bundled me out of St Luke's grounds. The cottage door slammed shut behind us.

'I told you not to say anything.'

'I didn't... Not like that. They have my intentions all wrong.'

'Damn your intentions!'

Tim's volume set Samuel squirming. The child let out an ear-splitting wail as the front door opened and Howard and Mildred crept inside. Tim whirled towards the window, one hand on his hip, the other driving into his forehead.

'Powell is a poisonous hag.' Howard eased himself into the nearby chair. His words were no comfort to me, although I was grateful that he was on my side.

I rocked Samuel in my arms, shushing him, but it was not working. As he cried, I felt my own resolve unravelling too. I swallowed and blinked, but I was losing myself.

'Take the child, Mildred,' Howard said.

She prised Samuel, hot and sticky, out of my aching arms. The child quietened as his grandmother paced about the parlour with him.

'I'm sorry.'

'Don't let them upset you, my dear.' Howard gave me his handkerchief.

Tim swivelled around. His anger had dissolved; he seemed nothing more than exhausted. 'You are an intelligent woman, Louisa; I knew that when I married you.'

I did not take it as a compliment. Mildred tutted behind me.

'Your brain… it cannot be idle. That is why I have spoken with Squire Buckley.'

Howard drew himself upright. 'You've done what?'

'He's back?' It must have been him – the stranger in the front pew. It explained the villagers' interest in him.

'He arrived the day before yesterday. You are to be his daughter's governess. Starting tomorrow.'

I could not understand a thing. The world had tumbled upside down, and I could make no sense of it.

Beside me, Howard protested on my behalf. 'She is a married woman, a doctor's wife. Are you really going to let her work for her bread and butter, Tim? It's scandalous. And what about Samuel? He needs his mother here, taking care of him.'

'I can do that,' Mildred interrupted, and held her husband's gaze.

'This is ridiculous!'

'I have made my decision, Father. Louisa's mind needs stimulation. I am sure Miss Sybil will provide more than enough.'

'Tosh!'

'Father,' Tim warned, his voice wavering. 'She is my wife. I will decide. She starts tomorrow.'

13

1900

Without Samuel and his pram acting as a defence, I felt peculiarly vulnerable walking along Church Street. A terrible ache in my head had plagued me since yesterday afternoon, a result of too many tears. Even now, the image of Samuel kept popping into my mind, of Mildred clawing him out of my embrace this morning. I could still smell him, that lovely baby scent, and I choked on the lump in my throat.

Don't be so silly, I told myself. *You will see him tonight.* Yet, it was if I were in mourning for him as I stepped along the Buckley property.

The day was quiet, and a blanket of grey cloud dripped into the air before me. The lush green of the grass and plants, once I emerged into Buckley's garden, was muted and grotesque in this dull light. As I passed ferns, water droplets wept from their tips and blotted my gown. The gown I thought I would never wear again. The gown I had every intention of selling but something made me push into the bottom of my trunk instead. The gown that had had water marks on it before, the salty kind.

I peeled my gaze off my sleeve. It went straight to the upper-floor window of the manor. A pale face watched me, half-hidden behind the frame. Our eyes locked. We two strangers regarded each other warily, knowing we were soon to collide, for better or worse. The child broke away, leaving only the sky's reflection in the glass.

It was some comfort to discover the daughter of Madam Buckley had survived. As was knowing I had not imagined the face at the window. Yet again it had been proved to me that ghosts did not exist.

But why did no one speak of the child? It was as if she had been forgotten, marooned in the manor house. Why had Tim and Howard failed to mention the girl they had saved all those years ago?

I climbed the stone steps. One was cracked, and as I placed my weight on it, it shifted and I grabbed for a trail of ivy lining the nearby wall to steady myself. Something scuttled inside the foliage – a plump, brown wren hopping away from the disturbance.

Once level with the manor, I could see a dozen mirror images of myself stalking towards the door. Vainly, I took a second to observe my reflections in the windows. A sombre grey gown, a round and pale face, dirt-coloured hair pinned back a bit too severely. I pinched some colour into my cheeks, then knocked.

There was no sound beyond the painted wood. Waiting, I glanced behind me at the gardens. Bushes gambled across the lawns, the signs of their flowers only just beginning to show; I wondered how colourful they would be in summer. Clusters of daffodils splashed yellow and sprouted under the shade of trees: oak, beech, ash, fir, and slender silver birch. Tufts of bright-green shoots speckled bare branches, and a squirrel dashed up a tree trunk.

'Mrs Edwards, isn't it?'

I spun around. The door was open. A woman, not much older than myself I guessed, observed me. She had a long face, not ugly but not beautiful. Unremarkable. She wore a gown of faded pink, which did little to complement her skin.

'That's right. And you are?'

'Miss Stone. Miss Sybil's nurse.'

I stifled my groan; nurses could be terrible creatures. I was sure this one would be no different.

Movement ruffled her skirts. She was not alone. A child hid behind her, peeking out to stare at me.

'You'd best come in.' She retreated into the gloom.

The hallway was tiled, and a chandelier bedecked with dust and spider webs hung from the high ceiling. Three doors forked off the hallway, leading left, right, and straight ahead, and all were closed. A wide staircase fanned skyward, and Miss Sybil granted me a full view of herself as she climbed to the middle of the steps.

The first thing of note was her hair. It was as black as a crow's plumage. The second thing was her eyes. They pierced the shadows between us and stabbed at my attention. They were like sapphire gemstones, burning with an unseen light. They were trained on me, and though I knew I should not show weakness to my charge, I could not help but look away first. She would take it as a victory, no doubt.

'I'm to show you Miss Sybil's chamber and schoolroom.'

'Am I to see Mr Buckley? I understand my husband arranged this situation with him, and I wondered if I might have a word?'

'The master is busy. This way.' Miss Stone ascended the stairs, holding out her hand for the child. The girl took it easily, turning her back on me as I followed.

Once on the first floor, we marched down a long corridor where yet more closed doors led to forbidden areas. It was the very end door which brought us into Sybil's quarters.

Miss Stone showed me Sybil's chamber, where the walls were plastered with pink-and-white patterned paper. Handmade soft toys lay neatly on a small four-poster bed, and a fire guard showing a picnic scene stood before an empty grate.

Next, Sybil's old nursery now contained nothing but a small table and two chairs where, Miss Stone informed me, Sybil and herself dined. A wash room and a water closet were stationed opposite Sybil's chamber, and at the end of the corridor, a very thin door led to Miss Stone's chamber. She didn't allow me to look inside.

'This is where you will spend most of your time.' She let me inside the schoolroom. A desk and chair sat before a bare blackboard. Bookshelves lined the narrowest wall. Lying carelessly at the foot of a pianoforte was a child-sized violin. Another table, near the bay window, held a globe as well as a box of brushes and watercolour paints. The walls had been decorated with the child's artistic attempts.

As I took in the state of the place, a murmuring started up behind me. Sybil was whispering in her nurse's ear, twisting from side to side, her blue eyes glazing with water. Miss Stone mumbled something in return, and I was certain, though it was only fleeting, that she kissed the child before straightening.

'I'll be up with lunch for the both of you at one o'clock.'

Sybil clung to her hand. Miss Stone prised her off, then left.

The child stared at the closed door, then faced me as if I were the monster from her nightmares come to life.

'Right,' I said, forcing myself to smile. 'Where to begin?'

* * *

'What's it like?' Jenny pushed herself off the Buckley Manor gates, behind which she had been hiding, and scurried to my side.

'I thought you said it was a bad idea to come out in the dark, what with Madam's evil spirit loose?'

'It's not proper dark though yet, is it?' She pouted, but her eyes rolled worriedly upwards at the moon in a navy-blue sky. 'So? What's the house like? Mary always told me to mind my own whenever I asked. I bet it's grand, isn't it?'

'I've seen less than half of it.'

Jenny harrumphed. 'Then what about him? Buckley.'

The church loomed ahead, a silhouette in the dusk. I wanted only to be home, to have my son in my arms, to close my eyes and be alone. I quickened my pace.

'I have not met him.'

'What? That's odd, isn't it? You're in the same house.'

'It's very large.'

'Yes, but—'

'Why didn't you tell me about Sybil?' I turned on her. Fatigue made my voice brittle, although I did not mean my question to sound so much like an accusation.

Jenny faltered. 'Don't know anything about her. Never seen her.'

'But your sister must have when she worked at the manor after the mistress's death.'

Jenny shook her head. 'Mary never saw no baby. It was only ever Miss Stone, and she was an odd thing, so Mary said. Quiet as a church mouse and scared of her own shadow. Tell the truth, plenty of folk in the village suspected there never was a child, but I suppose you've proved that wrong.'

'No one at all has ever seen Sybil?' I couldn't believe it, but Jenny confirmed it. 'Why?'

'I told you, he doesn't like Bodnem, nor the people in it. Perhaps he doesn't want his daughter mixing with us. I know the reverend has had words with him. It's not right for a child to have never set foot in church. She wasn't even christened.'

A cool breeze made me shiver. The world around us had darkened, and the moon glared white from above; we started walking again.

'Oh, I bet you haven't heard, what with being cast off up there.'

'I wasn't cast off,' I objected, but Jenny was right. She had the simple habit of saying what was plain, no matter how tactless.

'Daisy Powell's got herself engaged. Farmer Jacob Hunt is to be the unlucky fellow.' She giggled and glanced at me nervously. I smiled so that she knew we were allies on the subject of the Powells. 'It'll be a summer wedding, I should think. By autumn, we'll be rid of her.'

'One less,' I whispered as we reached my gate.

Through the leaded windows, lamplight glowed, and the scent of boiled potatoes infiltrated the air. My mouth watered. I shooed Jenny away and watched her dash down the south road before she disappeared. A pang of panic knotted my stomach; although I did not fear the ghost as Jenny did, a killer was in the village. And so I waited, holding my breath and straining to listen, just in case Jenny screamed.

'All right, dear?' Howard stood in the doorway in his smoking jacket. 'Cold tonight. Come in before you catch your death.'

He opened his arms to allow me inside. Pipe smoke hit me after a full day in the scentless space of the schoolroom, although I did not find it as offensive as I once did. Somehow, it was comforting. Howard, always ready with a smile, felt more fatherly than my own ever had.

I threw my cloak on the stand, eager to see Samuel. He was sleeping in the parlour beside Mildred, who briefly met my eye before returning to the stocking she was darning. Tim touched my arm, as if he would kiss me but had thought better of it, and replaced his hand by his side. He looked too large in the small space. How tiny the cottage now felt, after only a day amidst the palatial rooms of Buckley Manor.

'Mother has left a plate for you in the oven,' Tim said, as Howard settled himself into his seat and picked up his book. He drew the oil lamp closer on the table next to him and fixed on his nose the lenses which hung around his neck.

'I'll get it in a minute.' Food could wait for my child. I leaned over Samuel and gazed at his angelic face, brushing the back of my finger along his silken cheek.

'I've only just got him down,' Mildred snapped, but I took no notice. Holding him against my throbbing chest, we went upstairs. My mother-in-law could tut all she liked; nothing would dampen my spirits now Samuel was with me once again.

I laid him on the bed as I removed my skirt, blouse, and corset. The pads against my breasts were wet, my chemise damp and sour. To ward off the chill, I shrugged on my dressing gown, then scooped Samuel up once more. He found the nipple easily and suckled. Mildred may feed him powdered milk all she liked, but she would never be able to give him this.

Tim tapped on the door before he entered and shied away when he saw what I was doing. 'Your dinner will be cold.'

'Bring it up. I will eat it here.'

'That is hardly…' He gave up his argument.

Since church, all we had done was argue, if we had not been silent with each other. Perhaps the atmosphere was grating on him. Perhaps he was tired of it. Well, good. Let him be tired. Let him mope. I was in no mood to be a jovial wife.

'How is the child – Miss Sybil?'

'Fine.' I did not want to think of Sybil or Buckley Manor; all day, I had been consumed by them. Enough was enough.

'What is she like?'

I did not comment.

'Is she a happy child? Does she mourn her mother?'

'How can she mourn a woman she never knew?'

Tim flinched at my insinuation of his failure as a doctor. He turned towards the door, and although I brewed with anger, I knew I should not torment him about such things. He had ammunition to use against me if we were talking about failures in our professions.

But it was too late to apologise; the moment had passed. Tim was already halfway through the door. I swallowed my apology as he mumbled that he would bring up my dinner right away.

* * *

Sybil sat in front of the window overlooking the grounds. Miss Stone had plaited her long black hair and had tied the tips with scarlet ribbons; they appeared like wounds against her cream day dress. Watercolours lay on the table before her, and she nibbled the end of her paintbrush as she gazed at the view. After a moment, she dabbed her brush in the pot of water, loosened the green paint, and began working on her paper. I sat and recuperated while she did so, noting forlornly the other sheet of paper with illegible inky scribbles upon it.

A knock came at the door. I checked the clock – eleven. Usually our only disturbance came in the way of tea and lunch, but it was not yet the appropriate time.

'Come in.'

Miss Stone entered. 'Mr Buckley wishes to speak with you.'

Sybil dropped the brush. Paint splattered from its tip and speckled her pale frills. 'Does he want to see me too?'

The hope in her voice was pitiable, almost painful. Miss Stone tried to smile.

'Just Mrs Edwards for now.'

Sybil jabbed her brush into the water pot and glared at the scene outside.

I rose, feeling guilty, as if my going to Mr Buckley was betraying my charge. 'Will you…?' I gestured at Miss Stone to take my place, and she did so without hesitation. 'Where will I find him?'

'In his study, in the west wing.'

I made my way downstairs and hesitated in the hallway under the chandelier. There were two doors either side of me, shut, as always. Opening the one to my right, I was met by another gloomy corridor, lit not by sunshine but by buzzing gas jets. Although the passage was large in a modern way, I curled inwards as I paced along its carpeted floor. Its walls were bare of anything save the lights – no paintings or photographs to indicate homeliness. A faint banging noise came from somewhere, a door rattling in its frame. The further I crept, the louder it became until I found the culprit.

I wavered. There was no sign as to what lay behind the door. I could not be certain it was the study. I knocked gently and held my breath to listen.

The door shook in its frame so violently that I opened it without thinking.

A great room greeted me, dull because of the drawn curtains. Its size was staggering, with tall ceilings carved in intricate plasterwork and giant white mounds of covered furniture.

My heels echoed as I stepped onto the floorboards; the carpets had been rolled aside. Peeling back a corner of a sheet, I revealed an oriental silk chair leg the colour of a robin's egg. Next, a chestnut table, as cold and smooth as ice. The white marble fireplace had not been concealed, but the mirror above had. On the opposite wall, something else, the same height and width of the mirror, was hidden.

I hesitated before peeking under the cover. I was spying. I was creeping around where I had no permission to be.

Leave, I told myself. *Leave, before any harm can be done.*

Yet, my fingers were already upon the cloth...

To my horror, the sheet came clean away. I reeled back, cursing under my breath, for now there was evidence of my spying, but my voice petered to nothing as I saw what stood before me.

Madam Buckley.

She was life-size, though made of canvas and oil rather than flesh and bone. Her gaze bored into me, knowing of my trespass. Such shining, glowing eyes. Exact replicas of her daughter's.

She posed against a familiar backdrop – the grounds of Buckley Manor. The gardens were in full bloom: mountains of blue and pink hydrangeas, rose bushes frothing in peaches and cream, clouds of lavender. And yet, despite the brilliance of the flowers, Madam Buckley defied it all with her beauty. Golden hair curled around a delicate face. She smiled demurely in a pink printed gown with ruffles on the bodice, and she held a matching parasol. Her other hand rested on her stomach, suggesting she was pregnant with Sybil at the time.

My heart ached to see her happiness, the abundance of

life within the gilded frame, knowing only months later she would never smile again.

The door slammed shut.

How long had I been staring? Mr Buckley was waiting. Would he have started searching for me? Nausea squeezed my stomach when I imagined him finding me ogling his dead wife.

The curtain billowed, startling me yet again, but soon my mind was working rationally. I ran to it, and though I was blinded by the sun when I drew it back, soon I saw why the door was rattling in the first place. A square pane of glass had broken.

There was nothing I could do about it, and neither could I restore the sheet to Madam Buckley's portrait, for it was too tall for me to reach. I dashed out of the room, through the corridors, and finally arrived at an open door.

I felt like a child rather than a governess as I stood before Mr Buckley in a beam of sunshine.

His mahogany desk consumed the room, and his scratched, green leather chair was throne-like as he sat upon it. It was the first time I had seen his face, and I was disappointed; Sybil had inherited none of his looks, fortunately for the child. He was large, but I was unsure whether muscle or fat lay beneath his skin. His hairline was too high and, being clean shaven, his face was comparable to an egg. His eyes were his best feature – a rich, coffee shade of brown, almond-shaped and framed by long lashes. They would have been attractive had they not observed me so coldly.

'A governess.' His first words revealed a low, rumbling voice. 'You do not look old enough.'

'I am four and twenty, sir.'

'Mmh.' He pressed his fingers together in his lap.

'My experience is satisfactory, sir.'

'Only satisfactory?'

The sun fell hotly through the glass. My armpits prickled, and I retreated into the shade.

'Tell me again the name of your previous employer.'

'Pendleton, sir.'

'That's right. Your husband did say. They lost a child, didn't they? I recall the write-up in the newspaper.'

I nodded and hoped he would continue to talk, but he did not. 'Matthew,' I said. 'Scarlet fever.'

Mr Buckley grunted. 'He was the only child?'

'No.'

'Why did you leave, then? A year has not yet passed. Did you not think you should have supported the family in their time of grief?'

Despite the shade, I continued to sweat. 'They had no need of me.'

'So you married Mr Edwards instead.' His words were intended to wound. He speared them through me, and his mouth twitched when I flinched. 'I thought Mr Edwards had gone away to Birmingham for good. I had quite a shock when he turned up outside my door last week, begging a position for you.'

'I am sure my husband did no such thing.'

His eyes grew keen at my clipped tone. Was it my imagination, or were those brown eyes smirking at me?

'It seems strange for a man such as your husband to desire his wife to earn her own living.'

'Mr Edwards understands my mind needs stimulation.' I parroted Tim's words and heard how feeble they sounded.

'That is the only reason you are here?' The question was charged. It was not as simple as it appeared, but I could not fathom what lay in its hidden depths. I swallowed, and my anxiety from his questions turned into irritation.

'I am here to educate your daughter, Mr Buckley. And I believe I have arrived in the nick of time.'

'What are you implying?'

'I imply nothing. I am telling you that your daughter can barely hold a pen. She cannot even attempt to spell her own name and can read nothing at all.'

'Are you saying she is a delinquent?'

'No. At least, I do not think so. But the nurse has taught her nothing.'

'Miss Stone is not a governess.'

'Precisely why she should no longer be here. She is a distraction. She will hold the child back. They are too… sentimental with each other.'

He rose from his chair and ambled to the window. A forest of overgrown bushes and tangled willow leaves pressed against the glass. 'Now I see why no one likes you.'

He did not notice how he winded me, and for that I was grateful. But I should not have let the truth hurt, for hadn't I always been friendless? Even my own sisters never liked me. Now, my husband merely tolerated me. What did it matter? I had never needed anyone. I was happiest alone.

'You are making enemies in the village. You should ingratiate yourself to the people, if you want to stay.'

'The people are stupid and ignorant.' I did not check my words. I reasoned that if he sacked me for impertinence, at least I would be home with Samuel before lunchtime. 'And they do not hate me any more than they hate you.'

With that, he turned to face me. 'How so?'

'They blame you for your wife's death. For her ghost coming back to haunt them.'

He clawed the back of his leather chair. 'Country folk have their own peculiar superstitions.'

'Quite.'

His gaze slid off me and to the desk, his jaw crunching beneath his cheeks. 'Do what you can with the girl, but let Miss Stone love her.'

With that, he gestured at the door and I returned, my head swimming, to the schoolroom.

14
1900

I had not spoken to Mr Buckley since our meeting in his study. I had not even seen him, something which I was rather grateful for. Not that I could forget him altogether; Sybil had not stopped asking questions about him.

Was he well? How long was he staying? Was he going to see her? It was the most she had ever said to me.

To placate her, I said I would report on her progress at the end of each week and tell her father how impressed I was, as long as she continued to practise her handwriting. As a result, she had been most diligent.

Now, Miss Stone bustled into the room with a silver tray, smiling for Sybil. She did not glance at me as she ushered Sybil away from her desk and pushed a glass of cream-topped milk and freshly baked biscuits towards her. My stomach grumbled at the scent of cinnamon as I threw my cloak about my shoulders.

'You will spoil her dinner,' I said, wiping off today's letters from the blackboard. Miss Stone glared at me. 'Goodnight, Sybil.'

Sybil dropped her biscuit, rose from her seat, and curtseyed. I met Miss Stone's gaze with a smile. It was somewhat cruel of me, but the nurse had a habit of riling me without even opening her mouth. I pushed her silly jealousy from my mind as I glided down the stairs and off the Buckley estate.

'Good evening.' Once again, Jenny startled me as she appeared on the other side of the Buckley gates.

'Jenny, you do not need to wait for me every night.'

'I'm making sure you get home safe. Especially around here.' She glanced towards the lake, the water a hazy blue in the dusk light, the shadow of a moorhen slipping over its surface. I did not understand why she found it easier to fear a ghost rather than a real person, but then I had been raised on fact and logic. Country superstitions had left Edgbaston a long time ago.

We reached the churchyard and Jenny paused. 'It would have been her birthday today.' Her eyes were glassy as she gazed towards her sister's grave.

Candlelight shone from the windows of my home. Samuel would be in his cot, warm and sleeping. He would be perfectly content, whereas the child beside me was not.

'Come on.' I opened the lichgate and offered Jenny my arm. She sniffed as she took it and guided us towards a small headstone with the simplest of engravings: her sister's name and dates. There was no mention of how she had died. In one hundred years' time, no one would ever know that Mary Carr had been murdered.

A small posy of flowers from Jenny's mother lay against the stone. It was clear the woman kept the grave clean and tidy, for there was not a spot of lichen or moss on it, unlike the others around it, including Connie

Smith's. The engraving on hers was almost indecipherable, and I promised to bring up a scrubbing brush soon. Shame on the reverend for not doing so already.

Jenny wiped a tear off her cheek and kissed Mary's stone. I helped her back out of the church's grounds, but we lingered in the road. I could not help but look at the wall on which Mary's body had been found, the way the rocks protruded at sharp angles, and thought how uncomfortable it must have been to have lain upon.

'Where did you say Georgina Witcombe's body was found?'

'Next to Madam Buckley's tombstone.'

'And Connie Smith?'

'On the south road, just outside the village.'

'Close to the lake.'

Jenny nodded.

'They were all discovered within yards of the lake.'

'Because it's her,' Jenny urged, 'the spirit. That's where she lives. Madam Buckley was always there when she was alive; it was her favourite place. That's why they threw the bottle in there, after. And that proves it was her who frightened Betty to death this time, no matter what Inspector Quinton says.'

I couldn't stand the sight of the water for another moment. I marched on and Jenny trotted behind, but near the crossroads we stopped, our gazes falling on the Black Heart Inn. Betty's body lay inside in an open casket. For a second, I believed I could smell the embalmer's fluids and almost gagged, but it was only my memories floating in the breeze.

'Daniel Griffith isn't invited to the funeral either,' Jenny whispered. 'Why do you think that is?'

There could only be one explanation, though no one in the village would admit it. They knew what he was to Betty. Mr and Mrs Crook, despite all their ravings and the white ribbon on the door handle, knew Betty was no virgin.

'How do you know he hasn't been invited?'

'I hear things.'

No one minded their words when Jenny was about. They treated her as if she had no brain at all. 'Jenny, how would you like to take on a secret mission for me?'

Her eyes flashed brightly for a second, then clouded with suspicion. 'What?'

'Keep your ears and eyes open. Particularly around Pat Dunn.'

'You still think he has something to hide?'

'I don't know,' I said with a sigh. My brain ached with the effort of juggling my suspicions. 'But if he's as cruel as you say he is, then I don't trust him.'

The door of the inn opened. Mr Crook showed out Mr Dunn, who carried a box and tripod. I hadn't known the pharmacist was an amateur photographer, but there were enough chemicals in his shop to make the hobby an easy and inexpensive one.

Mr Crook's gaze fell on Jenny and me. He snarled, his eyes red-rimmed, and skulked inside once again. Beside me, Jenny shivered.

'I'll be glad when it's all over,' she said, then scurried home.

* * *

I watched the procession from the parlour window, peering through the drawn curtains. The reverend led the way, but there was no hearse; Mr Crook and three other village men carried the coffin feet first through the Black Heart doors, their steps synchronised as they paced towards the church. Behind them came the mourners. Mrs Crook wore black crepe, and her veil quaked as she sobbed.

It was nowhere near as grand as the last funeral I had seen. There was no quartet of oily black ponies draped in velvet. There were no ostrich feathers in sight. There were no children dressed in white, stark against the sorrowful adults, dutifully promenading behind a small, glass-sided hearse which shimmered with gold finishings and bouquets of white lilies.

Still, the streets were quiet, and overhead the clouds threatened rain.

Behind the closest family and friends, Mr Buckley walked on his own. Next, the rest of the villagers shuffled out, and Tim and Howard and Mildred were near the front, heads bowed and lips pursed. Out of all the women there, my mother-in-law was the only one with dry eyes, although she was deathly pale. Rather than sombre, she appeared exhausted.

Pat Dunn walked in the centre of the crowd behind his parents. He wore a grey suit with a black hat and a black band around his arm. The set of his face never wavered; his brows were tight, his eyes mere slits. He glared at the coffin, and as the people surrounding him parted, I made out his hands – he wrung them. I imagined them doing the same around Betty's throat and had to turn away.

The black-bordered invitation lay open on the parlour

table, my name obvious by its absence. How Mrs Powell must have rejoiced when she learned I wasn't invited! Part of me was relieved. I was not ready to witness another coffin descending into the earth so soon after the last.

I occupied myself by sewing Samuel a summer cap. The baby slept in his blankets beside me, and I concentrated on my needle, although I could hear the mourners' feet on the road outside. The church bells chimed for the dead, and rain pattered on the windowpane.

I sewed, trying to distract myself, but it was useless. I set down the cotton and slipped into the kitchen, went through the scullery, and opened the back door a crack. From there, the funeral was just visible. Black umbrellas shielded faces, and the reverend's voice was drowned out by the downpour as the pall-bearers lowered Betty into the ground. It was only then that I noticed a man lingering at the back of the congregation. Inspector Quinton.

Inside, I watched once more from the window as the family returned to the Black Heart and Mr Buckley talked with the inspector. I headed outside, tiptoeing as quietly as possible, but Mr Buckley saw me and faltered. He bid the inspector good day as I approached.

'Mrs Edwards.' Quinton turned to me. 'You are getting wet.' He did not offer me his umbrella.

'Rain on an open grave. There'll be another death.'

'I thought you weren't a superstitious woman?'

'I'm not, but others are. If I might speak with you?'

He nodded, although I was all too aware that he would rather have declined. We started up the road to where a pony was tethered outside the smithy.

'I've been thinking.'

He groaned.

'Don't you find it odd – strangling someone in the middle of the street?'

'Murder is always odd.'

'Quite. But to murder her on the crossroads was… bold.'

He did not answer.

'Are you any closer to finding the killer?'

'Posters are in every town between here and the coast. Officers are on the lookout. We are doing everything we can.'

'Posters? Liverpool? Are you saying you have a suspect?'

'Someone remembered something. As I said they would.'

I paused, confused. 'When?'

'Last week. Haven't you heard?' He was enjoying this too much.

I tried to hide my surprise, but I was too curious to protect my pride. 'I have been busy. So,' I prompted, when Quinton's lips remained pursed, 'who is it?'

'An Irishman.'

'Not local?'

He shook his head. 'He was passing through on his way to Holyhead. Going home, I suppose.'

We had reached the pony, who was as wet as I was now; rain rippled off its flanks and puddled at its feet. Inside the smithy, Daniel Griffith banged at some metal; the pony was shoeless on two hooves. Quinton peered through the smithy door and asked how long he would have to wait. Daniel grumbled something about it being done when it was done, his sourness at not being invited to the funeral apparent in his glaring countenance and heavy-handedness.

'You think an Irishman, who just so happened to be passing through Bodnem on the twenty-second of March, strangled Betty Crook outside her family's inn in plain sight?'

'It would have been in plain sight if anyone had been awake, but they weren't.'

'And she didn't scream or fight this stranger who was attacking her?'

'If she did, no one heard. Apparently.' He peered at me, accusingly.

I ignored him. 'But what about the copycat theory?'

'The cases were all over the national papers. He could have read about them.'

'That seems hardly likely.'

'But possible.' He checked his pocket watch.

'*Why* kill her?'

He shrugged. 'Too much to drink? Maybe he tried it on with her. He is Irish. He got angry. When he realised what he'd done, he ran away. Mrs Crook never saw him the next day. He never paid for his room either.'

I turned to the pony and stroked its muzzle. 'Why did no one say anything sooner?'

He shrugged again, but I knew why. The ghost of Madam Buckley had blinded them.

'So, he was staying at the inn. But surely, if it were this man – this stranger – why not move Betty's body somewhere more discreet? It would give him more time to make his escape.' Questions and doubts muddled through my mind. Quinton said nothing about my concerns. 'Who did come forward?'

'A few men who were drinking that night. Your husband put me on to them.'

'Tim?' I turned my face to the pony so Quinton did not see my shock. Why hadn't Tim told me? 'Do you have any proof it was this man? No one saw him actually kill Betty, did they?'

Quinton peered through the smithy door again. 'Hurry up, I want to get back in the light.'

Daniel shouted something indistinguishable back, and the inspector reeled on me.

'Suspicious behaviour. Several witnesses confirmed his unwanted attention towards Miss Crook that evening. Mrs Crook says she heard Betty and a man downstairs after closing. That puts him as the last person to see Betty.'

'It could have been any man talking to her. And if Mrs Crook had had any suspicions, she should have gone down to see what was going on. She clearly didn't think there was anything wrong.'

Quinton glanced away, blushing. 'I don't like what you're implying, Mrs Edwards. You should be careful of your words. I hear you've got yourself into enough trouble as it is.'

The smithy door opened before I could respond. Daniel stalked out, two horseshoes in his gloved hand. The pony beside me shuffled uneasily.

Betty's body flashed in my mind, the way she had lain at the crossroads, angelic looking. If it had been an impulsive act of rage, why would the Irishman have only strangled her? Surely a beating would be more likely.

'It does not make sense that a stranger would—'

'Mrs Edwards, you are not only being a nuisance to me but to the whole village. I have received several complaints about your behaviour. I will warn you now – stop. Stop interfering in things which firstly are not your concern and secondly you do not know anything about.'

He turned to his pony as Daniel pelted the final shoe into place. He dropped coins into Daniel's blackened hands, as if he'd been born better than he had, before jumping into the cart. He whipped his pony's rear. I had to jump out of the way before I was trampled.

15

<small>1956</small>

Iris grimaced at the sheet of rain pouring from Smedley's gutters. Lifting her coat over her head, she had no choice but to step out into it. It doused her immediately, soaking through her clothes and showering her face. Shaking droplets from her nose, she scarpered into the night.

'Would you like a lift?'

She barely heard the voice; she had certainly not heard the car from which it came. Abigail had opened her window an inch and was squinting at Iris through the downpour.

'I'm going into town,' Iris called. 'I thought you'd have gone by now.'

'Wanted to see if it would stop.' She nodded at the black sky and the buffeting branches. 'Doesn't look like it. Come on, I'll take you in.'

Iris wasn't going to argue. It was a short ride with Abigail or a long, damp slog on the bus. Shivering, she slid into the passenger seat and fogged the windscreen. They waited a moment for it to clear.

'What are you doing in town?'

'The shops have a late-night opening. I need to get someone a present.'

Abigail raised a brow. 'Someone special?'

'Yes, actually.' Iris fiddled with the seat belt. 'An old friend.'

Smirking, Abigail shifted into first gear.

'So?' Iris wanted to change the conversation. 'You still keen on going to Bodnem?'

'After what we've just read this afternoon? Absolutely. I'm more like my mother than you realise, Iris. Once I've an idea in my head, I will not let it go.'

'She got herself into trouble too.'

'She was absolutely right though. It makes no sense to pin such a crime on a stranger. That girl's murder was personal, somehow. Don't you think?'

'Well, yes. The way the body was laid out might even suggest a fondness for the victim.'

'Exactly. It had to have been someone who knew her, at least for more than a few hours. I was thinking we could visit next Saturday if you're free?'

Iris didn't answer. She tried to think of an excuse but failed. By now, Abigail knew Iris was as friendless as she was.

'It'll be an adventure.'

She didn't like the excitement in Abigail's tone. It reminded her of childhood birthdays; expectations would soon be dashed. Tears usually followed.

They parked in the street.

'Can I join you?'

'If you really want to.'

Was Abigail putting off going home to her father? Each

day, she seemed to spend longer at her mother's side, ruminating on the latest section of writing.

The store was just beginning to sparkle with Christmas goods. A saleslady stacked dolls and board games beside packs of crackers and snow globes in the window. Hardback books lay on the tabletops beside displays of baubles and miniature Christmas trees. Well-dressed women milled between the aisles, inspecting saucepans and festive tableware, readying themselves for the season.

They found the cards section. A small area had been left for birthdays, but the selection was sparse. Painted cartoon girls smiled back at Iris with bright white teeth and too-big eyes. Most mentioned ponies or showed young women in ballooning skirts blowing out candles on a tiered cake. She gazed at them, plucking the dry skin on her lip, wondering which might be appropriate.

Last year, she had not faced this conundrum. She had picked the brightest, most elaborate card of them all, but that was when she and Shirley's friendship had been easy. This year, she needed something more sedate. In the end, she chose the dullest she could find, which had a bouquet of flowers on the front and some plain lettering.

'I suppose I should start writing mine, or else I'll never send them all out on time.' Abigail sighed as she flicked through the mountains of Christmas cards. If she was anything like Iris's mother, card writing was an Olympic event which could last weeks, filling in the most distant acquaintances on the year's events. Her gaze roamed to Iris. 'A birthday?'

Iris nodded and gestured at the chocolate-box station, leaving Abigail to peruse robin-fronted stationary.

Shirley liked anything sweet. Strawberry fondant centres were her favourite. Caramels came a close second. She used to urge Iris to let the chocolate melt on her tongue: *You must find the pleasures in life anywhere you can, Iris. No one is going to give them to you just for the sake of it.*

A woman bumped into her, interrupting her memories. Iris scooped up a box of Black Magic chocolates before she changed her mind altogether.

She met up with Abigail, who had a hefty stack of cards in her hands, and made for the tills. Over the crammed displays, something drew her attention: a head, taller than all the others, topped with a grey-rimmed hat. A soft jawline, a straight nose, a pair of deep-set eyes. The lips peeled into a smile as the person before him pointed at a plush garland of tinsel.

Iris stopped.

Not today. She couldn't see him today. She wasn't ready, wasn't prepared. She searched for an exit, an aisle to dive down where she could wait for him to leave, but Abigail was sailing along obliviously, her path set to collide with his.

Iris called her name, but the hubbub of the shop drowned her voice. Running, she caught Abigail's arm and was about to whisper in her ear when Simon's attention drifted from the ornaments and fell directly on her.

'Iris,' he cried, before the surprise of seeing her wore off and he remembered his manners. And his companion.

The woman who turned to Iris with a sparkling length of silver tinsel had delicately curled auburn hair, a mint-green coat nipped in tight at the waist, and slanted, hazel eyes which speared straight to the heart of Iris's confidence. Shrinking back, acutely aware of her drab black coat and the brown water marks on her shoes, Iris tried her best to smile at the lady who now approached.

'This is Ava,' Simon mumbled.

'How do you do?' Coral-coloured lips spread into a smile, not too wide to show teeth, not too small to be considered hostile.

Iris nodded. It was all she could do. Speech was currently unavailable.

'Abigail Edwards.' Saving Iris from social suicide, Abigail introduced herself and made some small remark about the decorations. The women exchanged pleasantries, appraising the selection of baubles and tree toppers and marvelling at how fast the year was passing. Meanwhile, Iris's gaze lodged into Simon's lapel, and only the familiar rumble of his voice roused her out of her embarrassment and forced her to face the situation.

'How are you?'

She took a breath and looked up. He had not changed a bit since the last time she had seen him, now several months ago, when the weather was still warm and winter was a distant threat.

'Well.'

'Your mother?'

'Oh, you know my mother. Always at her best.'

The skin around his eyes crinkled. 'I've been meaning to call in and see her, but…'

She nodded, her eyes flicking to Ava. The woman edged closer to Simon, and a delicate white hand with painted fingernails wrapped around his arm. There was no engagement ring. Iris could breathe again.

'Have you seen Shirley?' Simon lowered his voice.

'No. You?'

He shook his head. 'You know they're married?'

She'd seen the announcement in the local paper at the start of September. It had taken all her strength not to throw the sheets onto the fire. 'Did you go?'

'No.'

That was some comfort.

'Who are you talking about?' Ava asked, her clear-cut voice slicing the air.

Simon smiled down at her. 'Just a couple of old friends. No one you know.'

Ava lifted her chin a fraction, swallowed. Simon had no idea the slight he had just given, but Iris was all too aware. Heat rose from her collar and encroached on her throat.

'She was a girl I used to work with. We... lost touch,' Iris explained as she rolled her thumb over the chocolate box. 'It's her birthday soon. I wanted to give her something, but I haven't the faintest idea where she lives.' She laughed. After saying it aloud, it did seem rather silly to buy someone a gift when she didn't even have their address.

'Number nine, Chester Road.' Simon scratched his neck.

'You've visited?'

'No. I haven't seen John for months, but he still banks with us. Don't tell anyone I told you that.'

Silence descended between the four of them. Abigail cast her gaze to the decorations. Ava set the tinsel back on its hook.

'Right. Well...'

'Yes.' Simon pushed his hat down, although it was already firmly in place. 'We'd better head off. It's getting late.'

Ava pushed past Simon, clawed Iris's shoulder, and pulled her in for a peck on the cheek. She smelt of orange blossom and cinnamon. Iris dared not think what she smelt of. Most likely the smoke that lingered on her coat from Bonfire Night.

'Lovely to meet you, Iris. It's so nice seeing Simon's other friends, although he tells me so little of them.'

'You too.' Iris's gaze alighted once again on Simon's lapel and stayed there as he wished her good day. She prised her lips into a smile as Ava tugged Simon out of her line of vision.

'So, that's Simon.' Abigail fingered the tinsel which Ava had been holding.

Iris feigned interest in it too. She did not want to see Simon and Ava at the till together, spending money together, rushing out of the door together. Silly, of course. She should be glad for him. Ava was a beauty. Far superior in looks than him. Middle class as well; those manicured hands had never scrubbed a piss-soaked floor or gathered up soiled bed linen for the laundry. Those soft hands would be able to stroke a baby to sleep and set out fragile glassware for a supper soirée.

Abigail dropped the tinsel. 'He seems like a very nice young man.'

She nodded and gathered the courage to peek over her shoulder. Simon and Ava had gone. She offered Abigail her arm and made the smile, which had inadvertently slipped off her face, reappear. 'And you sound just like my mother.'

16
1900

Flesh touched mine. Peculiar. The sensation was foreign, unwanted. It fluttered from my shoulder, towards my neck, and prodded into my chin. Someone was moving me, turning me. I fell backward and woke with a start.

Everything was too dark. Something blocked my vision. A scent of mustiness, the sickly sweetness of alcohol. Tips of hair tickled my cheek, my forehead, as fingers fumbled against my chin, dropped to my neck, and pressed against my airway. I broke away, beating off the figure.

'What was that for?' Tim shielded himself from my fists. Crouching on the bed, his silhouette looked like a devil in a Renaissance painting. Relief flooded through me when I realised it was not the murderer come to strangle me to death.

'I was dreaming.' I rubbed the nightmares from my eyes with the heel of my palm. 'You scared me.'

He crawled up to me once more, his body enfolding

mine. He was too hot. I wriggled away from him, pushing my leg out of bed and into the cool air, but he followed. A sticky hand slid under the covers and dug into my hip before sliding lower and pulling up my nightgown. His lips aimed for mine, but he missed and latched on to my cheek instead.

'Tim, stop.'

He grunted something which sounded like a question. His fingers prowled up my bare thigh. His weight crushed me.

'Not tonight.'

'I need you. I need to…' Finally, his wet lips found mine, and I tasted the whisky on his tongue.

'No.' I managed to free my head, but only by pinioning myself against the pillow. He remained just an inch away.

'It's been months.' His tone changed; he was trying to be charming. Once, I had been lured in by it. Once, I had let myself go, as I imagined other women might do when faced with such a handsome proposition. Once, I had wanted to feel the burn of desire and passion, to quell a curiosity, to be seen as something more than a barren spinster.

'The baby.'

'He's sleeping.' Tim nuzzled my neck. Nothing stirred within me.

'Your parents will hear.'

'Don't care.'

For a moment, I considered letting him get on with it. If I lay still, he could do what he needed, and it would be over in a matter of minutes. But the thought of Howard and Mildred in the next room, listening, made me nauseous. I clamped my legs together and struggled against his persistence.

'No.'

'Come on, Lou.'

'I said no.'

'I want you.'

'Why didn't you tell me about the Irishman?'

I pierced his alcohol-addled brain. He rolled away. Cold air collided against my sweating skin, and I inhaled shakily, grateful that the darkness concealed the panic which lingered on my face. Tim's breathing slowed as he lay beside me, sobering.

'Didn't want to worry you.'

'Liar,' I whispered. He didn't object. 'What happened the night Betty died?'

'Now isn't the time.'

'It's the perfect time. Just you and me.' Not even Mildred could hear us through the cracks in the door. 'Tell me, Tim. I won't stop until you tell me.'

I heard him rub his whiskers. 'We were drinking. Betty was singing. The Irishman couldn't take his eyes off her.'

'Why didn't you tell Quinton about him from the start?'

He sighed. 'I don't know. I'd forgotten, I suppose, in the shock of it all, and what with doing the post-mortem. I wasn't thinking straight.'

'Talk me through the night.'

'I couldn't look at Betty, not after what she'd asked of me about the baby. But she seemed the same as ever. It made me sick. I went outside to… relieve myself.' He quietened. I feared he would succumb to sleep.

'Carry on.'

'When I went back inside, Dad was drinking with the Irishman, talking to him about… I don't know, something about going home to his family. I think they were ill. I wasn't taking much notice, but I remember him saying something about Betty, that she was pretty and… well, something like that anyway.'

I rolled my eyes at his embarrassment. 'Everyone thought she was pretty. That doesn't mean he killed her.'

Tim pulled the covers up to his chin. 'I never said he did.'

'But you told the police.'

'I put Pat Dunn on to the inspector.'

'Pat Dunn?' I turned on my side and poked Tim in the arm, for he was growing too drowsy. 'Don't you think that's a bit convenient? Pat Dunn suddenly remembers an Irishman taking too much of a liking to Betty, the girl he was sweet on.'

'He didn't remember. Not until Dad and I started talking about that night. We needed to stock up on some supplies – that's why we were paying a call to the pharmacy. All four of us were talking about it, and that's when we remembered him.'

'But it was Pat Dunn who said the Irishman killed her?'

Tim sighed and rolled over, his back to me. 'Others have agreed with him.'

'There's no proof. Did anyone see him do it?'

He mumbled into his pillow, 'No.'

'Did anyone see Betty with him?'

'We left her behind the taps alone, as usual.'

'Then why, for heaven's sake, are you all so convinced it was the Irishman?'

'Jesus, Louisa!' he snarled over his shoulder. 'That's enough. Go to sleep.'

I fell onto my back. There was no point pushing for more; he had closed up. He had said more than I expected anyway, one blessing of too much whisky.

I ruminated on his story, trying to make that night come alive in my mind. Out of everyone there, an Irishman on his way home to his sick family seemed the unlikeliest suspect.

Tim began to snore. To my left, Samuel stirred in his cot. Before long, he was wriggling and mewing. It had been hours since his last feed.

The room, which before had felt delightfully cool, was now chilling as I peeled back the bed covers. Shivering, I found my robe before easing Samuel into my arms. I crept downstairs as the clock chimed two.

* * *

I wrote an *S* on the blackboard and waited for Sybil to copy it onto her own board. She sat before me, her white dress pressed up to her desk, her porcelain fingers fidgeting as she struggled to grasp the chalk. Her brow furrowed and her lips puckered as she concentrated. With effort, she managed a shaky attempt.

'Well done.'

She exhaled long and slow, and drooped like a flower in a heatwave.

'And now the *Y*.'

The door to the schoolroom crashed open. The globe

on the desk trembled as the door handle slammed into the wall, and the water in Sybil's glass rippled. Both the child and I gasped, but it took only a split second for the intruder to become clear.

Sybil jumped up and dropped into a curtsey. 'Mr Buckley.' Her red-ribboned plaits dangled beside her dipped head as she waited for her father to acknowledge her existence.

Mr Buckley seemed surprised to find his child in the room. Fury lay within his balled fists, his blanched lips, his shuddering composure, but as he regarded his daughter, that rage bled away. With difficulty, he swallowed, and the sound of it was grotesquely loud in the silence. He forced his hands behind his back.

'Good morning.'

Sybil smiled and Mr Buckley looked away, as if her gaze caused him acute pain. He glared at the floor as he addressed me.

'I will speak to you, Mrs Edwards, outside. Immediately.' He barged out of the room.

Miss Stone's face appeared on the other side of the door frame before she rushed to Sybil, who, I only now noticed, was weeping. Miss Stone dabbed the girl's cheeks with the corner of her apron and swept her into an embrace. I did not need to ask the nurse to watch over her while I was gone; already, it was as if I were no longer in the room.

With as much serenity as I could muster, I made my way out of Sybil's quarters. The front door opened once I reached the top of the stairs, and a cool draught billowed against my skirts as I descended. Outside, white light momentarily blinded me. Shielding my eyes, I scanned the area for Mr Buckley, but could not see him. Then, birds flew up from below; he was pacing at the foot of the stone steps.

'Have you been in every damn room in this house?'

Carefully, I made my way down to his level. 'No.'

'Did you have any reason to enter the drawing room, or was it just to satisfy your own morbid curiosity?'

The fallen sheet had given me away, as I feared it would. 'The door was rattling. I thought it might have been the study, so I entered.'

'Yet, upon clearly seeing it was not my study, you went inside anyway and meddled with things you had no right to see.'

I squared my shoulders. 'A pane of glass had broken, as I am sure you are now aware. It was this which caused the door to bang. The sheet covering the painting, to which I assume you are referring, was already on the floor when I arrived.' My cheeks flushed as I pushed the lie through my lips.

'Nonsense! You were spying.'

'I was doing no such thing.'

'You are a deceitful woman. I will not have you around my daughter.'

'Fine.' I turned on my heel and pounded up the steps.

'Where are you going?'

I did not answer but headed for the front door.

'I said' – he ran at me, blocking my access – 'you are to leave.'

'I am getting my things,' I hissed into his face. 'The faster you move, the faster I can be out of this wretched place.'

'Wretched? The only thing wretched here is you.'

The cord inside me, which had been holding me together ever since I arrived in Bodnem, snapped. No matter how much I tried to stop them, tears trickled over my cheeks. I bit my lip, hoping the pain would halt the flow, but it only made it worse.

It was only exhaustion making me powerless over my emotions. Sheer exhaustion and frustration and an inexplicable feeling of fear that had plagued me for months. The insult had made it all well up and topple over, and I stumbled backward, searching for something to take my weight.

My feet scattered the gravel as I made for the far end of the patio where a stone bench was set against the greenery. I saw the smattering of moss over the seat just as my vision began to blacken, and I collapsed upon the bench just in time.

Wretched woman… whore… murderer…

Images somersaulted through my mind.

Betty's corpse. Her coffin. The funeral procession.

And then: a dented pillow where a head should be, another open casket, a crimson handprint on a cheek.

Was it my breath I heard scraping down my closing throat or his?

'Mrs Edwards?' The voice was distant. I barely felt the hand upon my shoulder.

I leaned forward, and my corset cut into my pelvis. Blood pulsed in my temples.

'Mrs Edwards?' The voice was close to my ear. The hand squeezed harder. 'Mrs Edwards, should I call for your husband?'

Mr Buckley dragged me out of myself. I stared at the tips of my kid boots, at the jagged, honey-coloured mosaic of stones beneath my soles. With his help, I sat upright. The breeze cooled the streaks of tears on my face, and before I could find my own, another handkerchief appeared before me.

'I will go.' I tried to stand, but he held me down.

'What just happened?'

I swallowed. 'I apologise...' Again, I tried to stand, but he did not let me.

'Just sit. Until I know you are recovered.'

His hand slid off me. I should have been reassured that he had let me go, but instead my skin felt dreadfully cold.

After a moment, I was recovered enough to speak. Too embarrassed to explain my emotional outburst, I turned the subject back to the painting. 'I am sorry for prying. I should not have looked at the portrait. It is private.'

Mr Buckley sighed, as if he had been pierced with a pin.

As we sat, the birds that Mr Buckley had scared away started to return. Their chatter whispered through the air, accompanied by the rustle of leaves in the breeze, and sunshine rained over us. I let its heat warm me and thought of the oil painting again, Mrs Buckley radiant in her summer garden, the pain too far away to glimmer in her eyes.

'She was beautiful.' The word seemed inadequate yet wholly encompassing.

'An Irishman, so they think,' Mr Buckley said, changing the subject. 'The murderer, I mean. The copycat. I doubt they'll catch him now.'

I wiped away the last traces of salt water on my skin. 'I believe that is the point.'

Mr Buckley raised a brow.

'They catch him, and they will learn he is innocent. Then what will they do?'

Mr Buckley gazed past me, his attention absorbed by the undergrowth.

'Doesn't it matter to you? What some say about your wife – her evil ghost being the real murderer?'

'She's gone. Nothing matters anymore.'

In part, I understood. Death made everything so concentrated yet so diluted at the same time. Everything mattered. Nothing mattered.

'Surely you do not agree with the villagers about a ghost enacting revenge upon young women?'

He laughed, but with no humour. 'My wife was the gentlest soul you could meet. Everyone loved her.'

I offered him his handkerchief back, but he refused. I secured it underneath my sleeve instead. The silk slipped around my wrist like water.

'Reg Smith was only convicted of his wife's murder, so I believe?'

'He was a violent drunk. He deserved to hang for what he put his wife and children through.'

'But you believe he killed the other two as well?'

He ground his teeth together. 'There wasn't enough evidence for them. He'd abused his wife for years and everyone had seen it. The police concluded that he had tried to poison Mrs Smith, and when that didn't work, he strangled her and dumped the body.'

'Poison?'

'Belladonna. There was a bunch of the berries in the kitchen in a bowl of blackcurrants. Your husband's post-mortem found it in her stomach. Or has he not told you that?'

I did not answer; Buckley saw the surprise on my face.

'But you have no doubt it was Mr Smith who killed all three?'

He cleared his throat, swallowed, considered the question, then stood and strode away without another word.

17
1900

Sybil was talented for her age. With regards to painting, of course. In every other aspect of academia she was still frightfully lacking. Luckily for her, her father had failed to follow through on his threat of sacking me.

No longer did the unsubstantiated promise of her father's praise hold allure. She refused to lift her head off the desk most of the time, complaining about the weather, which had grown too warm, and when I pushed a piece of chalk her way she simply stared at it.

If I had shown such defiance to my governess, I would have been whipped. Even now, the memory of the rod against my knuckles made me smart.

Where was my old governess? Did she think of me and my red skin the way I thought of Catherine Pendleton and her stinging cheek? Did she wish she had never lifted that cane the way I wished I had closed the door properly? Did she wish she had stopped, when I had started to wail in agony, the way I wished the silence had alerted me to what was happening in the neighbouring chamber?

I would never know.

But I could no more change the past than she could; I could only move on. And I would not punish Sybil with whips or canes or leather-bound books or dunce's caps no matter how much she tested my patience.

With the chiming of midday came a knock on the door. Mr Buckley entered. Sybil jumped from her chair, hands clasped behind her back, anticipation shimmering in her eyes.

'I hear you have not been reading your books like you ought.'

Pink spots flamed Sybil's cheeks. She lowered her gaze.

'Spell your name.'

Sybil's chin trembled as she struggled with the first two letters. The seconds stretched, and I had to avert my gaze. I found a red spot of paint on my cuff – I must have smudged it on one of the child's paintings – and tried to pick it off.

'How are you supposed to take over the running of this estate one day if you cannot even spell your own name?' Mr Buckley snapped.

Sybil's tears slipped. Her long, black lashes turned to wet spikes against her porcelain cheeks. She gave up.

Mr Buckley inhaled slowly. The skin under his eyes was dark and puffy. He was not accustomed to being in Bodnem for so long, so Miss Stone had told me. He grew restless and uneasy; he preferred the hubbub of the city, the constant noise and chatter and smoke and steam. I hazarded I knew why. It was easier to let all of that commotion cram your mind, to distract you, rather than face a long, lonely night with your grief.

'A walk,' he exclaimed, forcing a note of cheeriness to his voice.

Sybil's eyes widened and a smile appeared.

'If that suits you, Mrs Edwards?'

I nodded, too stunned to speak. Sybil rushed from the room and to her chamber, where she collided with Miss Stone and shouted that she must have her walking shoes.

'Again?' Miss Stone tutted as she bustled into the schoolroom with Sybil's sturdy boots before pinching her lips together upon seeing Mr Buckley. She dipped into a curtsey. 'Excuse me, sir.'

'The weather is fine. You should come too, Miss Stone. Sunshine will do you good.'

The three of us followed Mr Buckley like ducklings after their mother. In silence, we headed out into the sunshine, all of us squinting until our eyes adjusted. Mr Buckley headed down the stone steps and turned right, and we began the climb of the garden.

'Go off and play with Miss Stone,' Mr Buckley ordered, and Sybil did not have to be told twice. She streaked ahead, vanishing amidst unclipped grasses and ferns and bushes as Miss Stone tried to keep up. Mr Buckley slowed his pace to widen the distance between the two parties.

The heat was shocking after a cool spring. There was barely a whiff of breeze, and it was a relief to head into the wooded area where oak trees made dappled shade.

'You caught her off guard, Mr Buckley. She can spell her name now; it was just the shock—'

'They've found him. The Irishman.'

I stopped. Mr Buckley stopped. We stood beside a weeping willow, and he ran his fingers through its branches as if it were his lover's hair.

'Where?'

'In his homeland. They've brought him back. He's awaiting trial. He's saying he saw Betty dead before dawn from his window. That's why he ran.'

'Why not alert someone?'

We veered right and meandered between the bluebells.

'He's spent time in the hulks.'

I took my frustration out on the nearest flower, snapping off its head.

'You cannot be certain he is innocent,' Mr Buckley said.

'Of course he is. A rogue Irishman passing through a random Shropshire village on his way home to a sick family would not have murdered Betty like that. It has to be someone who knows the place. Knows where they can get away with killing a girl like Betty in the middle of a street. Knows all about the ghost of Madam Buckley.'

'You have been searching for weeks, Louisa. What have you found?' His gaze slid my way. A tongue peeked out to wet his dry lips. The question felt like a test.

'Nothing. Yet. But unlike the police, I have not given up. Just because you want this all to disappear so you can get back to London doesn't mean that a young man's life should be sacrificed.'

Footsteps came from behind. Sybil ran for us, arms spilling with a bouquet of wildflowers. Miss Stone paced after her, her usually sallow skin mottled the same shade as her pink gown. Sybil offered the flowers to her father, who stared at them as if they were a bunch of drowned kittens.

'Thank you.' Buckley cleared his throat and stiffly accepted his daughter's gift. 'Run along.'

Sybil gambled deeper into the woodland as Miss Stone puffed after her.

'Imagine her splayed out before your door, her lips blue, her filmy eyes staring at the sky.'

'Mrs Edwards, I would remind you of your situation.'

I needed no reminding. 'Imagine her, ten years from now.'

'I will dismiss you if you continue—'

'Imagine her strangled to death because you couldn't be bothered—'

'Stop!' He grabbed my arms and shook me. His fingertips cut into my flesh and yet… I was not scared. I was not scared because his anger disguised something else.

Fear.

He was just as petrified of the whole thing as I was.

With effort, he released me.

'Did you know Betty thought she was pregnant?' I whispered.

He stalled. 'What has that to do with anything?'

'I believe it is important somehow. It was her secret, and secrets are powerful.' I pulled my collar away from my neck, searching for a cool slice of breeze.

Damn, the weather was hot. I plucked at my collar again and unfastened the buttons on my cuffs. Buckley glanced away as I rolled up my sleeves, hiding the red spot which I could not scratch out.

I pressed my thumb into the soft, veined flesh of my inner wrist, imagining all the blood protected by such a thin layer of skin. If I were to push the nail down hard enough, I could cut myself open and bleed out.

Life was such a delicate thing.

I focused on my pulse. It raced more quickly than

usual. When I looked up once more, Buckley was gazing at my naked skin. I pulled down my sleeve.

In the distance, Sybil's laughter drifted in the still air.

'There'll only be one way to prove it wasn't the Irishman,' Buckley whispered. 'Another body.'

* * *

It came in plenty of time. For the Irishman, at least.

Not so much for Daisy Powell.

Her body was found on the north road, several hundred yards from Daniel Griffith's smithy, at the end of a searingly hot May.

'Ma told it. Rain on an open grave.' Jenny chattered into my ear as the body was covered up and taken away. 'Daisy and Betty were second cousins.'

As I had presumed. Everyone in the village was related to each other.

Inspector Quinton muttered to his sergeant, head down, fingers to his mouth. He didn't glance in my direction, but when he started walking off, I caught him up.

'You'll let him go now? The Irishman.'

He turned to me, squinting from the sun in his eyes. Already, he was sweating, his brow slick and his sideburns wet, and it wasn't yet midday. 'Why do you think that?'

I was sure he only asked such a dense question to rile me. 'Even you cannot twist things enough to prove that he escaped gaol just to come and murder Daisy Powell.'

'Different cases, different killers.'

He only said it to save face. I could tell by the sheer hatred in his eyes and the gauntness of his cheeks that he knew the mistake he had made. And so would those above him. I left him and the morbid scene behind and headed home. Jenny scuttled to my side.

'You still think Pat Dunn might be involved?'

'In all honesty, I have no idea.'

'Can't be Pat.' A smirk pinched her lips.

'Why?'

'Because I was watching him last night.'

'Jenny, you must be careful. You shouldn't be out at night, alone.'

'You said—'

'I didn't tell you to put your life in danger. What time were you out?'

'Maybe midnight.' Her smirk fell as I tutted in disapproval. She studied the cobblestones. 'I was only out because of Da, getting him home. Don't you want to know what Pat was doing?'

'Yes, of course I do.'

She looked up at me, eyes sparkling. 'He was in the graveyard, by Betty's stone. He goes there lots. He cries.'

'Cries? Are you sure?'

'He gets in a state. He falls to his knees, saying he's sorry.'

'Sorry for what? Why does he have a guilty conscience?' Was he sorry for the way he had treated her? Sorry that he hadn't protected her? Or sorry for killing her? 'Jenny, you need to tell Quinton about this.'

She shook her head.

'It could be important.'

'No,' she shouted. The people who had gathered to gawp at Daisy's corpse turned to stare at us. Jenny scowled at them and marched for the crossroads, and this time I had to hurry to keep up with her.

'I won't go to the police. I won't.'

'All right.' I grasped her arm. 'I'm sorry.'

After a few moments, I thought I was forgiven.

'No more sneaking around, do you understand? I don't want you anywhere near that boy again.'

'But I'm helping.'

'No.' Even I had taken advantage of her naivety, to my shame. 'Do not go out at night, even for your father. It's not safe. Do you want to end up like Betty and Daisy?'

Beside us, the front door opened. Howard found us, and we jumped apart.

'Everything all right out here?'

'Jenny was just a bit upset.'

'Does she want to come in?'

Jenny shrank back from my father-in-law's imposing presence. She changed when she was around men. The chatter which constantly fluttered from her lips when she was with me bled away.

'It's all right.' I squeezed her shoulder. 'It's safe. Do you want to come in?'

'I've got to get back to the farm.'

Without looking up at either of us, she scurried out of the gate and into the street.

'You shouldn't have gone, my dear. A murder scene is no place for young ladies.'

I stumbled into the hallway, shrugging off my cotton shawl. 'Where's Tim?'

'Preparing.'

In the medical office, the kitchen table was already set up. Tim and Mildred stopped whispering as soon as I entered. Mildred could not look at me and left for the kitchen. Tim's eyes were red from crying, although he would never admit it to me.

'Samuel is sleeping.' A wet and creased handkerchief quivered between his fingers.

'It's not the Irishman.'

He sighed and turned from me.

'Who do you think it is?'

'I don't know.' He put the handkerchief to his nose and blew, avoiding my gaze.

I fled for the stairs. 'I won't come down until the body is out of the house.'

18
1956

'Won't you stay? We can't leave it there,' Abigail said, groaning when Iris hopped up from the armchair.

She'd already stayed well past her shift. Nurse Carmichael had had enough of Iris spending too long with the Edwardses and had threatened to move her to another ward if she continued to shirk her other responsibilities. Hence why the last several days she had sat with Abigail only after she had clocked off. As if her life hadn't been consumed by Ward 13 enough already, now it was eating into her only free time.

'I'm sorry, Abigail, but I need to deliver this present. It's Shirley's birthday tomorrow and I need to take it before…'

Abigail raised a brow, but Iris didn't want to explain about John. It felt like a betrayal of Shirley's confidence.

'I'll see you tomorrow.' She gave Abigail a quick squeeze, ignoring the disappointment in her face as she closed the notebook, then dashed through the ward.

She navigated her way to number nine, Chester Road. It was a neat little semi-detached Edwardian house on the edge of town. Mature trees draped across the driveway and fallen leaves had been heaped up neatly by the side gate.

Iris couldn't imagine John gardening, stooping so low as to pick up nature's mess. Perhaps he employed someone. Perhaps Shirley had a cleaner now too. Would John have thought of that? Would John allow another woman into their home? Was he so confident that Shirley would keep his secrets of violence close to her heart? Probably.

Through the large bay window, the lights had been turned on but the curtains had not been drawn. Shirley sat in the front room, leafing through a magazine. Everywhere was so tidy, not at all how Shirley's old bedroom had been. Blood-red chairs sat beside an old, tiled fireplace, decorated with patterned cushions. A green sofa faced a television set – Shirley could watch her favourite Hollywood stars in her own living room. But was it only there so she no longer ventured to the picture-house?

This was Shirley's life now. A housewife. Was there something cooking in the oven? Had she been out to the shops this morning and bought a little something special for John tonight? Had she eaten lunch alone before the television set, ensuring she cleared away so nothing would be amiss when John returned from work? Was she glancing at the clock on the mantelpiece now to see if it was time to change her clothes, neaten her hair, and spritz perfume on her skin for her husband's imminent arrival?

Iris was running out of time. Shirley needed to find the card and gift before John got to them first.

Hugging the shadows, Iris dashed for the porch. She set the wrapped chocolates on the mat, placed the card on top, and rang the doorbell. Then she scurried back to her hiding place behind the tree.

Shirley had already left the room by the time Iris was safely out of sight. The hallway light shone through a semicircle of stained glass above the front door. There came the clinking of metal, the latch lifting, and then there was nothing between her and Shirley but cold, winter air.

Iris's breath puffed out before her – a white globe of shock. She blinked, trying to clear her vision. Surely not. Not yet. She couldn't be…

Iris clasped her hand over her mouth to stop the emotion bubbling up into a cry.

Although as made up as ever, Shirley was more rounded than last time Iris had seen her. Gone were the slender calves and the cinched waistline. Instead, her ankles were swollen, the skin bulging over the kitten heels. Her once-ample bosom had now ballooned and stretched the fabric of her cashmere sweater. And it was all because of one thing.

The baby in her belly.

Shirley glanced around and peered into the night. When the gift at her feet caught her attention, she stepped sideways to pick it up. Like that, Iris could make out the bump more clearly. Shirley and John had been married almost three months, but the child had evidently been conceived well before that.

Iris thought back to what felt like the distant past. To the heady heatwave of summer. To the sickness Shirley had complained about. To the pale clamminess of her skin. To the tears and tantrums. Iris had thought it had all been down to John's abuse, but obviously John had left Shirley with more than just bruises.

Was that why she had gone back to him? Had she known, right from the start, that there would be no getting away from him?

After all Iris had said to her – begging her to leave him, telling her what a vile man he was – had Shirley agreed but known there was nothing she could do about it?

How Iris wished she could turn back the clock and use a different tack. They might have discussed options together. Although illegal, there were methods of getting rid of babies. Iris would have been with Shirley every step of the way. She would have done anything to save Shirley from the man she had felt obliged to marry.

A faint smile lit Shirley's face as she saw the box. She grinned, lifted the lid, and ran a finger over the contents before plucking out one black cube of chocolate. Sighing with pleasure, she held it in her mouth, letting it melt for a moment.

She turned her attention to the card and ripped open the envelope with as much excitement as a child, but when she read the words, she froze. With effort, she swallowed the chocolate. She stepped out from the porch.

For a second, Iris thought she was going to search for her, but she did not have to worry. Shirley was not looking for her; she headed for the dustbin at the side of the house. She lifted the metal lid and placed the chocolates and card inside and rummaged around as if arranging the other rubbish on top.

She was making sure John would not see them.

Back in the doorway, Shirley lingered. Now nothing but a black silhouette, she raised her hand, as if about to wave, before setting it on the door and shutting it. The light in the hallway went out. Shirley walked into the front room, straight for the bay windows, and closed the curtains.

19
1900

I held Samuel close as I gazed up at the first star, a brilliant white dot in a cobalt sky. Beside it, the moon hung like the curl of a clipped fingernail. A flutter of black wings passed my head, and a bat's silhouette vanished across the gravestones.

Everywhere was hushed now another girl was dead. There was no laughter or music from the Black Heart Inn. People talked in whispers as they enjoyed the late, light nights before rushing home when dusk settled.

I headed back inside as a chill flushed over my skin.

In the scullery, Mildred was drying the plates. I ignored her and joined Tim and my father-in-law in the parlour. Tim read aloud from yesterday's newspaper beside the oil lamp, while Howard peeled one of last year's shrivelled apples. He carved off the yellowed skin in one long reel.

'How old were you, if you don't mind my asking?' I interrupted and nodded at the photograph of Howard on the wall.

'Twenty-five, I think. No more than twenty-seven because my father is alive.'

A tall, thin man stood next to a young Howard. They bore little resemblance to each other but for the darkness of the hair and eyes. Behind them, the sea rolled out, bleached white with sunlight.

'Where were you?'

Howard chopped off a side of the apple and bit into it. 'Sidmouth.'

'Holidaying?'

He swallowed, then bit again. 'We lived there.'

His answer surprised me. 'Have you not always lived in Shropshire?'

'No, my dear. All over the place.'

Tim closed his paper. 'Should you like coffee, Father?' Howard nodded, and Tim got to his feet and removed Samuel from my arms. 'Louisa. Coffee.'

'Where else have you lived?' I asked, settling myself into a chair, much to Tim's annoyance. He flounced into the kitchen with a growl.

'I can't remember them all. I was born in Broseley. That's where I met Mildred. Edinburgh while I was studying. When I'd qualified, we all moved to Sidmouth where that photograph was taken. A stint in a Cotswolds village. Then Birmingham, but I couldn't be doing with the city. Well, it was a town back then. Still. So ugly. Sorry, I know Tim liked it there, and it is your home.'

'Not anymore.'

Tim stomped into the room and shoved Samuel into my arms again. His mother followed and carried a silver tray with cups and saucers and a coffee pot. She started to pour.

'Have you a photograph of your mother?'

Mildred slammed the pot down before handing Howard his drink.

'No. But you should not be disappointed. She was nothing special.'

'Is she still alive?'

He sipped his coffee. 'I don't know. She left us.'

'Left?'

Mildred held the cup before my face. I had to peep around her to see Howard speak. He stared into his drink, and the liquid rippled as he blew across it.

'One morning she wasn't there. Another man. She was that sort.'

Mildred tutted as she sat beside her husband. I had expected her to try to comfort him, for his distress was clear in his features, but she remained as straight as a rod.

'I'm very sorry,' I whispered.

'Better off without her. She was a difficult woman to live with. My father was a different man afterwards, in a good way, although his heart had already been damaged.'

'Have you decided if you would like anything for your birthday tomorrow, Louisa?' Tim gulped his coffee, gasping each time he did so. It was cringingly annoying.

'As it happens, yes.'

He raised his brows.

'I would like a photograph taken of Samuel while he's still a baby. I want to capture him as he is now. Perfect. Before anything can happen to him.'

* * *

I packed Samuel's christening gown, checked myself in the looking glass, then joined Tim at the foot of the stairs. He had washed himself free of the day's grime and had oiled his whiskers. He wore his best suit and a silk top hat. How he had used to look – how he had been when I first laid eyes upon him – back when his clients were those in the upper echelons of society. He hadn't tried as hard since moving to Bodnem. The way he glanced up at me, exactly like that first time I descended the Pendletons's staircase to greet him, made my breath catch in my throat.

'You look lovely,' Howard said from the parlour doorway.

I wore my wedding gown. A peach silk dress, trimmed with lace from Honiton, with buttons made of shimmering pearl at the wrists. The most expensive gown I had ever owned. Tim had bought it for me after having my measurements sent to the dressmaker's in London.

Mildred placed Samuel in the pram outside the front door. She looked me up and down but didn't say anything. She came to her husband's side instead, held on to his arm, and guided him into the parlour.

The villagers gawped at us as we made our way down the high street. I didn't suppose they'd seen anyone dressed so well in years. I took no notice of their jealous sniggers, although Tim cleared his throat and touched his hat too often to appear unperturbed.

The pharmacist's shop was closed to the public, but Mrs Dunn was waiting for us on the other side of the glass door.

'Oh my, don't you look wonderful!' She joined me as I scooped Samuel up and left the pram outside.

The stench of carbolic and other potions clung to the

back of my throat as we entered. Samuel sneezed and wriggled. Behind the counter, Pat was clearing away for the night, wiping down the shelves and sliding away the pill maker. He nodded at me and Tim through the lens of the carboys.

Mr Dunn said little as he led us into the back rooms and up the stairs, a mere black figure passing through the shadowed corridors where framed photographs blocked all evidence of wallpaper. In the dim light, it was hard to make out who or what stared out from the papers. Were they pictures of the living or the dead? A fleeting thought of our photograph being used as a memento mori made the flesh down my spine twitch.

Mr Dunn showed us into a room at the end of the corridor. It was spacious enough, dominated by a box and tripod. Several pieces of furniture were stacked against its walls, and a backdrop hung on a high rail. A whiff of burning chemicals tinged the air.

'That all right for you?' Mr Dunn nodded at the backdrop. It was a shabby scene of an orangery, with lush potted plants fanning out at all sides and arched windows giving out a dusty yellow light.

'What other ones do you have?'

Mr Dunn rummaged in his trunk. 'There's a landscape, a staircase, or a plain velvet.'

All were as tired as each other. 'The orangery is fine.'

Samuel began to cry as Mr Dunn readied his camera.

'I need to change him.'

'Why didn't you bring him ready?'

'It's his christening gown, Mr Dunn. I will not run the risk of it being ruined by going through the street.'

Mr Dunn rolled his eyes but pointed to their chamber, the door on the right in the corridor.

I changed Samuel quickly on the bed. The room was small – Mr Dunn had clearly commandeered the largest for his hobby. It overlooked the backyard and the laboratory, and with the windows opened because of the heat, there was an unfortunate smell emanating from the alleyways.

When I returned, the chair and neck brace had been set up. Tim assumed his position behind the seat, one hand placed on the chair back, the other waiting for me. I sat and arranged Samuel as best I could, tilting him so his face was showing and splaying out his white gown across my lap. He ogled the photographer with fascination as Mr Dunn tinkered with the flash powder and dived in and out under the camera's cloth. When Tim's hand came to my shoulder, I flinched; it had been so long since his fingers had caressed me.

'Ready?'

I tried to nod, but the neck brace forbade it. With a swoop, the cloth was lifted. Blinding light exploded. A sliver of smoke curled up towards the ceiling. The shock of it all made Samuel cry.

'Done.'

The heat from Tim's palm dissipated. To my surprise, I wished it would come back, that we could return to and linger in those seconds before the flash. I wondered if the camera had managed to capture a tenderness between us. They did say it had a habit of lying.

Mr Dunn ushered us out of the room, locked the door behind him, and marched for the stairs.

'I need to change Samuel again. I shan't be a moment.'

He hesitated on the top step, but Tim was already heading down and talking about a recent article in *The Lancet*, forcing Mr Dunn with him as he went.

As soon as they disappeared, I darted into the room on the left. Pat's chamber. It was tiny, with one bed stuffed against the inner wall and a wardrobe and set of drawers on the other side next to the window. A note of perspiration rose from the bedsheets.

I clutched Samuel close and headed for the drawers. I did not know what I was looking for, but such an opportunity would not come about again. If Pat Dunn could hide his bullying nature so well, what else could he hide?

Linens and underclothes filled the first two drawers. The bottom was crammed with nothing but old socks. The wardrobe was almost empty but for a few jackets which had seen better days. I turned to the bed and pinched the pillow up at arm's length. From the case, a square piece of paper fell onto the mattress.

A photograph.

I flipped it over. Betty stared at me. Her black hair cascaded all the way to her naked waist, barely concealing her breasts. She wore only a thin pair of drawers, and her slim silhouette struck against a dark background – the velvet one from Mr Dunn's trunk. One hand rested on her hip; the other hung stiffly by her side. Her lips were pinched, but her eyes were as fierce as I remembered.

She didn't want to be photographed.

'Don't think bad of her.'

I jerked back, dropping the picture and pillow. Pat stood in the doorway, his eyes blank. 'I wanted to have something to remember her by. She never stayed with me long enough.'

My grip around Samuel tightened. He began to wriggle and groan.

'She was happy about being photographed naked?'

'She was happy taking the money for it.' His voice was as hard and cold as steel. 'I loved her.'

'So you keep saying.'

'Are you interrogating Daisy's fiancé as much as me?'

'Does he have nude photographs of her hidden under his pillow too?'

Pat smirked. 'How should I know?'

'Daisy was not a whore. Her fiancé didn't have to buy her affection, unlike some.'

His eyes narrowed, and he stepped into the room. 'Did my father allow you to come in here?'

I swallowed. 'I needed to change Samuel.'

Pat gestured at the bed, then at my son. 'Go ahead.'

It was a power game. Would I expose my child in front of him? Did I trust him enough to do so? Was I brave enough to turn my back on him?

Jenny and Daniel Griffith had been right. Inside this feeble-looking boy there was a bully.

'You'd best hurry. Your husband is waiting for you downstairs.'

'I'll change him when I'm home.'

He stepped aside, leaving a narrow gap for me to pass. At the last minute, he placed his hand on Samuel's leg and rolled the silk between his fingertips. 'Such a bonny lad,' he breathed. 'I hoped Betty would give me a son.'

I barged past him and scurried downstairs as Samuel began to wail.

20
1900

Jacob Hunt's farmhouse was three miles north of Bodnem. Even so, it sat in Buckley land and was a ramshackle building of clumsily placed bricks and narrow windows. Livestock chewed on grass in the surrounding fields, or else grain rippled in the breeze.

Daisy had made a good match.

'I'll wait here,' Mr Buckley said beside me in the carriage.

He hadn't wanted to come. He had thought it improper to call only days after Daisy's murder. Let them grieve, he had told me, but he should have known how unguarded minds were in the swirling days following tragedy. Now was the perfect time for questions.

'Tell your father all about the wives of Henry VIII, Sybil,' I said as I slid out of the carriage. 'I'm sure that will pass some time.'

The track to the front door was stony and uneven. Rocks pierced into the soft arches of my feet, and I raised my hem to stop it dragging in the dust. A dog ran at me, gnashing its teeth and raising its hackles, but a chain around its neck choked it back.

Taking in a shaky breath, I continued. The door was splintered and rickety in its frame as I knocked. Weeds crawled from the cracks in the gravel around the base of the house, and some of the window ledges had split.

Perhaps it wasn't as good a match as I had thought.

Jacob's mother opened the door. She was wrapped from head to toe in black crepe, and her face had pruned from crying. She did not look long for the grave.

'Mrs Hunt, on behalf of myself and all of the Edwardses, I would like to extend our condolences to you and your son.'

She peeked around my shoulder at the carriage. 'Is that...?'

'Mr Buckley thought it best if I spoke with you, on account of the delicacy of the situation.'

She nodded. Then she frowned. 'What are you doing here?'

'I would like to speak to your son.'

'Why?'

'To try to understand what happened that night.'

'The police have already asked their questions.'

'Yes, but—'

'Let her in, Ma.' Through a door to the left, Jacob's voice saved me. His mother stepped aside, putting up no objections. The frown on her face, I now realised, was not from animosity but confusion.

She allowed me into a tight hallway, where the scent of wet dog and cow muck simmered in the air. She gestured for me to go through to the kitchen while she crept up the stairs, gnarled fingers gripping the bannister for support.

Jacob Hunt sat at the kitchen table with stalks of dried herbs hanging from the beams above his head. Dirt dusted the quarry tiles, and thin balls of hair and fur tumbled across them in the breeze from the open back door. A bowl of grubby new potatoes and early summer greens waited before him, ready for preparing.

'It's Mrs Edwards, isn't it?' Jacob didn't stand on my arrival. 'What do you want to ask?'

The only signs of his grief were in the black band around his arm and the rawness of his eyes. He nodded at the chair opposite him, and I sat gingerly. It juddered with my weight.

'You were with Daisy the night she died?'

He swallowed. A fleece of light-brown whiskers covered his cheeks and throat, all the way down past his open collar. 'Yes. Until eleven. Then I drove her home in the cart.'

'That is late for her to be here with you, alone.'

'She helps. Helped.' He pushed himself to his feet and fiddled with the range, checking the coal. He lifted the kettle off the hot plate and filled it. 'Ma is… Daisy was going to take care of us. Take care of everything.' With his back to me, I could not see him cry; I only knew he was sobbing by the way he folded in on himself. I focused on the potatoes in the bowl until he had recovered.

'You drove her straight to the shop?'

He set the kettle back on the hot plate. 'No.'

'Why not?'

Dropping into his seat, he met my gaze for the first time. His eyes were the colour of split wood. He was surprisingly handsome beneath the unkemptness. 'It was late, as you said. People talk.'

I sat up straighter, understanding the implication in his words. 'Where did you leave her?'

'Just before the stables. I turned around in the road and came back.'

'Did you see anyone else?'

He shook his head.

'Why didn't you watch her home?'

'She didn't need me to.'

'There is a murderer in the village.'

'Yes, a copycat, so I thought she'd be all right. She wasn't like Betty. She wasn't like any of the others.'

He licked his lips. Behind him, steam was beginning to pour from the kettle's spout.

'What do you mean by that?'

He grabbed the bowl of potatoes, trying to avoid the question, but I stopped him with my hand. Both of us froze. He glanced at me, a question in his eyes. An unwelcome question.

I released him. 'Sit down, Mr Hunt. Now tell me what you mean.'

'She was a good girl. There'd been no one else. She was... you know... pure.'

'Are you saying the others weren't?'

'Well, Betty.' He laughed, just one loud bark; he startled himself with it.

'And Mary Carr? Georgina Witcombe? Connie Smith?'

'Connie was on the game. Had been for years. Everyone knew that.'

I blushed at my ignorance. 'But she was married.'

'He made her do it.'

'Who? Her husband?' I could not hide my disgust. 'But Mary and Georgina weren't...'

Water bubbled up the spout of the kettle and plopped on the hot plate. Jacob made a pot of tea.

'They weren't like my Daisy. No matter all Georgina's airs and graces, no matter all her crying over her friend's tombstone, everyone knew what she really wanted.' He scowled at the carriage through the window before finding two chipped cups and saucers. 'Mary was the same. Money. I wouldn't wonder at the things those girls did for it.'

He poured the tea. Standing on tiptoes, he retrieved a box from on top of the cupboards. From it, he brought out a vial of chloral hydrate and poured a teaspoonful into one cup. 'Best for her to sleep while I'm working,' he said as he stirred it in. 'Then I know she's safe.' He turned to me. 'If that's all, Mrs Edwards, I've work to be getting on with.'

I stood. It seemed too easy. I was expecting more of a fight. 'Why did you let me in?'

'Mrs Powell doesn't like you. Daisy didn't either. Sticking your nose in where you shouldn't. Questioning things you shouldn't. But you seem to be the only one who cares enough to ask.' He smiled and sipped from his cup. 'Will you go to the inquest?'

'What do you think?'

He laughed and, with that, showed me to the door.

I stumbled out of the house and shivered at the thought of his mother lying upstairs in her black dress, unconscious for the rest of the day.

Again, the dog barked as I passed. I scurried for the safety of the carriage. Sybil wittered away to her father as I entered, so much so that she barely noticed me. Somehow she had got on to the subject of dolls, the intricacies of the relationships between all of her favourites, and I remembered just how small she was. Of course she didn't want to talk about kings and queens with Mr Buckley.

He sighed with relief as I sat beside him, and Sybil's chatter drifted into silence. 'So?'

I glanced at the house, at the drawn curtains in the upstairs window. 'What's wrong with her?'

'She was never the same after her husband died. Melancholic? Demented? I don't really know. It's for him she wears black.'

'Her son should send her to an asylum. She might get help.'

Mr Buckley banged on the carriage roof. 'You have obviously never been to an asylum.'

21
1956

The Morris Minor's heating system was no match for the November wind. It seeped into the car, making Iris scrunch her toes and sit on her hands.

By her watch, it was now half past ten, and the suburbs of Shrewsbury had long faded away. It was all narrow country lanes here, hemmed in by hedgerows devoid of autumn berries. Beyond the brambles, barren fields stretched over the gentle hillsides in corrugated mud lines. A single jackdaw fluttered its jet wings against a sterile sky.

The map slipped off Iris's lap as they rounded a tight bend. Righting it, she saw they were less than five miles from Bodnem. She sat upright, peering through the windows, trying to see over the tops of the hedges as Abigail cut her speed.

A house was coming up on the right. Cow sheds surrounded it, and it made a sorry sight in the bleak landscape. The rendered walls had been soiled grey from years of muck on the wind. On the top floor, a window had been boarded up.

'Is this...?'

'Jacob Hunt's house,' Iris answered, certain this almost derelict building had once been the quaintly ramshackle farmhouse they had just read about. 'What do you think? Should we ask?'

'Can't see how it would hurt.' Abigail pulled onto the cracked, concrete driveway and led the way to the front door.

'Yes?' A girl answered, no older than Iris. She wore an apron dusted with flour, and her fingers were crusted with dough. A wireless played inside the house, and an infant shouted for its mother. The girl winced. 'What do you want?'

Abigail froze. Her gaze rolled past the girl to the wooden bannister beyond.

'Sorry to bother you,' Iris began, stepping forward so the awkward silence didn't continue. 'Are you any relation to a Mr Jacob Hunt?'

The question caught her off guard. The child within yelled again. 'I'll be there now,' she called to it with a Welsh lilt, then turned back to Iris. 'No. But the name sounds familiar. Why do you want to know?'

'Miss Edwards's mother used to live in the village. She knew him. We were passing and thought we'd enquire on the off chance. He lived here with his mother in 1900.'

'The woman who threw herself out the window?'

Abigail looked up and pinched her coat tighter around her throat.

'We aren't sure.'

The girl leaned against the door frame; it creaked as if

close to snapping. 'Must be. We only got this place a few years ago, auctioned off from the big house's estate. No tenants had lived here for decades. As you can tell.' She threw her hands up, shook her head. Picking the crusts of dried dough out of the creases of her knuckles, she continued. 'My Bob got it for a steal, so everyone said. Only a steal because no other daft sod wanted to take it on. People say it's haunted, but the only thing that goes bump in the night is a burst pipe. There's plenty of them too.'

'Haunted by the woman who killed herself?'

She nodded. 'Mad, so they say. It ran in the blood too.' The girl's gaze jumped to an ant climbing up the splintered frame. She crushed it with her palm, then brushed off its splattered remains. Iris edged away as it fluttered to her feet.

'Why do you say that?'

'Her son ended his days in an asylum. Died just after the war, I think. The first one.'

'Do you know which asylum?'

She shrugged. 'The nearest one, I suppose.'

The child shouted again. The girl stood up from slouching. There was no chance of a warming cup of tea or further conversation. She stared pointedly at their car.

Iris thanked her and began to walk away, looping her arm through Abigail's because the woman looked as if she needed some support.

Abigail slumped into her car seat and picked at the stitches on the steering wheel. 'Sorry about that. Suddenly, it just all seemed…'

'Too real?' The boarded window caught her attention once again. Had the last time it had been intact been the seconds before an old woman broke through it, too defeated by the world to spend another moment in it? 'Do you want to continue?'

Abigail took a breath. 'Yes.' She reached for Iris's hand. 'Thank you for stepping in. I really couldn't do this without you.'

Iris squirmed out of her grip, making the excuse of fastening her seat belt. Abigail started the engine.

'It has to be Smedley, doesn't it? The asylum Jacob Hunt ended up in. It was the only one for the county.'

Iris agreed, sensing the conversation was yet again going somewhere she didn't want it to.

'I wonder why he was put in there?' The question lingered between them. 'I wonder if it had anything to do with the murders. Maybe he was mad enough to kill?'

Iris fixed her gaze on the passing hedgerows.

'If only we knew someone who worked there,' Abigail said. 'Perhaps they could trace his file and find out.'

* * *

Bodnem was bigger than she had been expecting. Newer houses had been built and fanned out from its centre, post-war judging by their flat, squat faces. They were an ugly addition to the village, which, for the most part, retained its old-fashioned charm. Iris was half expecting to see a pony cart trotting up the street as they parked on the side of the road.

It was easy enough to get their bearings once they reached the crossroads. The public house remained, although the name had been changed. The high street stretched out before them, the shops cloistering together in the centre. A grocer's, baker's, butcher's, pharmacist's

– everything as Louisa had described, but, like the pub, they no longer held the names from generations ago. St Luke's Church towered above its congregation at the head of the village, its golden stones frowning as a drizzle of rain fogged the air.

'Something isn't right,' Abigail muttered, turning back and forth, taking Bodnem in. 'Where is it?'

The church's grounds extended to the crossroads. A memorial for the fallen soldiers from the village had been erected at the corner point, an inscribed monument whose cross arrowed skyward, surrounded by flower beds which now held nothing but dirt and poppy wreaths from the Remembrance Sunday service.

The doctor's cottage that had once been Louisa's home was gone.

'Perhaps something happened to it during the war.'

Iris led the way to the churchyard. A woman was visiting a grave over on the other side, so Iris veered left to give her some privacy. She scanned the names on the stones. A few popped out as recognisable from Louisa's tale. A Carr here, a Powell there, another belonging to Griffith the blacksmith. When she came across a more familiar name, she stopped.

She shouldn't have been shocked. Of course, Timothy Edwards's parents must have died a while ago, and yet being confronted by Howard's grave made her chest tighten.

'He died before I was born.' Stepping closer, Abigail brushed her fingers over the curve of sandstone, flicking off dropped yew-tree needles. 'I never knew anything about him until Mum's story.'

'Your father never mentioned him?'

She shook her head, then crouched beside the grave, picking off browned leaves and old stems of cut flowers. 'Someone's been keeping an eye on him.'

'Is your grandmother here too?'

'No. She's buried in Broseley. We go every Christmas.' Abigail eased herself up, rubbing the droplets of dew off her fingertips. They took a moment to listen to the silence, the song of a robin, the pitter-patter of rain off one of the saints' faces carved into the church.

'Lovely man.' They turned towards the voice. Behind them, the woman who had been visiting another grave pushed up her umbrella. The handkerchief tied around her grey curls had darkened with the damp, and she untied it and slipped it into her handbag.

'Did you know him?' Abigail asked.

'Only when I was very little, but I remember him well. You?'

Abigail stepped forward, finding the confidence she had been lacking back at the farmhouse. 'I'm his granddaughter, Abigail Edwards.'

'Rosie Smith.' They shook hands. 'I haven't seen you here before. I hope you don't mind. I've had a little tidy up.' She nodded at Howard's grave. 'The weeds shot up over the summer.'

Smith – the name was familiar. Iris interrupted the pair's polite introductions. 'Are you any relation to Connie Smith?'

The woman swallowed. 'My mother.'

'You were sent to the workhouse.' It was a tactless thing to say. Rosie backed away, alarmed at how much a stranger knew about her.

'My mother has been telling us about her time here,'

Abigail explained, trying to right Iris's wrong. 'She… talked about the deaths.'

Rosie eased back her shoulders. 'Oh. Yes.' She cleared her throat, her eyes flicking towards the grave from which she had just come.

'You came back to Bodnem?'

'It was my home. It was all I ever dreamed about when I lived at… Tell the truth, I can't remember much about my mother. I was five when she died. That time is murky. Like looking through water. But sometimes… just the smell of bone broth and it's like she's in the room with me.' Rosie's smile creased her face. 'That's the last thing I remember of her. Feeding me bone broth, of all things.'

The conversation petered to nothing. None of them mentioned Rosie's father, the man who had hung for murder. If Rosie didn't bring him up, Iris wasn't going to embarrass herself for the second time that day.

'Lovely meeting you, Abigail. If you ever want to chat, my house is down the south road. The old cottage. You can't miss it.' Rosie's eyes didn't quite reach Iris's before she headed for the lichgate.

Overhead, the church bells chimed midday, although the light was already fading. They continued around the gravelled paths, pausing to read inscriptions as they went.

The Buckley obelisk was a shaft of granite, rising well above Iris's head. Water droplets frosted its smooth surface, trickling like condensation on glass. It was a superior monument compared to those around it, obscurely modern amidst the softened and rounded sandstone graves which slumped in the wet grass. It seemed Mr Buckley was doing his best to distance himself from his village in death as he had done in life.

In loving memory of
My beloved father
Philip William Buckley
Died December 24th, 1917
Aged 57 years
"Remember Me As Thou Pass By
As Thou Art Now
So Once Was I
As I Am Now
So Thou Wilt Be
Prepare Thy Way
To Follow Me."

Shuddering, Iris edged away from the monument. The drizzle had morphed into a downpour. Any more exploring would have to be postponed.

'Come on.' She offered Abigail her arm. 'Let's find a tea room before we're washed away.'

* * *

It was a quiet evening. Abigail had been and gone. Medication had been administered. Food had been forced down. Now the slow process of getting Louisa changed into her nightgown began.

She sat on the side of her bed holding the photograph of her, Tim, and Samuel. Iris perched beside her.

'You were very beautiful.'

'I wasn't.' Louisa ran her thumb over her photographed face. 'You don't need to lie just because I'm old.'

Iris smiled and shook out the fresh nightdress, wafting the smell of laundry soap in the air.

'It's not mine.' Louisa nodded at the gown.

'I know. Sorry.'

She sniffed and returned her attention to the photo. 'I'd have done anything for him.'

'Then you were a good mother.'

She shook her head. 'Not for long. I… It was his fault.' With force, she set the frame face down on the bedside cabinet. Her mouth worked, as if chewing something between her teeth. The next time she looked up, it was as if she was seeing Iris for the first time.

'Matilda.' She reached for Iris's hand. Papery fingertips brushed over Iris's dry knuckles. Iris didn't correct her. 'I was wrong.'

'About what?'

'It wasn't him.' She studied their two hands, lines grooving deep between her brows. 'Whatever happened to little Jenny? Sometimes it's so clear. I can see their faces and then… someone breathes on the glass.' Her hand fluttered off Iris and ran over her scalp. How the memories must have been fighting inside her brain, all jostling for first place, causing carnage as they struggled.

'I couldn't tell you. I have done things.' Her brown eyes bulged and darted to the pillows on the bed. 'I never meant it. It was an accident. It was…'

The ramblings were getting worse. The confusion was edging further back, into the deepest recesses of her mind.

Iris cleared her throat and held up the nightgown. Louisa jerked her head at the sound. Red veins began to throb across her eyes. Timidly, she raised a hand to Iris's forehead, as if checking for a temperature.

'He was so sick. He just needed to sleep.'

Iris pulled back, snapping the spell between the two of

them. The emotion switched off on Louisa's face, leaving a blank. Her shoulders rounded in. Overhead, the clock chimed – night galloped towards them. With sleep, Louisa's brain would try to heal itself. Her confusion was always worse at the end of the day.

'Where is Abi?'

'She just left, do you remember? About an hour ago.' Iris stroked her hair, trying to emulate the way Louisa's daughter did it, hoping it would give some comfort. Slowly, Louisa started to relax. 'She'll be here again tomorrow.'

'Tomorrow,' Louisa whispered, as if securing a promise. 'Tomorrow I'll remember.'

22
1900

I was not to see Jacob Hunt at Daisy Powell's inquest. The day following our meeting, Quinton had him arrested.

Tongues had wagged through Bodnem. People had never trusted him, living out there all on his own, with only his mad mother for company. They talked as if he were their very own Bluebeard, though mere days before they had whispered their condolences and preached of his honest and hard-working nature.

Once again, the Black Heart teemed with people. Warmer now than when Betty had died, their scents fogged the room with filth and sweat. I stayed by the door out of choice this time, propping it open a crack with the toe of my shoe to get a wisp of fresh air.

The female reporter was back again and sitting in the spot she had before, notepad at the ready. Behind her, the jury of men wriggled in their seats. The coroner scowled, perturbed at having to return to such a cramped establishment in such a short space of time.

Daisy lay on the table in her best Sunday gown. No

matter the styling of her hair or the fineness of her dress, she remained plain and portly. Were the other villagers comparing her pale corpse to that of her cousin, as I was? Even in death, women could not escape scrutiny. I set my gaze on the witness box, ashamed of my criticisms.

Mr Powell was called as the first witness. He was a small man next to his wife, one used to keeping in the background, and he squirmed as everyone studied him.

'When was the last time you saw the deceased on the night of her death?' the coroner asked.

'She left for her fiancé – Jacob Hunt's – house just after five in the evening.'

'And you did not see her again after that?'

'No, sir.'

'You did not see her until her body was found the next morning?'

Mr Powell coughed, glanced at his wife. 'That's right.'

'Did you not think it odd when she did not return?'

'I… My wife and I retire at ten. Daisy usually… used to come in some time after that. She did the housework for Jacob and his mother. It was a lot of work for her.'

The coroner grunted. 'Was the deceased content with her intended?'

'Yes. She was looking forward to the wedding next month.' He broke off, shielding his face in his elbow.

'You never suspected the accused of the murder?'

Mr Powell regained himself. 'No, sir. Jacob was always very good to our Daisy. To us as a family. I cannot see him hurting her.'

With that, Mr Powell was dismissed.

To my astonishment, the next witness called was Pat Dunn. Folk stepped aside as he made his way to the stand.

He smiled apologetically at the Powells, but their son, Will, turned away and scratched scribbles into the bar as soon as he started speaking.

'I saw the deceased the night she died.'

'At what time?'

'Must have been around half past eleven.'

'Where did you see her?'

'Near where her body was found. She was standing by the wall of the common field with a man.'

Gasps fluttered around the room.

'Did you know who the man was?'

'Jacob Hunt.'

The gasps dropped lower.

'Where were you, Mr Dunn?'

'I'd just come out of here. I was by the crossroads.'

'Yet you are sure, from that distance, it was the accused?'

Pat licked his top lip, considered. 'They were close. The man was tall, like Jacob. Broad and well built. I'd seen her with him there before.'

'Did you see any violence? Any struggle?'

'No, but I didn't watch for long.'

I wished the coroner would ask him where he went after. Would he have said the churchyard, to cry over Betty's grave? What would everyone have made of that? Or would he have lied on oath? Then I could have been sure what he implied was all lies.

But the coroner only dismissed him. My husband came next.

'Dr Edwards, you assessed the time of death to have been between midnight and six o'clock in the morning, is that correct?'

'Yes. Rigor mortis had set in by the time her body was discovered at eight.'

'Have you concluded the cause of death?'

'Asphyxia by strangulation. A thin cord of some kind would have been the murder weapon, but this has not been found.'

'Any signs of violence pre or post death?'

'None.' He was about to say more, but the coroner silenced him and sent him away. A flush of irritation reddened Tim's cheeks, but he did as he was told. He filed through the crowd and, on passing me, took me by the wrist and dragged me outside with him.

'I told you not to come.'

'I wanted—'

'Enough, Louisa.' He snatched off his top hat and ripped his fingers through his hair. 'When will you start to listen to me?'

I didn't commit myself to an answer.

We lingered underneath the glare of the sun.

'Do you think Jacob killed her?'

He hissed out a breath. 'It doesn't matter what I think. And it doesn't matter what you think. The sooner you realise that, the better it will be for us all.'

* * *

'Did you hear? There's a female reporter staying in the village.' Howard scraped butter across his toast, getting half of it on his fingers. 'Asking about the murders.' He laughed. 'Sending women to write up about such horrid things... The world nowadays. Mind you, she seems rather thrilled with it all, from what I've seen of her.'

'You've talked to her?' Mildred asked. It was unusual to hear her voice; mostly, she was a silent creature. I glanced up from my plate and found her watching her son. Tim licked tea residue off his lips and, feeling himself under scrutiny, fiddled with his tie.

'I met her in the street yesterday,' Howard said.

'It's shameful,' Tim muttered.

'Perfectly pleasant girl. Very young.'

Tim rose and wiped his fingers on his napkin. 'Please don't speak to her again, Father.'

Howard dropped his last mouthful of toast. It clattered against the plate. 'I'll speak to who I damn well like, boy!'

Never had I heard Howard shout so. Never had I seen him lose his temper so quickly and violently. And at his son, the man who usually did anything and everything for him.

Tim froze. Mildred didn't breathe.

Howard sighed and ran his crumby fingers through his hair. Grease glistened in the blackness. Turning to me, he smiled, then suddenly laughed. I jumped at the noise.

He got to his feet. 'I'll go out today, Tim. I fancy the ride, now the weather is warm again. It'll do me good. You stay here.' He patted Tim on the shoulder, filled and lit his pipe, and strolled out of the room.

No one spoke after he had gone.

I helped Mildred clear away the plates while Tim slunk off to the medical office. With the cleaning done, I went to him.

'Is something wrong with the baby?' He busied himself with his diary, scribbling down illegible notes. He was forever filling in that thing.

'No. I came to see if you were all right.'

Ink blotted the page. He set the pen in its holder. 'Fine.'

'Your father seems a little... Is he well?'

He leaned back in his seat. He looked tired. Like me, I didn't think he slept much nowadays. 'His mind is not what it was.'

I had thought as much. It was somewhat of a relief for Tim to believe it too. 'What will you do?'

'There is nothing I can do.' He picked up his pen again. 'You'll be late.'

* * *

The sun was still shining as I headed off the Buckley estate. Roses bloomed in the bushes beside the manor's road. Pale pink petals spread wide and perfumed the air. A bee purred past my face, landed on a flower head, and dusted itself in pollen.

'Stop... Stop it!' The voice was distant and drew my attention away from the bee. I stood on tiptoe, but still could not see over the hedgerow.

I walked on, picking up my pace as I realised it was not just one voice but two. Judging by the sounds, there was a fight going on: whimpering, thudding, splashing.

They were by the lake.

I was breathless by the time I saw them. Two boys tumbled at the water's edge, snapping reeds and setting insects aflutter.

'Stop that now!'

They took no notice of me. I could not walk on and leave them. One of them clearly had the upper hand and was forcing the other deeper into the water.

I had no choice but to climb the wall. Leaving my bag on the road, I hitched up my skirts and clambered over the stones, feeling a snag in my stockings. My ankle twinged as I landed with a thump.

The grass was high and wild, baked to a golden green. Wildflowers splintered up towards the sun, and butterflies of all sizes flickered amongst the stems. Jenny had said this was one of Madam Buckley's favourite spots, and for an instant, I saw a flash of trailing blonde curls and a billowing cotton skirt.

The boys had not noticed me. I made it all the way to where the hard earth turned spongey before the child getting beaten up pointed at me and made his foe falter. To my horror, I recognised the child despite his developing bruises and split skin. He was Jenny's youngest brother, John.

'Let go of him this minute.'

The fighter dropped his victim, and John splattered into the water, gasping for breath. I grasped the fighter's shoulder and spun him around. Will Powell, Daisy's little brother. There was not a single mark on his face, but his podgy knuckles were bleeding. The two of them were roughly the same age, no more than eleven, surely too young for such savagery.

'What is going on?'

Will showed me his teeth, but the fire in his eyes was drowned by tears. He clenched and unclenched his fists, grinding his jaws together. 'It's his fault.'

'I'm sorry.' John wept into the water, and Will turned to kick him, but I pulled him back just in time. I shoved him towards the wall, then helped John to stand. The boy had to wrap his arm around my waist as he hobbled towards the road.

'Wait there,' I said. 'Don't you dare try to run.' Will had nimbly skipped over the stones but did as he was told. I gave John a boost, then lifted my skirts to my knees and climbed over. Both of them looked away. 'Now,' I said, brushing grit off my gloves, 'are you going to tell me what that was all about?'

Will sniffed back his tears. John doubled over coughing and spat out a tooth. He picked it up with trembling fingers and slipped it into his pocket. Neither of them answered me.

'Right. Well, we'll see what your father thinks of all this. Come on.' I yanked Will along by his collar. John staggered behind us and, at the crossroads, broke off for home.

The Powell's grocery store was closed. Will took me in around the back, leading me down the alleyway and in through the yard. The back room was stacked full of produce and smelt of moulding fruit. We passed child-sized sacks of flour and potatoes, trays of carrots, and giant tins of tea and sugar, and climbed the stairs. He went to the parlour but, on opening it, saw it was empty.

'Where are they?' I asked.

He shrugged.

'I'm not leaving until I tell them what you were doing.'

He pushed past me. 'Then you'll be waiting a while.'

'William Powell, tell me where your parents are.'

'I don't know,' he yelled. 'The inn. Probably. It's where they usually are, after Betty and now Daisy.' His lower lip trembled. He shuffled into another room, and although he tried to close the door after himself, I followed him in.

It was a small room, where two narrow beds took up most of the space. Will crawled into one and curled up in a tight ball. I perched on the other bed. Daisy's bed: dark strands of hair matted her pillowcase.

'You will need to wash that,' I whispered, nodding at Will's torn hand which he cradled in his lap. 'But I should say you deserve the pain.'

He put his knuckles to his mouth and sucked, then fanned out his fingers and winced. He reached for the drawers between the beds, on top of which there was a tiny, framed photograph of Jacob Hunt facing Daisy's pillow. He retrieved a brown bottle and a tarnished spoon. He poured himself a measure of laudanum.

'She won't be needing it now.'

'That was Daisy's?'

He nodded.

'She was in pain?'

'Broke her wrist about a year ago.'

'And it still hurt?'

He shrugged. 'Doctor gave her a bottle then, and she's kept having it ever since.' He knew as well as I did that Daisy's wrist would have healed a long time ago. The laudanum was not for pain.

'How often did she take it?'

He hugged his pillow to his chest as he leaned against the wall. 'Most nights. Sent her to sleep easier, she said. Only, some nights she wanted to stay awake. She didn't take any the night she died.'

I sat up. 'How do you know she didn't take any that night?'

'I saw her.'

'She came home?'

Will nodded.

'When it was dark? Daisy came home after eleven o'clock the night she died? You're absolutely sure of that?'

Again, he nodded. 'And then she went out.'

'When?'

He stared at his bleeding hand.

'Will. This is important. What time did she leave?'

'I heard the clock strike two.'

'Did she say where she was going?'

'I pretended I was asleep. I thought she was… going to be with Jacob.'

'Did she say that?'

He shrugged. I gripped a fistful of blanket so I didn't try squeezing the truth out of the boy.

'She didn't say anything. But before that night, when she used to go out to meet him, she said it was all right because they were to be married.'

He broke off, unable to hold himself together. I sat beside him and wrapped my arm around his juddering shoulders. His tears dripped onto my skirt.

'I should have made her stay. I should have told Da.'

I shushed him and rocked him back and forth.

Had Jacob lied to me? Had he come back to meet Daisy? But even if he had, it didn't mean he had killed her. Even if he hadn't loved her, he had needed her; she was going to take care of him.

Unless it wasn't him she was meeting.

Jenny said Daisy's murderer could not have been Pat because he'd been at the grave at midnight. But she hadn't watched him all night.

'Will, did your sister have anything to do with Pat Dunn?'

'No,' he said, snivelling into my shoulder. 'She didn't like him.'

'Why was that?'

He shook his head. 'Don't know. She said he was a peeper.'

'Peeper?'

'You know, a peeping Tom.'

Will unfurled from my embrace. 'I want to sleep now,' he said, yawning. The medicine was kicking in.

From the drawer, I found a clean vest and soaked it in water, wringing out the excess. I bound it around his knuckles as he settled himself under the blankets. By the time I closed the door, he was already sleeping.

Outside, the sun was no longer in the sky. The street was deserted as I clomped towards home, my brain a fog of questions.

The door of the Black Heart opened. Shoes clicked my way.

'Mrs Louisa Edwards?'

I stopped in the middle of the crossroads. The female reporter I had seen at the inquest faced me. The one Howard had spoken about. The one Tim had warned us all to stay away from.

I guessed she was similar in age to me, if not slightly younger. Her pale dress glimmered in the dusk light, and beneath her straw hat, dark curls framed an elfin face. Her eyes were keen as she took me all in, a little disappointedly.

'Matilda Tindall.' She extended her hand, and I shook it. She had a firm grip, despite her delicate appearance. 'From the *Birmingham Daily*. I wondered if I might speak to you about the murders?'

I should have said no. Tim would not like it if I went about whispering gossip to reporters.

I glanced about myself. No one was around, but that didn't mean they weren't watching. Any moment, Tim might glance out of the window and see us.

'Not here.'

I walked up Church Street and, after waiting a few minutes, Matilda followed. We paused at the Buckley gates.

'I don't have much time. Neither do I have anything to tell you. I know very little.'

She set her bag down on the wall and retrieved a notepad. She flicked it open and licked the end of her pencil. 'It's my father who owns the paper. His father before him. He used to take me out with him sometimes, and that sparked my love of stories. Scandal.' She eyed me, smirking. 'I know when someone is lying to me.'

'I've only been here—'

'Since March. You're the young doctor's wife. You used to be governess for the Pendletons in Birmingham, but you left following the funeral of their son. Now you work for the squire, Philip Buckley, and teach his daughter. You haven't settled in well here and are not particularly liked except by a simpleton girl named Jenny Carr. You are also the only person in the whole world who is trying to find the real murderer of innocent girls. Apart from me, of course.' She raised a brow. 'Am I right?'

I didn't know whether to be unnerved or impressed. 'Why are you interested? Bodnem is in the middle of nowhere. I can't see your city readers being bothered.'

She waved her hand dismissively. 'Everyone enjoys murder. Especially when it's not on their doorstep. We sold thousands when Jack was about. Although I don't think Jacob Hunt has the same kind of glamour as the Ripper.'

'It's not him. He loved Daisy.'

'Then hopefully they'll let him go when they realise their mistake, as they've done with the Irishman.'

'They have?' I perched on the stone wall.

'Quinton's not a popular man with his commissioner. First arresting the Irishman, now Hunt, and all because of one boy's testimony. No other witness came forward at the inquest. Shame your husband wouldn't let you stay to see it.'

I blushed, but she continued quickly.

'For what it's worth, I don't think it is Mr Hunt either. Why kill the only girl who was naive enough to marry you? Besides, say he did kill Daisy. He had no motive to kill Betty. According to the locals, he never came to the public house; he was always too busy at home.

'So that means the real killer is still out there, and Quinton hasn't a single idea who it is. And that's because he's not listening to you.' She sat beside me. 'This village is as tight as a clam. It doesn't like outsiders. I know how you're feeling, believe me. Really, you owe them nothing. So why are you so desperate to find the killer?'

'I could be his next victim.'

She shook her head; a curl tickled her brow. 'You're not his type.'

'What is his type?'

'Oh, come on. I know you've been thinking it. Too prudish to say it out loud?' Her cockiness was an unfortunate habit; I would not humour her with an answer. She laughed. 'Young women of dubious moral character, I should say.'

'Not Daisy.'

'How do you know? People do all sorts of things behind closed doors.'

I looked away from her feline green eyes.

'And anyway, I don't believe self-preservation is your only reason.'

I couldn't speak of the urge inside me to save whoever might be next. I could not say it was part of my own redemption.

'All right. You want to know what I think. I understand. Well, I believe the lack of a struggle suggests the victims knew their attacker. The Irishman was a cheap shot from the start. The murderer lives amongst them, as you have been saying all along. He would have to be strong too, but gentle. Strong enough to hold them secure, gentle enough not to leave too many bruises. You've thought that too, I assume?'

If she knew so much about me, there was no need to answer her question.

'Oh, fine. You know the main thing I suspect? There is no copycat.' She smirked at me, her very own Cheshire grin.

'What are you saying?'

'That there is no copycat because Reg Smith was not the original killer. I saw him at the trial on the day of his sentence. I can tell you, I have seen enough murderers at court to know a brute like Reginald Smith would never be so kind as to gently strangle his wife. Not that I was sad he swung, but he did not kill those women. Which means that the real murderer never left.'

I laughed. 'Absurd. Why would he stop for three years in between?'

'Because the ghost was exorcised. What if the ghost was his scapegoat all along? Now she's out, he can start again.'

Her theory lodged like a cold slice of ice in the pit of my stomach.

'What can you tell me of Philip Buckley?' She pressed the pencil against the paper. The page was blank, waiting for my words to fill it. 'Come on, I've told you my ideas. It's only manners to give me something back.'

'I don't have anything to tell you about the squire.'

'There are rumours he hated his wife, that he was a jealous husband. Probably why he keeps his child locked up in the manor now, so she doesn't get out like her mother did.'

'Lies. He loved Madam Buckley very much. He loves his daughter too.'

'You're not suspicious at all? Even though both Georgina Witcombe and Mary Carr were either living or working at the manor when they died.'

'Before you go accusing him of such crimes, I have already made up my mind about Mr Buckley. He is innocent, I can assure you.'

'You know he was questioned by the police for the original murders?'

I stood. She was a vile woman. I should never have agreed to speak to her. 'They question everyone.'

'They stopped pursuing him because he said he was not in the village when Connie Smith died. He said he was in the city.'

'Yes. He goes to London regularly.'

'And yet I can find no evidence of him there. I can find no evidence of him anywhere, for that matter.'

I reached for my bag. 'That doesn't mean anything.'

'He also had an alibi which placed him at the manor when Mary Carr died.'

'There you go, then.'

'The alibi was from Miss Anne Stone, his child's nurse. The only woman who lives in that house with him and his daughter. A friendless spinster.' She pushed her pencil behind her ear and cocked her head. 'What would she do if Buckley were hanged?'

I ignored the whisper of doubt in my mind, turned my back on her, and marched towards home.

'What if there weren't just five victims?'

I halted.

'What if there's another we haven't accounted for? The ghost who started all of this.'

'You cannot imagine Buckley killed his own wife.'

She shrugged. 'Perhaps not like the others. Perhaps just with a simple instruction. Save the baby.'

I swallowed as her words sank in.

It would have been the easiest thing to do in all the world. Women died in childbirth all the time. A convenient tragedy.

A convenient excuse.

'Why are you so sure it is the pharmacist's son?' Matilda asked.

Her quick change of questioning left me dumbstruck. Briefly, I recognised the reporter traits in her: the fired accusations, the mocking attitude, the half-said truths, all to make one uneasy and put one at a disadvantage. I closed my mouth before I uttered anything I would later regret.

'Seems like an odd choice, unless you know something I don't? Although I admit, his damning evidence about Jacob Hunt could be proof of him trying to shift the blame before it falls on him.'

She sighed at my reluctance to talk, shoved her blank notepad into her bag, then came to my side. 'We both know things we aren't telling each other, Mrs Edwards. Things which might save the next girl he is planning to kill.'

Was she bluffing? Perhaps it was a ruse to get me to speak.

'Very well. I shall be staying at the inn, until they throw me out. There's a flower pot with carnations in it on the south side; you can leave a note for me there if you want to speak again.'

23
1956

Louisa listened to her own words being read back at her with dull eyes and offered no further comment. The only thing she questioned was the woman reading to her, as if she had never seen her before.

'So, that's Matilda,' Iris said.

'You must remind Mum of her.'

Iris didn't know if that was a good thing or not.

Abigail packed away the notebook. 'Have you found out anything about Jacob Hunt yet?'

'I can't access the files.'

She snapped her handbag shut. 'Someone must be able to.'

Iris sighed, glancing nervously at Nurse Carmichael who was watching her from the other side of the room. 'I'll see what I can do.' She rushed away to help Maeve who was battling Nurse Bennet for a teacup.

When her shift ended, she crept down the corridor to the reception desk. Miss Horracks glanced up from her paperwork and smiled.

'How are you this evening?' Iris asked, leaning against the desk.

Miss Horracks nodded, and her gentle curls sprung either side of her face. 'Well, and you?' The question came out stilted. In all their working lives here together, these were the most words they'd spoken to each other.

A timid little thing, reaching five foot nothing, Miss Horracks sat behind the protection of the Victorian desk and whispered to patients as they came in and out for the day. Nobody paid her any attention, which she liked. She could be more discreet that way.

Iris's fingertips patted on the wood. 'Look, I'm really sorry to ask…'

What was the best way to approach this? Flattery might work, but Iris guessed the girl would see straight through that. Plain girls could always catch a faker; Iris had had enough years' experience to know that when someone started finding her face pretty and her jokes funny, they usually wanted something. Miss Horracks and she were not the Shirleys of the world, who would have accepted roses thrown at their feet as an everyday occurrence.

So, not flattery.

She would start with the truth and ask for a simple favour.

'Do you have access to all patients' records?'

'Yes.'

'From before the war?'

Her eyebrows stitched tight. 'I suppose so. They'll be in storage, though.'

Iris lowered her voice. 'I need to know if and why someone was admitted here.'

Miss Horracks leaned back. 'You know I can't do that.'

'I know you *shouldn't* do it, not that you *can't*.'

She folded her thin arms. 'What's it about?'

'A woman on my ward knew somebody who, I believe, was incarcerated here. I need to find out why.'

'Surely if she knew them she can find out for herself.'

'She's an eighty-one-year-old demented woman with a husband who swears she's talking nonsense.'

'Aren't they all?' Miss Horracks whispered under her breath.

Iris bristled. Miss Horracks was not as timid as she would have people believe. 'This man might have murdered several girls.'

The smirk slid off Miss Horracks's face.

'Or, he might not have done. But I need to know why he was considered mad enough to be thrown into a pauper lunatic asylum and left there to die.' She inhaled deeply, letting the information sink in to Miss Horracks's mind.

Still, the receptionist was not softened.

'It's just a file about a man whom nobody cares about anymore. I won't tell anyone. You'd be doing me a huge favour, and I think it could really help. Please?'

Miss Horracks grimaced.

'I really wouldn't ask unless it was important.'

She tapped the end of her pencil against the desk. Iris had the urge to snatch it from her and snap it.

'You live about ten minutes away, don't you?'

Miss Horracks frowned at Iris's question.

'I see you sometimes, when I'm walking home. I've seen you with Nurse… Evans? Is that her name?'

Miss Horracks turned rigid, her cheeks beginning to flame.

Iris took a breath and forced herself to continue. 'Do other people know about your relationship?' It wasn't a question; it was a threat. Both of them knew it. In all honestly, Iris hadn't expected to blackmail her way into getting anything. The words stuck in her mouth like a stain.

Miss Horracks cleared her throat. 'Never knew you were such a bitch.'

She should have expected some recourse, but the insult hit her hard. 'I need that information.'

Slamming down her pencil, Miss Horracks glared at Iris. 'I'll see if I can find it.'

24
1900

All night, I replayed mine and Matilda's conversation.

There were so many questions.

I kept coming round to her accusation of Mr Buckley.

I shifted my chilled arms under the blankets. Beside me, Tim did not snore. He lay on his back, and I was sure if I were to glance his way I would have found his eyes open, staring at the ceiling. I scrunched my eyelids shut.

Say I humoured Matilda's suspicions. What if Buckley had murdered his wife by telling my husband to save the child? Had Georgina known about it, and was that why she had died? Had Mary been suspicious too?

It was possible.

Connie Smith didn't make sense, though. She and Mr Buckley had never been connected. But perhaps she was just an odd piece in the puzzle. Perhaps her husband really had killed her.

And what about the recent victims? The idea that Buckley had harmed Daisy Powell was ludicrous. She was a shopkeeper's daughter. She was to be married to a man who paid Buckley rent.

Neither had there been any connection with him and Betty Crook. When would they have spent any time together? They were from different worlds and barely crossed paths. He was a gentleman, and she was a—

I sat up.

I could not stomach the thought.

Betty Crook. A prostitute. Like Connie Smith had been. Buckley, a lonely, single widower.

What if Betty thought she was pregnant by Buckley? A bastard child, with no doctor willing to help get rid of it…

I glanced at Tim. He was silent. Too still. Awake.

Perhaps I should have consulted him. We could have talked everything through together. He could have told me just how silly I was being, like usual.

He would not have believed a word of it, like usual.

I kept my lips closed.

* * *

It took all my strength to walk up Church Street and beyond the Buckley gates. It was a cloying day, the sky cloaked with a thin, bright haze and the breeze non-existent. My gown was like a cotton coffin, my petticoats clinging to my stockings, my stays making my back sweat.

Sybil watched from the window. Forcing a smile, I lifted my hand to wave. But no, she was not looking at me. Her gaze drifted beyond me, into the undergrowth. I glanced back. There was nothing there. Hurriedly, I climbed the steps.

'Who were you looking at, Sybil?' My bag slapped

on the table, disturbing the palette and almost knocking over the water pot. Yet again, another sheet of paper hung on the wall, a new painting of the view from her eyrie. She didn't answer me but sat at her desk, ready for our morning routine of handwriting practice.

I scanned the landscape. Hydrangeas bloomed in shocking pink and garish blue, rising high beside the trees. Roses clutched branches for support, trailing unrestrainedly in a dense wilderness of green. Ferns wilted like dogs' tongues in the patches of shady ground.

It was all too lush. Ripe with too much life.

Mocking.

I closed the curtains and plunged us into a grainy gloom.

We worked by oil lamp for the rest of the day in the stifling heat. Sybil's hair was stuck to her forehead when Miss Stone rushed in and threw open the curtains, clucking over Sybil's scarlet cheeks.

I dodged the nurse's scowls and escaped into the corridor. At the top of the stairs, I stopped and, clinging to the bannister, breathed in the cooler air which rose from the hallway below. A strand of loose hair tickled my cheek, and as I brushed it behind my ear, my attention fell on the other corridor. The other wing of the house. Mr Buckley's domain.

Tiptoeing, I headed into it. So many rooms! Most bare of furniture, others with sheets to cover what lay beneath. Bed chambers, dressing rooms, bathing rooms.

And then a boudoir, papered in swirling green patterns, with thin cream curtains. What I assumed had once been Madam Buckley's private salon. Nothing was covered. Everything was bare to the eye, exactly as she had left it.

Indeed, there was too much of her in that room. She lived through the William Morris wallpaper; the empty, gilded terrarium where ferns might once have flourished; the softness of the chaise longue; the thinness of the patterned rug in the spot where her footstool sat.

Tapping came from the window. The curtains shivered. My breath faltered.

But I was not a superstitious woman, I reminded myself.

Before I had time to shy away, I marched to the glass and peeled back the silk curtains. A wall of willow branches confronted me; it was their fingers which scraped on the panes. Through the slivers of leaves, the woodland was visible and full of giant-leafed plants and spiky brackens, where the browns and reds of chaffinches and sparrows flashed by. I turned my back on it, imagining all the times Madam Buckley had stood in my place, smiling at the creatures in the wild.

A door in the corner of the room led to her chamber. To her death place. My palm grew cold as it rested on the doorknob; the last person to have touched it might have been her.

The chamber was like the boudoir. It had the same decorations and furnishings but for the bed. It was bare, stripped of the bloodied and soiled sheets it had once been dressed in, although some fluid had sullied the top mattress. On the sideboard, a cup was stained brown from how the tea had dried out over the years. Crepe covered the looking glass, but her dressing table still held her perfume bottles, brushes, and a porcelain hair collector littered with honey-blonde strands. The window overlooked the gardens, and a painting of Madam Buckley and her husband hung on the opposite wall. Had she stared into his painted eyes as hers had closed for the final time?

'Looking for something?'

I had been studying the portrait; now I turned to find Mr Buckley made of flesh and bone in the doorway. He leaned against the frame as if he needed its support. His hair was a mess, sticking out at all angles from the sides of his head. His eyes were bloodshot. He smirked at my shock.

'There's a board right there' – he pointed towards the door that led to the boudoir – 'that jolts. I haven't heard it do that in five years.' His words were slurred, showing he was the worse for drink. 'I thought she'd come back.'

He stared at the bed and breathed deeply. The scent of alcohol wafted towards me. 'Miss Stone cleared it all away before I could see it. Georgina said it was for the best.'

With effort, he stepped into the room and mechanically made his way to the bed. He brushed his fingers over the stain. 'Is there a worse end? I heard her agony from below. For hours. Until they gave her the ether.'

I recalled my own ordeal, the lack of anaesthesia; Tim wouldn't allow it. For an instant, I felt a pang of jealousy, then reminded myself who was alive and who was dead. It was all too easy to slip under, that was what Tim had said, as I had begged him to douse the cloth with chloroform.

'That's the last thing I remember of her: the screams and then the silence.'

'But the child survived.'

He nodded.

'And that's all that mattered to you.'

His eyes scrolled upwards and found mine. 'What do you mean?'

I edged backward, nearer the door, ready to escape if needed. 'Everyone loved her. That's what you said. Were you jealous?'

He removed his fingers from the mattress, rested them in his pocket.

'Was it some kind of petty revenge, telling them to save the child and not her? Was it a convenient way to have done with her?'

'I don't know what you're talking about.'

'You told my husband to save the baby, knowing full well what that meant in such circumstances.'

'I did no such thing.'

'So they are lying?'

'Who is lying?'

'Everyone! Everyone in this village. You must know that is why they blame you for her death, because you gave the order.'

It was as if I had taken a hammer to his chest. He clutched it as he stumbled backward, slamming into the wall; I was not sure if it was from the shock or the alcohol.

'I would never… It is a rumour, like everything else in this damned place.' His fist smacked into the sideboard. The teacup rattled in its saucer.

'Is that why you can't stand to see your daughter? Because every time you look at her you are reminded of what you did to her mother.'

He shook his head violently.

'Her cousin, Georgina, knew. She would have seen the guilt in your face. A perfect opportunity to blackmail you and get what she had always wanted – Madam Buckley's life, her riches, you. Is that why you killed her?'

'I cannot believe you are asking such things.'

'Mary – she was in love with you too. All three women who loved you have died.'

He shoved the heel of his palm against his eyes. 'Stop.'

'And Betty Crook. Pregnant with your child. Did you think she would hold it against you? I imagine she would; she was that sort of girl.'

'Stop!' In his rage, he swiped his arm across the sideboard. I swerved the cup just in time. It smashed against the wall, splitting the wallpaper as it shattered.

I ran as he lunged and slammed the door shut behind me. He thudded into the back of it. Hurtling down the staircase, my toes caught in the hem of my dress and I fell on the last step, crashing into the tiles. My knees and wrists took the weight, creaking and snapping, and as I hauled myself to my feet, pain shot up my thigh.

But he was coming.

I raced out of the manor, across the gravel, and down the lane, until my lungs burned and my vision darkened at the edges. Staggering out through the Buckley gates and holding out my hands like a blind woman, I crashed into someone.

I had not the air nor the energy to scream, but the shock kicked my knees from under me. On the ground, I tried crawling, knowing I must get away from the estate, from the lake, from the churchyard, from the murder sites, so I did not become a victim myself.

A hand squeezed my shoulder. I tried to bat it away, but it did not work. Another hand came to my other side, slid up to my face, and held my chin. Fingers brushed my lips. I would be next.

'Breathe, Mrs Edwards. Calm yourself.' The face came into focus, and I collapsed with relief. I hugged the hand to my chest, not wanting to let her go. 'What's wrong? What's happened?'

'I've been a fool,' I choked. A fool for confronting him. A fool for ever believing he was harmless.

'What are you going on about?' Jenny brushed my hair out of my face.

I looked into her eyes. 'I know who killed your sister.'

25
1900

'I won't go.'

'You must.' Tim snagged his tie into place, intent on his own reflection. 'You have a duty.'

'Not anymore.' I clutched Samuel closer. 'I won't step on Buckley property again.'

'You're already on it. Everybody in Bodnem is on it.' He dug his fingertips into the corners of his eyes. 'Why don't you just tell me what happened? You never tell me anything.'

'Because when I do you don't listen.'

He slumped on the bed beside me. I studied his hand on the sheet. Such smooth, fine skin, speckled with shiny black hairs. I wished to hold it. When was the last time I had held Tim? Had I ever? Ours had never been a tender marriage. Just a burning heat which fizzled out to ashes. We were never right for each other, not from the start.

But I could not bear a lifetime of this. A frigid sea between us. Like two trains passing each other beside a platform, we never properly met.

My fingers crawled towards his. He was hot where I was cool. I gripped him, just gently, testing how far we could take this. He gripped me back.

'I don't trust Buckley,' I whispered, not wanting to break this moment between us.

'Has he done something to you?'

'He lies.'

'What do you mean?'

'He will not tell the truth. I know… things. I am sure. But there is no proof.'

'About what?'

'The murders.'

Tim's heat vanished. He marched to the waistcoat stand. 'Louisa, you are only harming yourself.'

'I must find out the truth.'

'You must let the police do their jobs.'

'Why? They never got the Ripper, did they?'

Tim snorted. 'It's hardly another Jack here in Bodnem.'

'Women are being murdered, Tim!' I laid Samuel on the bed and faced my husband. He would not meet my gaze as he fastened his buttons. 'The killer is getting away with it, as he did four years ago. He knows he can. But why? Somebody knows something. *I* know something, but it's just not clear…'

He let me drain out, then turned. 'What do you mean – as he did four years ago?'

'I don't think it's a copycat, Tim. I think it's the same killer.'

He did not blink. After too many seconds, I shrank away from his stare.

'You are worrying me, Louisa.' His gripped my arms.

His heat seared. 'Women are vulnerable after the birth of a child. The mind does not always work the way it should. It is not your fault.'

'I—'

'Stop, Louisa. You must stop and rest. You are right; you should not go back to Buckley. You will stay here, where you know you are safe. I will take care of you. It is my fault that I have let this continue for so long.'

'Tim—'

'You will remain here. Mother will check in on you. You will soon start feeling more… yourself.'

'I can't do nothing.'

His fingernails snipped into my flesh. 'For the sake of your health, your mind, and our child, you *will* do nothing. Do you understand?'

* * *

Tim grunted as Samuel started to cry. 'See to him, will you?' He buried his face into my pillow as I lifted Samuel from his cot; I wouldn't be needing it.

My dressing gown hung ready. My slippers, too, were laid out for this moment.

'I'll take him down.'

In the parlour, the child suckled as I watched the inn. Not a single light shone from its windows as the clock chimed one.

Maybe Matilda was already waiting for me. Earlier, after Tim had gone out and while Howard and Mildred were busy, I had left a note for her in the pot of carnations, telling her to meet me tonight. I hadn't said a time;

it would have been too hard to keep to it using the ruse of the child. Maybe she was watching from her window also. I imagined she would stay awake all night if it meant progressing the case.

Samuel grew sleepy against my breast. His once-balled fists relaxed, his fingers unclenching like cabbage leaves. His black lashes fluttered against his moonlit skin.

I wrapped my cloak tight, bundled Samuel in the blanket from the back of the chair, tiptoed to the kitchen, and felt my way towards the drawer with the knives. I took a small one so that it fitted into my gown pocket, but it was sharp – the knife Howard used to peel the skin off his apples in one long reel. If I were to meet the murderer, I would aim for his throat.

Outside, there were no street lights, unlike in the city. Only the moon painted the road and muted the colours of summer to monochrome. The wind had picked up, and every so often it blew a cloud across the sky and shut off the light. The breeze buffeted my narrow gown, buzzed in my ear, and rippled through the heavy, laden branches so the leaves chattered to each other and blocked out the soft patter of a murderer's light tread. I knew it had me at a disadvantage. As I scurried past the stone wall beside the lake, every other second I glanced over my shoulder to make sure I was not being followed.

It took only a few minutes to reach the designated spot on the south road. The sight of the lake was shielded by swaying silver birches, and the houses thinned to nothing. Ghostly spectres of sheep speckled the fields around me.

I waited. Matilda would come soon. I was sure of it.

But what would I say? I had no more evidence of Buckley's crimes than she had. I had no more chances to gather any either; he would not let me cross the threshold again.

I cursed myself for my outburst, my weakness. I should not have shown him my playing cards.

And yet... there was something which still did not feel right.

I could easily imagine him instructing the doctors to sacrifice Madam Buckley for the sake of the child. After all, so many wives died at their husbands' hands, one way or another.

Georgina Witcombe, from what I had heard, had been a heartless woman intent on personal advancement at any cost; not many men would take kindly to being blackmailed into marriage, as I could attest to.

Even Mary Carr, an hysterical girl with an unrequited obsession, was somewhat easily understood. Betty Crook, too, might have been so minded.

But why Daisy Powell? By all accounts, she had nothing to do with Buckley. She was due a quiet life in the countryside, no bother to anyone.

I shook my head. Too many thoughts. I was dizzy with them all.

Samuel jumped in his sleep. I rocked him gently, for he needed to remain quiet. Time was pressing on. My feet were itching, my lower back gnawing.

She should have arrived by now. She should have been watching from her window.

Although a mild night, I was growing chill. The wind bit against my bare ankles. When a sheep bleated, a scream hammered at my throat. I found the outline of the blade in my pocket for reassurance.

I waited until the church bells chimed two, then the

opportunity had passed. It was too risky to stay out any longer. I headed back, wishing I had written a time on that damned note. I didn't know when we would get another chance like this to meet.

The Black Heart Inn, when it came back into view, was as dark as it had been before. No sign of movement, of any life at all.

A gust whipped up from behind, shoving me forward, making the trees around the lake to my left creak. A falling branch crashed into the water, the splash echoing too loudly in the dead of night. Entranced, I watched the waves ripple, snatching shards of moonlight from the sky and drowning them. The quivering reed heads held my attention for a moment before something pale caught the corner of my eye.

Across the water, a whiteness lingered.

Without realising, I held Samuel tighter and stepped closer to the stone wall.

I squinted into the gloom, blinking to make the image clearer.

It was moving. I was sure it was moving, almost… dissipating.

A cloud passed overhead and all fell dark. I kept my eyes trained on the spot, not daring to close them for an instant in case I lost it.

Another second later, the cloud rolled away.

Nothing.

Had it ever been there at all?

My vision swam and swirled. I blinked quickly, scanned the scene again, searching for something unknown and unwanted. A trick of the light, surely. It must have been.

There were no such things as ghosts.

A shadow slashed across my face. It happened too fast for me to do anything about it. It was only when it held my throat that I realised it was a hand. A large, strong hand, which drew me back against a hard chest and clamped around my neck.

I was too late to take a breath; my scream was silenced. Open-mouthed, I writhed against the body, instinctively clutching Samuel tight while I struggled to find my knife. I could not get a purchase on anything. My fingers slipped over my dressing gown as clouds shrouded the moon.

My lungs started to burn. My pulse throbbed against my attacker's fingers and thumb. Saliva pooled around my gums.

Samuel started to squirm, awake now, and through checkered vision I glimpsed his eyes open. He stared at the murderer behind me.

I had killed my child.

Samuel wailed. The scream splintered through the pounding in my ears.

And then I was released.

It was as if all the blood had drained out of me. Ice hit me, dazzling, blinding. Air thrust into my chest, leaving me dizzy.

Knuckles cracked into my right temple. The grey world turned black.

I was on the floor the next time I opened my eyes. Samuel was crying, screeching as if in agony. He was a foot away from me, in the long grass next to the stone wall. With shaking hands, I peeled him towards me, dreading what I might see; had he fallen against the rocks? Was he a bloody mess of broken skin and bones?

His face was intact, scrunched into familiar wrinkles. I cried when I saw he was unharmed.

Then I turned.

There was no one anywhere. No running shadows. No shutting doors. No footsteps in the distance.

The wall took my weight as I slumped back, composing myself as best I could before dragging myself to my feet. With limp limbs, I staggered home.

I was shaking too much to be quiet. I clattered through the gate, then the back door, and dropped at the table in the kitchen. Sobs reverberated around me. My numb fingers assessed the sore flesh of my throat, and images flashed in my mind of the rustling trees, the skimming clouds, Samuel's wide eyes.

The door opened with a bang, startling me and the child all over again. Above a candle's flame, Howard's face floated in the dark. Behind him, Mildred's profile was only just visible. They stared at me in their nightclothes, horrified, before Mildred rushed to the child. She snatched him up and glared at me.

'What have you done?'

'Nothing,' I cried, my mouth barely able to form the word.

Howard set the candle on the table, put his arm around my shoulder, and squeezed tight. I leaned into his sweet, tobacco scent, pressing my wet cheek against his cotton nightshirt.

'My dear, what's happened?'

'I... It was him... He tried to kill...'

I trailed off when I noticed another figure loitering in the doorway.

'You went out,' Tim said. His voice was dead.

'I'm sorry.'

He shuffled to his mother's side to check the child. Satisfied with Samuel, he turned back to the door.

'Tim, I'm sorry,' I wailed, but he had already gone.

26
1956

'Oh, Mum.' Abigail dropped the notebook and hugged her mother. Louisa had started to cry after listening to her lakeside attack. 'It's all right,' Abigail breathed against her scalp as she perched on the arm of the chair. 'You're safe now. Samuel is safe. Dad is safe. We're all safe. No one can hurt you anymore.'

Iris crept away, giving them a moment alone together, and refilled the teapot.

'What is it, then?' Nurse Bennet sidled up to her, resting her hip against the trolley and making the scalding liquid splash. 'Why are you here on your day off? We all want to know.'

Iris glanced behind her. The other nurses turned away and pretended to be busy when she met their eyes.

'Miss Edwards is reading her mum's old diary to her. Sometimes it makes her sad.'

'So you're the shoulder to cry on, eh?' Nurse Bennet sneered.

'I'm just here as a friend.'

'But you're not a friend; you're a nurse. You're not supposed to get attached. Haven't you learned that after the last one? Look how well that turned out.'

Iris tried to ignore the sting of that last remark. 'Kath, you mean?'

Bennet shrugged. Iris placed the teaspoon down carefully, though she felt like pelting it at the nurse's head.

'I'm not attached, but unlike some here, I do have a heart. I will be there whenever the patient and her family needs me.'

Bennet turned on her. 'Quite the martyr, aren't you?' She leaned closer and lowered her voice. 'I wonder if it's just for the patients that you're spending your free time here, or if you're trying to make the rest of us look bad.'

Iris bit her teeth together as irritation flared up her spine. Her voice came out sickly sweet. 'How could *I* make *you* look worse?'

Bennet shoved herself off the trolley, sending the tea crashing over the rims of the cups. 'Carmichael doesn't like brown-nosers.' She sauntered back to the other nurses and called over her shoulder, 'Neither do we.'

* * *

The next day, Iris hadn't seen Abigail arrive; she'd been too busy with the lunch plates, clearing up another patient's messy accident, and avoiding Nurse Bennet at all costs. Her head was light from the stench of bleach which clung to her nostrils as she rushed for the chairs by the window.

'Abigail,' she breathed. The threat from Bennet had only made her keener to be there for Louisa and Abigail.

'I've been thinking.' She'd been mulling it over all night. There was nothing much she could do for Louisa other than care for her as a nurse, but Abigail needed Iris's full support – after all, she wasn't getting any from anybody else. She needed Iris on her side as she struggled through the confusion and turmoil of her mother's story. Iris had to stop shrinking away. She needed to get her head around it and do something to help.

'The best person to ask about all this has to be Matilda. We should find her.'

The lump in Abigail's throat lifted up and down. Iris should have sensed by the woman's stiffness to keep her mouth shut, but it had all come pooling out. Only now did she notice another visitor. A man shrunken against the wingback chair, black eyes peering at her.

'How do you know about Matilda?'

Iris faltered. She glanced at Abigail, but she was too busy knitting. The needles tapped faster.

Tim glared at Louisa, whose gaze was as milky as the sky outside. 'What's she been saying?'

'She hasn't *said* anything,' Abigail mumbled under her breath.

Iris shot her a warning look. Tim saw it.

'Tell me what is going on.'

The needles ceased clicking. Abigail chewed her cheek, as if considering her options. She took a deep breath and faced her father. 'She wrote me a letter years ago. We only just found it.'

'What does it say?'

Abigail hesitated, then retrieved the notebook. 'She wrote about Bodnem. And the murders.'

Tim laughed, shaking his head. 'Tell me you don't believe a word of it.'

Abigail's silence was his answer.

'You know she always talked nonsense.'

'So what is the truth?' Iris interrupted, settling herself into the nearest seat.

'Girls died. They found the killer. Girls stopped dying.'

'She believes they got the wrong man.'

'Which is peculiar, considering how she hunted him down the most.' He clasped his hands in his lap, gently stroking the swollen knuckles. 'They found him because of her. She played some part in his execution, you might say. She will have made a mountain out of the whole thing because she couldn't live with herself.'

'Why do you say that?'

'Have your actions ever led to someone's death, Miss Lowe?'

Iris shook her head, not liking the way his voice had hardened.

'You have never killed someone, however inadvertently?'

'Dad—'

'I'm asking a perfectly reasonable question, Abigail. If you have never done such a thing, then you will not have experienced the consequences of it. It is something I, as a doctor, know well. Something your brother will know too. And you, Miss Lowe, will feel it soon enough if you stay in this place. I pray you are spared, Abigail.'

'What is your point, Dad?'

'Guilt is a powerful, mind-altering sensation. Men cope easier with it than women.'

Iris scoffed.

'I have seen it happen. I know it.' He splayed out his hands. 'You want the truth, Abigail? The truth is your mother hounded her suspect for weeks, and eventually she got what she wanted. When that meant a noose and a short drop, she changed her mind. She liked the hunt, you see. Thought of it as a game. But lives were at stake. It was all very well trying to stop a murderer, but what happened when she realised she was just as bad as he was?'

'She was protecting young women.'

'Exactly, and she succeeded. So why, Miss Lowe' – he flicked his head her way, as quick as a snake – 'do you believe her delusional tale of him being the wrong man?'

She eased away from his ferocity. It felt as if he had bitten her. Bitten her with his hatred, but with the truth also.

'Why did you never tell me this?' Abigail whispered. 'You never let her speak.'

'It was in the past. Your mother had a habit of dwelling on things, making things worse than they were. You didn't need to deal with all that.'

'But women did die, Dad. You and Mum were right there, through it all. Don't you think, if we'd have talked about it, we could have helped her? We could have made her see that what she did was right. We could have taken that guilt away.'

'Always talking,' Tim muttered. 'It's all you and she ever did. Did it help you? Did you get what you wanted by talking to her?'

Abigail set her gaze on the floor. Tim took a breath.

'Now you will stop this. Both of you. She is here for rest.'

'It wasn't him,' Louisa whispered, but her husband ignored her.

'Why do you never visit Grandfather's grave?' Abigail asked.

The colour drained from Tim's face. His jaw slackened, and for the briefest moment his fingers began to tremor before he clasped them together.

'How do you...?'

'We went to Bodnem. We saw his stone. Why did you never tell me?'

He closed his eyes. For a moment, Iris thought he was ignoring his daughter, but then he glared at her. 'You've been gossiping about your own family?'

'It wasn't gossip—'

'Shameful.'

'I wasn't—'

He turned on Iris. 'You've made her do it. Meddling where you have no right.'

'It was me, not Iris.'

'Take me home. Now!'

Abigail jumped to her feet, stuffing the notebook and her knitting into her bag and throwing it over her shoulder. She lifted her dad out of the seat and settled him into his wheelchair. The commotion made Louisa agitated too.

'Where are you going? What's happening?'

Iris rushed to her side, trying to calm her.

'Where is Abi?'

Abigail didn't try to explain who she was to her mother. She grimaced apologetically at Iris over her father's head as he slapped her arm, urging her forward.

'Leave my wife and my daughter alone,' Tim hissed. 'If

I hear you've been upsetting either of them, I'll make sure your matron dismisses you within a week.'

* * *

'What is it, love?'

Iris picked at her food. The pork chop was as tough as leather and cold from being cooked several hours earlier. The crispy fat on it had turned to rubber, and however much she chewed, it remained intact. She swallowed it whole, washing it down with a mouthful of milk. Giving up, she fell back in her chair.

'You look as tired as a dog.' Mum sat opposite her, rubbing a damp tea towel around a soap-studded cup. She eyed the full plate, and Iris lifted her fork once more, forcing lumpy mashed potato between her lips.

'Abigail's father hates me.'

'What've you done to him?'

'Nothing really.' She speared a carrot. 'Insinuated he's a liar, maybe?'

Mum laughed, shook her head at the teacup. For the first time since her altercation with Tim Edwards, Iris laughed too.

'Someone else called me a bitch the other day too.'

Her mum tutted at the language. Easing herself up, she set the dry cup on the sideboard.

'I was. A bitch to them, I mean.'

Mum filled the kettle. 'Did they deserve it?'

Iris considered Miss Horracks, the receptionist. She recalled the time she'd seen her and Nurse Evans holding hands down a dark alleyway, a peck on the lips when they thought no one was around, but Iris had been shuffling some way behind in the shadows. Iris had smiled at the time, after the initial shock.

No, Miss Horracks had not deserved it.

'I needed something, and they didn't want to give it to me. So I blackmailed them.'

Her mother stalled halfway to the pantry. Recovering swiftly, she fetched the milk from the pail and poured a little into a jug. 'Well. It's done now. No point fretting over it.'

Iris cringed at the disappointment in her mother's tone. She set the knife and fork together on her plate, not able to stomach another bite.

There was nothing but the buzz of the kettle, the water humming against its iron walls. Both of them watched the vibrations, the splutter coming out of the spout, like a patient coughing up phlegm. Like Kath had done.

Iris turned away. Through the window, there was nothing but black. Night had swallowed them hours ago.

How she hated winter: the endless dark, where days were held hostage and shadows reigned; the frozen lanes, where frost-webbed cobblestones preyed on the unsteady; the chilling, wet air, where disease hung on droplets and infected the weak.

She could feel those droplets all around her, as good as rain, soaking her skin and weighing her down. A pain throbbed at the back of her head, pulsed through her brain and to the backs of her eyes. She winced as the kettle whistled, and she pushed hard against her temples.

'You're doing it again.' Mum poured their tea. The china creaked.

'What?'

'It's that place. No, don't roll your eyes. I'm telling you

because you can't see it yourself.' She carried the cups to the table and dropped a sugar cube into Iris's. 'You're getting carried away in things like last time.'

'Abigail needs me.'

'Abigail is a grown woman. She can fight her own battles.' Mum tested Iris's forehead with the back of her hand. 'I worry about you.'

Iris had slumped in her chair; now she forced herself straight. She poured milk into her cup and watched it make snowy swirls in the tea. 'I'm fine. And actually I'm not sure she can fight her own battles. The way her father treats her...'

'You're only supposed to be a nurse, Iris. If I'd have thought you were going to get yourself caught up in all this sort of stuff I would never have let you go.'

She bit her lip in irritation. Her mother hadn't wanted her to work at Smedley in the first place, but she hadn't been able to stop her. 'You know I won't leave.'

'I know.' Mum's elbows pressed into the table top, holding her weight. She, too, looked exhausted. 'You're good at your job, love; I can see that now. I can see how much it means to you. But you're twenty-two. You've a whole lifetime of work in front of you. A whole lifetime of women like this, with all their pasts and whatnot. You keep on like this and they'll end up outliving you.'

'I'm fine,' she repeated, although it was a lie. Flu still lingered on her bones. She felt its debris in the base of her lungs, in the cough which was too pronounced for her liking. The skin of her eyelids resembled pebbledash whenever she blinked these days. Only when her head hit the pillow did oblivion descend, giving her hours of blissful nothingness.

'At least you had Simon when you were dealing with that Katherine woman. You had some relief, some happiness. When was the last time you went to the picturehouse? Or a walk in the park?'

'And who would I go with?' Iris snapped, although she hadn't meant for it to come out so harsh. 'Shirley won't let me near her. Simon is busy with... None of the other nurses talk to me. I've got no one else. And I'm not going out on my own. For God's sake, Mum, you've got more friends than I have.'

Eyeballs aching, she bit her lip, trying to stop the tears. It didn't help that her mum was gazing at her pityingly, head cocked to one side, trying to find something reassuring to say. It didn't help that the pain was now seizing her skull and crushing it.

'I get the feeling sometimes...'

'What?'

'No one likes me,' she whispered, voice breaking.

Mum rushed to her side, hugging her tight against her pinafore. She smelt of cooking fat, of childhood. 'That's not true. We love you. Alan loves you—'

'You don't count.'

'Oh, thank you very much.'

Iris sighed. 'There, you see? I always say the wrong things. I'm always asking the wrong things. Getting on the wrong side of people.'

Her mum smoothed the wet off Iris's cheeks with her palm. 'You ask what people don't want to answer. That's all it is. Just some things people don't want to hear.'

Like Louisa, Iris thought. Louisa had asked difficult questions, had made a nuisance of herself. Was there anything worse than a difficult woman? In the intervening decades, nothing had changed in that respect.

In that moment, despair choked her. She didn't know how to be anything else. For so long she had fought against turning into her mother, into Shirley even. Callouses had grown and crusted over any feminine softness.

She couldn't change that now. She had moulded herself into what she had become, thinking it would make her happy. But to have a lifetime of it? Of this loneliness which cocooned her, which might, eventually, make her end her days in a place just like Ward 13…

'You've had a long day. Not a very nice one either, by the sounds of it. It's got on top of you. You need a hot drink and a good night's sleep, and you'll feel better in the morning.' Mum kissed her forehead.

Iris nodded, sniffing back the tears. All she wanted to do was sleep. She felt as if she could stay in bed for a week.

Bones crunching, she pushed herself to her feet.

'Wait a moment.' Mum shuffled into the living room and returned with a box. On closer inspection, Iris could see why it looked familiar. Black Magic chocolates.

Her stomach tightened. Had John found out she'd left them for Shirley and sent them back? Was it his custom to rifle through their bins, trying to catch Shirley out? Had her well-meant gift resulted in more bruises for her best friend?

'You didn't let me finish before. There's someone else who likes you.' She handed over the chocolates. 'Simon said he'd seen you buying them as a treat for someone and thought you could do with a treat yourself.'

Relief made her smile. 'He said he'd been meaning to call in. He wanted to see you.'

Mum laughed and shook her head at her.

'What?'

'Nothing. Go and get yourself to bed.'

Iris set the chocolates on the table after popping one in her mouth. She hugged her mum quickly, mumbled goodnight to her dad, and trudged up the stairs, letting the chocolate melt on her tongue as she went.

27
1956

The next day, Abigail didn't visit her mother. Louisa sat in a chair next to the piano and watched life go on around her. After lunch, Iris checked if she was all right.

'He won't let her come back.'

'Who?' Iris perched on the nearby seat. The pianist had just arrived and was setting up. Soon, their voices would be drowned out by music.

'He never liked her. Poor child.'

'Do you mean Abigail? Your husband never liked her?'

She nodded. The baby blanket, which she was always clutching, rippled as she dragged it to her face. Closing her eyes, she brushed it against her cheek.

The pianist checked the pedals and began. The sudden noise made Louisa flinch. The blanket fell from her grasp. Panic gouged her face. She reached for Iris with claw-like fingers, her nails scraping down Iris's bare forearms, and tugged her close.

'The picture on the wall.'

Flesh stinging, Iris snatched herself free. Red slashes ribboned her arm, the skin around them torn and flaked.

'I didn't mean to hurt you. I didn't mean to do anything,' Louisa said, choking, the tears thickening in her throat. 'It was an accident.'

Iris rocked her gently. It would be best to calm her like this. She didn't want other nurses getting involved, bringing in pills or needles.

She gripped Louisa's quivering body close. Louisa smelt of this place, this ward with all its disinfectants and bodily fluids and boiled foods. Once, she would have smelt like her daughter, of the faint sickliness of mothballs and pot pourri. Odd, how bodies resembled sponges. Did Iris smell like Ward 13 too? She must be a mix of bleach and old ladies and her mum's beeswax polish and laundry soap.

Louisa ran someone else's handkerchief against her nose. Iris touched her shoulder, and she glanced up, dribbling eyes now confused again.

'Where is Abi?'

* * *

In the living room, the electric fire buzzed. Rain spat on the windows, reflecting sparks of street-lamp light in each droplet. Kneeling on the floor, her dad was building a miniature spitfire for Adam's Christmas present out of bits of anaemic wood, tongue poking out as he dabbed glue onto part of the wing. Mum was working on her umpteenth baby garment underneath a pile of soft pink wool. Iris tried to focus on the words in her book, but each time she reached the end of a paragraph, she hadn't a clue what had happened.

The doorbell rang. All of them stopped what they were doing. Who would be out at this time on such a wretched night?

Iris hopped up, grateful for the distraction from the novel. The wind knocked the door open as soon as she turned the latch, lashing her with a splatter of rain. On the doorstep, her brother held an umbrella over Abigail's head.

It was such a bizarre sight that she didn't do anything for several seconds. Alan barged past her in the end, ushering Abigail inside too and closing his brolly. Water flecked the floor where he rested it against the wall.

'It's only me, Mam.' Alan clomped into the living room, dripping all the way. 'I brought a guest.'

Iris gestured for Abigail to step into the warmth; she shuddered with relief as she stood before the flames. 'Sorry to intrude like this.'

'What are you…?'

'I didn't know where you lived and I needed to see you,' Abigail explained. 'I remembered your brother's house and asked if he'd mind giving me directions.'

'Couldn't let her go driving round the whole of Shrewsbury getting lost.' Alan beamed at Iris. 'Not on a night like this.'

Abigail smiled her thanks at him. There was a beat of silence.

'Would you like some tea?' Mum asked, readying herself to make for the kitchen.

'No. I can't stay long. I just wanted to apologise for my father yesterday.'

Iris flushed. She focused on the splayed pages of her novel.

'And I wanted to tell you to take no notice. Because I'm going to take no notice.' Glancing up, Iris saw the blood pool in Abigail's cheeks. She took a breath, swallowed, as if psyching herself up for a fight. 'I think there is more than he is telling us.'

'I told you she could fight her own battles,' Mum muttered.

'I've found Matilda.' Abigail laughed at Iris's shock. 'It took all day. It's a wonder I can see straight. But I found her through the yellow pages. We're meeting her next week, if you'll come with me?'

Alan picked a chocolate from the box and threw it into his mouth. 'Who's Matilda?'

'Miss Matilda Tindall. A reporter.'

Alan shook his head, still none the wiser.

'What about your father?' Iris asked.

She swiped the air. 'I am almost sixty years old, Iris. I'll take tea with whomever I like. I'll drive wherever I wish.'

Abigail's proclamations sounded like something more suited to the lips of a teenager. Disobeying her dad was clearly not something she was used to. She sounded almost giddy with the thrill of it, yet there was a tremor of fear there too.

'I want to go back to Bodnem, see the manor house, take flowers for my grandfather, look around. Perhaps we could go on your next day off? There's a reason Dad doesn't want me there, and I want to find it.'

Alan cheered. 'Good for you. Though you'd best get it in quick. You heard they're rationing petrol soon? That bloody canal. I blame the Tories.' He scooped up another chocolate, completely unaware of the tension in the room. 'Where are these from?'

Mum spoke, relieved to divert the conversation away from politics. 'A present from Simon.'

Alan nearly choked on his mouthful. Abigail's eyebrows rose.

'It's just a little gift from a friend.' Iris slammed the lid on them so Alan didn't siphon away any more. 'They don't mean anything.'

Alan smirked at his mum.

'I should be going.' Abigail found a pair of leather driving gloves from her coat pocket. 'Sorry again to intrude.'

Iris showed her to the door. 'Abigail, look, I'm not sure you should. Are you certain about this? Your dad was so angry.'

'Yes, but he's angry most of the time over something or other. It wasn't like that when I was little. My parents never argued. There were never any rows, never any raised voices. We never wanted for anything. And yet, something felt not quite right. I could never understand it. For all the privilege we had, there was something underneath it all, as if we had forged a bridge over an icy stream. And I never tried peering over that bridge. I made the walls of it higher, if anything.'

She shook out one leather glove and peeled it over her hand. 'Just because you can't see the water doesn't mean it isn't doing any damage. Over the years it's eroded us. And now look at what we've become. A mother in a madhouse. A brother who can't stand to come home. A father who hasn't smiled for years. And me... left to deal with it all.'

She slipped on the other glove. 'Secrets do that. They eat at you, like regret, like all the mistakes you've ever made. Mum wanted to try to put things right. If Dad's been hiding something, I won't let him take it to both their graves.'

She brought her handbag before her and pulled out a stack of palm-sized books. 'Dad's diaries. I found them in the attic when he was taking his afternoon nap. There's a whole trunk full of them, but these are from the Bodnem murder years.'

Iris baulked at them. Tim would be furious if he ever found out his daughter was not only gossiping about their family but showing a stranger his most private thoughts.

Abigail flicked through the pages. 'He doesn't say much. Just notes about patients and treatments, the odd landmark occasion. I don't know how much help they'll be, but we can compare his story with hers. You keep them for now, and take this too.' She brought out Louisa's notebook. 'I've read on a few pages while I was away.' Her breath trembled. 'Prepare yourself. It's not pleasant.'

28
1900

My head was a pillow, a thin sack of feathers. Light filtered through them and I blinked, trying to understand, but it was too much effort.

I stared at the clock face long enough to make out the black hands, and several moments later I understood it was thirteen minutes past two. Panic should have swept over me, but I felt only its distant tendrils stirring the base of my stomach.

Tim sat near the open door reading a newspaper. Noting the pinkness of his complexion and the sheen on his forehead, I surmised he only sat so far away on account of the fire to my left. Surely there was no need of a fire on such a fine day in June? Through the window-panes the sky was sapphire, and the air above the road shimmered like water.

Water…

I shuddered as the memories of my attack by the lake fought their way into my consciousness. I ran my finger-tips over the bump which had formed on my temple.

'How are you feeling?'

I winced at the loudness of Tim's voice. He slapped down his newspaper and knelt before me.

'Why are you not out working?' I whispered. He flinched at the scent of my breath.

'Father is doing the rounds so that I can stay here with you. You've hardly surfaced for two days.'

Two days? How could so many hours have passed without my knowledge? 'Did you give me something?'

'Chloral hydrate. Just for the pain.' Tim walked to the window, blocking the light. He changed the subject before I had chance to object to the drugs in my system. 'The reverend is exorcising the ghost tonight. There will be a crowd.'

'It won't work.'

'It will give some comfort. Hope.'

'Then they deserve to die.'

Tim turned, shocked by my acidity.

'If they had sorted it before, the killer would never have attacked me.'

'If you had obeyed your husband, the killer would never have attacked you.'

He stared me down. I did not argue.

After a moment, he gazed once more into the street. 'I've called for the inspector. He should be here within the hour.'

Tim made himself busy for the next forty-five minutes, bringing me beef broth and a hot, wet flannel to freshen up with. At three o'clock, knuckles rapped on the front door.

From the hallway, Tim peeked in at me. 'Mother doesn't want him in here, so…'

My command to move.

My bones groaned. I stood, and the room vanished. Tim caught me before I thudded back into the chair, one firm arm around my waist. His breath licked my throat as he guided me into the dining room and eased me into a seat opposite Quinton.

The inspector's face was as bland as milk pudding, wet like it too. Even with the dull confusion that followed a sedative, I recoiled at the sour stench of sweat on his old wool jacket. 'You were attacked, Mrs Edwards?'

I did not answer. Such stupid stating of the obvious did not require a reply.

'What were you doing out at that time of night?'

'I know who did it.'

Tim scraped the chair over the floor and sat beside me.

'Well?' Quinton asked.

'Buckley.'

Tim coughed, laughed – something between the two. His outburst drew Quinton's eyes off me for a second. 'She's suffered a blow to the head. She doesn't know who attacked her.'

'It's Buckley. The killer of all the girls.'

'Louisa,' Tim whispered, before smiling at the inspector and shaking his head.

'There is no copycat. You hanged the wrong man last time.'

Quinton's lip twitched with annoyance. 'Your husband is right. You do not know what you are saying.'

'He must have found the note. He was trying to stop me telling Matilda. It started with his wife for a reason. Three women who loved him were killed within months of each other. His alibi was his own servant.'

Tim rose, gripped my shoulder. 'Forgive my wife.'

It took all my strength, but I shook him off. 'Just consider it, please. I beg you. For the women of this village.'

Quinton's lip trembled. He sniffed and swallowed the phlegm. My stomach curled.

'Buckley thinks he's untouchable. You know why. Men like him. He thinks he's above the law.'

That worked, as I knew it would. A man like Quinton, a man from the gutter, would relish the chance to interrogate a squire. He got to his feet. 'Fine. I'll look into it. If only to prove you wrong.'

'Inspector, please—'

Quinton silenced Tim with a hand, then let himself out.

'You will only get yourself into more trouble carrying on like this, Louisa.'

'Then who is it?'

Tim examined the table, staring into it as if its wooden patterns were as readable as tea leaves. 'It can't be Buckley. He's a good man.'

'He doesn't think so highly of you.' I laughed, and the sound floated out of me; I watched it on the air. It was a long time before it vanished. 'No more sleeping draughts. I don't like them. They make me... unreal.'

'It is for your health.'

'No, Tim.' I pushed myself up. The ground waved like an ocean.

'Where are you going?'

'I have been in that room for two days. I need fresh air.'

It was hotter in the yard than inside, but it tasted

better. The mineral breeze landed on my tongue as the spire of St Luke's speared a clear sky. Tim marched out with a dining chair in one hand and my hat in another. He set the chair in a slither of shade, forced me into it, and slapped the hat on my head.

By the time the church bells tolled five, my brain was stumbling out of the fog. Pain gnawed at the backs of my eyeballs and clamped the sides of my head, but pain was good. Pain was real.

I was alive, I reminded myself. I was the only one to survive the murderer, the only woman who had felt her lungs expand after being under his tight grip.

I was the only one who could stop him from doing it again.

* * *

The next day, I was determined to go out of the backyard. I had tried yesterday evening, but such violent tremors took over my body as I reached for the latch that I could not do it. I had to lean against the wall and recover myself in secret; if Tim had seen me, he would have ushered me before the fire again and spiked my cup of tea.

My fear was not irrational. I had been attacked for what I knew, for the threat I posed. Buckley must have had spies everywhere; he was powerful enough. But I had never thought of myself as a coward. A fool, yes. Selfish, yes. Mean-hearted, cold-blooded, despicable – yes to all. But never a coward. If he thought he could beat me down, he would be sorely mistaken.

I filled a bucket with water and grabbed a scrubbing brush. I fastened one of Mildred's many aprons around my waist and headed out of the scullery. If I had a purpose, I knew I would be able to lift that latch.

'What are you doing?' Tim stuck his head out of the medical office's window.

'Cleaning Connie Smith's grave.'

His mouth popped open; disbelief bleached his face. I felt slightly sorry for him. It couldn't have been easy having a wife who was such an enigma, and a stubborn one at that.

'You should be resting.'

'If I stare any longer at those four walls, I will start talking to them. Is that what you want?' I looked away before I saw the answer on his face. Sometimes, it seemed he wanted me to go mad. It would have been easier.

The graveyard was quiet. A song thrush beat a snail on the cobblestones, cocked its head at me approaching, and flapped off with the shell dangling from its beak. I followed it, and my gaze landed on my home, on the falling curtain at one of the windows. Somebody inside was watching me. The notion was both relieving and unsettling.

I made my way to Connie Smith's grave and got to work.

I had only cleared the first of the letters before heavy footsteps and snivelling came my way. Jenny had pulled her bonnet so low that her face was hidden. I recognised her by her hair and walk – no other woman in the village walked like her. It was a lumbering gait, all over the place. It was a wonder she was not perpetually dizzy.

She rubbed a fist into her eyes, slowed her pace, and finally glanced up. She was not heading for me intentionally; she was heading to her sister's grave, which I sat beside. I expected her tears to dry when she saw me, for a smile to spread as it usually did, but there was nothing. Her lips hung open, slippery and red, and she assessed her escape route.

'Jenny? Jenny, come here.'

She hesitated, then threw herself at me and sobbed.

'What is wrong?' She ignored me, but she could not have spoken even if she had wanted to. I stroked her back. She was hot and damp, giving off the scent of cow muck and musk. 'Please tell me why you are so upset.'

Gently, I tugged on her shoulder and coaxed her upright. Her face was as tight and red as a cherry. I removed her bonnet and brushed back her wet hair. With the tip of my apron, I wiped the mucus off her top lip.

She inhaled and her breath caught all the way up her throat. 'Can't.'

I held her hands. They were chapped, the skin broken between the knuckles, her fingers like little fat earthworms. She had bitten her nails down to the quick. So very different to my own porcelain hands, and for the first time in my life, I wished I could have swapped places with her. I wished I could have taken the pain from her, for she had endured so much already and deserved none of it.

'Did your father hurt you again, Jenny?'

She shook her head.

'Did someone else hurt you?'

She shoved her fingers in her mouth.

'You can tell me what happened. You can tell me anything. I won't be angry.'

'You will.' She choked on her words, gulped a mouthful of air.

'I won't. I promise. Tell me who hurt you.'

She swallowed. 'Pat.'

I held still, trying to remain calm. 'How did he hurt you?'

'He said he was sorry.' The words were staccato, cut off by gasps. 'For calling me names. He said we could be friends.'

'When was this?'

'Three nights ago.'

Ice trailed down my spine. The same night I had been attacked.

'What happened?'

'He was drinking. He gave me some. And then...' She scratched at a running tear, leaving nail marks on her cheek. 'I didn't know what he was doing...' She trailed off, bending forward so her head rested in my skirts.

She sobbed harder, the pain and fear and shame sheathing off one layer after another. I didn't move, only touched her knee to let her know I wouldn't abandon her.

'I couldn't stop him.'

I combed my fingers through her knotted hair. 'Oh, Jenny. I told you not to follow him at night.'

'I didn't.' She balled her fists and pushed herself up to face me. 'You promised you wouldn't be angry.'

'I'm not' – I cupped her face – 'I'm not. But it's my fault. If I hadn't set you after him—'

'I was waiting for Da outside the inn. I don't like going inside, not a place for girls, Ma says. But Da sometimes needs help getting home. Pat saw me. I wasn't spying on him. Since what you said about Buckley, I thought he was safe.'

I opened my arms and pulled her close. 'Where did this happen?'

'Their laboratory.'

Sickness curdled my stomach. 'Have you told anyone else about this?'

She shook her head. 'When I got home, Da beat me for going off.'

'You need to tell the police.'

She pushed against my chest so hard I almost fell back. 'No! Please, Mrs Edwards, no one. I'll die... Da'll kill me.'

'He won't—'

'No!'

And I knew she was right, although it made me want to tear the earth in two.

'All right.'

She glowered, but the hatred in her eyes was not for me. It was for Pat. It was for her father. It was for her sister's killer.

Between us, we may have had all the rage in the world, but there was nothing we could do except hold each other and weep.

29

1900

On the fourth day of cleaning Connie's grave, I was again accompanied. I had been waiting for Matilda's visit, hoping each time I stepped through the back gate with my swinging bucket that she would be looking out of the window for me. She was.

'How are you?'

I dug my nail into the lichen in the snaking S of Connie's family name – it was too stubborn for the brush. 'Why didn't you meet me?'

'When?'

I glanced over my shoulder to where Matilda sat against the wall. Her pretty face was stitched in confusion.

'I left a note. Behind the carnations.'

'I never found it.'

'Then he got there first.' The tip of my nail snapped back with the effort. I sucked it and spat out the dirt, but a thin line of blood surfaced. 'The killer.'

'You know who it is?'

I took up the brush again and scrubbed at the last few

flakes of lichen. They clung fast, putting up a good fight, but in the end, I won. Murky water splashed onto my skirt as I dropped the brush in the bucket. I was sweating as I leaned back, taking the strain out of my burning thighs and forearms.

'I was certain it was Buckley after what you said. I'd had it out with him at the manor, seen the guilt all over him. I was going to talk to you about him the night I was attacked.'

'But you're no longer certain?'

'Quinton saw me yesterday. He's questioned Buckley. He said Buckley has a witness for the night. Stone again, no doubt. Her word doesn't mean anything, and I told Quinton that. It made no difference. I am to cease making all these accusations. I sound like a madwoman, apparently. I asked him to turn out his pockets so I could see his coins.'

Matilda snorted. 'Good girl.'

I shook my head. 'I made it worse, as is my habit. Taunting inspectors is not the way to solve this. And, in truth, I do not think Quinton would be bought. He's too… bitter.'

'So, what? You believe Buckley's alibi, or you only believe that Quinton believes it?'

'Buckley's hiding something. That's the one thing I'm sure about. But what if Stone is actually telling the truth? I mean, would he really be capable of killing all those women? He has a temper. He has reasons. But to be capable of such evil…'

'That is the way of the devil, Louisa. He comes in all forms. Sometimes he's hard to spot.'

I knew one devil who was not hard to spot. 'Jenny Carr

has been raped.'

Matilda sighed, as if this kind of news no longer had the power to shock her, only disappoint.

'By Pat Dunn. The same night I was attacked. If he can do that to her—'

'What else can he do?' She snagged the hat off her head and used it to fan her face instead.

'He has a picture of Betty Crook. A compromising one.'

'The little pervert.'

'Betty thought she was pregnant. That's what I wouldn't tell you before. I didn't want you putting it in the papers.'

'*Thought* she was pregnant?'

'A phantom child. Tim says her womb was empty when he examined her body. But whether it was phantom or not, it's important.'

'Who was the father supposed to be?'

'No one really knows. I don't think she knew. But Pat told me he wanted her to keep it and that he'd asked her to marry him. She said no.'

'A perfect motive.'

I nodded. 'But if he is the murderer, why did he not kill me? I'm certain he hates me, although he tries to hide it. Why stop when he was attacking me?'

'Your baby.' Matilda swatted at a circling fly. 'I heard your child crying. By the time I'd woken, understood where the noise was coming from, and got to the window, you were already running home. It was the baby's noise that stopped him doing anything worse to you.'

I stroked my neck instinctively. My little Samuel, the boy who depended on my protection, had saved my life.

'I don't know… Sometimes I think I have it, but it is like sugar slipping through my fingers. First I thought it was Daniel Griffith, then Pat Dunn, then Buckley. I'm not sure about anything anymore.'

Matilda squeezed my arm. 'Whoever he is, we're getting close. He's making mistakes – leaving you alive, for one thing. But we won't get any further here. You've done all you can, Louisa. You need to take care. He knows you're a threat.' She pushed herself to her feet and replaced her hat. 'I've outstayed my welcome at the Black Heart. I'm going back to Birmingham.'

'You can't leave.'

'Only for a while. I know people there, people who can find things for me, with a little persuasion. I'll dig up all their secrets, Louisa, you can rest assured. But you must promise me to stay safe. If he wants anyone dead right now, it's you.'

* * *

Matilda's words struck at my heart. I didn't leave the house for almost a week.

Jenny called a couple of times after sneaking off the farm, saying she'd a headache. We had tea in the parlour. Mildred didn't like having her inside, but Tim overruled her; he thought I would go out to meet her otherwise.

'She's only a child,' he whispered to his mother, his palm on her shoulder to guide her away from the parlour door. She told Jenny to leave no later than midday, on account of Howard returning for lunch.

We stared at the walls. What could we say to each

other? Where once Jenny could prattle endlessly about nothing, now she barely opened her lips.

Multiple times I marched to the front door, hat in hand, shoes on, determined to storm to the pharmacy and out Pat Dunn. The whole village should have known what scum he was, but they would only blame Jenny. So was the way of our world.

At church on Sunday, she did not greet me. She stuck to her father's side, her skin sallow under the light from the stained windows. Her eyes never lifted higher than the pew before her, and I was glad for it, for otherwise she would have seen Pat ahead, singing hymns as if the words should not have set his tongue to flames.

In the churchyard, I waited while Tim and Howard talked to the villagers. Even Mildred now chose to experiment with idle chatter just so she did not have to stand with me.

Alone, I felt Mr Buckley's gaze pattering over me, like falling autumn leaves. He was lingering – he usually left as quickly as possible – and was garnering interest. A few village women approached him, tipping their heads, but he batted them off with monosyllabic responses and marched towards me. I didn't have a chance to dodge him.

'Mrs Edwards, I had hoped I would see you here. How are you, after what happened?' The sound of his voice was like spiced plums in syrup. For an instant, it warmed me, delighted me even.

'You have an alibi for that night, so I believe.'

His jaw muscles quivered in his cheek as he took a breath. 'I would never hurt you.' By his sides, his hands started to tremble. 'Please, come to the manor.'

I laughed, but it was the high-pitched, breathless kind

– it did not hide my anxiousness. He heard it and glanced up, pained. More veins skidded across his eyeballs than when I had last looked at them. Dusky pink shadows smudged the skin around them too, as if he had been punched with a puff of whore's rouge.

'I will explain all of it if you come.'

'Tell me now.'

He shook his head. Amidst the crowd, Tim watched us.

'I do not trust you.'

'I know. I should have explained sooner. But there are things which seem too important to a man to give up so easily. Pride, for instance. But I will give that up for you now, if the truth is what you really want.'

Tim pushed his way through the congregation. He would be with us soon. I had only seconds to decide.

My husband, or Mr Buckley.

'I will try,' I breathed, and Mr Buckley's face lightened. He slipped out of the side gate, as smooth as water, melting into the foliage and disappearing up the road.

'What did he want?' Tim asked, hooking my arm through his. 'Did he scare you?'

'Why should he scare me? The inspector says he has an alibi. You, yourself, said he was a good man.'

'Why must you always fight me? I am only trying to care for my wife.'

I removed my arm and walked out through the lich-gate, this pretence of his tiring me: the doting husband, the good doctor, the one above secrets and suspicion.

If he thought I did not know he still poured chloral hydrate into my evening cocoa, he was more of a fool than I was for drinking it.

30
1956

The sun was a pale, watery globe. It dusted the roads with a cold light and made Iris's clouds of breath sparkle in the air. She inhaled deeply, and late November air snipped at her lungs as she looked at the periwinkle sky. Her mind fell blank, and all that mattered was the endless blue above.

But then she heard the car.

Nausea rolled in her stomach. Despite the sunshine, foreboding lingered in the air.

'Did you read it? What happened to Jenny Carr?' Abigail asked as they drove away.

'That poor girl. What a life.'

They sat in silence until Shrewsbury town was behind them.

'Do you think it was Pat Dunn who hanged in the end?' Abigail fiddled with her sun visor as they rounded the corner.

'I hope so. If only for Jenny.'

Her grip tightened and her leather gloves whined against the steering wheel. 'But for the murders?'

There seemed little point speculating at the moment. 'We haven't heard the rest of the story yet.'

Abigail concentrated on the road. Once again, they passed the farmhouse where Jacob Hunt used to live. Iris's gaze fled to the boarded window. She imagined a woman beyond a thin pane of glass, taking a breath in anticipation and charging.

She turned away.

Soon, St Luke's church spire loomed above the rooftops. Smoke peeled up from the chimneys, just as it had done in Louisa's time. The crooked buildings smiled as they had always done. The murders were a blot on the village's long history, had been absorbed and digested until not a mark was left. Did the children who ran along these narrow roads know their ancestors had once dropped to their knees in despair? Did the newcomers realise their slice of country life came with a murderous reputation?

This time, Abigail did not park by the crossroads. She turned onto Church Street and drove between the open Buckley Manor gates.

'Sybil Buckley. I thought I recognised the name when I saw it, but I couldn't place it. You know who she is?'

Iris shook her head.

'The artist.'

Still, Iris hadn't heard of her in that context.

'I only realised the other day. I was putting a log on the fire and I saw the signature. We have one of her paintings above the mantelpiece.'

Iris straightened in her seat. It wasn't just the way the

overgrown brambles scratched the sides of the car which made her feel uncomfortable. She rummaged in her mind for the image of Abigail's parlour. It came back in snippets. A silver expanse. A white orb. Fingers of darkness.

'A lake scene at night?'

'That's right.' Abigail's voice was chipper, too forced. 'It looks like the lake by the crossroads. It's my favourite out of all of my parents' pictures, actually. If I recall correctly, Dad bought it for Mum for their twentieth wedding anniversary.'

'Why would he have done that?'

Abigail shrugged. 'It's a beautiful painting.'

'But why buy a picture of a place where girls had once died?'

Abigail dropped down a gear. They had crested the hill and now were descending. 'Maybe it was just a nice painting done by a child whom Mum had once taught. Dad might have given it to her to show that Sybil had done well for herself after they'd left.'

The road swept right. The grounds were dense, the trees crowding next to the bushes, the grass straggling up to knee height. Autumn leaves stifled the place, the frost on them twinkling silver. It was beyond unkempt; it was wild. The formal gardens aspired to by Sybil's mother had vanished. This was a jungle before them.

The road ended in a circle of gravel at the base of an ivy-clad wall. They parked next to a couple of other cars, which, judging by the leaves on their roofs, hadn't moved for a while.

Emerging, neither of them muttered a word as they climbed the short flight of stone steps between which summer flowers had sprouted and since set seed. The manor bore down on them once they reached the top. A block of green with the odd patch of red brick struggling for air – ivy covered its facade, with only the windows kept clear of the shaggy growth.

'Can I help you?'

They turned to their left. A man stepped out from the bushes; through the evergreen leaves, they could see his stool and easel sitting in the shadow of a laurel tree. A paintbrush was secured behind his ear, half-hidden by his long hair. He was bundled up in loose-fitting knitwear, and his nose gleamed red from the cold as he held an empty coffee pot.

'Is it possible to see Miss Sybil Buckley?' Abigail smiled as warmly as she could. Iris wondered if she had ever seen such a dishevelled young man before.

'Of course. I'll show you to her. I need more coffee anyway. So, are you artists or admirers?'

'Definitely the latter.'

He gestured for them to follow him through the front door. Tiles remained on the floor, as they had in Louisa's time, but the glass chandelier was gone, replaced by something modern and unassuming. There was no need for a pompous chandelier anymore; the most breathtaking thing about the hallway was how every inch of wall space was taken over with pictures. From the size of her palm to bigger than a doorway, paintings assaulted Iris's senses.

'They're all hers. All the public spaces hold her work. We have our own in our rooms.'

'You live here?' Iris asked.

'There's seven of us here, all working on our masterpieces.' He winked before mounting the stairs. 'She'll be in her rooms.'

'Like a commune?' Abigail said, a hint of horror in her tone as her palm skidded over the polished bannister.

'That's right. Miss Buckley shares her home and her talent with us, and we keep the place ticking over. It's a big house for just one lady.'

'You could do with a gardener by the looks of it.'

'She won't let us touch anything out there. She says we'll cut the heart out of it if we give it a tidy.'

Upstairs, they veered left and walked down the corridor. Despite the state of the place outside, inside was spotless. The carpets were plush, the picture frames dustless, the windows without a stain from winter rain.

'So, it's just you artists and Miss Buckley? No staff?'

'We wouldn't be doing our share if she needed staff. There's old Miss Stone, of course, but I don't think she counts. We call her the ghost, the way she haunts this place. Not to her face, though.' They reached the end of the corridor, and he knocked on the door. 'Miss Buckley? You've guests to see you.' He nodded at them both. 'Go straight in.' His gaze lingered just a little too long on Iris before he sauntered down the corridor.

Smirking at Iris's frosty expression, Abigail opened the door. It led to a smaller corridor and a variety of doors. They approached the only one which was open.

Like elsewhere, paintings served as wallpaper in this room. A tired sofa was slumped in front of a fireplace. In the large window, an easel and chair overlooked the grounds, and an assortment of paints, palettes, knives, and brushes were splayed out on a nearby desk. A Persian rug was sprawled across the floor, its blue and red colours weaving yet more garden designs. Colours were everywhere, all jarring and clashing against each other in a headache-inducing display. Iris's gaze fell gratefully onto the only muted patch available: Miss Sybil Buckley herself.

She rose on seeing them, fingers twitching the buttons on her skirt. All in black, she cut a svelte and severe figure. If Iris's maths was correct, she should be sixty-one years old, but she didn't look it. Her skin was fine and smooth, her face carefully painted with makeup, her hair thick and black. Her luminous blue eyes shone.

'Was I expecting you?' Her voice was as sharp as her gaze. Iris felt as if she were being dissected where she stood. The artist's eye.

'Sorry, no. My name is Abigail Edwards.' Stepping forward, Abigail offered her hand. Sybil accepted it without hesitation but showed no sign of recognising the name. 'My mother was your governess for a few months. Mrs Louisa Edwards.'

'Oh.' Sybil smiled, but she was still none the wiser. 'What year was that?'

'1900.'

'Gosh, a lifetime ago. Is something wrong? Is that why you're here?'

'No. Well, not really. She's suffering with her memory a little, that's all. She's been talking about Bodnem, and you and your father, so I thought it would be nice to see the place for myself. I hope you don't mind?'

Sybil gestured to the sofa for Abigail and a blue silk chair close to the fire for Iris before disappearing into the corridor. 'Anne will bring us some tea,' she said on her return, rubbing her ringed fingers together as another black figure slid past the door. Iris caught the white arc of a face peeking in.

'We have one of your paintings,' Abigail said as Sybil settled beside her on the sofa.

'Which one?'

'The lake under moonlight. It's my favourite. My father bought it for my mother. She would never have guessed what a great artist you would become.'

Sybil shook her head demurely.

'Can you remember her?'

Caught out, Sybil had no choice but to answer truthfully. 'Afraid not. I went through so many governesses, you see. I think I was quite a brute with them. Do pass on my apologies.'

'On the contrary, Mum says how quiet you were.'

'Well, I suppose I was only very little then. Tell the truth, it was their leaving which used to upset me. Father would send them on their way within a year. In the end, it was better to hate them than to love them.' She picked the button at her waist. 'Father and his peculiar ways.'

'We saw the grave,' Iris said. 'He was not an old man when he died. I'm very sorry for your loss.'

Sybil shrugged. 'My father was not a man who loved well. There was only ever one thing he cherished in this world and I was not it. It was the death of him.'

A shadow appeared at the door. It moved silently into the room with a silver tea set. Miss Stone placed the tray on the table before the fire. Gnarled hands lifted the teapot. Her cataract gaze slid up and skimmed warily over Iris. When it landed on Abigail, her grip on the pot loosened. It crashed against the cup, making tea spew over the rim and out of the spout. Abigail and Sybil jumped in fear of scalding liquid catching their stockings. Miss Stone soaked up the spillage with a handkerchief from her apron pocket and handed Abigail her cup and saucer.

'This is Mrs Abigail Edwards,' Sybil said, nodding at the sugar cubes.

'Miss,' Abigail corrected, and once again offered her hand. Miss Stone did not take it but busied herself with the sugar.

'She's one of my governesses' daughters. Do you remember a Mrs Edwards?'

Miss Stone straightened her spine, although the hump which had formed over the years was painfully exaggerated. 'You had so many.'

'Yes, that's what I was saying. Sit down, Anne; you look terribly pale. Always working, she is,' Sybil told Abigail. 'Never had a day off in over sixty years.'

'You stayed here after Mr Buckley died,' Iris said, bringing her cup to her lips.

'I couldn't let her leave.' Sybil's paint-stained fingers brushed against Miss Stone's arm. 'She's been like a mother to me.'

Miss Stone shook her head, as if embarrassed, but her features began to soften with something akin to pride.

A gust of wind hissed down the chimney. The flames spluttered, reaching out towards the fire guard like tongues. The door slammed shut in the draught, making Iris and Abigail jump.

Sybil and Miss Stone did not move.

'Do you know anything about the murders of 1900?' Iris's question seemed to shatter in the room, its shards splintering off and striking blows at Miss Stone. She had to ask though; after all, that was the main reason they were here, not just so Abigail could fawn over the talented artist.

'I was so small when all that happened.' Sybil drank her tea.

'A man hanged for them, I believe. Do you know if your father thought they got the right man?'

'My father kept me here like something out of a fairy tale, and I never knew why. He was not one to explain himself. I only learned about the murders when one of my governesses happened to ask me about the ghost of my mother. It was the first I'd heard about any of that. When I asked my father, he refused to speak of it.'

'Did you find his reluctance odd?'

'He never spoke of anything from the past. He couldn't even use my mother's name. To be honest with you, in any snatches of time he permitted me, I made sure not to rile him. For all his faults, I loved him. Time was too precious to waste on such things. All I know of those murders is that the villagers blamed my mother. The evil spirit of Madam Buckley didn't leave when they hanged that man either. Any time anyone died before the age of seventy there were whispers: Was the ghost back?' She laughed bitterly.

'You don't believe in ghosts?' Abigail asked, trying to lighten the tension that was weaving strings across the room.

Sybil glanced at Miss Stone. 'Some things are inexplicable, I suppose. What can one expect out here in the middle of nowhere?'

'And you, Miss Stone,' Iris prompted, 'did you ever believe in vengeful spirits?'

Miss Stone drained her cup, crunched some grains of

sugar between her teeth, then got to her feet and made for the door. 'If ghosts could kill, wouldn't we all be dead for our sins?'

* * *

They headed back to the car in silence. Taking one last look at the manor, Iris thought she saw movement in a ground-floor window; the curtain swayed ever so slightly. Most likely it was one of the artists, and she checked the shady spot underneath the laurel tree to find the easel and stool were now gone. The thought of that man watching her from the window was enough to make her quicken her pace.

Abigail started the engine and made a U-turn on the drive. She peeked up at the house and waved; Sybil stood in the top window.

'Can you imagine living somewhere like this?' Abigail breathed as they crashed through the bushes.

'What did you make of Miss Stone?'

Abigail shrugged. 'Doesn't seem that different to how Mum describes her.'

As if she were stuck in those old Victorian days too, Iris thought.

'It's not right, though. This place. Just something about it feels… off.'

'You're only saying that because we were talking about ghosts.'

Abigail laughed. 'Probably. But didn't you feel it too?'

Iris shook the shivers off her skin. 'No.'

Abigail didn't question anymore. Once again, they crawled along the lane, with the brambles scraping the paint off the car, and emerged in the village. Iris took a deep breath and felt as if she could fill her lungs properly now she was out of the manor's clutching embrace.

They turned to the right, down the south road. Like elsewhere, new houses had been built where fields had once stretched. They lined the road in ugly grey squares but fizzled out quickly enough. A hundred yards or so after the final one, another house came into view – a thin, red-brick structure, its back garden marked out by neatly trimmed hedgerows, the fields beyond bearing a shorn crop of wheat. Unlike the newer builds with their deep-set driveways, this cottage's front door opened straight onto the street, and empty hanging baskets swayed in the wind above a narrow line of pavement.

Abigail slowed the car. Just as they peered at the windows, a net curtain fluttered back. Rosie Smith glared at them but, on recognising Abigail, smiled.

Abigail parked on the road side. From the boot, she brought out an old Christmas biscuit tin. 'I made you a cake.' She thrust the tin at Rosie as soon as the door opened.

Rosie motioned them into the front room, taking the tin as she went. 'What for?'

'Looking after my grandfather's grave.'

'Oh, there was no need.' She lifted the lid, grinned, and headed to the kitchen, calling over her shoulder, 'Take a seat.'

The parlour was cramped, packed with too many mismatched chairs, knick knacks, rag rugs, and rickety tables holding hardback novels. A fire dominated the space and coughed out coal dust from its open face.

Just in time, Iris realised what she thought was a

cushion on one seat was actually a cat. She nudged it awake, although it didn't budge. It stared at her with hostile eyes until she perched on the edge of the chair to save her skin from claws and teeth.

Rosie brought in plates, cups and saucers, a teapot, and the cake which was now free of its tin. Its golden sponges oozed strawberry jam, and Rosie carefully cut three large slices.

'How long have you lived here?' Abigail asked as she skewered the sponge with her fork.

Rosie wriggled back in her chair, moving her feet closer to the flames. 'Moved in just after the last war.'

'Who lived here before?'

'John Carr.'

The piece of sponge fell off Iris's fork. 'This was the Carr's cottage?' She glanced to the hallway, half expecting to see Jenny tumbling down the stairs in a cloud of red curls and dirty skirts.

'That's right. John remembered me, even though I didn't him. He was a few years older than me when… Anyway, he was trying to sell this place, and I snapped it up before anyone else could. I'd been waiting for a house to come up here for years by then. The war stopped people buying and selling.'

'What was he like?' Iris couldn't imagine the little boy from Louisa's story all grown up, living out his father's life in these walls which held so many bad memories.

'He was a survivor.'

Iris knew the veiled meaning of that word. Abigail set her gaze on the flames.

'His older brother had died at the Somme, so he told me.'

'And his mother and father?'

Rosie chewed and swallowed before she spoke. 'Mrs Carr hadn't lasted long after the murders. Old Mr Carr...' She shook her head. 'Well, he's buried in the churchyard like all the others. I believe it was put down to the influenza – better for everyone that way.'

'John was the only one left?'

Rosie nodded. 'He went to Australia, needed a fresh start. I couldn't blame him for that. I knew how he felt.'

The cat prowled onto Iris's lap and nosed the plate, claws extending and snipping her thighs through her skirt. Iris stuffed the cake into her mouth before it had chance to pounce.

'What about your brother?' Abigail asked gently.

'Died in the workhouse orphanage.' Rosie set her crumb-speckled plate on the table. 'About a year after we'd arrived, but I hadn't seen him since we were both in the infirmary together. Separate blocks for boys and girls, you see.'

'I'm so sorry,' Abigail said.

'Do you mind my asking why you were in the infirmary?'

'We were just getting over scarlet fever when we went to the workhouse. But it was consumption that killed him in the end. He was always a sickly child, and that place felled some of the strongest. They didn't allow me to go to the funeral. I must have been no more than six, but I can still taste my rage. So strong. But at least I can visit his grave now.'

'How do you know where he is? I thought those who died in a workhouse were buried in unmarked graves,' Iris blurted, before she realised how callous it sounded.

'He has a stone.'

'How…?' She was trying to think of the most diplomatic way of asking how an orphaned child, abandoned to the workhouse, with not a penny to his name, could have procured such a burial.

'I don't know,' Rosie said, before Iris had to say any more. 'Some distant relative, I assume. The same one who left me enough to buy this place.'

'Sorry?'

'A solicitor found me just after the war and told me I had inherited some money. No name. No person to thank, or hate. I couldn't understand; if someone had thought enough about me to leave me such a sum, why couldn't they have saved me from that terrible place when I was a child?' Rosie sniffed before she lost herself. 'I shouldn't think badly of them. But still, I would have preferred a warm hand to hold on to.'

She couldn't imagine how awful it must have been for a little girl to go from having a home and a family to being all alone in a Victorian workhouse.

'Sorry, I didn't mean to get all maudlin.' Rosie laughed too loudly. 'I hardly ever have visitors and look what I do! And you made such a lovely cake. Thank you, Mrs Edwards, it was delicious.'

'Miss,' Abigail said for the second time that day. Iris wondered how tired she got of correcting people and how each time she did so, another layer of sadness was draped over the word.

31

1900

It was not until the following Wednesday that I could leave the house. A whole three weeks since I had been attacked, and yet it could have been months. The hours had all merged and blended, and the more I looked at the hands on the clock, the less sense they made.

It was the first day Tim had taken out the cart and done his rounds since my attack. Howard had grown tired from doing it. He loped about the house, yawning, scuffing his slippered heels on the rugs, and making Mildred tut. He avoided the medical office, so it was easy for me to slip inside and write a note.

Taken Samuel for fresh air. Will call at the Carr's.

I bundled Samuel in his pram and strode off up Church Street before anyone could stop me.

Sybil was not at the window. Miss Stone did not answer the door. They could have been ghosts, their presence was so absent at the manor. Instead, Buckley let me in.

'I didn't think you were coming.'

I raised Samuel out of his pram. Buckley led the way to his study. A chair sat opposite his, and I wondered how long it had been there, waiting for me. When I sat, it sighed with relief.

Buckley tapped his nails on his desk. It was clear of paperwork, the mahogany wood naked and glimmering. Not even a dirty teacup, just a vast expanse of darkness to separate us. I was grateful for the barrier.

'Well?' I said.

'I thought you might be too frightened—'

'I believe there is a very real possibility you tried to strangle me. My coming here is not an act of forgiveness or bravery. You said you would tell me the truth. That is all I want. All I have wanted from the beginning. I do not trust you, Mr Buckley, but quite frankly I don't trust anyone in this village.'

The skin about his eyes crinkled. 'I won't tell you again, then, that it was not me who attacked you.'

'Is this going to take long?'

'Probably.' When I glanced up, his smile had drained. 'Do you know why you came here, Louisa?'

'My husband wished to keep me occupied.'

He shook his head. 'Your husband knows I have neglected Sybil. Not to any detriment, just kept her at a distance. I believe he sent you here to keep an eye on the child, see she is faring well. Prospering, if you will. I believe your husband values your intellect and expects your loyalty as his wife. A governess and a spy.'

I rolled back my shoulders. 'You were supposed to be telling the truth, not accusing me of treachery.'

'I do not accuse you of treachery in the slightest. You will not have understood any of it. Why would you?'

'If you are going to keep talking in riddles, I will leave.'

'Timothy is Sybil's father.'

The room became a vacuum. It sucked the breath from my lungs. 'What?'

'My wife and your husband had an affair.'

I shook my head. There were too many thoughts and questions tumbling in it, making me dizzy. 'He would have told me.'

'Would he?'

I looked down at Samuel.

Another baby.

How could Tim have kept Sybil quiet?

'Mine and Dorothea's was not a union of passion but money,' Buckley said, drawing my attention. 'My father had debts which he kindly passed to me. Her family was new money, and they had a lot of it too. You might say she got the rough end of the deal, but you should have seen the other options. She got Bodnem. She got a home she adored. All of this was her doing. Just a hunting lodge before. She had everything transformed within two years of our wedding and loved every second of it.'

'Madam Buckley and Tim?' I couldn't picture it.

'You are thinking of her as the spirit, as the ghost – the legend – she has become. I told you, everyone loved her. She was forever in and out of the village, paying visits, giving alms. I imagine that is how she and Tim met.' He took a moment and stared unseeing at the space between us. 'I loved her. I was jealous. Angry, for a while. But I ignored it. I occupied myself with other things.'

He pushed out his chair and walked to the window. The willow branches framed him.

'Habits are so easy to form, yet they harden like chains. When the baby came, I had been unconscious for several hours. Tim tried to wake me, but it was impossible. They had cleaned and moved the body by the time I surfaced. I thought I was still dreaming.'

He lifted his hand to brush his forehead, and his fingertips quivered.

'I never told them to save the child and sacrifice Dorothea. I never told them anything, you see. Couldn't. I was too far gone already. I can't even remember the last time I kissed her, nor her final words to me.'

He faced me. 'Drink is my vice, Mrs Edwards. As you saw the other day, to my shame.'

He returned to his seat. 'Miss Stone was already here before Dorothea died, ready to feed the new baby. Her own had died at two months old, only a week before she arrived – only a month after her… fellow had disappeared one night. After Dorothea passed, she became a nurse to me too. Would put me to bed when I fell asleep here. Would clean me when I didn't know I was filthy. Would feed me, even. She hid my monstrous self from the rest of the village and kept the child away, for she saw how she upset me – reminded me of what I had lost. Miss Stone grew as protective of me as she did of Sybil. She was the only person I let close. That's why she is the only person who can say she was with me the night Georgina and Mary died.'

'And Connie Smith?' I stuttered. 'Miss Stone said you

were not here when she died, you were in London, yet there is no record.'

He sighed, and a faint, resigned smile softened his features. 'In Dorset, there is a house. Smaller than this place. It prides itself on discretion for people like me. Not a neighbour for miles. Just fields and trees and beaches. They say in another fifty years it will have fallen into the sea, and no one will know it had ever existed.'

There was a clacking sound – his tongue sticking to the roof of his mouth. He tried again to swallow. His throat writhed with the effort.

'The sea air does me good. The locks on the doors are better. A few days there and things start to clear: the mind, the cravings. Each time I think I have been cured, and yet… there is always a next time. I hope I shall be dead before it falls into the sea.'

'You were at a madhouse the night Connie Smith was murdered?'

He flinched at my brutal use of the term. 'A sanatorium, they call it. But yes, I was there. And I was there the night you were attacked. I left after our… altercation and returned as soon as I heard about what happened. I needed to see that you were well.'

I felt as if all my strings had been snipped. Everything that had been holding me together broke. Tears slugged down my cheeks and dripped onto Samuel's gown. Buckley could not stop his own from falling either.

'I thought… I was convinced it was you who attacked me.'

He nodded.

'But why didn't you tell me about Sybil? Why didn't Tim?'

'Tim and I agreed, not long after Dorothea died, that I would raise the child as my own. He was a young bachelor with his sights set on the city. Everything here was set up for a baby. I could give her the life, the wealth, the opportunities that Tim never could. And it wasn't just that. She was my last piece of Dorothea. Even if it pained me to look at her, I couldn't let her go. It would have finished me.'

He took a breath. 'She was to be kept a secret for fear any of the villagers saw a trace of her real father in her. How could she become the lady of this place or marry well or be accepted if she were known as a bastard? Tim only let you here because you are his wife. You would keep the secret too, if ever you realised.'

I sniffed back the last of my tears. How foolish I had been. How had I not seen it for myself?

Tim. Poor Tim. In that instant, I wished to take back all the hurt I had caused him these last few months. I wished to erase the suspicions I had cast on him. On Buckley too. Both of them had done nothing more than love their child.

'I did not kill those women, Louisa.'

I reached out for him, but the desk blocked me. 'I'm sorry for ever thinking it.' He regarded my bare fingers upon the polished surface. Silence descended.

The chiming of the clock snapped us back to reality.

I stood, urgency coursing through my veins. Buckley was not the killer, which meant I needed to send Matilda a telegraph. There was no point her wasting time on him; she needed to focus on Pat Dunn.

* * *

Rain picked at the windowpane and blotted into the thatched roof. Samuel was soothed by its steady patter and slept well, and Tim and I listened to it absently as we stared at the black ceiling.

'I understand,' I breathed.

Tim's hair ruffled against his pillow as he glanced my way.

'Sybil will want for nothing. A life you could never give her.'

He paused. 'So you were lying in your note. You didn't visit the Carr's.'

I shifted onto my side, better to trace his outline in the shadows. 'You could have told me before about Sybil.'

'You would not have gone.'

I touched the edge of his shoulder and found the cotton of his nightshirt warm and worn against my fingertips. 'You love your children. We both know that is how I came to marry you.'

Air slid against my cheek; Tim laughed softly, without making a sound.

'I'm sorry I can't be more like Dorothea.' Emotion broke my last word. Truly, I wished I could have been what he longed for. Being a constant disappointment was wearing for both of us.

Tim slipped his hand on top of mine. 'I'm sorry. For this. For what is happening. I should never have brought you to Bodnem.'

'Your father needs you. I can see it now.'

Neither of us spoke. It was only the sip of his breath that hinted he might have been weeping. I reached blindly for his eyes. Water seeped over his temple.

Opening my arms, I brought him close. His forehead

pressed against my breastbone, the air hot and wet between us.

For what did he weep? Dorothea, his true love? His father's decline? The victims? For being bound to me, forever? Or perhaps, like me, he was just exhausted by everything.

32
1956

Abigail had stared at the wall while Iris read aloud about Tim's love child. Not a muscle had twitched as she had discovered that the artist whom she so admired, that the stranger with whom she had taken tea with only three days earlier, was in fact her half-sister.

'I'm sorry,' Louisa whispered, crooked hand held out to her daughter.

Abigail kissed her mother's knuckles. 'Rest now, Mum. We've heard enough for today.'

Louisa's eyelids lowered. Her chin sunk to her chest. Abigail laid her hand in her lap, pulled the baby blanket over her shoulders, and strolled to the window.

'Are you all right?' Iris whispered, checking that the other nurses weren't eavesdropping.

'That's why he didn't want me to go.' Gloomy dusk light made the water glimmer on the rims of Abigail's eyes. 'How can you keep something like that a secret for so long? Both of them... How could she bear it, knowing he could never love her like he had loved Dorothea? She was always second best.' A tear broke the dam and skimmed her cheek.

'They were different times,' Iris reasoned, before trying to make herself useful. She hurried to the nurses' station to find her bag, grabbed her hanky, and dashed back to Abigail, ignoring her colleagues' suspicious glances.

Abigail dabbed her cheeks. 'That's the reason for the painting.' She was losing her control; her shoulders juddered and her voice scaled higher. 'It wasn't for love. He was tormenting her. Every day she's looked at that painting, and she's seen what she could never be. He was reminding her how he could never love her. Every single day.'

Abigail broke off with a gasp and clutched the handkerchief to her face. Protected from view, she took three deep breaths before she exposed herself again.

'He can be a difficult man, but I've never thought him cruel.' She turned to Iris, dazed. 'How do people do it? Hide themselves for years. How can you spend decades with someone and never really know them?'

She didn't have the answer. No matter how desperate she was to reassure Abigail, Iris could not lie for Tim Edwards. He had made his wife a pawn in his game, and although it might not have been intentional, there was a bitter taste of mocking that came with it.

Was that really why he had bought Sybil Buckley's painting, and why he had set it over the mantelpiece for both of them to stare at each day? It did seem like a small slice of torture to remind his wife of his lost love, of his first child, of the place which had split their marriage in two.

Abigail trudged to her seat and slung her coat over her shoulders.

'Will you go home?'

'Where else do I have?'

Iris didn't like to see her leave like this. 'You could go to my house? I'm sure Mum would be delighted for someone to eat my dinner while it's still hot. She's always moaning that it's ruined by the time I get home.'

Abigail lifted the wet handkerchief. 'Do you want this back?'

'It's yours.'

She stuffed it in her pocket. 'I shan't eat your dinner, Iris. I have to go home at some point. Might as well get it over with.'

'Will you tell him you know?'

'I imagine he'll guess for himself as soon as I step over the threshold.'

They hesitated at the ward door.

'You did warn me. I've found something I don't like.'

Iris squeezed her arm, then checked her watch as discreetly as she could. She'd need to sort out the dinner any time now. Already she could hear the nurses talking pointedly in her direction and the clatter of the food trolley.

'Thank you for being with me for that. I know I've pushed you into this when it isn't your problem.'

Iris shook away the gratitude. 'I could have stopped if I really wanted to.'

'Do you want to stop now?'

Iris considered, then smiled. 'Your problem is my problem now.'

Abigail laughed breathlessly.

'Sybil, the affair – they don't mean your dad loved you or your brother any less.'

'Perhaps,' Abigail said, unconvinced. 'I'll see you tomorrow.'

She stumbled down the corridor, her heels grinding against the tiles as if it were too much effort to lift her feet.

'Miss Lowe?' Nurse Carmichael stood in the middle of the room, hands on her hips. 'Not keeping you, are we?'

Her shift had run over. There'd been an incident in the toilets, one of the ladies refusing to leave the cubicle in fear of those who were waiting for her on the other side. Iris was a bruise or two heavier now after catching a pointy wrist to the cheek. The throbbing in her lip mimicked that in the soles of her feet, the base of her spine, the back of her head.

Some days just seemed to be out to destroy her.

She yearned for her bed as she loped towards the hospital's exit, cursing the long and cold walk home which lay ahead.

'Miss Lowe?'

Iris braced herself. Since blackmailing Miss Horracks, the two of them had studiously avoided each other's gaze. Iris hadn't picked up the nerve to ask her to hurry along her investigation.

She approached the reception desk. Miss Horracks stood behind it, smiling as sweetly as she always did on account of the other nurses and doctors heading home for the night.

'You've found it?'

Miss Horracks nodded. She ripped off a page in her private notebook and thrust it at Iris. 'Thought it best to write it down. Didn't want to forget it and have to go back.'

It felt like a forged note slipping into her bag. Miss Horracks returned to her seat and tried to look busy.

'I'm sorry.'

Miss Horracks ignored her.

'It was just really important. I never would have done anything.'

'But I didn't know you were bluffing, did I?'

She cringed. What to say? Was there anything she could do to absolve herself?

But perhaps that was the point. Why should she be absolved? She didn't deserve it; after all, she had wanted that information, and if she'd had a second chance, she would have gone about getting it in the same way. Her apology meant nothing.

Perhaps that was what Tim had realised years ago: that apologising made no difference. It hadn't stopped him loving Dorothea, or grieving for her, or using his wife as he had done. So he had buried that side of him instead.

Iris did the same. Without another word, she stalked into the November night and huddled close to the building, using the light from one of the ward windows to illuminate Miss Horracks's scrawled note.

Jacob John Hunt
   Admitted 2nd Sept 1910
   Died 23rd June 1920
   Case notes from post-mortem conclusion:

> *Male, 45, duration of insanity 9 years and 10 months. Form – at first mania, latterly dementia with paralysis. Cause of death – GP.*

She slumped against the wall. Jacob Hunt had died only yards from where she stood after years of suffering from a disease that could now be easily cured. General paralysis was a diplomatic way of hiding the true cause of that illness which started from a moment of passion and led to a gradual decline into deathly insanity.

Like so many men and women before and after him, syphilis had killed Jacob Hunt.

But had his mania from it made him a likely suspect for killing his beloved and innocent fiancée? It was a possibility. Delusions were common in such patients. Violence sometimes too.

She shoved herself off the wall and started her trek home.

33
1900

A week later, a carriage arrived in the street. It stopped on the crossroads and the driver dismounted, tugged open the door, and helped Matilda descend. I ran out and met her in the graveyard.

She held the smell of the city, of oil and smut, no matter the rose water she had doused herself in. Coal dust coughed out of her carpet bag as she joined me on the bench and set it by her feet. Heavy skies and greasy faces simmered in my mind. Blasting furnaces, deafening factories, a mass of people as dense as an ocean. My childhood memories stirred.

'Thank you. For not putting it in the papers.' I had checked every morning since I sent her the telegram about Buckley's innocence.

Matilda looked skyward. 'I came for the killer. Chronic drunkards and illegitimate children in society's upper echelons are hardly newsworthy.' She sighed. 'Sorry. I'm in a foul mood, and none of it because of you.'

'Have you found anything?'

'Nothing that will mean something to those who matter. Pat Dunn is as clean as a cat's arse. Not a single misdemeanour. No fines, no cautions. Never been arrested for anything at all. But the Dunns do have family in Birmingham. A second cousin is a clockmaker, has a little shop down a back alley. Pat visited last spring. The man says he comes a few times a year, if the weather is fine enough to travel.'

'Right… I'm sorry, I don't quite know what that has to do with anything.'

Matilda peeled off her lace gloves and laid them over her powder-blue skirts. She picked at them, and the bones in her hands lifted and twitched like piano keys. 'It is not just in Bodnem where girls are dying.'

It took a moment for me to comprehend what she was saying.

'Girls – prostitutes. It's been happening for several years now. Just the odd couple every now and again. No one takes any notice. Prostitutes die all the time. But these… They're strangled. No sign of distress. No violence. Not even robbed. They look as if they're sleeping.'

'That's why you came here. You think they've been murdered by the same person?'

She was paler than when she left. The planes of her face were sharper too, chiselled like knives.

'When did this start happening?'

'Four years ago. The first on the third of October 1896.'

'Connie Smith died in August that year. The successful exorcism was September, so I believe.'

She nodded.

Neither of us spoke. The information sunk into my mind, solidifying as heavy as steel.

'He never stopped,' I breathed.

'Now you see why I came to the same conclusion. The bottle, the ghost – it's an excuse. If it had never been found, never been opened, he wouldn't have started again here. He's trying to pass the killer off as an evil spirit intent on revenge because he knows that's what the villagers believed last time and that they'll believe it again.'

I leaned forward, holding my stomach. My gaze was trained on Betty's and Daisy's stones. Mrs Powell was right; Jenny had let the devil loose on the streets. I had the urge to weep for all of them, but for Jenny most of all. She could never find out.

'The clockmaker confirms Pat visited for three days last May, from the twenty-second. A prostitute was found dead in her rented room on the twenty-seventh. There was no serious post-mortem, but it was estimated she had died in the previous two to three days – confirmed by friends who hadn't seen her – and from strangulation. That was it. She was in a pauper's grave by the weekend.'

'The others?'

'Same story. But the clockmaker can't be sure of any other dates Pat visited. He only remembers those because his wife had gone into labour on the Friday. Their first son.'

She reached for her bag and fished out her notepad. She leafed through the pages until she found what she was looking for.

'Third of October 1896. The next was not until April in ninety-seven. Again that year in August. Then May,

August, and September in ninety-eight. And last year, May, then July. None so far this year.'

Gooseflesh rippled over me as I thought of myself so close to the city for all those deaths. July last year was the final time I had seen my parents.

Thrown out, I had roamed the streets of Edgbaston before taking an omnibus into the city centre and passing hours in a tea room where women ogled my reddened eyes. Afterwards, I had gone to a music hall, spent the last of the Pendleton's pennies on gin and acted like one of the women who sat with their bloomers showing.

With nowhere to sleep, I had drunk and wept and staggered the whole night. As the coal-choked sky had lightened with dawn, I had slumped by the canal and ignored the glares and smiles of the boatmen.

Then I had found Tim.

Had I seen the victim that night? Had I passed her, heard the tinkle of a false laugh, smelt sex and disease on her breath? Had I even been considered myself, for there was nothing which separated me from her kind that night?

Life was as thin as a piece of thread.

'There is something we are missing,' Matilda said, disturbing my thoughts. 'He plays God, but he is not the Almighty. He'll make a mistake. We must make sure we are watching when it happens.'

* * *

Jenny came again the following Wednesday. I took her outside on account of Howard resting in the parlour.

Mildred shut the door on us, flapping a cloth at an imaginary fly and sucking her teeth.

We sat on the wall. The uncut grass from the churchyard border rolled behind us, tickling our shoulders. Bumblebees droned past us and took refuge in the clumps of purple-pink wildflowers that sprouted amidst the overgrown lawn.

'How are you?' I asked.

She lifted a shoulder, let it drop. 'You?'

I made an indistinguishable grunt.

'Two lambs died. Dog got them last night. Da put them out of their misery just now.' She swallowed, and the sound was like a squashed frog. 'Such a mess. So much blood.'

She ground the heel of her hand into her eye socket, a veil of tears forming. Again, she swallowed and blew a trembling breath up into her face. There was a sheen to her skin, like puddles of grease skimming a pail of milk.

'Come. Let's find some shade.'

Without the need to speak, both of us wound our way onto Church Street and perched on the stone wall. Oak and ash trees let through ribbons of light and glimmered golden green on the moss. Behind us, the lake buzzed with heat and ripened the air. A moorhen paddled out from amidst the scorched reeds, its bleats piercing the silence.

I could not tell her what she had done, yet the secret weighed down the space between us. If only she had never found that damned bottle! It was as if the water had spewed it out on purpose, knowing Jenny was nearby. I wished the sun would burn it dry.

'Is there anything I can do, Jenny?'

'Like what?' The words were muffled, barricaded by her fingernails.

'You look…' How could I explain it? The greyness of her flesh. The sudden gauntness, as if her skin were too heavy. The sour stench of her. 'Thin. Are your family struggling?'

She spat out a rind of nail and shook her head.

'You can tell me. Your father should not be too proud to take charity for the sake of his children.'

'We've plenty. I just don't feel like eating.'

I turned towards the nearby dog roses and found relief in their perfume. Further up the road, a pair of wood pigeons hopped around each other. One flew up, hauling its plump body off the ground and onto the stones. The other followed it. The first strutted away, but again the other chased.

Their whooping calls wrapped around my head as the second pigeon bent forward, dipping its head low, raising its tail feathers and spreading them wide before drawing them shut, like a lady's fan at a ball.

My saliva thinned.

'Jenny, why do you not eat?'

'Can't stomach anything.'

I dragged my gaze off the pigeons. 'When did you last have your… menses?'

'My what?'

'Your monthlies.' I wiped the prickle of sweat off my brow. 'The curse.'

'Oh.' She frowned at her feet. 'I don't know.'

'Try to remember.'

She shook her head.

I trawled through my memories for dates. 'Had Daisy died when you last had the curse?'

She considered. 'No. It was before Daisy was found because Ma sent me for some broken biscuits, because that's what she likes when we're… Our treat, she says. And Daisy packed them up for me.'

'Have you bought biscuits for your mother this month?'

'Ma sent John, what with Mrs Powell hating me like she does.'

'When did John go?'

She shrugged. 'A week or two ago, I suppose.'

'And did you have any of the biscuits?'

'One. But it made me sick.' Her nails flew to her teeth again. 'Why are you looking at me like that?'

'Did you have the curse when you ate that biscuit?'

She shook her head.

How to say it? I could hardly bring myself to think it. Could I turn back the hands of the clock, never see those pigeons, never notice the slickness of her skin, never detect the scent of vomit on her breath?

But what would happen then? In three, five, nine months' time? When would her mother realise her rags never needed washing? When would her father try beating the baby out of her?

'Jenny. Why does the bull go in with the cows?'

'So there'll be calves for market.'

I gently lifted up her hand. It was like a lump of chilled butter. 'I think you might be with child.'

She stared blankly.

'When Pat Dunn… did what he did to you, I think he might have made a baby inside you.'

Her fingers fell away. 'No.' The sour tang of vomit filtered into the air as her mouth hung open. 'What will I do?'

I dragged her close as her words disintegrated into sobs.

'Hush, Jenny.' I wiped her tears and mucus away with my skirt, even though they returned just as quickly. 'I will sort it.'

'How?'

'I will find a way to sort it. You trust me, don't you?'

She nodded and dragged her sleeve across her nose.

'You do not need to worry. There is nothing to worry about.'

I didn't know if I was saying it to reassure Jenny or myself.

'I will fix it.'

34
1900

I refused to go to church the next day. I would not share the same space as that vile rapist. I gave the excuse of a headache, then, as soon as Tim and his parents left, ran to the medical office and scoured the bookshelves. Perhaps if I'd taken an interest before, I would have known instantly what to give Jenny, but as I scanned the pages in a copy of *Pharmacopeia*, the words crumbled to dust in my mind. I slapped it back on the shelf.

Cabinets lined the walls. Scalpels and butchers' knives sat behind Mildred's polished glass, the shine of the metal muted by the dullness of the day. My gaze lingered on a pair of forceps, and I shuddered. Was that how they delivered Sybil, or were blades involved?

Blades. The surest way to get out a baby.

No. I would not use knives on Jenny – I'd kill her and the child both.

In the next cabinet, medicines were lined up in uniformed rows. A shrunken pharmacist's shop, and all a mystery to me. I spied the chloral hydrate which Tim had stirred into my tea and turned away.

Tim's case was propped up against the wall. The leather was the shade of ox blood and softened by use. I remembered it sitting at the foot of Matthew Pendleton's bed, its mouth yawning open, showing its teeth of metal and glass. Now, I picked it up. It was heavy, and I used both arms to hug it close. It smelt of Tim; Tim smelt of it. Of stripped and waxed hide, of other people's houses, of medicine mixtures and carbolic acid for cleaning.

I noticed the cough syrup first. A new bottle, judging by its fullness and the boldness of the label.

A wonder cure. Safe, he had said.

He was still using it.

I snapped the bag shut, repulsed.

It was no use rifling through medicine bottles I had no knowledge about. I needed to speak with someone who did.

Tim would not help, and if I asked him I would have to tell him what had happened to Jenny after I had sworn not to. Neither did I want to confide in Howard about such a delicate matter; if he had the same principles as Tim, he would not allow such an abomination to take place.

There was only one person whom I might be able to persuade.

* * *

'You're going back?' Tim asked the next morning, blundering into the bedroom after using the privy.

'Sybil needs an education, like you said.' I lifted

Samuel out of his cot. 'Will your mother be all right with him?'

'I'll have him.'

'Does Howard not still suffer?'

'The migraine is passing.' Tim brushed my arms out of his way and embraced his son. He kissed Samuel's forehead, lips ruffling tufts of black hair. Samuel ogled him, fists clenching around his tie, head-butting into his neck.

I could not watch. I could not bear it.

Downstairs, I found my bag and made my escape.

The grey gown clung to my skin as I marched through the high street. Too hot. I snatched at the collar. But it was appropriate, a dress of death, and I did not wish to tarnish another one with such sin.

In the shop, Mrs Dunn was filling a jar of liquorice while her husband saw to a customer at the other end of the counter. She started when she saw me entering, a flicker of tongue against her lips, like a serpent tasting the air for its prey. She had a morbid sense of excitement. Perhaps that was where her son got it from.

'Mrs Edwards, how can I help you?'

'Where is Pat?'

'Out. Why do you ask?'

'You should keep him on a leash. You don't know what harm he is doing.'

'What do you want?'

'Something to loosen a baby.'

Her breath hiccupped up her throat. 'We do not meddle in that sort of thing. Try the newspapers. There are advertisements for all sorts of pills if you know what to look for.'

'I do. And I know they're as useful as a lump of coal. I

need something more reliable. You must have learned something while working here, or are you as stupid as you look?'

'Dunn's pharmacy does not—'

'Violate simple girls?'

Her voice cut out. The light drained from her eyes.

'If you want to know who the medicine is for, I would suggest you consult your son.'

'Everything all right?' Mr Dunn called. Both he and his customer were peering at us from the other end of the counter.

I edged closer to her, pressing my skirts against the glass. 'Perhaps you should take me somewhere a little quieter while you sort out what I need. Wouldn't want any rumours spreading.'

She swallowed, then turned a garish smile at the two men. 'Fine. Mrs Edwards has a tight chest. I'll make her up a plaster.'

Mr Dunn nodded and faced his disappointed customer to continue their consultation.

'Can you return in an hour or so?'

I did not move.

She busied herself again with the liquorice sticks, turning her back on her husband and whispering to me, 'Meet me in the laboratory.'

She set the lid on the liquorice jar, then walked stiffly behind the counter, past her husband, and into the back rooms. Mr Dunn did not return my clipped smile but kept his eyes on the pills he was rolling as I slipped out of the front door and down the alley.

A rough brick building crouched just yards behind the Dunns' back steps. Cobwebs coated its thin windowpanes, which were speckled with curled black carcasses quivering in the slow breeze. Mrs Dunn shoved open the door and allowed me inside first. Old wooden cabinets lined the whitewashed walls, bedecked with various bottles containing white powders and jars with plants suspended in liquid. At the far end, a black curtain concealed a small portion of the gloomy space.

'Who is it? The girl.'

'Doesn't matter.'

'She is lying.'

'We both know she is not.'

Mrs Dunn flushed, pushed her hands into her hips, and paced before the window.

'He did it here, you know. In this fetid place. On the floor, no doubt. Not even a fire to warm her bare flesh.'

'Stop.'

'Then find me a medicine and I will sort it. It will be over within days.'

I wound my way to the work desk where beakers and glass tubes lay beside a rusted set of scales and an apparatus clutching two empty flasks. The scent of gas grew bitter on my tongue as it wafted up from the Bunsen burner below. I imagined the whole building blowing up with the lighting of a single match.

'Ergot extraction.'

'What?'

'Ergot extraction might do it. It's been used for centuries. Hastens a birth. Or a death.'

'You have some?'

'Inside.' She lingered.

'Well? Go and get it.'

She hurried for the door.

'Wait. You're sure it is the best option?'

'Not as good as a needle or blade, but better than gin.'

'Is it safe?'

'Meddling with death is never safe.' She reached for the handle. 'If anything happens, I will deny it all. There is no proof you had it from me.'

I laughed. 'I would expect nothing less.'

She scurried away silently. Bored, and not a little agitated with the thought of securing a vial of poison, I occupied myself with opening the drawers. Glasses rattled under my disturbance; spiders ran for cover; papers rustled as I lifted them out. Words had been scrawled between symbols: meanings I could never fathom but what I assumed to be notes from the experiments done here.

Curiosity beat my nerves as I ambled towards the black curtain. My fingers curled around it, hesitating as I imagined a ghoul jumping out as soon as I peeled it back. With a deep breath, I stripped it away, exposing a makeshift red room. The light was off, and the trays were dry of chemicals. Beneath the table there was another set of drawers, but when I tried to open them, they were locked.

'What are you looking for?' I whirled around; Pat stood in the doorway. 'You already received your photograph. Are you not happy with it?'

I edged towards the desk in order to put a barrier between us. 'Why are the drawers locked?'

'Privacy.'

'Are there other pictures in there? Pictures like the one you have of Betty under your pillow?'

A smirk played on his lips. Thin lips. Physiognomists

would have branded him peculiar for it. So would I. Peculiar habits. Peculiar desires. The thought of those lips against mine, of those fingers against my flesh, made the room swirl about me. Poor, poor Jenny.

'So, you were spying. Not enough to send your little bitch after me, now you're sneaking around too?'

'I know what you did to Jenny.'

He crossed his arms, lifted his chin. The softness he had once presented to me was gone.

'Did you do the same to Betty?'

His eyes narrowed, and when he next spoke, his voice was quieter. 'Betty was a slut. She did anything she was told. Oh, the things she did, Mrs Edwards.'

He stepped into the room, shutting the door behind him and closing the space between us. My clammy fingers gripped a bottle on the desk, the only thing I had as a weapon if I needed to defend myself.

'What do you want?' he asked.

'You. On the end of a rope.'

He laughed, and his stale breath blew into my face. 'They don't hang rapists anymore.'

'The police don't. The Crooks and the Carrs might find a way.'

'But that would mean they'd have to believe you.'

He reached into his jacket and removed his hip flask, and as the lid came off, the bitter scent of gin stung my nostrils as it had done the first time we'd spoken in the alleyway. He took a sip, then belched. I leaned back, stretching to get away from him.

'If you've finished in here, you should go. Unless you'd like to join me?' He lifted the flask. 'Jenny drank all of it.

Such a small thing, but she guzzled it down like she was sucking on a teat.'

'Son?'

Reluctantly, Pat turned away from me. His mother was waiting by the door, holding a vial.

'What have you got there?'

Mrs Dunn hid it behind her back.

'Now, don't keep secrets from me, Ma. Does Father know about that?'

I stepped forward, pressing my skirt against him, for he still blocked my way. 'We can tell him, if you like? Tell him why your mother is finding a medicine to kill a child conceived by rape.'

His smirk fell. Mrs Dunn's free hand fluttered to her cheek, her lips, not knowing where to stop until she fixed it behind her back once more.

'Or should I tell her to take it away? Let the child live.'

Finally, he stepped aside, leaving a narrow gap for me to pass. As calmly as I could, I squeezed through and hurried for the door, swiping the vial from Mrs Dunn with trembling fingers as I went. Outside, the air was close and humid but cleaner than in the lab.

'If your little bitch comes near me again,' Pat called, 'I'll put her down.'

I didn't turn but ran for the alley, my heartbeat slamming against my ribs. Movement caught my eye: Mrs Powell creeping into the back of her store. For a second, our eyes met.

35
1900

The church bells chimed nine o'clock as Jenny joined me by the manor gates. We did not wish each other good morning – we both knew it would not be. Nothing but the drag of cotton over cotton and the clicking of heels followed us up towards the house.

Miss Stone answered the door. Confusion clouded her face when she saw Jenny.

'I need to see Mr Buckley.'

'Does he know you're calling?' She was even more hostile than usual. Was that because I had walked out on Sybil and never come back? Or was it because I had accused her employer of the most heinous things imaginable?

'I am sorry.' An apology was so unlike me that she baulked. 'I am so sorry for everything, Anne. How I treated you and Sybil. How I behaved to Mr Buckley. You do not need to forgive me, but I do need to speak to him. Please.'

She was too shocked to reply but moved aside all the

same. I grabbed Jenny's elbow and pulled her down the corridor towards his study. She tripped over her feet, too busy eyeing the grandeur of the place.

I knocked once on the door, then entered.

Buckley was bent over his desk. He was expecting Miss Stone, I imagined, and surprise made him stand to attention. He smiled on seeing me, but the smile vanished when he noticed Jenny cowering behind.

'We had nowhere else to go. We need a room for the morning.'

* * *

He showed us upstairs to an old guest chamber, stifled with the scent of musk, the bedclothes damp to the touch, a patch of brown staining the wall where it met the window. I threw open that window and let in the air of the woodland beyond, though thunderclouds were brewing over the tips of the birch trees. A throbbing was starting between my brows, from the weather or what I was about to do, I was not sure.

'Sit on the bed, Jenny.'

Buckley lingered in the doorway. Bloodshot eyes sought out mine, questioning me, doubting me, understanding me. He did not ask what my purpose was.

'We will need water. Towels too.'

He nodded and left. I placed my bag on an empty dresser and retrieved the vial. In a couple of minutes, Buckley returned with a ewer, a glass, and two towels over his arm.

Our eyes locked after he set everything down. He knew what I was about to do.

From his waistcoat pocket, he produced a silver flask and handed it to me. I lifted the lid to smell brandy.

'I don't—'

'Not for you. For her.' He nodded at Jenny. 'It's all I have left.'

Jenny reached for it. I let her sip, but not too much. She gasped and put her fingers to her lips as if bees had stung her there.

Buckley left quietly.

I didn't let myself hesitate. If I had, I would have run away and abandoned Jenny. I poured fresh water into the glass, then the ergot extraction.

'Get yourself comfortable.'

She kicked off her shoes and lay propped against the headboard.

'Drink this.'

She took it from me with quivering fingers. 'Will it kill me?'

'No. Only the baby.' My voice sounded surer than I felt, which was good. What was the point of scaring Jenny now? It was this, a quack's rusted blade, or a bastard child.

She took her chance.

I perched beside her, set the empty glass back on the table, and grasped her hand.

Then we waited.

There was no clock to tell us how much time had passed. Outside, thunder rolled closer and rain battered the windowpane.

'How do you feel?'

Jenny swallowed, ran her tongue over her teeth. 'Sick.'

She was pale, but then she was always pale nowadays.

My fingers slipped to the pulse in her wrist. It was strong. I thanked the Lord.

'Talk to me,' she said, shifting in the bed, wrapping her free arm over her stomach. 'I don't want to think of this.'

'I am no storyteller, Jenny.'

'What happened before you came to Bodnem?'

Her fingers slid over mine, both of us damp and clammy. She gestured for more water, and I poured it into the glass and held it to her lips.

As I had done with Matthew Pendleton.

'I was a governess. Nothing special.'

She winced at something going on inside her. 'I wish I could have had a governess. One like you.'

'You don't.'

'How did you fall in love with Mr Edwards?'

'Love.' I breathed a laugh. 'It wasn't… Love is a rare thing, Jenny.'

'But you do love your husband, don't you?'

'Not everybody marries for love.'

Her head fell back. She gazed dreamily at the silk canopy. 'Then why do it at all?'

The knuckle in her throat bobbed up and down. The colour of her skin was changing, bruising like the clouds outside. 'I think I…'

I was not quick enough. She lurched forward. The purge was a violent one, splattering onto the rug under my feet, flecking the bottom of my skirt. She dragged in a breath, her lower lip trembling and dripping vomit, her eyes round and glassy as she looked at me, trying to apologise.

'It's fine. The medicine is working. We need a bowl.' I raced into the corridor as her wails of terror scratched at my back. I ran all the way into Sybil's quarters. Bursting into her room, I grabbed the basin, leaving the jug behind, and sprinted back to Jenny.

She had curled onto her side. Another layer of vomit was pasted on to the old one. Her eyelids had closed. She was beginning to shiver.

'I'm here.' I set the bowl into the nook of her stomach.

'It hurts,' she whimpered.

'Where does it hurt?'

But another purge silenced her. There was little left in her stomach now. She retched a yellow, watery bile, and I climbed onto the bed and wiped her lips with a clean towel.

'Not long, Jenny. Some hours of discomfort and it will all be over.'

I leaned over her. A cold sweat clung to her forehead and made black curls of her hair. Her breathing was too shallow.

'We should put you under the covers.'

She didn't move.

'Jenny, you're cold. Shift this way and we can get you covered up.'

But again, she did not move, only grunted at me.

I forced her onto her back. Her arms flopped by her sides, but she was conscious. She looked at me, wet her lips.

Then she buckled.

Her whole body juddered, snapping in and out like a wet sheet in a stiff breeze. I could do nothing but watch as she cried.

Whole years elapsed in those few seconds before she grew still again.

'Jenny?'

'Where...?' She tried to lift her head but failed – I saw the strain of it in the tight, raised bones of her neck. She frowned at the room around her, widening her eyes and then squinting, as if the world was blurred.

'We're at Mr Buckley's manor, remember? We're safe. You're going to be fine.'

I lifted her limp wrist, checked the pulse again. It was weak, barely noticeable, and slowing down.

'Jenny?'

Her eyelids shut. I slapped her cheek gently, then harder when she didn't rouse. A blue slither of eyeball appeared.

'Jenny, say something. Talk to me about something.'

Only the flutter of her chest remained, the involuntary twitching of her legs. That was all there was to tell me she was alive.

'I... I'm going to see if anything is happening.' Under her petticoats, blood slowly seeped over white flesh.

And then I was sick.

With relief, with worry, with realisation.

I gulped a glass of water, forcing it down, though it bubbled back up my throat. I moved back to Jenny's side, leaned against the board, and cradled her head. Beneath her lids, her eyes rolled. As long as they kept rolling, as long as her body kept twitching, I knew she was alive.

So I waited. I waited with her in my arms, silent, as good as dead.

My thumb rolled down her slick cheek, over her lips and chin. My fingers washed over her throat. I pressed lightly against her neck. She did not stir.

Now I understood.

* * *

'Can you walk?'

Jenny tested her feet on the floor and pulled herself up by holding on to the bed posts. She swayed too far forward, and I rushed to catch her before she fell.

'You should lie down for a little longer.'

As if it pained her to do so, she shook her head. 'Ma'll be wondering.'

The clock had struck three already. She had been here over six hours.

She held up her arm, and I looped it over my shoulder. Together we staggered out of the chamber, through the corridor, and down the stairs one step at a time. At the bottom, Buckley lingered in the doorway to his wing.

'I can ready a carriage for you.'

'No,' Jenny whispered.

'It will seem suspicious,' I explained, for Buckley seemed wounded by Jenny's rejection. 'Anyway, the fresh air and the walk might do her good. Help it all get out of her system.'

And so we stumbled together, alone but for the birds and the spots of rain which persisted after the downpour. The scent of the wet world was sweet after so long in that chamber, where sweat and blood had soured the air.

'Will I be all right?'

'Of course you will.' I squeezed her waist gently. 'It's over now. You need never worry about it again.'

'I feel sick.'

We were coming up to the church. She would have to walk by herself soon, so as not to arouse interest.

'Do you think you can manage on your own?'

Carefully, I peeled her arm off my shoulders. She clutched at the air for a moment, searching for something solid.

'Take my hand.'

We walked, hand in hand, to the crossroads and down the south road. Glancing up, I could see Matilda in her chamber window of the Black Heart. She nodded once, a sign of solidarity and compassion.

It took longer than usual to reach Jenny's cottage. We had to stop every so often for her to get her breath, blink the dizziness out of her mind, and check her skirts to ensure there was no more blood than before.

'What if something happens? What if I need you?'

'Send your brother to the cottage. If you feel you need a doctor, Tim will see you. But do not go out on your own.'

She nibbled her lip. Sweat persisted to cling to her brow, and her flesh refused to find colour.

'You must rest now. Tell your mother you have a sickness coming, a fever, anything, just so she will let you stay in bed. Keep warm. Drink tea.' I stroked a damp strand of hair off her temple. Her wide blue eyes bored into my own. 'You will be fine, Jenny. You will be safe.' I kissed her chapped knuckles. 'Go on, before you fall down.'

Obediently, she crept to her cottage. Each time the wind buffeted, it almost knocked her over. At the door, she turned back. A smile whitened her lips before she disappeared inside.

* * *

Mrs Crook did not let me enter the inn. She kept me on the doorstep as she called for Matilda, who clutched a shawl around her shoulders as she rushed to me. 'What is it?'

'I have found the missing piece.'

She glanced back, but Mrs Crook remained guarding her establishment. We made for the churchyard instead and huddled together under the yew tree.

'He drugged Jenny before he raped her.'

Matilda's eyes drew slowly up to meet mine.

'She took a drink from him, and then she couldn't move. I gave her ergot extraction just now and it was the same. I think he gave Betty ergot too, to get rid of the suspected baby. It explains the vomit in the yard. It explains why there were no defence marks and why she didn't make a noise. It wasn't just because she knew him; it was because he'd sedated her. And I think he did the same to the others. You need to tell Quinton.'

'But the others – why would they trust him enough to take a drink from him?'

I plucked a needle off the nearest branch and rolled it between my finger and thumb. Its poisonous juices wet my skin.

'I don't know. But Jenny once told me that Georgina Witcombe was taking chloral hydrate so she would sleep and that Mary Carr was taking chlorodyne for her cough. They would have got their medicines from the pharmacy. Pat might have dealt with them. Daisy Powell had a laudanum habit too. Think about it. He has direct access to all the drugs he needs. And who would suspect him? He's young, quiet, the son of a respected pharmacist. And if the drugs had ever shown up in the post-mortem, they could be explained away as regular medication.'

'My God.'

I flicked the yew needle at the ground.

'It's him, Matilda. I know it is. We just need something solid to prove it.'

36

1956

Birmingham city centre glimmered in the bracing winter sunshine as they piled out of the train station. Taken with the swell of the crowd, they emerged amidst the market stalls and into an ocean of people scouring the wares under shop canopies.

'She's meeting us at St Philip's,' Abigail repeated for the third time since the train had rolled into its destination. She forced her way through the throng of bodies and into the road, jumping back just in time as a bus whirred past, leaving her in a fog of fumes.

Iris took the lead and guided them safely out of the chaos.

'I thought it was supposed to have quietened down,' Abigail moaned as they twisted their way along the pavement.

Iris didn't want to point out that for Birmingham, this was quiet. Shops had begun closing in the last eighteen months with all the talk of redevelopment set to take place.

'Horrid place,' Abigail snapped. Iris had never seen her so perturbed. She was sure it wasn't just her distaste for the city that was making her snipe; she hadn't been right ever since reading about Jenny's abortion. Though she'd clutched her mother's hand and told her she'd done the right thing, the greyness of her complexion and the horror in her eyes had said otherwise. Iris had reminded her who the real villain had been in the whole ordeal. The poisoner, rapist, and potential murderer, Pat Dunn.

St Philip's Cathedral reared before them. Its long, arched windows caught the light and made the sand-coloured structure shimmer beyond the thin veil of bare trees which lined its grounds. They crossed the street and marched alongside the black iron railings.

'Where will she be?'

'West side, she said. By the statue.'

Inside the cathedral's grounds, several old gravestones protruded from the waterlogged grass. People sat on the benches, resting their weary legs and arms while loaded shopping bags slouched by their feet.

In the slanting sunshine, they waited underneath the soaring face of the church, the clock tower telling them it was now three minutes past eleven. Matilda was nowhere. Abigail strode to the statue and peeked behind its plinth, as if Matilda might have been playing a game of hide and seek.

'She definitely said here.'

'Did you get her address?'

Abigail shook her head. 'Just a phone number.'

A few more minutes passed.

'Do you think she's changed her mind?'

'God help her if she's made me trek all the way out

here on a freezing day,' Abigail muttered, and Iris tried to hide her smirk. She didn't want to be on the receiving end of Abigail's annoyance.

'Miss Edwards?'

They searched for the voice. It was coming from the nearest bench, on which sat an old lady and a West Highland terrier. She peered at them over half-circled spectacles which perched on a thin nose. With the dog lead in one hand, she was using the other to hold open a copy of the local newspaper – the apparent source of her previous attention.

'Matilda Tindall.' She didn't get up but smiled and beckoned them over. 'How long have you been standing there?'

'Ten minutes.' Abigail's snarl skimmed Matilda's head. The woman merely shook out the paper, folded it, and placed it in her shopping trolley.

'Do come and join me. This is Charles, named for my father. He's just as ill-mannered.' On cue, the dog growled at their approach, knowing they'd soon be stealing his seat and demoting his position to the floor. 'Thought I'd bag us a bench before the youths got them all.'

Abigail wiped the seat of stray dog hairs once Charles had reluctantly moved out of her way. Iris squeezed in on the other side and had to lean forward past Abigail to get a good look at the infamous Miss Tindall. It was apparent she had lost none of the temerity from her younger days as she eyed Iris and Abigail keenly.

'Your daughter?'

'Oh, no. Iris is a nurse. She's taking care of Mum.'

'Louisa Edwards,' Matilda breathed the name. 'I always wondered what happened to her. You wouldn't think someone with such a sharp mind could lose it so suddenly.'

'Well, it's been a long deterioration actually.'

Matilda fanned the air, closing that strand of conversation, and rummaged in her cognac-alligator-skin handbag for a packet of cigarettes. She pushed one into a dainty black holder before striking a match. Her fingers didn't even tremble as she lit the end. 'Why did you ask to meet me?'

Abigail veered away from the stream of smoke blown her way. 'Mum believes they got the wrong man for the Bodnem murders.'

'Is that why she went cold, then?' Matilda shifted back in her seat, catching Charles with her heel. The dog jumped up and moved to the other side. 'We'd spent weeks hunting that little rat Patrick Dunn, and when we finally caught him, she just disappeared without a bye or leave. She and her husband moved away less than a week after Pat was arrested, and I never heard from her again. She didn't even go to the trial. I assumed she was just one of those people who liked the chase, that for all she said she cared about avenging those girls, the only thing that really mattered was sticking her nose into business that wasn't hers. There's plenty of folk like that, and I should know after a lifetime in journalism.'

'So, they *did* arrest Pat Dunn?' Iris asked.

They waited for Matilda to take another drag on her cigarette. 'They gave him a sore neck too. The twenty-first of April 1901. I remember the date better than my own birthday. I drink champagne each year to celebrate.'

'And you definitely think he was the murderer?'

'Oh, absolutely.' She flicked ash onto the grass. 'If the

police had taken notice of your mother sooner, he would never have killed that last poor little thing either. But, of course, your mother and I were women. What did we know? It took a whole host of witnesses who suddenly declared they'd never trusted him and had always seen him lurking around where he shouldn't, and a stash of photos, to get him sent down.'

'What photos?'

'Pat had a hoard of photographs of Betty Crook hidden in their laboratory. Not the kinds of things you'd want your vicar to see, if you understand me? And it wasn't only Betty. Daisy Powell too, although she at least had some clothes on. It was clear he'd taken them when she wasn't aware she was being photographed.'

'That was enough to prove his guilt in court?'

'It was a start, and pretty damning. It showed his true character, after all. Nasty piece of work. The final piece of evidence came from the last victim's post-mortem. There was a substantial amount of liquid in the girl's stomach contents which proved to be a cough syrup made of heroin.' Matilda shook her head at Iris's shock. 'It was a new thing back then, a miracle drug. The Dunns sold it in their shop, and the police found it mixed with gin in Pat's hip flask. Anyway, Pat denied it until the end, as of course someone as cowardly as he would, but it was enough to convict.'

'And he went down for all the murders?'

'Those committed in 1900, yes. Jacob Hunt was finally released from custody, but from what I heard, he never had much to do with the people of Bodnem after that. Can't say I blame him.' Matilda reached the end of her cigarette. She threw the stub on the floor and screwed her heel into it.

'What about the other murders? The original three at Bodnem and the prostitutes in Birmingham.'

'The police never went digging into those. In their eyes, Reg Smith had killed his wife and Georgina Witcombe and Mary Carr, and they were sticking to that. They'd have hanged an innocent man otherwise. As for the prostitutes, no one cared enough about them. I told Quinton my theories, that I'd a witness that put Pat Dunn in the city around the time of one of the deaths, but it wasn't good enough. He said bringing that up would only weaken the case against him, so I didn't push it.'

'Didn't those women deserve justice too?'

Matilda levelled her gaze at Iris. 'They were dead. No one loved them; no one cared for them. There was no grieving family to comfort. They didn't need justice, but others like them needed a woman-killer on the end of a rope. And that's what they got.'

Iris shrank back and didn't ask another question.

'So,' Abigail probed after a moment of uncomfortable silence, 'do *you* think he killed the other Bodnem women?'

'Yes.'

'But you had a theory it all started with Dorothea Buckley.'

A smile slithered onto Matilda's lips. She grazed Charles's head and gazed out towards the tombstones. 'I was young and eager. I saw murder everywhere. But the truth was – and still is – that sometimes there is no baddie. We aren't living in films or novels. Although it would be easier to blame a murderer, we have to admit that life is not and never has been guaranteed. Most of the time, people just die.'

Iris couldn't help herself. She sat up again and took a deep breath. 'Don't you think Buckley's behaviour was odd, though? Shutting Dorothea out of his life like that. We spoke to his daughter last week, and even after Pat was arrested he remained aloof. He never talked about his past at all. What if there was something in the theory of his guilty conscience?'

Beside Iris, Abigail examined her fingernails. The mention of Sybil Buckley had reddened her cheeks. Matilda noticed it too.

'Guilty? Well, aren't we all of something? Some of us cope better with our decisions than others. He blamed himself for not being at his wife's side when she expired. By all accounts, he was a terrible husband and an even worse father. Drink does that to people. You know he committed himself to a sanatorium for the last decade of his life?'

Iris shook her head. Abigail was still studying her hands and had begun pinching off dead skin around her nails.

'That kind of place costs a fortune. That and the drink had practically bankrupted him by the time he died. Sybil inherited debts like you wouldn't believe. That's when she started selling her paintings and letting those… artists… inside her home. I visit every now and again. I wrote an article about her first painting which sold for one hundred pounds, and we became friends despite that ghastly woman always hovering in the background.'

'Miss Stone?'

Matilda grunted. 'Never liked the woman. Always had

her clutches in Sybil. It's not right for a maid.' Once again, she unclipped her handbag and found another cigarette. Abigail bristled as another plume of smoke wrapped around her head. 'You'll have seen them, then, if you visited. The paintings. Wonderful, and not a little macabre – just how I like my art.'

Abigail shot out of her seat as Matilda's fogged breath drifted her way. Charles leapt up in fright and launched himself at her, but Matilda gripped the lead just in time.

'Macabre? How do you mean?' Iris asked, aware that her time with Matilda was running out; Abigail was close to bolting.

Matilda smirked. 'You haven't noticed? The spirit of Madam Buckley is in every one of them. A whole house full of ghostly faces peeking out from the canvases. It's Sybil's signature.'

'You're wrong,' Abigail snapped. 'We have one over the fireplace, and there's no ghost in that.'

Matilda took another drag, her smirk growing. 'Then you haven't been paying enough attention.'

* * *

'Are you sure you don't mind?'

Iris shook her head as the train stopped in Jackfield. They hopped out onto the wooden platform alone before the carriages rumbled away on their journey to Bridgnorth. The weather had clouded over, and now a white mist hung low over the river.

'It's a short walk, but all uphill.' Abigail set off with the wreath she had bought at one of the stalls in Birmingham. 'Thought I might as well do it now, seeing as we've been on the train all day, as have to come back.'

'I've never been here before.'

'Dad and I come every year at Christmas to do the grave. Before that, we'd visit Grandmother once or twice during the summer and play in the graveyard – every spare minute she had was spent at church making herself useful. Otherwise she was cleaning the tile factory over there.' Abigail pointed at the giant brick building which sat beside the banks of the river. 'Samuel and I used to come down here and play in the water. Surely you must have heard of the Jackfield landslip a few years ago?'

Iris had a vague recollection of some houses sliding into the river, not that she'd taken much notice. 'Won't your father want to come?'

'He's too ill.'

Already, Iris was beginning to feel slightly sweaty, but she rushed to keep up with Abigail who strode up the hill. 'What did you think of Matilda?' She hadn't dared ask the question on the train; it had seemed to take the whole journey for Abigail to calm down after wishing Miss Tindall a swift good day.

'Typical journalist.'

'The photographs and heroin all point to Pat Dunn. Perhaps your dad was right and they did hang the true murderer.'

'We haven't got to the end of the story yet.' Abigail dragged her coat sleeve across her forehead. From this angle, Iris couldn't see her face, but she imagined it was quickly turning scarlet. 'And anyway, the police get it wrong all the time. Newspapers should never be trusted either.'

It was impossible to continue a conversation at this pace. Iris focused on breathing as they marched upwards, ignoring the lightness of her head, until they reached the plateau and she could rest against a wall. Abigail didn't pause; she headed to the church at the bend in the road.

When her pulse had ceased throbbing, Iris strolled through the church's gates and spotted Abigail at the far end of the graveyard. She had already laid the wreath against the stone and was staring at the ground with her lips set tight and her gloved hands clasped at her waist.

The stone was well tended, despite the fact Abigail only visited once a year. Someone else in the parish must have been taking care of it. The inscription was clear and told of three bodies beneath the surface. Mildred May Edwards had been buried with her parents in 1946 at the ripe old age of ninety-four.

'This is where your grandparents were born – I'd forgotten. I wonder if Howard's mother is here.'

'Grandmother never said.' Abigail edged closer to Mildred's grave.

Sensing she was intruding on a personal moment, Iris took the opportunity to check out the other stones. Wandering across the grass, the years rolled back and she found a familiar surname.

Emily Jean Edwards had a small stone which reached no higher than Iris's knee. It sat in a shaded corner where drizzle dripped from a branch onto its head. Emily had died in 1865, aged only forty-one.

'Are you a relative?' Weaving towards Iris, the old reverend smiled and nodded at the stone.

'No. But my friend might be.' She gestured at Abigail who hadn't moved.

'Miss Edwards,' the reverend called, jolting Abigail back into the real world. Hastily, she swiped at her cheek and smiled as the reverend greeted her. 'So lovely to see you. How is your father?'

'Sound of mind, but his legs…'

The reverend nodded. 'And your mother?'

'Not so fortunate.'

'She will be in my prayers tonight.'

Abigail smiled as best she could, eyes alighting on Iris in a way that meant assistance was needed. Iris stepped forward and shook the reverend's hand. 'Iris Lowe. A pleasure to meet you. That grave I was just looking at – I don't suppose there's any possibility of it belonging to Abigail's great-grandmother.'

'Iris, I told you—'

The reverend laughed. 'Why, yes.'

Words failed Abigail.

The reverend looked between them, confused. 'Mildred was always taking care of it, so now I make sure it's looked after too. I thought you knew?'

Slowly, Abigail approached the gravestone and brushed her fingers over it. She started to sway, as if her legs no longer had the strength to hold her. The reverend asked if she'd like to have a seat inside the church, but Abigail shook off his offer with a laugh.

'It's been a long day, that's all.'

'I see.' He hesitated, but in the end he got the hint. 'I shall let you have some quiet. Good afternoon.'

After he'd gone, Iris guided Abigail to a wooden bench pushed up against the church wall. They stared out at the fields which sloped steeply downhill into the valley.

Woodland rose up beyond, a whole ridge of trees spiking against the horizon.

'All these years coming here, and no one ever told me about her,' Abigail whispered as the sky lost its brightness. Iris checked her watch. It was fast approaching three o'clock.

'Dad should have mentioned her.'

'Your father wasn't even born when she died. Maybe he didn't think it was important.'

'Not important?' Abigail's eyes bulged at Iris. 'She was his grandmother. His flesh and blood. The least Dad could have done was tend the grave.'

She pulled a handkerchief from her pocket and wiped her sore eyes. The day had taken its toll on her. All the anxiety and annoyance and shock had left their marks. She curled inwards, as if she'd received too many blows to the heart.

'It's as if he's able to just shut a door and close off parts of his life. How many others has he shut?' Abigail pinched the bridge of her nose and closed her eyes. She sniffed back her emotions.

'He cried when my grandmother died. He cried at her funeral too. Mum never did.' Abigail's gaze drifted to Mildred's final resting place. 'I hated my mother that day. I hated the way she never even tried to comfort him. I wished her dead. The only time in all my life I've ever thought such a thing.'

A single tear dripped down Abigail's cheek and landed on her coat. 'I always wondered if that's why he sent her to Smeldey. A form of revenge for being so cold.'

Iris now realised why the date on Mildred's grave seemed familiar. It was the same year that Louisa had penned her letter. A month after her mother-in-law's death, Louisa had written about what had really happened at Bodnem.

Abigail stuffed the handkerchief back into her pocket. Daylight was rapidly failing. The street lamps would be coming on soon.

'We'd best get going.'

Abigail nodded and tiptoed to Emily's grave. 'I'll bring you flowers soon.' At Mildred's, she kissed her fingers and laid them over the stone. 'Merry Christmas, Grandma.'

37
1900

Matilda walked me back from St Luke's churchyard towards the doctor's cottage. Both of us seemed a little dazed by the horror of Pat Dunn's calculated killings.

At the gate, she paused. 'I haven't asked – how is Jenny?'

I tried to shield my face, knowing my worries and fears were writ all over it.

The door of the cottage opened. Tim stood under the lintel, glaring at me. Matilda and I froze.

'What's wrong?'

He stormed out, grabbed me by the arm, and dragged me inside. 'Why did you take Jenny to the manor?'

'What—'

'She's been there all day, and she comes back unable to walk.'

'How—'

'You think people don't have eyes in this village, Louisa? You think secret meetings in laboratories and mansions don't get whispered about?'

'It has nothing to do with them.'

'Rumours are spreading. What were you doing?'

I shrugged out of his grasp. 'It is none of your business.'

'You are my wife. You will not keep secrets from me.'

'But you can keep them from me?'

We stared at each other, neither of us relenting. The longer I remained silent, the more Tim shuddered with rage. Still, I did not expect to feel the back of his hand across my cheek.

'What have you done to Jenny?'

Reeling, I held my stinging skin. 'I have helped her.'

'Tell me what you have done!'

'What you would not do for Betty! I have saved her from a life of ruin.'

His skin bleached. 'She was with child?'

Further down the hallway, Mildred and Howard watched us. Neither of them moved.

'My God.' Tim brushed his hand over his face. 'What did you do?'

'Gave her ergot extraction.'

'You might have killed her.'

'She lives. She is at home. She will recover.'

He dashed to the medical office and grabbed his case.

'What are you doing?'

'I will check on her.'

'You cannot. Her father cannot know.'

Without speaking, he shoved me out of the way. My shoulder smacked against the wall, my head following shortly after, but I recovered swiftly, spearing my question at Tim before he disappeared. 'Were there drugs in Betty Crook's system?'

He halted, hand on the doorknob. Slowly, he faced me.

'What about Daisy Powell's? What about the other three women?'

'What are you talking about?'

'It was Pat who killed them. He drugged them first, then strangled them. Why didn't you see it in the post-mortem?'

Shock slackened his features. 'They were strangled. I did not test for poison. They did not die from poison.'

I met his gaze. 'I never said they did.'

He was out of the door before I could stop him.

My ragged breath was the only sound in the hallway. Slowly, I turned towards my in-laws. I didn't know if the disappointment in their eyes was for me or Tim.

Howard stalked into the parlour. Mildred crept into the kitchen with my son, closing me out. I was not welcome, so it seemed. Would I ever be welcome again?

For the second time in my life, I had nowhere and no one.

Except Buckley.

* * *

'What's happened?'

I fell across the manor's threshold. Buckley caught me, lifting me up against his chest as I sobbed.

'Is it Jenny?'

I shook my head.

He guided me into the corridor. Instead of taking me to his study, he led me into the room beside it. The library. Books filled every wall, and a small ladder was propped up against the shelves. A sideboard held a fruit bowl and a drinks set, and a Persian rug cloaked the floor. I dropped into one of the sagging armchairs before the empty grate. Buckley poured us both a glass of spring water from the cut-glass decanter.

'Sorry there's nothing stronger.'

We sipped.

'Will you tell me what is wrong?'

My tears were drying. I sat shrivelled in the chair like a piece of ash. 'They think I'm evil.'

'Who?'

'My family. Tim. They know what I did to Jenny.'

'How?'

I couldn't answer. I hadn't the energy to relive what had just happened.

'You did what you thought was right.'

'Why do you say it like that? Do you think I was wrong?'

He shook his head and smiled softly at my paranoia.

'I heard you talking to Jenny earlier. About Tim.' Buckley eyed the bottom of his drink. 'That you didn't marry for love.'

I fingered the lump that was forming above my left temple and the tenderness of my cheek, then pressed the cool glass against it. 'Neither did you.'

'No. But you can't say yours was for money either. So, what was it?' When I didn't answer, he continued, 'Samuel, I assume. It explains you helping Jenny like that, and your sudden departure from your old governess situation. He was an accident?'

I drank again. 'I told Tim I'd throw myself into the canal if he didn't marry me.' My breath grated in my throat. 'I would have. Couldn't bear the shame of it otherwise. My parents had disowned me. I would have been destitute, no better than a whore. To my astonishment, he agreed. I think we all would have been better if he'd refused.'

He let the idea settle between us, then, 'Why are you so unhappy?'

'I have just put a girl's life at risk.'

'No. You have always been unhappy, all the time you have been here.'

I flinched. I did not want to think about what had been plaguing my life for months.

'I understand grief, Louisa. I have lived with it for the last five years. Even more, I understand guilt. I see it in you too.'

I closed my eyes. Catherine Pendleton's scarlet cheek. The dented pillow. The syrup bottle.

'Tell me,' he whispered.

'It is too dreadful.'

'I was honest with you.'

'This is different.'

He waited.

My tongue barricaded the words inside me, but it was weakening. The story that I had been swallowing day after day was pushing its way out.

'Matthew Pendleton had suffered scarlet fever.' Just his name on my lips felt treacherous.

'His father had called the doctor, and that is how I met Tim. I showed him to the child. Tim dealt with him straight away, and then… he lingered.'

I pictured him now, in that dim corridor, his hand slipping from the child's bedroom door and resting by his side, his other holding his case. I had walked him downstairs, listened to him explain his course of treatment to the Pendletons in the drawing room, and led him outside.

Dusk had wavered in the warm air and wrapped the scent of early summer roses around us. We moved in silence and glanced up in unison as a bat swooped over our heads. Mr Pendleton's groom had Tim's pony and trap ready and doffed his cap before leaving us alone.

'All my life I have been considered plain, Mr Buckley. Too serious. Too intelligent. What good are those things for a woman? I thought, when I became a governess, that I would find a place for myself. That I would fit. But nothing changed. Again, I was this odd thing, floating between somewhere and nowhere. Hated, ignored, passed over.'

As I was now.

'Tim was the first person to see me. To... want me. I am ashamed of my vanity. My weakness to want to be wanted.'

Buckley's fingers stretched to mine. 'Everybody longs to be loved.'

I studied his skin. His hands had not done what mine had done.

'Matthew was so terribly ill. Coughing, feverish. I stayed up with him for nights on end. No one else did. Tim came every day.'

I prepared myself to say it.

'I just wanted to feel something else. Forget the pain and exhaustion and fear, just for a moment. Matthew was sleeping. I thought he was sleeping...'

A handkerchief appeared before me. Buckley dabbed my cheeks with it – I was crying again.

'The old nursery had been made up for me, the room

next door to Matthew's. We were in there only minutes. Just minutes. And then Catherine saw us. She'd come looking for me after finding her brother alone and... dead.'

I hid my face with the handkerchief, for I could not look Buckley in the eye. 'It was my fault he died.'

'No.'

'I wasn't there.'

'It was an accident.'

'That means nothing.'

'That means everything.' Buckley's arm wound around me. His warmth cradled my side. 'His blood is not on your hands, Louisa. He was a sick child. There was nothing you could have done.'

I could not bear to hear any more.

My lips stopped his from speaking.

In a second, we broke apart.

Was I going to do it again – lose myself, as I had done with Tim? It didn't feel the same this time. Tim was like putting my hand on the stove top – searing and instant. This was like sunshine on an autumn day.

In the end, I didn't have to decide. Buckley did it for me.

The leaves were black eyes winking against a watercolour sky. They fluttered against the windowpane, tapping like raindrops. Beyond them, the first stars of the night began to shimmer, like diamonds scattered in water.

Buckley's shirt lay open to his chest; his collar and waistcoat were discarded on the floor. He was all shadows in this light, but the sight of him, the feel of him, was imprinted on my mind and body.

He picked a grape off its vine and rolled it between his fingers, warming it. He tore through the crisp skin, the soft flesh. I bit into a slice of orange and tasted Spain on my tongue.

It would have been the life Dorothea could have had if she had lived. If she had loved Buckley instead of my husband.

I dropped the peel. 'I should not be here.'

I needed to return to the cottage and find out what had happened with Jenny. It was cowardly to stay.

What would I tell Tim, though? How would I explain what I had been doing? Terror, guilt, longing – would they be as readable as newsprint when he looked at me?

My stockings hung over the arm of the chair like shed snakeskin. I unfurled, and Buckley watched me slide them on. Despite the falling temperature, I flushed against my chemise and reached for my petticoat and stays. Each garment was a piece of real life coming back, heavy and constricting.

'I will walk you back.'

'You mustn't. Think how it will look.'

'I will not let you walk alone at night when a killer is loose.'

I smiled down on him, cupped his cheek. Odd, how it seemed so easy to touch him. As if he were mine already. I had never touched Tim like that.

'At least I would know to run if I saw Pat approaching.'

When my stays were fastened, Buckley lit an oil lamp on the sideboard. I flinched against the brightness, my gaze falling on the fruit we had devoured.

'Some part of it is not making sense.'

I had told him about what had gone on at the laboratory, then what I had realised as Jenny lay drugged and paralysed on the bed. I had explained how Pat must be the killer.

'You don't believe me?'

'No. Not that,' Buckley said. 'But what about Connie Smith? It doesn't fit with your theory about drugs from the pharmacy.'

'She had belladonna in her stomach. Jenny said they'd been out picking blackcurrants. Perhaps Pat saw them, and the idea struck him.'

'But belladonna berries were found in the bowl in the house. If you are saying Pat planted them there, he would have had to have gone inside. I can't see how he would have done that.'

'Well' – I threw up my hands – 'I don't know. Perhaps she really did pick the wrong berries, and it was a coincidence.'

I fastened my skirt. I didn't want to think about the murders after what we had just done.

Buckley returned to his chair and stared into his empty glass. I stepped around him to the mirror above the mantelpiece and tried to remember how my hair had been styled before Buckley had tugged it out of its pins. It fell in limp waves to my waist, the same colour as mud. Not at all as spectacular as Dorothea's hair. Not at all as thick and soft and glimmering.

'Georgina certainly does not fit.'

I abandoned the notion of trying to style my hair and grabbed my blouse instead. 'You confirmed she was taking chloral hydrate.'

'Yes, but she never bought it from the pharmacy. Georgina never stepped foot in any of the village shops. She never so much as bid good day to any of the villagers. Pat had absolutely no link with her.'

'Perhaps he got talking to her in the graveyard.'

'She would never have accepted anything from the likes of him.'

'She must have got her medicine from somewhere.'

Buckley paused. 'Tim prescribed it for her.'

I had missed a button on my blouse; it was all askew.

'I asked him here to see Mary too. See if anything could be done for her cough. He recommended the chlorodyne.'

My fingers fumbled as I unpicked my buttons from the bottom up.

'Louisa?'

I pulled too hard; a button snapped off.

'Did you hear what I said?'

'Yes!'

My knees crumpled. The chair slammed into my backside, saving me from the floor. 'You can't possibly think my husband—'

'He would have had access to the drugs too. No one would question what they took from him. If they met him outside at night he could say there had been an emergency.'

'He had no reason.'

Buckley sat beside me, elbows piercing his thighs, thinking.

'The first was Georgina. She knew the truth about Sybil, and she was mad enough to talk about it, in the end. That is the first motivation. Mary… she wanted this place. She would have seen Sybil, would have found out the truth eventually.'

'He had nothing against Connie Smith.'

Buckley swatted away my argument. 'It stopped when he left and started when he returned.' Buckley leaned back, frowned at the ceiling. 'What if you are right about Betty Crook being poisoned with ergot, but by Tim, not Pat? What if the baby was real? After all, we have only his post-mortem which says otherwise.'

'Why would he lie?'

'Because it was his.' He laughed. 'It's not the first time he's got the wrong woman pregnant.'

'But he told me…' Could he have lied all along? I had witnessed him do it before.

'Perhaps Daisy Powell knew. She and Betty were cousins,' Buckley whispered, ruminating on his own thoughts as my ribs felt close to snapping.

'He didn't find the drugs in the bodies on purpose?' I whispered. Air would not come to me. My vision blackened.

I was in the Black Heart Inn, squashed between the door and a farm worker. The bell was banging against my hat. Tim was standing beside the window, half his face in the light, the other in the shadows. He was talking over Betty's corpse, saying *copycat killer*.

Copycat killer.

He had been the one to first utter those words. He had planted the idea from the start. To cover himself.

I pressed my fingers to my lips, uncertain whether I could contain my nausea.

I had known all along, hadn't I? From the moment I had seen the grey pallor of Betty's skin in the dawn light.

From the moment he had told me to stop interfering. From the moment I had smelt his scent lingering in the air when I lay bruised and shaking by the lakeside, reaching out for his son.

The bottle meant nothing. Tim was living in Bodnem when Georgina and Mary and Connie had died. There was no exorcism; there had been a job opening in Birmingham. There was no releasing of a trapped spirit; there had been an ailing country doctor who needed his son back.

I had known what Tim was capable of since he had hidden that syrup bottle the first time, since he had diagnosed pneumonia as the cause of Matthew Pendleton's death. That was the true reason why he married me: because we were the same.

We were murderers.

38

1900

'You can't go back.'

'He has my son.' I fastened my shoes.

'Louisa, please.' Buckley grabbed my arm.

'Call Quinton. Tell him what you have told me.'

'There is no proof.'

'Women are dying!'

He looked at the fireplace, avoiding my blazing gaze.

'Fine. I will do it.'

Again, he stopped me. His fingers burned my wrist, pinched at the thin bones there. 'Think about what you are doing. Think of your life. Of your son's life.'

'Samuel is better a bastard than the son of a murderer.'

'It will be your word against Tim's. Only hours ago you were saying it was Pat Dunn, absolutely convinced of his guilt. Now you have changed your mind, accusing your husband, a medical man, a doctor! Everyone knows you for a troublesome woman, a troublesome wife. Paying Tim no heed, cuckolding him, looking as if—'

'What? What!'

His grip vanished. He rubbed his face. 'You will look hysterical.'

The sideboard cut into my hip as I backed away from him. The truth was a sword I never thought he would wield so brutally.

'I will gladly look mad if it stops him hurting anyone else.'

'Don't you see? If you appear mad, you won't be able to stop him at all.'

Buckley returned to his seat, leaving me clutching the wall for support. He was right. The threats had been in Tim's words before. No one would blame him. No one would stop him from sending me away for a while, to recover, to rest, to cease these hysterical thoughts and ways. Would I ever see my child again?

'You need to tell Quinton.'

He said nothing.

'Philip? Did you hear me?'

'If it comes from me, they will have to know other things.' He squeezed his knuckles. 'The truth. All of it.'

I paced to the window. All was black beyond; the night had fallen in on us. 'You will let others die for your pride?'

'Not my pride. For Sybil. What would her life be like? Known as an illegitimate bastard, her mother an adulteress, her father a murderer.' He cleared his throat and buttoned up his shirt. 'Anyway, if anyone found out about what you and I... They might say we framed Tim. No. If Tim is to be punished for his crimes, he will have to be caught properly.'

The clock struck eleven. We listened to every chime in silence. By the end, I still could not believe his cowardice.

Shoes clipped towards the door. Bones knocked on wood. Neither of us moved.

The light from the corridor blinded us. Miss Stone's silhouette was pushed out of the way, and Tim crashed into the room.

* * *

Tim blinked with shock and removed his hat. Fiddling with the rim of it, he smirked. He addressed Buckley. 'Your way of getting back at me? I should have known.'

I waited for Buckley to deny it. He did not. 'We know you killed them.'

'What?'

'You killed them all.'

Tim's laugh cracked through the room. 'You think I am the murderer now? How?'

'Poison,' Buckley said, taking the word from my lips. 'You sedated them, then you strangled them. Georgina with chloral hydrate. Mary with chlorodyne. Connie with belladonna.'

'How many whiskies have you had today, Philip?'

Buckley snarled but continued, 'Laudanum for Daisy.'

Tim was still laughing, although it had long left his eyes. 'This is absurd.'

'We can't decide if you used ergot for Betty's unwanted child, or if you were telling the truth about the phantom pregnancy.'

'I am not a killer.'

'Did it start with Dorothea?' I asked, finally finding my voice. Both of them jumped at the sound of it, as if they had completely forgotten my presence. 'Did you kill her after she had given birth to your child?'

Tim's cheeks stained red. 'I could never—' He pinched the bridge of his nose. 'I loved her. And I love my daughter.'

'Swear it,' Buckley said. 'On Sybil's life, swear you have not killed any of those women.'

They held each other's gaze, and once again, it was as if I had vanished.

Tim's lips parted, showing a slice of white teeth, and the words slithered up his throat. 'I swear on my daughter's life that I have not killed anyone.'

'He is lying,' I said.

'You will be quiet, Louisa.'

'Or what? You will punish me for not being the good little wife?'

'God knows you deserve some punishment!' Tim towered before me. 'Setting me up as the murderer. Which number am I? How many have you accused now?'

'We know it is you.'

'Always looking for someone to blame, aren't you? Because that way you won't blame yourself.'

The words struck me, as good as any fist. I limped back.

'You want her?' he asked Buckley. 'You think having her will get at me, the way Dorothea and I got at you?'

Buckley growled. They were like stags locked in horns. And I realised that none of this had been about me. This was between them. Years of anger at each other over a love for one woman and one child. But never me. I had been a pawn for them both.

Did Buckley really believe Tim was the killer, or was it

an idea which sprang from the jealousy that coursed through his veins?

'I will say it again: I did not kill anyone.' Tim glanced between Buckley and I, geeing himself up. He was going to say it. I saw the words pulling at his lips. Vengeance for bringing his lies to the surface. The surest way to condemn me. 'There is only one murderer in this room.'

The wall met me. Tim's eyes were black, as black as they had been that night. Black with lust, with anger, with fear.

'I wonder if he would kiss you if he knew the truth.' His eyes glistened. 'After all I have done for you. All I did for you back then. How I have tried to love you, make you happy, keep you safe. And you accuse me of this?'

'What are you talking about?' Buckley asked.

'Tell him about Matthew Pendleton.'

I edged back, but there was nowhere to go. Tim blocked my exit. Trapped. In one stifling room, like that night. With death on the air.

'Tell him!'

'I can't!' I cried.

How Matthew had cried that night. How there had been nothing but crying and the scraping of air through clogged lungs. Endless. Whimpering and whining, beating my efforts away as he always did, as the pair of them always did. Scorning me. Working against me. Despite my care and attention, which they never received from either parent.

'Louisa?' Buckley asked, turning from Tim to stare at me.

'Tell him!'

'I just wanted ten minutes. Just for it to stop. Just to be with you.'

'Excuses. Always.'

'I didn't know it was dangerous. You prescribed it. You said it was safe.'

'I told you, just a drop.'

I shook the thought out of my head. The bottle. The teaspoon. Just to ease him. To make him sleep.

'What did you do?' Buckley said.

I couldn't say it. If I did, it would all seem too real.

'The child was suffering,' Tim explained. 'Last year, there was a new drug available.'

'You're still using it.'

Tim stiffened but ignored me.

'Heroin. Better pain relief than morphine, no chance of dependency. Aided breathing, helped give rest, that sort of thing.'

'I just wanted him to sleep! Some peace, for him and me.' My face was wet, sopping with tears.

'She gave him too much.'

'It was an accident!' But when they looked at me, I knew they did not believe me.

'That is not what you told me,' Buckley said.

'How could I tell you? You wouldn't understand. And it *was* an accident. I never meant to kill him.'

'But you did,' Tim said. 'And you made sure you covered your tracks.'

I felt Catherine's cheek against my palm, the sting of it. She'd seen me fucking her family's doctor as her brother lay dying in the next room. The threat had been in her eyes – to expose us. The violence only kept her quiet for so long, until just after the funeral, when her mother's embrace finally loosened her tongue.

But Mrs Pendleton had only thought it negligence. Matthew had died of pneumonia, as Tim had declared on the death certificate. And what good would it do to let everyone know they had let a whore watch over their sick son because they could not be bothered to do so themselves? Because his own mother could not bring herself to love such a petulant, whining, spiteful child.

Tim's reputation had dwindled. The money had stopped coming in. Because of me.

Because of me, Tim had accepted the plea from his father to come back here.

I brought him back.

I killed Betty and Daisy.

My knees collapsed. I slid down the wall and thumped into the floor, unable to get a wisp of air into my lungs.

'You get notions, don't you?' Tim's voice was distant in my ears. 'You get sad too. You were sad at the Pendletons', with Matthew, and you wanted it to stop.' He stepped closer; I peered up at his legs, at his hand reaching out for me. He touched my cheek, raised my face so I met his gaze. 'I did not kill those women.'

Lies slipped easily from his lips. I had seen them do so before. He shifted back, knowing I didn't believe him.

'Get out of my house,' Buckley whispered, standing and rousing us both.

'Please, Philip, believe me. It was an accident. He is lying.'

'Leave!' Buckley crushed the back of his chair; his eyes told me he wished it were me instead.

Tim dragged me to my feet and hurled me along the

corridor. I did not fight. I could not fight. All my strength had bled away. My bones felt hollow, my brain scooped out. Only once we were outside did I shrug out of his grip.

'Come home.'

I did not move.

We glared at each other before the wall of windows.

'Fine,' Tim snarled. 'Stay here. But you've lost him, Louisa.' He glanced towards home. 'And if you don't come back, you'll lose everything else.'

39
1956

Abigail slammed the notebook shut. She had started to cry a while ago; now her tears scored down her cheeks in torrents. It was causing a fuss. The other patients were becoming agitated and were making their way over to see what was going on. Abigail ran for the toilets.

By Iris's side, Louisa looked at the wall. Her face was blank, her eyes half-closed. One might believe she hadn't understood a word of what her daughter had read. One might believe she had thought the story was something from a novel. One might believe her mind was as soft as cotton inside that skull if it weren't for the way her fingertips drove into her thighs.

'You could have saved Pat's life,' Iris whispered.

'I was wrong,' Louisa said mechanically. It was a phrase that had got stuck in the brain, as often happened with demented patients. A constant cycle of thought that they were unable to move on from. Iris knew that Louisa would be muttering this for the rest of her life. Until the day she died, she would be living with the guilt of allowing the wrong man to hang.

'Did Tim hold it against you – what you did to Matthew? Did you keep quiet to save you both from the noose?'

Louisa took a long, quivering breath.

How could Louisa have lived with Tim when she believed he was a killer? How could she have let her child be raised by such a monster? How could she have let him close enough to father Abigail?

Iris swallowed. She pinched her lips tight before she said something she would regret. She dashed for the toilets instead and heard Abigail weeping in one of the cubicles. As Iris knocked on the door, the weeping ceased momentarily before she said who it was.

'Can I come in?'

The lock flicked back. Abigail bowled into her arms and sobbed on Iris's shoulder. There was no room for words just then. There was no point in muttering condolences. Nothing Iris could say would make this any easier.

Iris hugged Abigail tighter and rubbed her back. Her uniform soaked up the tears.

'I can't believe he was the murderer.'

Abigail grabbed a handful of tissue and pressed it against her eyes, disentangling herself from Iris as she did so. Her sobs had diminished and were now nothing more than pitiful sniffs. Before the mirror, she stared at her mottled skin and ruby eyes, then splashed water onto her face.

'For all his faults, my father could not kill anyone. Of that I would wager my own life.'

The loose flesh under her chin trembled as she tried to

remain in control of herself. She threw the spent tissue paper into the toilet.

'There's still some pages left to read,' Iris reminded her.

Abigail shook her head. 'I can't bear the sight of her. Not after what she did to that little boy…' Her chin began to quiver once more. No matter how ferociously she blinked, tears were forcing their way through. 'I'm sorry, Iris. I can't go back in there.'

Abigail rushed out of the toilets. However quick Iris ran, Abigail was faster. Iris stopped in the corridor and watched Abigail dash for the hospital's exit. She didn't try calling her back.

Inside the day room, the notebook sat in Abigail's seat. She took it to the staff room and slipped it into her bag.

The rest of the night passed in a blur. Iris went through the motions without realising what she was doing; one minute she was sloshing corned beef hash into bowls and the next she was tucking the women into their beds. Her mind was in Bodnem, running through the murders one by one.

Georgina Witcombe – Tim would have had reason to kill her because she knew about Sybil.

Mary Carr too, at a stretch.

Could Betty Crook have really been pregnant with Tim's child? Anything seemed possible.

But Connie Smith?

And always the most baffling of all, Daisy Powell.

The prostitutes only compounded the confusion.

What was the meaning of it all? Why had Tim chosen who he had?

Louisa sat in her nightgown on the edge of her bed.

Tentatively, Iris approached. Neither of them spoke as Iris brushed her hair and helped her between the sheets.

On her bedside table, the two photographs looked out. Iris felt a jolt of nausea as she stared at two murderers holding a baby.

Louisa murmured as she gazed at the ceiling. 'The picture on the wall.'

Iris flipped the photographs face down on the table before moving on to the next patient.

* * *

At home, she tipped the notebook out of her bag. She found Tim's diaries in her drawer and set them on her bed beside the notebook.

Downstairs, she made herself a cup of cocoa. Mum and Dad were already in their room and sleeping, if her father's snoring was anything to go by. She spooned two sugars into her cup, something she wouldn't get away with if her mum had been around, before trudging upstairs once more.

Her bedside lamp illuminated the room in a golden glow. Settling herself against her pillows, she drank her cocoa while staring at the books before her.

Then she began.

40
1900

The night was hot. The air as thick as soup, spilling into my mouth, my nose, filling up my lungs. Clouds had brewed and blotted out the stars, as if an ink pot had fallen on the world.

All was still. Unfamiliar sounds carried loudly towards me: shuffling, sniffing, snapping. Croaking frogs simmered from the lakes beyond the manor house. Not far away, something pawed at the woodland floor.

This was the time for night creatures and women-killers.

'I'm sorry,' I whispered into the darkness as I shifted down against a tree trunk. I had not meant to kill Matthew Pendleton. Out of everything, that was the only thing of which I was certain.

Yet I had poured the cough medicine. Two spoonfuls. And only an hour after the last. Because I knew Tim was coming, and I wanted to be alone with him.

Just two spoonfuls and everything changed. Forever.

I closed my eyes. No longer did I fear the night. What was the point? The worst things were already in my mind.

My chin dropped. Dreams fell through my mind, like grit being sifted for gold. Time became immeasurable.

At one point, my eyelids flickered open. The horizon bled as the sun dipped its toes into the day to see if it wanted to come out.

Sleep took me again. Nightmares screamed inside my skull.

Peering up, I could see the orange was brighter now, tainting the clouds. If I held my breath and listened very carefully, I could hear other noises. Voices. Shouts. Screams?

I pushed against the tree, rolled on the balls of my feet. My eyelashes were crusted together, and I picked at them until I could see more clearly. Each time I breathed in, something tickled the back of my throat. A familiar scent, one I should have known and yet couldn't place.

Staggering out of the woodland, I made my way past the manor house. Its windows were black. I checked the top right pane, expecting to see Sybil, but there was nothing. Everyone inside was asleep, or at least pretending to be. I wondered, if I were to have twisted the doorknob, would I have found it locked to keep me out?

I didn't ponder for too long. The scent had become clear. Smoke.

I was running by the time I saw flames licking up beyond the roof of St Luke's. As I clattered past the manor gates, yells of panic reverberated around me. Men dragged buckets of water, women clutched their children close, and all of their faces glowed red and yellow, their eyes mirroring the fire that raged.

The fire that raged from my home.

The cottage was ablaze. Already, it was being reduced to its wooden bones, the wattle and daub unable to fight. Structures shattered; floorboards crumbled; the thatched roof dropped like dollops of batter from a spoon. The heat scalded the air, pouring over me like water.

'Samuel,' I breathed. 'Samuel!'

I ran for the house. I would have plunged into the furnace and singed the skin off my bones if only I could have saved my son. Even as I went, I knew there was no way a baby could survive such a thing. But I ran on, because if I could not save him, of all people, then I would be glad to let the flames blister me to ash.

Someone caught me around the waist. I folded against them, kicking and punching.

'My son!'

They thrust me against the ground before wiping a soot-greased forehead and finding another bucket. When they turned, I scrambled to my feet once more.

'Stop!' The voice chimed with another arm colliding against my chest. It wrapped around me, pulled me against a body, reeled me back. No matter how I fought, it held me fast and dragged me to the stone wall.

'Let me go! Samuel!'

'He's here.'

I whipped around, blinked, and saw him. My baby. My boy. In the arms of his grandmother.

Mildred was barely holding him up. Her whole body shook in her singed nightgown, her tears clear on her cheeks where they had furrowed through dust and grime.

The arm around my shoulders belonged to Tim. He wore an ash-marked dressing gown and slippers.

'Where is Howard?'

His glazed eyes flicked towards the blaze. 'He was sleeping. We couldn't… It was too late.'

To imagine Howard in that furnace was impossible. I was too numb to feel the shock of it.

Someone screamed behind us, away from the fire. Tim gazed out across Buckley Lake.

We didn't move.

Another scream came.

Through falling embers and the grittiness of dawn light, faces turned to peer down the south road. Buckets dropped. Legs ran. Screams pierced over the roaring of the flames once again.

In a daze, I joined the throng. We ran beyond the edge of the lake, beyond the last few houses, to where the village turned to fields of sheep and grain, to where someone was weeping. I shoved past spectators, who removed their caps and whispered to their neighbours, and emerged on the other side.

A girl lay on the stone wall. An arm dangled down, the fingers gently curled. A brown skirt concealed her legs, showing only scuffed boots. A clean yellow blouse was buttoned up to her throat. Red hair tumbled over the stone, copper strands lifting and lilting in the breeze. The eyelids were closed, as pale as rose petals. She would have looked peaceful if it weren't for her swollen lip, the cut fresh and red, or for the patchwork of bruises against her jaw and hairline.

For a moment, I was suspended, held in the air by an invisible hand. I observed the scene from above, unable to understand any of it.

Sobbing brought me back down. A man and a woman

knelt beside the stones, tugging on parts of their daughter in despair. Bile rose in my throat as Mr Carr's fingers twisted through auburn curls. To my left, her brothers stared, unseeing, at a corpse they didn't recognise. Around me, voices whispered. 'What was she doing out?'

The older boy looked to the ground, wiped his cheeks with his sleeve. John spoke for the family. 'She ran away.'

Mr Carr winced. The bruises, then, were his doing. She would not have run after I had told her not to. She was more frightened of the devil within her home than the devil outside of it.

More villagers came. Mrs Dunn pushed through and halted at my side, hand to mouth, eyes popping at the sight of Jenny on the wall. Her son collided with her and stopped short.

'Madam Buckley,' Mrs Dunn whispered. 'The spirit's taken her. She let the spirit out. It was her fault all this started in the first place.'

Mrs Carr snapped her head at Mrs Dunn, eyes brimming with water and rage. Then she lunged. The two women tussled, dragging each other down to the ground, fists full of skirts and hair and skin.

'Stop it!' John screamed, when nobody else made a sound. The boy ran at them and yelled above their heads. 'It was us!'

The women peeled apart.

'We found the bottle. I opened it. It wasn't Jenny; it was me.' John sobbed into the crook of his elbow, turning away from the group. Will Powell went to his friend and placed an arm on his shoulder. John shrugged him off, but he persisted until both of them wept on each other's shoulders.

They blamed themselves.

I couldn't look at the body on the wall, at the person who, I now realised, had been my only true friend in this place.

At the back of the congregation, Pat edged away, but Mrs Powell saw him.

'I heard you. You said you'd put the bitch down if she came near you again.'

Pat whitened. 'That's a lie.' But for all his denial, guilt was clear in his face. The crowd grew hostile. He backed away, hiding behind his mother, until he bolted. Men followed; he wouldn't get far.

Overhead, the flames grew higher. I staggered back to the cottage, to the stone wall where Mildred held Samuel and Tim hugged his robe tight. He was not surprised when I told him what had happened.

My forehead hit his chest. I wept against him. I wept for everything. For a friend I should have saved. For a man I had loved better than my own father. For a mother-in-law who had protected my son. For a husband who was a murderer, but who was the only person who could comfort me now.

Tim pulled me close and planted his lips on my forehead. 'I'm sorry,' he whispered.

He brushed back my hair. Mildred eyed us before looking away. The tears had been burned out of her – she was like a crisped slice of pork skin. I took Samuel from her limp arms before he fell.

Tim hugged me and, in turn, hugged Samuel between us. After everything, after all we had done, all the horrors we had caused, Samuel was the one pure thing to come of it all. He was the only thing that both of us loved unconditionally. He was what bound us together, forever.

He was the only thing that could stop all of this.

He was my last hope.

I snuggled him closer, that innocent babe of mine. Some smuts had fluttered against his plump white skin, freckling his cheeks, but otherwise he was perfect. I kissed his nose, and as one of my tears dripped onto his scalp, I met Tim's wet gaze.

I swallowed. Took a breath. My voice was scorched as I muttered the words which haunted the rest of our lives.

'If you kill another girl, I will kill your son.'

41

1956

Iris had come to the end. There was nothing else. No afterword by Louisa. No apology to her daughter for the shockwaves this would cause. No mention of Howard's funeral or Jenny's post-mortem or Pat's arrest.

The words just stopped.

The clock by her bedside told her it was twenty minutes past one. Her eyes felt as if they were bleeding, they were so sore. She had an urge to weep, for Jenny's murder and Louisa's hopelessness.

But she was not finished yet. She could not stop yet.

Tim's diaries lay before her. She picked one up from 1895. The handwriting was almost illegible, so small and slanted. Every day he had written a brief sentence of what had happened. It was tediously boring, until she reached the thirteenth of April.

Girl delivered. Weight eight pounds two ounces. Healthy. Buckley too drunk to see her. Dorothea died from complications.

If it weren't for the way certain spots of the paper rippled, there would be no clue as to the heartbreak Tim had endured when he wrote those words.

Outside her room, a floorboard creaked. Looking up, she saw the doorknob turn and her mum peer in through the gap.

'What are you doing up at this time?' Mum entered the room with bare feet, her nightgown skimming her ankles. She winced against the light.

Iris held up the diary. Her mum sat beside her, rested her hand on Iris's leg, and shuddered against the cold. 'You look dreadful.'

Iris laughed quietly. 'I won't be long.'

Her mum sighed at the pile of notebooks beside her. 'Can't it wait until the morning?'

'I have to do this for Abigail.'

'Have you figured it all out yet?'

'Nearly.'

Mum smiled and got to her feet. She kissed the top of Iris's head and tiptoed out of the room. Iris listened to the gentle creak of her parents' mattress as her mum settled in for the rest of the night. She dragged the eiderdown closer against the chill and carried on reading.

On the third day when Abigail didn't come to see her mother, Iris decided she'd had enough of waiting. Her calls had not been answered. Abigail had gone to ground, so it seemed.

As soon as her shift finished, she bounded down the corridor. It was late enough already. She'd have to get a train to Ludlow, then hope there was some kind of bus route that incorporated the back lanes which led to Abigail's home. Who knew how long that would take? There might not even be a train back to Shrewsbury, but she had to go. She had to do it tonight. No longer could she hold on to the information that was burning inside her.

She had no idea what the evening would hold. The only thing she was certain about was who had killed Daisy Powell and why.

Rain drummed against the pavement as she dashed through Smedley's gates. A bus waited at the nearest stop, its last few travellers filing inside and handing over their pennies. Iris sprinted for it and made it just in time. Passengers ogled her as her coat made puddles on the floor and her wet hair dried onto her face. With as much dignity as she could muster, she perched on the front seat.

She was the first to hop out of the bus and dash for the train station. The town was busy and shone with the Christmas lights which had been switched on only a couple of days ago. Shoppers milled around the station, coming and going for the late-night shopping. The scent of cinnamon mingled with raindrops and washed through the night air. Somewhere, carollers were singing; she heard their voices in between bus engines and train announcements. She joined the ticket queue, her foot tapping restlessly as the hand on the giant clock sliced into her time.

'Iris?' She blinked at the face smiling down beside her. 'I thought it was you. What are you doing here?'

Iris checked around him to see if Ava was anywhere nearby. 'Buying a cow. What does it look like I'm doing?'

Simon smiled at her rudeness. She stepped forward in the queue as another person hurried off to find their carriage.

'I need to see Abigail. The woman I was with in Woolworth's. It's urgent.'

Simon dipped his hand in a paper bag and pulled out a toffee apple. He stuffed it in his mouth and took a bite, and juice dribbled down his chin.

'Where does she live?' he asked with his mouth full.

'Not far from Ludlow.'

'Are you staying over for the night?'

Iris shook her head.

'Then how will you get back?'

'I'll sort it.'

He swallowed and wiped his chin with his coat sleeve. 'I'll take you. My car isn't far.'

'Have you not heard? There's a petrol crisis.'

'I get extra allowances.' His eyes sparkled mischievously.

'No, really. It's too far. And besides, won't Ava be waiting for you?' She glanced at his face. The mischievousness remained, and a grin tugged at his lips.

'Come on. I'll let you have a bite of my apple.' He grabbed her hand. The touch of his cold fingers made her gasp. There was a moment when both of them hesitated, but neither of them let go. Simon pulled her out of the queue and headed for the station's exit.

* * *

Iris ran her finger over the dashboard, wiping away a thin layer of dust. They were out of the town now and heading into the countryside. Simon's headlights illuminated a slither of road ahead, but all else was black. Rainclouds blocked the moon, their droplets making rivulets down the windscreen.

'How have you been?'

'Oh, fine. I was in Wolverhampton today at one of our sister branches. It was dull, to say the least.'

Iris nodded. Her mind kept tumbling back to the last time she had been in his car with him – months ago, just after he'd waited for her outside Shirley's parents' house. She'd come out crying, and he'd handed her his pocket handkerchief, and they'd driven to Smedley in silence. He'd kissed her cheek before she got out, and when he'd said goodbye it was as if they had both known things would never be the same again.

'Are you all ready for Christmas?'

She forced herself back to the present. 'Tell the truth, I haven't given it much thought.'

'Another case, Inspector Lowe?' He nodded at her bulging handbag with a knowing smile. 'What is it this time?'

'Two men were falsely hanged for killing several young women and the only person who could have saved them has been lying about it for sixty years.'

Simon's smile disintegrated. He swallowed. 'What are you going to do about it?'

'Tell him I know the truth and that I'll make sure everyone else does too.'

Simon blew out his breath. 'How will he take it?'

'I've no idea.'

Simon flicked the windscreen wipers on faster. 'Just... be careful. Please.'

She ground her teeth together. 'How is the amazing Ava? How did you meet?'

'Friend of the family.'

Exactly as Iris had suspected. 'How long have you been courting?'

Simon laughed. 'We're not courting.'

'Does she know that?'

Once again, his smile fell flat. 'We're friends.'

'Friends who go Christmas-decoration shopping together on a weeknight?' She folded her arms, for despite the fan heater coughing out as much warmth as it could muster, her extremities were still turning numb. 'She's very beautiful. She'd make an excellent wife. I suspect she knows all about hors d'oeuvres and how to shake the best martinis. Have you asked her to marry you yet?'

'We're just friends.'

'You should be quick. A girl like her won't wait forever. She's probably expecting a ring for Christmas.'

'Jesus, Iris!' Simon's grip tightened on the steering wheel. 'How many times do I have to tell you? We are friends, nothing more. All right?'

'Fine.' Iris turned her face to the window and the blackness beyond. Her pulse throbbed in her chest.

Why, on tonight of all nights, did she have to bump into Simon? She was on edge enough as it was. She didn't need this hour-long journey filled with yet more confrontation.

She vowed not to speak to him again for the rest of the ride.

They drove in silence. Only the patter of rain against the car's tin roof softened the space between them.

But when they reached the sign for Ludlow, Iris was

obliged to mutter directions under her breath. The road narrowed into a single track and Simon cut his speed. Grey branches groaned towards them in the headlights before vanishing into the darkness.

'What about you?' Simon said, his voice almost back to its normal lightness but not quite. 'You seeing anyone?'

'Don't have time. Turn left.'

He shunted down a gear and rounded the corner.

'And you know I don't want to.'

They were on the right street now, dipping down into the valley. In minutes, she would be facing Abigail and her father. Her stomach clenched.

Simon eased on the brakes and peered at the houses that speckled the countryside. 'Perhaps we'll both end up alone, then.'

42

1956

'I'll wait here.' Simon cut the engine.

'I don't know how long I'll be.'

He waved his hand. 'Take as long as you need.' He reached to the back seat and pulled his briefcase onto his lap. 'I've got a torch in here and work to do. Go on, before they go to bed.'

She made a dash for the front door, pushed herself against it to shield herself from the rain, and rang the bell. Several minutes passed with no sign of movement inside. She rang it again, and finally a light came on.

Abigail peered through the stained-glass window before opening the door. She wore her dressing gown and a pair of woollen slippers and had wrapped her hair in a silk scarf.

'What on earth are you doing here?'

'I need to speak to you and your dad. And I need to see that painting.'

Abigail glanced behind her at the grandfather clock. 'But it's—'

'The sooner I start, the sooner I'll finish.' Iris pushed past her and strode for the parlour. Tim sat in the same chair as last time, with the fire roaring by his side. He'd been slumped back, half-asleep, a glass of scotch perched perilously on the arm of the chair, but as Iris barged into his home, he woke with a start.

'What are you doing? Abigail!'

He was too weak to lift himself up. He shouted from his chair and slammed his glass on the table. Iris took no notice of his protestations, nor of Abigail pleading for her to stop. She marched straight to the mantelpiece, to Sybil Buckley's painting of the lake, and lifted it off the wall. Stuck against its frame was a slip of paper. She plucked it free, tore it open, and sighed with relief.

It had been a guess at best. All the time Louisa had been muttering about the picture on the wall, it wasn't just the photograph she had been talking about; it was this. The final missing piece. The thing which had made her write in that notebook to start with.

'I think you should sit down, Abigail.'

'Iris, please. I can't do this.' It was true. She looked frightful.

'I'm sorry, but you should know. Everyone should have known, from the start.'

'Leave my house,' Tim hissed, his fingers scraping against his chair like talons. If he could, he would have hurled himself at her.

'Your wife believed you killed all those women in Bodnem.'

'She believed many fanciful things in her time.'

'You wanted her to believe it was you. It was easier that way.'

'Abigail, get her out of here.'

Abigail hovered between her father and Iris.

'I know what happened,' Iris whispered. 'Please. You'll be scared of him the rest of your life unless you listen to me.'

Abigail bit her lip. Shaking, she edged towards her seat, wincing as her father snapped at her to do as she was told. Iris spoke over his tirade.

'Louisa said she would kill Samuel if you ever hurt another girl.'

Silenced, he glowered at Iris, but he was not shocked. Abigail was the only confused person in the room.

'You let her hold that threat against you her whole life. She knew it was the only thing she could do to stop other women dying. Can you imagine how that must have plagued her? Threatening to kill her own child? She would never have done it. I don't think she was capable of knowingly murdering someone. But that didn't really matter, did it? Because you knew you would never hurt anyone else. So you let her believe it was her threat which was keeping people safe.'

Iris sat in the chair on the opposite side of the room to Tim. The chair Louisa had once used to ease herself into. The chair on its own, stuffed up in the corner.

'To protect herself, she hardened against Samuel, didn't she? It's the only explanation for her behaviour towards him after you left Bodnem, and the only explanation for why she's been begging him for forgiveness these last ten years. Ever since she read this.' Iris held up the piece of paper that had been behind the painting. 'She realised she never had any need to hold his life against you. Because you were never the killer.'

Tim neither accepted nor denied it. Abigail stared between the two of them, then stepped before the flames to look at the painting. 'Why did you buy her this?'

'A gift.'

'A warning,' Iris countered. 'You didn't murder those girls, but you did attack your wife that night by the lake. It wasn't Samuel's cries which made the attacker flee. There was never any chance of Louisa getting killed; that wasn't the purpose. Besides, the murderer didn't attack women. He befriended them, coaxed them. You saw Louisa going out and you wanted to frighten her so she would stop investigating. She was too close to finding out the truth. This painting was just another way of reminding her of what she thought you were capable of.'

'Dad?'

He didn't answer. Horrified, Abigail crept to the drinks cabinet and poured herself a measure. She gulped it down, then filled it again.

'Do you want to tell her or should I?'

Tim didn't speak. The rage in his eyes was beginning to wane. He sipped his scotch. 'I don't know what good you think it will do all these years later. There won't be justice.'

'Not in the typical sense, but there are still some people alive who deserve the truth. Rosie Smith. John Carr. Your daughter.'

'Iris?'

She turned to Abigail. 'You were right about your father. He didn't murder those girls. But he knew who did, and he's spent his whole life covering for him.' Iris took a breath. 'Howard.'

'No.'

'Please don't lie anymore, Mr Edwards. I know it was him and not you. I know because of one simple medicine.'

'I don't understand,' Abigail said.

'Your father gave Matthew Pendleton a heroin-based syrup when he suffered from scarlet fever in 1899. Only three years before that, two children had suffered with the same disease in Bodnem. They'd been ill, but they'd survived and recovered enough to make it through the workhouse infirmary. So, what had cured them? Surely, if your father had successfully treated two children with one medicine, he wouldn't then use a new, untested syrup for another? That wouldn't make sense.'

Tim cleared his throat. His black eyes started to shimmer.

'That's because Howard treated them. And he used belladonna.'

'What?' Abigail breathed.

'Doctors had used it for scarlet fever before, but many had discounted it for its dangers. Some, though, still tested their theories. What better subjects than two poor children?'

Tim's spine collapsed. He fell back against his chair, his breath knocked from his lungs.

'Howard gave the Smith children belladonna. He believed in it – he already used it in his pipe. Belladonna had been smoked for centuries as a treatment for asthma. That's why Rosie remembered him well enough to say what a lovely man he was – a strong opinion to form, considering she was only five when she was sent to the workhouse – because he had been their doctor.'

'But how did he kill Connie?' Abigail whispered.

'The berries in the fruit bowl had nothing to do with her death, did they, Tim? Howard drugged her with her own children's medicine before he strangled her.'

Tim drained his drink and stared at the fire.

Abigail shook her head. 'No. No, it couldn't have been Howard. He was ill.' She looked at Tim desperately, but found no reassurance.

Tim wet his lips, searched for the right thing to say. 'He was sick. He... didn't know what he was doing.'

'He *was* sick. You knew just how sick, although no one else did. Louisa wouldn't have known the signs to look out for. Perhaps Mildred didn't either. But I do. The failing eyesight. The deterioration of health that had been going on for years. The mood swings. The erratic behaviour. Your father was heading into the final stages of syphilis, wasn't he?'

Tim's grip on his glass tightened.

'How did it all start, Mr Edwards? What happened?'

He paused.

'Dad,' Abigail begged.

He bit his lip.

'Please.'

Tim took an unsteady breath. 'I'd told him about Dorothea and me, about Sybil. Georgina Witcombe was starting to talk – she'd gone mad with insomnia. She was... making threats. I told him.' He cleared his throat. 'If I'd never mentioned it, if I'd kept it to myself rather than gone crying to him, he would never have started.' He faced the flames, his jaw working beneath his loosened jowls. 'I told him about Betty too. Stupid... Stupid!' His voice broke, and he angled his face away from us.

Iris had wondered why he had kept his father's murderous nature hidden. Family loyalty could only account for it so much. This was the real reason. Tim blamed himself.

'But why the others?' Abigail asked. 'Why the prostitutes?'

Tim flinched. 'What do you mean?'

'They didn't know anything about Sybil.'

'What are you talking about? What prostitutes?'

Abigail looked to Iris for help; she couldn't bring herself to explain.

'Your father killed eight prostitutes from 1896 to 1899.'

Tim reeled in his chair. 'You're lying.'

Iris opened her handbag and brought out Tim's diaries. She flicked through to the relevant pages. 'Your father visited you several times while you were working in Birmingham. Never in winter – his health was too poor to go out at that time of the year. You dined together on each occasion, and then you escorted him to the train station. Except he didn't board a train.' She pointed out the relevant dates. 'Each victim was discovered a day or two after your father had been to see you.'

'It wasn't him. He'd stopped when—'

'When the ghost was exorcised?'

'He had stopped. He promised me.'

'He lied. He never stopped. He drugged those prostitutes the same way he drugged Georgina and Mary and Connie and Betty and Daisy and Jenny. He strangled them the same way too.'

Tim shook his head.

Iris didn't blame him for not believing it. He had held on to his notion of truth for the majority of his life.

'You believed he was sick. You believed this was... a new thing. But I don't think it was.' Iris closed the diaries. 'I rang Matilda Tindall the other day and asked if she could look something up for me. Any death reports in a Shropshire village in May 1865.'

Abigail's skin whitened.

Iris continued: 'On the seventeenth of May, Emily Jean Edwards was discovered in one of Broseley's jitties. She'd been badly beaten, but that wasn't what had killed her. She was strangled. Witnesses heard her and a man arguing several nights before she was discovered. Everything pointed to the man she was living with. He had a history. He was a simple man with violent tendencies. He was arrested, and though he pleaded innocent throughout the trial, it made no difference. He spent the rest of his life in Broadmoor.

'Now, if Emily Edwards was the vile person Howard said she was, why did Mildred tend Emily's grave for four decades and shun her own husband's?'

Tim didn't move.

'It was never your fault that your father started murdering anyone. But it was your fault that you allowed it to continue. Until, of course, you didn't.'

Tim peeled his eyes away from the fire. Fear blanched his features.

Once more, Iris reached into her bag. She pulled out the photograph of Tim and Louisa holding baby Samuel.

'It was on the wall. Louisa kept saying it. *It was on the wall...* Of a house that went up in flames. By accident, apparently. But if you were too late to wake your father, how did you have time to salvage a picture?'

Abigail's hand flew to her mouth. She bent at the waist and gasped for breath.

'Was it you or Mildred who started it?'

Tim's mouth gaped. He could not speak.

'Perhaps it doesn't matter who it was. Only that one of you put an end to it.'

She turned the photograph over so she didn't have to see those fixed smiles. Abigail curled up on the sofa, hugged her knees, and sobbed.

'The only thing that linked all the victims was a very loose idea of sexual immorality, as Matilda had once said. I believe his hatred of women like that stemmed from his mother. He despised her for abandoning him and his father for another man.'

'But Jenny and Daisy?' Abigail whispered.

'Jenny's name was tarred after what Pat did to her. Her fault or not, she was tainted. As for Daisy, Howard saw the signs in her too. The early ones. The mouth sores. The itching palms. I can't prove it, but I believe Daisy had contracted syphilis from her fiancé, Jacob Hunt. Perhaps she went to Howard for help. We'll never know.'

Beyond the door, the grandfather clock chimed midnight. The three of them listened to all twelve strikes.

Simon. She'd forgotten about him out there, waiting in a cold car with rain lashing against the roof.

She set the photograph on the nearest table as well as the stack of diaries. There was no point in keeping them any longer.

In the silence, she got to her feet. Tim couldn't look at

her. His tears had dried. He didn't move, hardly even breathed. Abigail continued to cry.

There was nothing left for her to say. Iris turned for the door and walked through the hallway. She didn't know if it was just the lack of books in her handbag or something else which made her feel as if she were floating.

'Wait!' Abigail yelled, before running out of the front room and dashing for the stairs. 'Just wait there.'

Feverish footsteps thudded overhead. The electric chandelier in the hallway flickered as doors slammed open and shut. Another moment later, Abigail bounded down the stairs in a skirt and jumper, a small travelling bag thrown over her arm.

'Take me with you. I can't stay here.'

Abigail grabbed her set of house keys and opened the door. She didn't hesitate as her father shouted for her to come back.

* * *

They didn't talk on the drive back to Shrewsbury. Simon didn't ask questions.

The roads were deserted. Their companions were foxes who slipped through hedgerows and owls who perched on branches. And the rain. Constant and dribbling. The windscreen wipers hypnotised Iris into a half-sleeping trance, where images of female bodies lay scattered through her mind.

It was after one in the morning when Simon stopped outside her house. Iris didn't want to move. The car cocooned her. Wrapped snugly in her coat, she was enjoying the thrum of the engine and knowing Simon sat beside her. Why hadn't she noticed his scent before? Lime and sandalwood sifted through the air, a freshness she had been lacking for a long time.

He turned to her and smiled. The animosity from earlier had gone. The little argument they had seemed to have bled away like raindrops down glass. She smiled back.

A light lit up her bedroom window, pulling at their attention. Simon waved at the person peering out.

'Your mum's waiting.'

Iris helped Abigail out of the car, taking her bag from her. She walked her to the front door, which was already open by the time they'd passed the gate.

Mum beckoned Abigail inside and bustled her towards the living room. Over her shoulder, Iris watched Simon drive away until his little red car had disappeared around the bend.

She went straight to the kitchen and filled the kettle. She took her time to set out the cups and saucers, the teapot, the sugar pot, the milk jug. It was easier to do this than face the devastation in the other room.

The kettle hissed. She poured the water, feeling the steam weave up to kiss her face. She lifted the tray and stopped. She couldn't move.

The crockery started to tap. Unbeknownst to her, she had been shaking.

She set the tray down before she dropped it, collapsed onto a chair, and wept.

With the climax over and the truth revealed, what was left? A wrinkled balloon, drifting to the ground. They were all spent and empty.

Abigail had nowhere to go. She was jobless. Her entire

life had come to revolve around her parents, and now all that was tainted.

Tim had been right. The truth would do no one any good. It wouldn't bring back the dead. It wouldn't save a wronged man's life. Tim and Mildred had punished Howard as best they could. And as for themselves and Louisa, they had spent the rest of their lives knowing what they had done.

Truth. She had asked her mother about it once before. She had listened before. Sometimes lies were better.

'Iris?' Mum tiptoed into the kitchen. 'She could do with that tea now.'

Iris jumped to her feet, shielding her face from her mother. She didn't want anyone to see her tears for fear that they would pity her. And she deserved no pity.

She wiped her eyes with her sleeve and picked up the tray. Abigail was scrunched up on the chair before the fire, her flesh wrinkled with tears. Iris poured the tea and dropped two sugar lumps into Abigail's cup. She joined her mother on the sofa and stared into her drink, letting it scald her hands.

'I'm sorry,' Abigail whispered.

'Nonsense.' Mum draped a blanket over Iris's shoulders; she was still shaking. 'You've nothing to be sorry about.'

All of them sipped their drinks. The clock on the mantelpiece clicked in the quiet.

'What was behind the painting?' Abigail asked.

Reluctantly, Iris found the piece of paper in her handbag. She handed it to Abigail. 'Your mum went home for a few weeks after her first month at Smedley. That must have been when she planted the notebook in the wardrobe. Perhaps she suspected Tim would find it, that he'd burn it or something. So she stuck this behind the painting too, before he sent her back to Smedley.'

Abigail's eyes skimmed the paper. 'Mildred's will. She left all her money to Rosie Smith.'

'I think Louisa realised Howard was the killer after reading this will, and that Mildred had known all along. Mildred had spent the rest of her life trying to atone for it.'

Abigail let the paper drop on the coffee table. 'A whole family of murderers and liars.' She picked at her nails and snagged one off, making herself bleed. 'Thank God Samuel and I have been barren.'

She shoved her wounded finger between her lips as tears began to pour again. Mum enveloped her in an embrace. 'Come on, come and lie down. Iris, find all the blankets you can and bring down your spare pillow.'

Iris did as she was told, grateful for the instructions. Upstairs, she tugged the eiderdown off her bed and bundled pillows and blankets in her arms. She would not need them; she knew she would not be able to warm her blood for the rest of the night.

Downstairs, Mum had settled Abigail on the sofa and slipped off her shoes and coat. She took the pillows from Iris and plumped them under Abigail's wilting head, then draped the eiderdown on top of her, tucking it in by her sides. She'd put a glass of water on the coffee table beside a short stack of tissue paper and turned the gas fire down.

'Now you get some sleep, my dear. It'll all seem different in the morning.'

Mum guided Iris to the hallway, gently shutting the door behind her.

'It's my fault.'

Her mum cupped her chin. 'You did this for her.'

'I shouldn't have carried on.'

Mum kissed her forehead. Wrapping an arm around Iris's waist, she ushered her upstairs. 'You need to rest. Maybe then you'll be a bit nicer to yourself.'

43
1956

Iris woke as a door somewhere banged shut. She hugged her knees close. Her fingers and toes tingled with the cold; her coat and single blanket had fallen off her some time during the night.

Groaning, she hauled herself upright. Her neck tightened and twitched from how she had been lying as she squinted at the clock.

Ten thirty.

She yanked open the curtains. Dense clouds rippled across the sky like curdled milk. Water droplets fell from the ledges and blotted the pavements. She shuddered just looking at it all.

She pulled on an old jumper and a knitted skirt, found her thickest pair of stockings and comfiest shoes, and crept downstairs. The door to the living room was ajar. Peering inside, she could see there was no sign that the sofa had been used as a makeshift bed. The cups and saucers had been cleared away. Abigail's glass of water was gone. All trace of her had disappeared.

Iris walked to the kitchen and stood before the range for warmth. A note lay on the table.

Porridge is in the oven. Rest today. I'll be back to make you lunch.

She found her breakfast and sprinkled some salt onto it. Bringing the spoon to her mouth, a wave of nausea gripped her, but she forced it down. Soon, she was shovelling it in. When had she last eaten? Yesterday's lunchtime sandwiches. When she got to the bottom of the bowl, she still was not satisfied. She poured herself a glass of milk from the pail in the pantry and drank it all in one before pouring again.

Gasping, she stood swaying before the sink. Her stomach bubbled. Cream flecked her top lip. She nudged it with her tongue, and she had to run for the back door. An old plant pot caught her vomit.

She fell against the wall and pressed her forehead against the bricks. Shuddering, she dragged herself back inside, ran herself a cup of water, and stumbled into the sitting room, flicking on the wireless as she passed it. She lay down and let the music soothe her, distract her, until her eyelids once again began to wilt.

'Iris?' Abigail sat in the nearby chair.

Blinking the sleep from her eyes, Iris checked the clock. One in the afternoon. 'Where have you been?'

'To see Mum.' Abigail wore the same clothes as last night, although she was better put together now. Her hair was brushed and set. The emotion from twelve hours ago was only visible in the puffiness around her eyes, but there was nothing else. 'I told her I knew what happened.'

'Did she understand?'

Abigail shrugged.

Iris pushed herself up. The wireless was playing something far too cheerful. The rock-and-roll notes danced in the air and seemed to mock them. She lunged for the switch and turned it off. The space turned brittle.

'You were right. I found out something I didn't like.'

'I should have left you alone when you wanted to stop.' Iris studied the green stripes on the sofa.

Abigail came beside her and plucked up her hand. 'I understand them better now, whether I like it or not. And I need to set things straight. A little girl needs to know her father was innocent, and I want to see my sister.'

* * *

Without a car, it took a train journey and a five-mile bus ride to alight in the centre of Bodnem. The weak daylight was already starting to dwindle, and the lights were twinkling on the Christmas tree which had been erected at the top of the high street.

'Which first?'

Abigail led the way down the south road. Ten minutes later, they were sitting before Rosie Smith's fireplace, and the cat prowled onto Iris's lap once more.

Abigail handed over the copy of Mildred's last will and testament. Rosie stared at it uncomprehendingly. Abigail never even flinched as she explained how her grandfather had drugged and strangled Rosie's mother, then allowed Rosie's father to die for it.

Rosie took a breath. She clasped the paper and screwed it tight before hurling it into the flames. She spat at it and dived into the kitchen.

Abigail and Iris didn't move.

The cat dug in his claws.

Crockery clattered. Cupboard doors opened and slammed shut. Rosie returned with a fruit loaf and three plates. She cut each of them a slice and resumed her seat.

'Any plans for Christmas?' Her voice was artificially bright.

Iris glanced at Abigail, afraid Rosie's calm facade would shatter at any moment.

Abigail shook her head. 'I don't know what I'll do.'

Iris stuffed her mouth so she didn't have to reply.

'You?'

'The usual. Just me and Jack.' Rosie nodded at the cat. 'How we like it.'

'I'm sorry,' Abigail said when she'd eaten the cake and the silence had stretched for too long. 'For everything.'

Rosie set down her plate on the table. Finally, her shoulders relaxed. 'It was a long time ago. None of it is our fault.'

'I wouldn't blame you for hating me.'

'Why should I hate you? You're the only one who's ever told me the truth.' She reached for Abigail's hand and patted it. 'None of us choose our parents, Miss Edwards. I am relieved, more than you could ever know, that my father was not a murderer, but he was still cruel. The memories I have of him were his own doing, no one else's. I still can never forgive him for what he did to my mother.'

The cat leapt from Iris's lap and onto Rosie's, where it head butted her chin before snuggling down and falling asleep.

'They may be our blood, but blood is all it is. We can

choose our own family, Miss Edwards. And I'm happy with mine.'

* * *

Through the gloaming, they made their way back to the crossroads. Abigail had slipped the note containing John Carr's Australian address into her handbag – she'd promised Rosie she would write to him and tell him everything. Perhaps then he might be able to stop blaming himself for finding that bottle all those years ago.

The church was a black beast in the twilight. Their gazes fell involuntarily on the graves there, the victims set side by side with their murderer.

'I don't know what to do about it.' Abigail nodded towards her grandfather's headstone. 'I mean, what *can* I do? Destroy it? Have him exhumed? Should I tell the police?' She shook her head, overwhelmed with the possibilities.

'Leave it,' Iris suggested. 'Rosie won't be tending it anymore. Let it fade. Let him drift into oblivion. They're all bones now anyway.'

Abigail didn't seem convinced. She nibbled her lip before turning away. Iris's gaze shifted to the granite plinth that marked Philip Buckley's grave.

'Tim and Mildred I can understand, to a point; they didn't want the shame or the heartbreak of having everyone know it was Howard who was the murderer. Your mother's reasoning for not telling anyone that she believed it was Tim is clear too: her guilty conscience over Matthew Pendleton, her dependence on her husband, her love for her son, her idea that she could save others. But Philip Buckley thought it was Tim. So why did he never say anything? He let Pat die.'

Abigail started up the street, heading for the manor's gates. Iris caught her up.

'It was to protect Sybil.'

'Could he really let a potential murderer just walk away?' Wouldn't Buckley have wanted Tim – the father of his ward, the old lover of his wife, his nemesis – to hang for what he had done?

Abigail rummaged in her handbag and pulled out a torch. Its light was pathetic, but it was something against the dark which descended around them. Every so often, a water droplet fell off an overhead branch and splattered on their heads, making them shudder and start. The birds had gone to roost. For a split second, the torchlight illuminated a weasel which scuttled across their path, but otherwise they were totally alone in the silent and still winter night.

Without saying a word, they quickened their pace.

Buckley Manor's roof was indistinguishable against the black sky. Yellow light shone from one of the ground-floor rooms, and as they approached, they saw the small group of artists gathered around Sybil who was prodding at a canvas.

Iris knocked on the door, and several minutes later Miss Stone appeared. Warily, she scanned the strangers, and the hostility in her features changed into fear.

'Sybil's teaching.'

'Might we wait?'

Miss Stone glanced behind her. She paused, as if she

were trying to conjure another excuse but then stepped aside to let them in.

The electric light in the hallway glared too brightly. Iris averted her gaze to the paintings and once again fell breathless. Wandering towards them, she picked one out to study.

A large canvas, it was ablaze with petrol blue and verdigris, all swirls and squares which portrayed a seaside scene that was somehow rather unsettling. Chaotic and rampant white sea foam sprayed up in sheaths against a blood-red cliff face. Gaping black chasms depicted caves. Plants and grasses and trees perched high above, teetering, as if about to plunge themselves into the waters and to their deaths. And finally she saw it – a white speck glinting in the dark. One might mistake it for a flick of paint, but if one looked close enough, one would see the blue flecks of eyes and the golden stream of hair. Madam Buckley.

She turned to the next one, a woodland scene. There, too, in the furthest and blackest corner, a tiny face peeked out from behind a tree trunk.

'Come up. She'll see you in her parlour.' Miss Stone led the way. Iris and Abigail relaxed into the same seats as last time.

'Sit with us, won't you?' Iris asked when Miss Stone turned for the corridor. The woman hesitated, swollen fingers wrapped around the door handle, but eventually did as she was asked. Gingerly, she lowered herself into the chair opposite Iris.

There were no electric bulbs here. Candlelight picked out the paintings and the faces in every one of them, which now Iris could not un-see. They were everywhere. Blue eyes staring out from every wall. How many eyes were in the manor? Surely thousands. Thousands of eyes constantly watching.

'Did you know Timothy Edwards was Sybil's father?' There was no point sugaring her question. Iris wanted it to shock, for in that second she could garner Miss Stone's true thoughts.

'This is not appropriate—'

'Then yes. You did.'

Miss Stone glared at Iris.

'Does Sybil know about her real father?'

Miss Stone sniggered. '*Real* father. He is only her father because of one night's actions. That does not make him a real father. Mr Buckley raised that child. Mr Buckley put clothes on her back and food in her belly and learning into her head.'

'Or he paid others to do so.'

'He was a good man. A good father. Always doing his best by her, any way he could. Anyone can make a child. Anyone can push it out of them. It takes love and sacrifice to raise them, to be a *real* parent.'

'Like you were?'

'Yes.' Miss Stone leaned back in her chair, clawing the arms of it.

'Did you know Mr Buckley suspected Tim of being the Bodnem murderer?'

Miss Stone examined her apron.

'You were his confidante, weren't you? He told you everything else, so I imagine he would have mentioned his suspicions about the real cause of those women's deaths.'

Miss Stone did not flinch.

'I can't understand why he never went to the police about it.'

'There was no evidence,' Miss Stone grunted. 'They'd arrested Pat Dunn by then.'

'But they hadn't hanged him. Pat didn't die until the following spring. There was plenty of time to save that boy. And yet he didn't. He let Pat die for a crime he thought Tim had committed.'

'Mr Buckley was no mean fool, as you seem to think. He was a father. He wasn't going to fix Tim up for murder when Tim had another child on the way. He wasn't that cruel.'

Iris paused. 'But how did Mr Buckley know about the child? If the child you are referring to is Abigail, she wasn't born until April 1901. Louisa and Tim moved from Bodnem less than a week after Jenny's death. Louisa would not have been showing by then; she might not have even known it herself. And they never returned. So how would Buckley have known about Abigail?'

Miss Stone plucked the hem of her apron. The silence stretched. Iris's confusion mounted.

Abigail stared at Miss Stone in horror. 'I'm not…?'

Miss Stone swallowed. 'There was a letter, September time, if I remember correctly. From your mother. She said she was with child. She said… it was Buckley's.'

Abigail took a deep breath.

'She wanted to leave Timothy and come here. Mr Buckley wouldn't allow it. He didn't want anything to do with her or the child. Louisa was to keep the baby and stay away, and in return Mr Buckley would never say a word about the murders – all of them, including the little Pendleton boy.'

Abigail was mute. Dry-eyed with shock, she focused on the fire, and the flames danced in her coffee-coloured irises.

Was that why Tim had never liked her the same way he had adored Samuel? Had he known from the start that she was never his?

The door opened. The three of them jerked their heads to see who had interrupted their despair.

Sybil wafted into the room, bringing with her the stinging scent of turpentine and the muskiness of oil paint. Her black clothes were speckled with colour, and a smear of gold shone on her forehead. She smiled when she saw she had visitors.

'Abigail, how lovely to see you. We weren't expecting you. Have you been here long?'

Abigail shook her head, rearranging her features into a more amiable expression. Sybil turned to welcome Iris, kissing her on the cheek.

'I hope Miss Stone has been taking good care of you.'

Miss Stone got to her feet as Sybil wiggled into the sofa beside Abigail.

'Is something the matter?'

Iris, Miss Stone, and Sybil waited for Abigail's response. After a long moment, Abigail shook her head.

'Not at all. I just came to see if I might buy another one of your paintings.'

* * *

It was almost eight o'clock by the time they alighted from the train. Shrewsbury station bustled with Friday-night activity as smartly dressed men and women headed out for the evening. Briefly, Iris wondered what film was showing at the picture-house and had a sudden longing for Rolos and lemonade and a comfy seat in the back of a theatre. She wanted to be filled with black-and-white images of romance and to feel Shirley's warm arm against hers as they shared a bag of sweets and swooned over the leading actor.

A lashing of cold air from the exit threw her back to reality.

'Will you stay with us another night?'

'I can't ignore him forever.' Abigail wandered towards the shelter of the wall, out of the way of the gale and the stream of people.

'Are you okay?'

'I don't know.'

Iris wanted to hug her. She would say she was sorry until she turned blue if she thought it would help, but she knew it wouldn't. 'What will you do?'

'I have no idea.'

'Will I see you tomorrow at Smedley?'

She shook her head. 'I think I need a break. This petrol rationing's been timed perfectly.' She laughed without humour.

Iris laughed as well, but it quickly turned into a bone-rattling cough. She found a handkerchief and pressed it to her mouth, feeling the iciness of her fingers through the cotton.

'You need a rest too, by the looks of it.'

Iris swallowed, shoved her handkerchief into her

pocket. 'I'm fine. If you ever want to talk about anything or get away, you know where I am.'

'Thank you, Iris.' She kissed Iris's cheeks, then turned back into the throng of the station.

'Abigail,' Iris called before she missed her opportunity and Abigail disappeared into the crowd. 'Would you like to come to ours for Christmas?'

44

1956

Adam careered around the kitchen with his toy aeroplane, zooming between the women's legs as they peeled carrots and potatoes. He made whooshing noises and several times collided with an open cupboard door. It didn't dampen his spirits. He was on his feet in a second and racing towards the living room where a harmonica played. The sound of that damned instrument set Iris's last nerve on edge. She'd only just got over her second bout of flu, and the noise did nothing to ease the headache which was her constant companion. She had a mind to march in there and shove a carrot in Alan's mouthpiece.

The doorbell rang, providing Iris with a much-welcome excuse. She dropped her vegetable, manoeuvred around Janet – who sat at the table with baby Jane in one hand and a glass of sherry in the other – and headed for fresh air.

'Leave it!' Iris halted Adam in his tracks; his sticky fingers scuffed the latch. He turned to her with a grin and opened the door.

'Hello, Master Lowe.' Abigail offered Adam her hand as she had done last time. He took it with just as much glee and shoved his toy aeroplane in her face.

'My granddad made me this.'

'Well then, what a lovely grandfather you have. Much nicer than mine.' Abigail caught Iris's eye.

'And look at my new bike.' He pointed at the trike propped up against the wall. Alan had bought it second-hand from one of his neighbours and had spent the last month painting it, putting new tyres on it, and making it shine all over. His efforts had been rewarded by his son's enthusiasm. 'What did Father Christmas get you?'

'Oh, well, I'm old, you see. I've had all my presents.'

Adam frowned. 'You've got to have a present. It's Christmas.' He sloped off, forlorn and confused.

Iris smiled over his head. 'Come in. Can I get you a drink?'

'Actually, Iris, I'm afraid I'm not stopping. I know I said I would, but…' She glanced over her shoulder. Behind her, the green Morris Minor held one miserable octogenarian. 'I couldn't leave him. Not on Christmas. And Samuel isn't coming up either – petrol rationing was a good excuse for him too. So, we're going to see Mum. Whether he likes it or not.'

Judging by Tim's expression, he did not like it. Iris smirked.

'Are you sure? They haven't seen each other for weeks, and not since… it all came out. What if something happens?'

'I've been dealing with the pair of them my whole life. The only difference is that before I didn't know what either of them was capable of.'

'Have you got your head around it yet?'

'I don't think I ever will.' She leaned against the door frame. From the car window, Tim scowled and drew his scarf closer to his neck. 'I've put them first my whole life. I've given up everything for them. My career, my fiancé, my hopes for a family. Did I ever tell you why I didn't marry?'

Iris shook her head.

'Michael was in the army. If we were to marry, I would have had to have moved away. God, how I wanted to. A fresh start. Away from Mum and Dad. I talked to Mum about it, asked her if she could cope without me. She never gave me a straight answer, part of her manipulation, you see. It made me feel even more guilty.'

Abigail stared at the trike, remembering. 'In the end, I made up my own mind. I was all set. I'd said yes to Michael. And then she had one of her turns. Dad sent her away for a rest and said it was the shock of my leaving that had made her worry herself into a bother. I wonder now if that, too, was a lie.'

She forced her attention back to Iris and inhaled deeply. 'I chose them, Iris. Over my own love. Over my own desires. I thought I was being a good daughter.'

'You were.'

'But what did it do for me? I lost the love of my life. I lost the family and the happiness I could have had.' She sighed resignedly. 'We'll have this Christmas together, and I will give them presents and I will kiss them and I will try to forgive them. I have been trying to forgive them… But then I'm taking Dad to the police station.'

Iris was stunned. She had thought Abigail would keep quiet.

'I don't know what they'll do, but it will be out of my hands. That's all I want now. No more secrets.'

The car horn beeped, startling them both. Iris glared at Tim. He might think he could still control his daughter, but he would be sorely mistaken when he realised what awaited him.

'Good luck,' Iris said, and dragged Abigail into a hug.

'Thank your mother for me. For everything. I hope she won't mind my not staying.'

Iris waved Abigail's concerns away. Her mum was too busy with two grandchildren and a roasting chicken to worry about anything else. Abigail turned for the car.

'Stop!' Adam yelled.

Iris was about to remonstrate with her nephew for yet again forgetting his manners, but he barged past her and stomped out to Abigail before she could say a thing. He shoved a kaleidoscope towards Abigail, one he had found in his stocking that morning. He'd spent hours twisting it round and marvelling at the colours and shapes.

'You can have this. It's pretty.'

Tears fogged Abigail's eyes. She crouched before Adam and thanked him and wished him a very merry Christmas. Before running back for his aeroplane, he kissed her cheek.

Abigail pushed herself up. 'You have a beautiful family, Iris. Never forget how lucky you are.'

* * *

Alan and Iris sprawled on the living room floor as the Queen finished her speech. Through the window, they heard Adam on his trike in the yard, talking to imaginary friends. Mum, Dad, and Janet were slouched in the chairs, eyelids drooping as their hands rested on their full bellies. Baby Jane slept in her cot beside the fire.

The clear-cut voice of Her Majesty faded into carols. Her dad poured them all another glass of sherry. Adam fell over and grazed his knee and came inside crying for his mum.

Then the doorbell rang for the second time that day.

All of them groaned. Finally, Mum hauled herself to her feet and staggered through the hallway.

Iris could tell by the tone of her mother's voice who it was. In that second, she sat up straight and uncreased her skirt.

'Look who's here!'

Simon stood in the doorway, his forehead tickling the straggly bit of mistletoe Alan had pinned to the frame that morning. He held a wrapped present and a card.

'This is Simon,' Mum said, widening her eyes at Alan, who immediately perked up and studied the visitor. 'This is our Alan and Janet.'

Simon nodded at them. 'Merry Christmas.' His gaze fell on Iris, and she could see the desperation in it. She hopped up as nimbly as she could after a three-course meal.

'Come and sit down,' Mum insisted, but Iris was already slipping past her and guiding Simon out of the room.

'I can't stay, Mrs Lowe. I just wanted to wish you season's greetings.'

Mum plonked herself down in her chair once more, disappointed.

'Iris,' Alan called, 'look up.'

She glared as he winked at her and did not look up at the mistletoe over her head. She led Simon towards the front door and out into the street, stopping to pick up the gift she had prepared and left at the foot of the stairs. Outside, his red car sat before the gate. In the sky, the moon had emerged and the sun had fallen beyond the horizon.

'Merry Christmas,' he said.

'I wasn't expecting you.'

'Thought you'd be used to me just turning up by now.'

She rolled her eyes. 'It's good, actually. I can give you this.' She thrust the gift at him. Awkwardly, he clamped the other present and card under his arm and tore through the wrapping paper. He laughed at the Black Magic chocolates.

'I never thanked you for the box you sent me. Or the lift the other night. Or anything, really.'

He gave her the present under his arm. He had wrapped it better than she had and tied it with a butter-yellow ribbon. Carefully, she removed the ribbon; she would wear it in her hair in the summer. The paper fell open and revealed Agatha Christie's latest release.

'I love her books.'

'I know. You told me.'

'Did I? I don't remember.'

'I do.'

She leafed through the pages of *Dead Man's Folly* before slamming it shut – she would not spoil it by reading the end first.

'Thought it might keep you occupied for a while, seeing as you've solved the Edwards case.' He rolled on the balls of his feet. Behind him, the street light came on.

'So, have you had a nice day?'

'Yes. You?'

'Yes.'

'Have you been with Ava?'

A flicker of irritation sparked in his eyes. 'No. Because she's at her fiancé's house.' He laughed at Iris's shock. 'You were right about her expecting a ring for Christmas. Just not from me.'

'If you'd told me she was already courting someone then I—'

'Would have believed me? Why didn't you believe me anyway? I've never lied to you.'

She scrutinised his tie so she didn't meet his gaze. It was a ghastly thing. All bright colours and clashing shapes. A novelty tie for the season. She was sure there was a spot of gravy on it as well.

'Here. Found this on the doorstep.' He handed her the card. 'I'd best get back. Mum will be wondering where I've got to.' He headed for his car.

Iris watched him go as Abigail's words rippled in her ears. The love she had sacrificed and lost, for the notion of a greater good. The biggest regret of her life.

But Iris didn't move. Instead, she plucked open the envelope.

A traditional Christmas picture of Victorian children on a sleigh greeted her. Inside, the words made her gasp.

Dear Iris,
Sending you and your family the warmest Christmas wishes.
Love, Shirley.
P.S. Thank you for the chocolates.

The engine made her start. Looking up, she swiped a tear off her cheek to see Simon pulling on his seat belt. She ran through the gate and hammered on his window.

'What's wrong?' he asked, rolling it down.

'Nothing!' Without pausing to think, she leaned in and kissed him. His lips were soft and unresponsive at first. The surprise had immobilised him. Then he kissed her back, his hand coming to her neck and pulling her closer. He tasted of marzipan and wine, and when she breathed in, she smelt his scent again: lime and sandalwood.

They broke off and stared at each other in silence.

Iris stepped back and cleared her throat. 'Right. Well. I'll see you soon.'

Simon placed his hands on the steering wheel and smiled up at her. 'You will.'

EPILOGUE
1895

Miss Stone's breasts ached, as if they were the only part of her that was able to weep. They were heavy with milk still, a whole week after her baby's last breath. Would that milk be sour when a child eventually suckled upon it? Would it be as sour as the rest of her, as if that babe might as well have died in her belly and stayed there to fester?

What had been the point of him taking his first breath? What had been the point of him opening his eyes to look at her if those eyes would never live long enough to recognise the woman gazing down at him as his mother? What had been the point of the agony of childbirth and, even more catastrophic, the ecstasy of it?

Tennyson was wrong. Far better to have never loved at all than to be left like this. A revenant, wandering the earth in a shell of a body.

Even the animalistic wails of pain coming from down the corridor did not stir her. Sitting on the top step of this ridiculous, grand staircase, Miss Stone never once flinched as she felt her new mistress's screams vibrate through the floorboards. She barely noticed when those cries reduced to simpering whimpers, or even when they fell to nothing at all. She did not sense her backside turning numb. She did not wince as needles prickled her toes. She did not see the housemaid switch on the gas lights around her.

She felt nothing.

Until the baby cried.

That shriek of life. Such a terrible sound. As if it knew that all its living was done, that it had been plunged into a long or short decline to death.

The noise broke the walls around her, shattered the staircase, until it was as if she were floating. Her pulse throbbed in her chest. Her stomach knotted itself into a ball of bricks. Every hair on her scalp quivered.

She slid down the corridor. Yellow light bisected the red carpet. Beyond the baby's cry, male voices talked, high-pitched and strained.

Someone was dead. No. Not yet.

That yellow slice grew wide. The bedroom door was cast open. A young man hurtled out.

'Where is Buckley?'

It seemed he was talking to her. She hadn't thought she was visible.

'Study,' she choked, her voice as hot and slick as oil as it spilled from her lips.

The man – the young doctor, she distantly remembered – disappeared and left her peeking into the room.

Before her, blood freckled and clogged white sheets. Copper scented the air, and the memories of her own labour groaned in the deep recesses of her mind. A woman lay on a bed, her legs stuck out crookedly from her torso, the toes pointing inwards. Her belly was puffy like a feathered cushion under her nightdress. She seemed carved out of cream, white and shimmering and wet. Golden hair rolled over her breasts, darkened with damp. Sapphire eyes looked out from swollen, limp folds of flesh.

Looked straight at Miss Stone.

More words. Another man. Saying everything would be all right.

The older doctor sat beside the woman on the bed. His voice gently pattered over her like the first flecks of snow. His fingers slid to the thread around his neck, from which dangled a pair of spectacles. He lifted it over his head and slipped it around the woman's throat.

For an instant, the sapphire eyes widened. The inward-pointing toes flipped out once, before falling back. The soft pillow rippled before settling again.

The doctor stepped aside.

The sapphire eyes lost their shine, like a wisp of cloud blowing across the moon.

The doctor turned and saw Miss Stone.

All was silent.

But for the baby.

It squirmed, mauve and slippery, in a cocoon of towels. Its arms lashed out as if it were blind. Its legs kicked as if it were done with the world already.

Exquisite.

The doctor lifted the child and carried it towards her. Rosebud lids peeled open, and sapphire eyes met hers.

'She can be yours forever,' the doctor said.

Her arms opened. The baby drooped into them, its

limbs ceasing their fight as its body pressed against her chest.

She freed her breast. Tiny lips nuzzled against her nipple and suckled.

Overhead, the portrait of a woman with sapphire eyes stared down and vowed to never leave.

THE FREE DELPHINE WOODS STARTER LIBRARY

Get three **FREE** historical ebooks when you join Delphine's newsletter.

The Butcher's Wife is a Victorian gothic thriller set in the stifling and stagnant streets of Wolverhampton.

The Last Flight of the Ladybird is a dark, twisting tale full of murder and betrayal in Elizabethan England.

Persephone's Melody is a short collection of deleted scenes from the novel, *Woman on Ward 13*.

Visit Delphine's website to get your free books.

AFTERWORD

Thank you for taking the time to read *Murder Under Moonlight*. I hope you enjoyed it and will consider leaving a review as it truly helps authors to get their work into the hands of those who will love it.

If you would like to find out more about my writing process and the history within my books, please visit my website.

ALSO BY DELPHINE WOODS

Convenient Women Collection:

The Butcher's Wife

The Cradle Breaker

The Promise Keeper

The Button Maker

The Little Wife

Convenient Women Collection Box Set

Iris Lowe Mysteries:

Woman on Ward 13

Murder Under Moonlight

Newsletter Exclusive Standalone Books:

The Last Flight of the Ladybird

Persephone's Melody

ACKNOWLEDGMENTS

Once again, thank you for reading!

I would also like to thank my family for being so supportive and encouraging me to follow my dreams. Thank you to my mother for always being there with constructive criticism and for being the first to read my work. Thank you to my father for all his technical support. Thank you to my husband for believing in me completely. And thank you to my dogs, for always providing the perfect excuse to get away from the desk!

Thank you to *The History Quill* for your editing services.

This book was a long time in the making. It all began after reading a local Shropshire ghost story about Madam Pigott, whose evil spirit was exorcised into a bottle. It has taken many shapes and forms since those initial notes with much painstaking research. Thus, my final thank you is to all the historians out there who make research fun, fascinating, and thrilling.

If you would like to read more about the various forms of inspiration behind this novel, please visit my blog.

ABOUT THE AUTHOR

Delphine Woods graduated with a First from The Open University in 2016, where she studied for an Open Degree, specialising in Creative Writing.

After a busy couple of years writing her collection of Victorian mystery-thrillers, she released her debut novella, *The Butcher's Wife,* in July 2019.

She lives with her husband in Shropshire where she writes in her spare room, her dogs by her feet to keep her warm. You can keep up to date with her news and get in touch with her via her website, newsletter, and social media platforms.

www.delphinewoods.com

Printed in Great Britain
by Amazon